Days Like These

Rebecca Tyrrel

Days Like These

Scenes from an ordinary life

MACMILLAN

First published 2003 by Macmillan
an imprint of Pan Macmillan Ltd
Pan Macmillan, 20 New Wharf Road, London N1 9RR
Basingstoke and Oxford
Associated companies throughout the world
www.panmacmillan.com

ISBN 0 333 90835 X

1 3 5 7 9 8 6 4 2

A CIP catalogue record for this book is available from
the British Library.

Typeset by SetSystems Ltd, Saffron Walden, Essex
Printed and bound in Great Britain by
Mackays of Chatham plc, Chatham, Kent

To Matthew and Louis.

I would like to thank the following people for their help and support:

At the office, Lucy Tuck, Dominic Lawson, David Jenkins, Kathryn Holliday, Tanja James, John Honderich, Jenny Brown, Johanna Gornitzki.

Not in the office, my mother, Mirabelle, my brother, Noel. Jonathan Margolis, Coleen Hatrick, Tanja Smith, Lynda Murray, Giles Kime, Lydia Burnet, Maggie Etheridge, Zuzana Vinarcikova, Camilla Musacchio, Davar Kheradvar and Hilda.

I would also like to thank Chris Heyworth, a most loyal reader.

Preface

The readers of the *Sunday Telegraph*, or at least the ones who wrote in, are to blame for this book. All those people sending nice letters saying that they tore the 'Days Like These' columns out of the magazine each week and kept them by the side of the bed next to Shakespeare and the Bible. In fact so many said this that I did for a while consider starting a small business manufacturing a hand-tooled leatherette folder for the readers to keep their cuttings in. I would have advertised it as a collector's item on UK Gold in between episodes of *Are You Being Served?* and *The Good Life*. In the end I thought that publishing a book was the better option. So here it is.

Many, many of the readers who wrote, dozens in fact, told me that they too had husbands like Matthew, which, though hard in itself to believe, was a tremendous comfort to me. There were others who said they had a Labrador as greedy and badly behaved as Izzy, and often I would be told by doting grandparents that they had a grandson just like Louis. It is through the column, indeed, that Louis has now made a friend called Harry, who has to be the only small boy in the world who has the same depth of feeling for Dr Who as he does.

And while nobody admitted to having a West

Highland terrier as unpleasant and mean-spirited as Steptoe, or a neighbour as delirious as Hilda, I did receive a sudden spate of letters a few years ago in which readers said that they too had fallen madly and deeply in love with their leaky twenty-year-old Mercedes estate cars that rarely started. All these readers' letters proved to me that my life was not odd at all, indeed my life was pretty similar to the lives of hundreds of other women, mothers, grandmothers, sisters throughout the country.

The 'Days Like These' column has been appearing in the *Sunday Telegraph* Magazine since February 1998. It hasn't always been easy to write, because its very aim is to parody the ordinariness of my life, and when a life really is as ordinary as mine it is sometimes hard to pluck any one particular thing from it as a subject for a column. The trick is to focus on the small things, which is exactly what we do in real life, sometimes in order to make the bigger things go away. We magnify small events, make dramas out of crises, or in my case column inches out of a Tesco's own-brand walnut cake. My favourite example of this came about one Sunday as Matthew and I drove to meet some friends for lunch and I sat beside him wondering what in the world I was going to write about that week. Then, like a miracle, I suddenly spotted the actor Martin Jarvis driving a big blue Bentley. Except that Matthew couldn't just agree that it was Martin Jarvis driving a big blue Bentley, he had to argue about it and then put money on it. The debate that then raged until I took the bull by the horns and phoned Martin Jarvis's agent made a column.

Other weeks I have gone right up to deadline without an idea. Whenever this has happened I have either phoned Lucy Tuck, the editor of the *Sunday Telegraph* Magazine, and sobbed gently, which is always effective because, showing endless patience and understanding, and probably to get me off the phone, she will then rush to get a stand-in; or I have resorted to writing about my imaginary psychotherapist. Because he was imaginary I was able to imbue him with any personality traits I chose. In fact I based him on Jack Favell, the wicked, debonair, philandering cousin of Daphne Du Maurier's Rebecca, as played in the Hitchcock film by George Sanders. George Sanders lived in the shed at the bottom of our garden. I would, in the columns, go to him whenever I was feeling wretched, which is, of course, exactly how I would be feeling in real life if I hadn't come up with an idea for a column that week. George would blow cigarette smoke all over me, pick flecks of dirt off his cashmere socks and tell me to stop simpering, which is probably what Lucy Tuck longed to do.

Although the readers' letters were always very complimentary about George, when I came to compile the columns for this book the ones in which he featured were not my favourites. I was making something out of nothing and the best columns make something out of something but nothing too big. I don't have any absolute favourites but I do have favourite characters. Hilda, who thinks we are harbouring her wartime lover, I really couldn't have made up – she is a gift. She is also very unpleasant to me: she hurls abuse at me when I walk down the street, which makes me feel better about exploiting her. I am also very fond of Barry the accountant, who is an expert in the art of long suffering and looks like Dennis Price.

My number one favourite character, of course, is Matthew, my husband, which brings me back to those readers' letters. Fifteen of them, presumably written by women who live with the kind of man who keeps a tidy sock drawer, accused me of making Matthew up. They don't think he exists. I admit I did make some things up – I never really drove to Truro looking for bread sauce – but Matthew is real. I promise. You have to believe me. I am telling the truth. The absolute truth.

1998

22 February 1998
Trish

'Oooooh! What you been up to then, saucy?' said Trish the cleaning lady with the filthy mind, in a tone suggesting that she had just found eleven jockstraps, a riding crop and a mountain goat in our bed. I was telling her that I was three months pregnant and this was the moment, I realize now, when it started, the moment the all-consuming hate arrived.

Eighteen months later, though, Trish is still with us, terrorizing our family, the cause of my daytime ostracism from society since no one – not family, not friends, not Jehovah's Witnesses – will visit lest Trish be here.

Built like a sumo wrestler – Mike Tyson's weight and half his height – she came from Manchester in the days when Ena Sharples held sway in the Rover's Return, Trish herself deemed too malevolent a gossip for a berth in the snug. She has a laugh that makes Sid James sound like Kiri Te Kanawa – a horrible, rancid, nicotine-laden, phlegmy cackle; an exclamation mark that punctuates all her countless single entendres.

'I'm off to the shops, Trish,' I'd say, 'would you like anything?'

'I'll tell you what I'd like, love, I'd like a man, I would. A man with a great big wad! Know what I mean?' Cackle, cackle. Her timing is faultless. Bernard Manning has nothing on Trish.

Trish never used to bother me but then Louis was born and we moved to a bigger house to accommodate the nappy-disposal unit. 'Oooooh!' she said. 'Look at you lot, in your posh gaff. Lord and Lady Muck. Won the Lottery, did we?' I should have sacked her then, come right out and done it. Once, in a futile attempt to assuage the guilt I would have felt if I had sacked her, I worked out that her disposable income was bigger than mine; she had four other 'ladies' and she took in ironing.

But still Trish came with us. She even popped round on moving day. 'Just thought I'd see if you needed any help,' she said. 'Don't want you doing yourself a mischief, in your condition.' Cackle, cackle. And then she propositioned the removal men in the bathroom. Four strapping Australians blushed crimson over Trish's quip about the sink plunger.

More rooms mean more hours: every other weekday from 9 a.m. until noon. Three days a week, I have to be out of the house, 'our house' Trish calls it, by 8.55. I go and hide at my parents-in-law's and leave the builder and the plumber to Trish. 'You've got a big wrench, love. Got anything else that big?' Cackle, cackle. The plumber left halfway through the job; the only decent, reliable plumber in the Greater London area, driven out by a squat, salacious sex-fiend of sixty.

When Louis was born, Trish bought me a baby-blue helium balloon with IT'S A BOY written on it. I left her a thank-you note and put a DO NOT DISTURB sign on the bedroom door. She walked straight in. 'Oooops, sorry, love, got your boobies out for the little 'un. Hardly Pamela Anderson, your mummy, is she?' Cackle, cackle. 'Aaah, bless 'im. Bless 'is little heart. The little angel.'

Matthew found me feeding Louis in the shed. Then Lynda the nanny complained. Not about Trish – she could just about cope with Trish – but about me. 'You're getting yourself in a state and it's making us all miserable,' she said. She's right. It's got to stop. I'm going to sack Trish now, today. I've learned my lesson. I'll go round to her flat. I'll pay her off.

Matthew had predicted she might turn nasty. 'She's dangerous,' he said. 'With those forearms, she could do real damage.' So he left town for the night to visit a friend in Brighton.

Trish stood in her doorway with her hands on her hips and a 'don't try it on with me, lady' look on her face; her eyes flashing, her jaw locked. And then I gave her the money, six weeks' worth. 'Oooooh, it's my lucky day. I'll get meself a toy boy.' Cackle, cackle.

I told her I'd decided not to go back to work, and couldn't afford her any more. I'd be doing the cleaning myself. I thanked her for all her hard work, said we'd miss her and that she must keep in touch.

Trish could not have been sweeter. Sweet as a nut, as she'd say, or a pair of nuts, cackle, cackle. She said she understood, she'd get by. I wasn't to worry myself, and could she have a photo of Louis just to remind her of the happy times she spent in 'our house'? And that was that. No more Trish.

Not long ago, our neighbour bumped into Trish in the supermarket. 'Oi, you,' she bellowed down tinned vegetables, preserves and table sauces. 'You know she's only gone and given me the boot. No notice, no money – and just before Christmas as well. Says she's going to do the cleaning herself, I'd like to see her try, Lady Muck. That nanny of hers is no better, sits about all day doing nothing while the little 'un cries. The old man's lost his job, that's what it is, but she won't admit it. Ooh, if I ever see her again, the bitch . . .'

The house is filthy, possibly condemnable. The laundry basket is impersonating the Leaning Tower of Pisa. You could grow organic parsnips in the downstairs loo. But 'our house' is 'our house'; it no longer belongs to Trish.

1 March 1998
I Do Not Smoke

I had forgotten, in the intervening twenty-three years, just how unrewarding a cigarette tends to be when smoked while leaning out of a top-floor window. The last time I did this, aged fourteen, it was Player's No. 6, and I was hiding from my parents. Now, at thirty-seven, it is Marlboro Lights, and it's Lynda I'm hiding from.

I only smoked half of it then I wrapped the dog-end in Kleenex and flushed it down the loo. And now the Kleenex has gone but the dog-end is still there, bobbing about merrily, in and out of the S-bend. Now I'm back at my computer enjoying a cocktail of Trebor mint and oranges, while choking on honeysuckle air-freshener and fumes of joss stick.

Last week Lynda watched me fill out a follow-up to pregnancy form from the Department of Human Science and Medical Ethics. *Since your baby was born have you smoked: a) not at all, b) occasionally, c) regularly.* I ticked 'a'.

If you are not smoking what helped you to stay off cigarettes? Lynda and I had one of our conversations about evil, dirty, smoking parents, so I wrote: 'It is very important to me that my child is brought up in a smoke-free environment.'

Today Lynda came home with yet another cot-death leaflet from the baby clinic and said, 'Apparently if you smoke you should never have your baby in bed with you. The fumes you give off, even if you haven't had a cigarette for weeks, can be a contributory factor.'

I've just had another one, in the boiler cupboard. It was extremely hot in there and I was driven out by a hideous, nicotine-yellow spider, probably sent to terrorize me by the Department of Human Science and Medical Ethics.

I threw the dog-end over the garden fence so now the neighbours will complain. I smell of cigarettes. I know Lynda will notice. She's probably found the dog-ends in the loo. The house has gone very quiet.

She's gone to the phone box to call Child Line. Esther Rantzen will be here any minute. Louis will be taken into care.

•

I know what a psychoanalyst would say . . . it's not Lynda that I am scared of owning up to but myself. 'Transference', the therapist would call it. But then that's why I have never been to an analyst: why pay someone £80 an hour to lecture me on the obvious when Matthew would be delighted to do it for nothing?

Anyway, it's only a matter of time before the game is up. Lynda must have guessed when last Sunday, while having a quick puff in the bathroom, in the dark, I triggered the smoke alarm. 'Weeeeeeee-w-ooouahhh' it went, like the radiation sensor in *Silkwood*, only twice as loud.

By the time Lynda arrived, almost forty seconds later,

to climb calmly on a chair and push the reset button with a broom handle, I had managed to light and blow out seven candles in the hope of creating what you could justifiably describe as a smoke screen. And it was at the precise moment the alarm fell silent that Sue Lawley introduced her castaway's next record – a particularly spooky Gregorian chant.

Lynda smiled the tiniest of smiles, switched the light back on and left the room. Either she thinks I am a Satanist, using Pentecostal candle circles and medieval religious music to rouse the demons of hell, or she knows. I'll have to tell her.

'Lynda,' I say, 'I'm not what you think I am. I am the devil's disciple.' Satanists probably get to keep their babies, with a bit of supervision from the council. Smokers are worse. Esther hates smokers.

•

If it had been up to me I would have smoked solidly throughout Louis's gestation. Giving up had nothing to do with willpower and everything to do with the fact that the combination of oestrogen and nicotine made me retch. When Trish, the cleaning lady from hell, left full ashtrays lying about I would stick one hand over my mouth and use the other to make theatrical wafting gestures. I became a traitor to my fellow smokers, a craven deserter in the war against personal choice.

So at Christmas, I had one cigarette. Then on New Year's Eve I had another. Then it was three a week, always other people's. I bought my first packet (of ten) two weeks ago. I made a pact with myself: 'I will only smoke one cigarette after meals or at times of great stress.' Now I'm so stressed about Lynda finding out, I'm up to six or seven a day and have been driven into hiding in my own house.

•

She just caught me in the shed. I didn't see her coming because I was too busy scrabbling about in the tool drawer, where I have hidden my Gold Spot breath-freshener. I heard the door open, turned round, hand tucked behind me – thirty-seven years old, and back behind the metaphorical bike sheds, trapped in second adolescence – smoke wafting over my shoulder. 'Your mother-in-law just phoned,' she said. 'I told her you were in the shed having a cigarette and she is calling back in five minutes.'

8 March 1998

The Baby Can Walk

I now know exactly how Al Capone felt when they finally caught him – all the bootlegging, all that gunning-down of gangsters in Chicago garages, and they sent him down for not paying his taxes. I am being punished for a lie which when held up against all my other lies could hardly be described as a lie at all, more an exaggeration. My Elliot Ness is a woman called Amanda, a woman whom I have many times in the past tried to cull from a short but minutely edited list of friends because, while wishing her no ill, I can't stand her. I've had no time for her ever since 1974 when I asked if I could borrow her Van Allen skinny-rib and she said, 'Never a lender or a borrower be.' I pretended to like her even after the Debenhams shoplifting incident (blue eyeshadow, cherry-flavoured lip-gloss and a Mary Quant mascara) because her father was a pop promoter and was one day going to introduce us to Woody of the Bay City Rollers. It never happened. All I ever got from sticking around Amanda was Leo Sayer's autograph and an inferiority complex born of the fact that she was prettier than me and had nicer clothes.

She now lives in New Zealand with her husband Rupert, who is a sheep farmer. (She was never a girl easily scared by the Sloane Ranger cliché; while I was selling roll-on girdles in Fenwick's underwear department, Amanda was learning to walk with a book on her head at Lucy Clayton's.) She fires off quarterly photocopied round-robin letters to her friends in England and occasional photographs of herself riding across apricot sunsets and clipping sheep. Rupert looks like Anthony Andrews.

Last April, just two weeks after Louis was born, Amanda and Rupert had Baby Charlie. The photograph showed them en famille on the veranda of the marital homestead, all wearing crisp white cotton. At Christmastime we were sent a round robin telling us that Charlie was already crawling and saying 'baah, like a lamb', accompanied by a photo of them all sitting on straw bales in Santa Claus hats. So when Amanda rang a few weeks ago, apparently for the sole purpose of telling me that Charlie was saying 'sheep', I had no choice but to compete.

'I suppose he's walking, too?' I said.

'God, no,' replied Amanda, 'not yet.'

'Oh, really? Louis has been walking for weeks.' And then Amanda announced the real reason for ringing. She was coming to London. That was on Valentine's Day, and Louis had precisely three weeks to learn to walk to save his mother from a massacre.

•

Louis's training becomes more intensive all the time, and we are now up to ten minutes, four times a day. I hold him under his arms and off we go – 'One step, two step . . .' After two weeks we've moved into the garden, bigger laps, although Louis's gait is a little stiffened by his padded all-in-one which he must wear if he isn't to catch a chill. My back is suffering slightly, but if Louis can walk just one tiny step on his own in eight days' time it will have been worth it.

As for me, I have regressed to the fourth form, to the days when Amanda had a fake-fur pencil-case and I had a green vinyl one, when she had platform soles and I didn't, when she spent the summer holidays in Florida and I went to Swansea.

•

One week to go and Louis is not walking. I have failed and will have to own up. If he ends up in calipers with a club foot it will be because of the enforced laps. If he doesn't walk until he is ten it will be Providence wreaking a terrible revenge. Like some hubristic creature in a Greek tragedy, I have brought a curse upon my own child.

The mental anguish of it all has prompted me to declare an amnesty on all my previous lies – a pact with the devil that Louis might be spared any kind of physical impairment – and I now ask for several hundred other lying offences to be taken into consideration, including the following:

1) My mother never had an affair with Simon Dee.

2) Noël Coward was not my brother's godfather.

3) I am not a member of the Tyrrell Formula One family.

4) I never had a pony.

5) I was never close to being selected for the Olympics.

6) I never met, let alone went out with, Midge Ure.
7) I have lost Louis's birth certificate.
8) I did forget to post Matthew's tax return.

Quite how I thought having a mother who ran off with Simon Dee would make me a more impressive/enigmatic person is a mystery now – perhaps I should update it to Jeremy Paxman. I am quite fond of the Midge Ure one, though, and only confess to it under extreme duress. I am sure everyone tells these kinds of fib, all the time. But not me, not any more. Never again.

•

When the doorbell rings I am prepared for a moment mentally rehearsed hundreds of times. I will admit I lied about Louis walking. Then, ignoring her gloating, I will be hospitable, and pleased to see her. And when she is gone I will banish her for ever from my list. It rings. We kiss. Her child is balanced on her hip. 'But where's your little one?' she says.

'He's upstairs in bed,' I say, 'with a hamstring injury – too much walking too early.'

22 March 1998
Another Funny Honeymoon

We met in a crowded car park on Richmond Common and it was pushchairs at noon as we walked towards each other – watery smiles of greeting as we gazed into the bags under each other's eyes.

'How are you?'

'Tired. So tired I'm hallucinating.'

'So am I. So tired I can't sleep any more. I've gone beyond sleep.'

'The Japanese used it as a form of torture,' said Sarah, bending down to stroke Louis's cheek.

'Sleep deprivation? I know. Only the Japanese didn't make you get up at six the next morning to watch *Sesame Street*.'

This might sound a bit unfair to the builders of the Burma Railway, I know, but nothing is fair in the Land Beyond Sleep.

We walked for about an hour and a half that day and each recited to the other, by rote, the pattern of our days and nights, calculating the hours of non-sleep caused by the teething pains, the colds, the random, nocturnal whims of the gummy little angels we were pushing in front of us; same age, same biorhythms, same eleven-month-old bags under their mothers' eyes.

By the end of our walk the Sleepathon had been intricately planned. We are going to rent a cottage in the country for a week, one nanny for each baby, two travelling days and six long, uninterrupted days and nights of non-stop sleep. We have a picture in our minds of nannies and babies playing happily outside while inside, under the eyes of some rosy, beamed cottage, two women sleep. That's what holidays have come to mean. Sleep. The cottage has been booked and the days are being counted. It's going to cost a fortune; we could be going to the Caribbean for less. But you cannot put a value on a six-day Sleepathon in Devon.

•

It never occurred to us that Matthew or Laurence would want to come. Matthew and I plan our holidays together around the following criteria:

My Needs: sleep and a bit of local interest.

Matthew's Needs: good restaurants, good weather, a casino or bookmaker, a sandy beach, in-room cable sports channel.

Matthew can go months without so much as a telephone bet but the minute the word 'holiday' is mentioned he mutates into the man who broke the bank at Monte Carlo. Or who thinks he will. He has only ever found his true holiday self while shouting, 'Deal 'em high,' over a blackjack table, or 'Come on, Trap Four, move yourself,' at a hotel room TV screen.

Our honeymoon was as good as it gets on the holiday criteria front. It began with two days at a monstrously luxurious hotel in Boston. Matthew stayed in bed watching American football and endless repeats of *Bewitched* and *Wacky Races*, while I went whale watching. We then drove through the Berkshires and I oohed and aahed over the colours of the leaves in the New England fall, while Matthew sucked his teeth in suspense as the Ryder Cup unfolded on the car radio. Then disaster struck. The authentic Shaker-style inn I had booked us into had no television, no alcohol and no smoking. We enjoyed what the brochure called a gracious stay, giving you time to enjoy the gentle pleasures New England has to offer, for three minutes, before Matthew checked us straight out and drove, in a determined but trancelike state, to the kind of roadside motel even Hunter S. Thompson in his most wasted moments would have avoided. The fifty-foot sign outside bore the legend '24-hour cable television in every cabin', and we stayed until the golf was over – three days during which I was able to sate my need for picturesque scenery and fresh air with daily walks across a five-lane highway to the nearest liquor store for Jack Daniel's (Matthew was by now living *Fear and Loathing*, only without the drugs because he didn't know how to go about getting them). Our next stop was to have been a health spa in Vermont, but in the interests of our six-day-old marriage surviving a full week, I agreed to a roundabout route that took us to Atlantic City.

In our suite at the Trump Taj Mahal, a giant TV screen rose from the bedroom floor at the push of a button, the marble-effect sunken whirlpool bath was banked with leopard and gold cushions, the sheets were black and shiny, the ceiling was mirrored and the casino was open twenty-four hours a day. I sought refuge on the boardwalk alongside middle-aged women of ample girth in Dame Edna spectacles and pastel home-knits, while old-timers in flat caps and white trainers shuffled back and forth to the All You Can Eat for $2.95 buffet tables.

Meanwhile, Matthew blew the deposit on our first marital home on the roulette tables. On the third night he started shouting, 'Come on, seventeen,' in his sleep (seventeen is his number; so, come to that, are four, ten, twenty-nine, thirty-two, thirty-three, thirty-five and thirty-six, but seventeen is his favourite), and by the following morning the honeymoon, as they say, was over.

•

These days, we holiday in two stages. I go rural for a week without Matthew and then we go off somewhere together that he likes. We've done Las Vegas once and Deauville three times (beach, two casinos, racecourse, sports channel in hotel room). I sleep and read, Matthew fries on a sunbed and reads and we meet up in the evenings for dinner. Then I go with him to the casino, just to watch the fat cats with their gold Rolex watches and their gold-skinned girlfriends, before retiring early to bed, leaving him there giving commands to the ivory ball to drop into seventeen.

Sometimes I covet the kind of holiday our friends go on – Tuscany, Thailand, Tanzania – but I know what's best for both of us in the end. So this year, after my Sleepathon, we are going to Deauville again, with Louis. In preparation Matthew has bought a toy roulette wheel from Hamleys. Louis is already prodigiously adept at spinning it, but then he's a very advanced baby. I may have been imagining it, but I thought I heard him say his first proper word the other day. 'Seventeen.'

19 April 1998
Bagel Ambition

Sounding eerily like Floella Benjamin in her *Play School* era, Matthew counted them out in big round vowely numbers: 'Tee-ee-nn unopened yellow envelopes from the accountant, ff-aii–ve brown ones [Inland Revenue] and tww-ellll-uvvv white ones [Lloyds Bank]. Anita Roddick didn't get where she is today,' he said, switching now into CJ from Reggie Perrin, 'by not opening her post and hoping it would go away.'

It's my fault, though. I should never have started him off. Three weeks ago I spent a blissful few days' holiday in Devon, sitting on a deckchair in early spring sunshine, watching Louis crawl naked on freshly mown grass, breathing clean air, and this was when I revived the get-rich-quick-and-move-to-the-country entrepreneurial plan. It is, like all the best plans, very simple. We open one Pret A Manger-style bagel bar (the Tower of Bagel), spawn a nationwide chain of 150 branches, sell out for £27 million to Grand Metropolitan and retire to Devon in two years' time. Apparently, though, this has serious flaws, some of which Matthew has helpfully listed: (a) I can't add up, (b) I am hopeless with money, (c) therefore I don't have enough money to open a bagel bar, (d) I don't even have enough money to risk opening one of these envelopes.

•

The Tower of Bagel stratagem was originally devised seven years ago with our friends Jonathan and Sue. Jonathan's distant cousin Motti Carmeli, of the celebrated Carmeli bakery in Golders Green High Street, was to supply the bagels. Sue and I would fill and sell them – smoked salmon and cream cheese, chopped liver, egg and onion, herring, bacon – and turn the shop into the kind of chic and eclectic little gem that would swiftly become a second home to the cast of *Friends*. We even found a suitable site, a former Sketchleys. Jonathan and Matthew went to see a bank manager, and Sue and I attended a single evening class in bookkeeping. The retirement fantasy in those days had Sue and me sipping tropical cocktails around a swimming pool in Essex, wearing rhinestoned swimsuits, while our husbands wore sheepskin car coats and drove to the dog track in Rolls-Royces with personalized number plates – Bagel 1 and Bagel 2. Devon, huge house and servants, though, is better; I cannot wait for Devon.

•

I still have the notebook I started at the time. It has 'Tower of Bagel Expenses' written on the front, and on the first page the one and only entry reads '£1.50 – return Tube fare to evening class'. I dug it out to show to Matthew as evidence of my good intent but he just did his head-in-hands thing.

'You can't even remember our phone number because

it's just that . . . a number!' he said. 'You got into a muddle timing your contractions when Louis was born.'

He is absolutely right. I can't do maths. I blame Mrs Drink, who sent me down a year in 1971. 'Rebecca, you obviously have talent,' she said. 'I gather from Miss Crisp in Domestic Science that your banana custard is outstanding. But you cannot do maths.' Thirty-two years on, though, I am determined to prove Mrs Drink and Matthew wrong. I shall conquer my numerical dyslexia, for that is what it is, with my *Math From Rock Bottom* study guide, purchased from a second-hand bookstall in Tavistock Market. It cost £1, an amount yet to be logged in my new double-entry bookkeeping ledger, leather-bound with Italian marbled cover (£43.99 from Liberty; a deductible expense, to be set against profits).

•

Matthew has kindly adapted some mathematical problems from *Math From Rock Bottom* to get me started. (1) 'If a bagel costs 25p wholesale and £1.50 retail, with a smoked-salmon and cream cheese filling costing 40p, how much profit will you make from the sale of twenty filled bagels, allowing 10p for sundries to include lemon juice, butter and black pepper?' Answer: umm. And (2) 'If rent on your shop is £35,000 a year, staff costs are £40,000 and you sell seventy-five bagels a day for six days a week, excluding bank holidays, how quickly will we lose the house and find ourselves in Carey Street?' Answer: go and see Barry the accountant.

Barry the accountant is non-judgemental, caring and looks like Dennis Price, and since Louis was born our conversations have occasionally veered from the benefits of Schedule D to his children, grown up now 'but always a worry'. I told Barry of my plan and he listened with no apparent sneer, making occasional notes on a Sun Alliance Post-It pad. His demeanour, patient and kindly, had something of the psychiatrist, and when I had finished he picked up my wad of unopened envelopes and said, 'Let's just have a look at these, shall we?' He started on the yellows, with which, unsurprisingly, he seemed familiar. 'This one is asking you to forward me your P60, so I can work out your tax for the year. Do you have your P60?'

'It'll be in one of the browns,' I said. So he started opening the browns, kicking off with one from the doctor's surgery, dated May 1994, telling me that they had detected no abnormalities in the mole on my back.

•

'What did Barry say?' asked Matthew as I laid the table for supper that evening.

'He was very positive and helpful,' I said.

'What exactly did he say?'

'He has suggested I do a course in business studies, have a detailed business plan and then go and see the bank manager. He said he wasn't partial to bagels himself but that he was sure plenty of people would be.'

'He was humouring you,' said Matthew. 'Why have you laid the table for six?'

'Because Jonathan and Sue are coming for supper, to talk about Tower of Bagel. You and me, that's two, Jonathan and Sue, that's . . .'

I tore up my Business Studies enrolment form and threw it in the bin. Devon can wait.

26 April 1998
World Cup

An enormous cardboard box, six feet by five feet, has appeared in the middle of our kitchen. I came home to find Lynda the nanny staring at it, wide-eyed, like a ham actress in a B-movie waiting for the green slime to ooze. Louis was practising his walking around it and the dog was growling at it.

'What on earth is it?' I asked.

'It's a telly,' said Lynda. 'It arrived half an hour ago from Peter Jones. Oh, yes . . . and there's a man upstairs steam-cleaning Matthew's armchair.'

Very slowly, like a hot flush, it dawned. This has happened before . . . new telly, clean chair, bulk deliveries of Budweiser from Majestic Wine Warehouse. It happened at exactly this time of year, four years ago. It's the bloody, hateful World Cup again. Like a badger preparing for winter, my husband is putting his house in order, battening down the hatches, squirreling away economy packs of peanuts and family-size bars of whole nut chocolate, buying his cigarettes in cartons of two hundred. In a month's time, armed with an ashtray and a roll of bin liners, he'll bid an emotional goodbye to his family and friends as he closes the door to his lair, draws the curtains and settles down to shout at his new thirty-two-inch screen.

I exaggerate, of course. Matthew will occasionally emerge, to bathe and sleep, bleary-eyed and blinking in the June sunlight, like Paul Newman in *Cool Hand Luke* after seven days in the cooler. After the first week he begins to look a bit drawn, two weeks in he's lost a bit of weight and by the day of the final he is positively etiolated. He will receive occasional visitors – his cousin, his father, his friend. They will arrive bearing pizzas and, as I meet them at the front door and show them in, I'll ask if they would be so kind as to convey my fondest regards and 'tell him his wife and child are well'. When I show them out a few hours later they will hand me a bin liner full of empty pizza boxes and spent cans and say, 'Matthew's fine and sends his love.'

•

In the early days of our marriage there was tension over the football, but that was before I truly understood the extent of the illness – that he is physically incapable of not watching a football match on telly; that he anticipates his lifespan not in years but in the number of World Cups he can squeeze in. He will be nine in June, and hopes to live to twenty-one. Once, stupidly, in a fit of football hate, I asked him what he would do if I were to die in early May and the funeral was on the day Spurs were playing in the FA Cup Final. He told me he would demand an autopsy, 'to delay it for a few days. Funerals are movable feasts. Football matches are fixed months in advance.'

I cannot claim I wasn't warned. We had been living together for exactly ten days when Spurs were in the Cup Final against Nottingham Forest. That Saturday he was up, showered and dressed by 6 a.m. When I asked him what he was doing rummaging noisily through a drawer, he told me in an 'I can't believe you have to ask' sort of tone that he was looking for his lucky 1948 shillings. He then set off for the northbound Northern Line platform at Embankment to tie his shoelace by the newspaper kiosk. He did this in 1981, he said, when Spurs played Manchester United and Spurs won, and he had done it ever since.

I am proud to say that I have never, not even in those early days, feigned even the slightest interest in football. I did once go to a match, against my will: the result of a lost bet. I sat listening to a talking tape on my Walkman. It was Jane Austen versus West Ham. Jane won, and I came away not knowing or caring in the slightest about the score. I was cold, wet and utterly miserable throughout.

•

'What was wrong with the old telly?' I ask when Matthew arrives home and starts stroking the box.

'Nothing, but I'll need more than one.' (That tone again.) 'There's Wimbledon and the Test cricket on at the same time.' An hour later, I overhear him discussing TV aerials on the phone. 'Yes, we have got cable,' he says, 'but as I am sure you understand there must be a contingency plan in case of technical problems.' Two hours later there's a man on the roof, the floor is littered with remote controls and wires, like mounds of squid-ink spaghetti, lie everywhere.

'We won't go anywhere, see anyone, communicate at all for a whole month,' I whine.

He says he is sorry but there is nothing he can do: 'Have I ever denied you your pleasures?'

My what?

•

Four years ago, just before the last World Cup, I got a dog for company. Now I've got Louis, but for how long? As with gambling and drinking, a predisposition to football is bound to be genetic, and already Louis's second favourite toy (after his roulette wheel) is a mini professional-standard football.

It's only a few years before my joshing visit from Shane Ritchie. I'll be expected to hold Louis's blue-white football shorts proudly up to the light in a Daz doorstep challenge. I am destined to mutate into an Oxo mum housewife, joining in the team kit-washing rota. 'Boys will be boys,' I'll say laughingly, as I shove another load in the machine. I'll send Louis and Matthew off to the match on a Saturday with a cheery wave and a warming flask of Cup-a-Soup and then set to preparing a wholesome meal for their return.

•

Kenneth Branagh has apparently stipulated in his next film contract that he gets cable in his trailer so he can watch the World Cup. He told Matthew this recently and I only mention it (a) to drop the name (they spent exactly forty-five minutes talking football at a recent theatre awards evening only interrupted at half-time by my asking for an autograph) and (b) because it illustrates the extent of my social ostracism.

'Do you like football?' asked Ken as he signed 'Happy First Birthday Louis' on my programme.

'No,' I replied. 'I hate it.' And there the conversation ended.

17 May 1998
Bank Holiday

The most stressful time of the year, according to leading psychologists, is the period after Christmas and New Year. The misery is caused, apparently, by the sense of anticlimax and having nothing to look forward to but a long and dismal winter.

For Matthew and me, however, public holidays of any kind are difficult. On Easter Monday, for instance, while Spartacus is dying on the cross and all the other slaves are shouting, 'I am Spartacus, I am Spartacus,' Matthew, as regular as the nuclear-powered clock in Zurich, chips in, 'I wish I was bloody Spartacus. At least Spartacus had some friends.' If, on the other hand, it's a film about Jesus, he waits for the Last Supper scene. 'I wish I was Christ,' he says, 'at least Christ had proper dinner parties.'

This year we started early, with *Ben Hur* on Good Friday. Charlton Heston was in the slave ship in chains, and rowing like mad at 'ramming speed'. 'I wish I was Ben Hur,' said Matthew, 'at least he had some friends on the neighbouring oars.' By the time Charlton Heston had been freed, and was making a name for himself as a premier-division gladiator in Rome, the traditional 'We have no friends' debate was in full swing. The motion, as ever, was as follows: 'This house believes everyone else in the world is spending the weekend with friends, either at home or at their friends' homes, or in a rented country pile, having fun and merriment, while we stay in watching *Spartacus/Ben Hur/*some film about Christ because everyone hates us.'

Opposing the motion, I argue that if we have no social life it is (1) because we are lazy; (2) because we are antisocial; and (3) – a new point this year – because we now have Louis and, like all mothers of one-year-olds, I am permanently tired. Proposing it, Matthew insists (1) we are loathed; (2) we are the most loathed couple in Britain; (3) no one will see us; and (4) no . . . one . . . will . . . see . . . us (an intonation he has borrowed from a scene in *Tootsie* – which we watched, alone, on video in bed, at 9.45 p.m., with a half-bottle of champagne, last New Year's Eve). 'No . . . one . . .' said Matthew for the third time, as Ben Hur made his way to Palestine to find his family, 'will . . . see . . . us.' Then the head went into the hands, and he started rocking gently to and fro, sighing, as he does when he wants me to think he is having a breakdown.

Kick-starting the social life of two people who make Howard Hughes seem like Christopher Biggins was never going to be simple. Going through the address book was a laborious task for all of three minutes and twenty seconds. I am putting everybody into categories: Work, Utilities, Friends and Family. 'A' then, in its entirety, is for Aunt (Matthew's), Aim Car Hire and, strangely enough, Jeffrey Archer, whom neither of us know or wish to. Jeffrey is getting his own category. 'Z' contains London Zoo (Louis is sponsoring a terrapin) and one friend (mine, Polish, living in Papua New Guinea). In between come fifteen London-based friends, counting couples as one entry.

My mission, if the sighing and rocking is to cease, is to phone them all and arrange to see them. 'This time next year,' I say, 'we could well be playing after-dinner consequences with fifteen fellow revellers in a rented Jacobean manor house near Stroud.'

•

Skipping the As I go straight to the Bs. The last time we spoke to the Bs was when Mrs B rang at nine o'clock one evening two years ago to ask if we were on our way.

'On our way where?' I asked.

'Here,' said Mrs B. 'We are expecting you for dinner.'

This, of course, was Matthew's fault because he never told me. By way of an apology I suggest we take Mr and Mrs B out to a restaurant. (Like just-released prisoners, Matthew and I must make our re-entry into society with caution. We are not yet ready to have people here and I am nervous about going to someone else's house for fear that force of habit will make us head straight for the television and fight over the remote control.) Mrs B, however, leaves me with no choice. She says she is far too pregnant with her third little B to go out but they would be happy to have us round.

It was a disaster. Matthew had a fight with the second little B over whether they watched Cartoon Network or the Paramount Comedy Channel. The child was sent to bed and Matthew, who refused to relinquish the remote control and actually put it by the side of his plate during dinner, was yawning and checking his watch before the cheese. Unable to bear the strained atmosphere a moment longer I feigned a migraine and we left. Mr and Mrs B are one of those modern, Continentally influenced couples who serve cheese before pudding so we were home by ten thirty and are now in bed watching *Silence of the Lambs*. Just as we get to the bit where Anthony Hopkins says to Jodie Foster, 'A census taker once tried to test me. I ate his liver with some fava beans and a nice Chianti,' Matthew turns to me and says, 'I wish I was Hannibal Lecter. At least Hannibal Lecter got to finish his supper.'

24 May 1998

Lynda Goes on Holiday

When Lynda the nanny tendered her resignation just before Christmas, we were angry, bemused and upset; angry that she had given only ten months' notice (how could she spring it on us like that?); bemused that she could quit for as flimsy a reason as wanting to go home to Australia; upset because all three of us love her, and cannot imagine life without her. Five months on I still find myself imagining the farewell scene. I'm holding Louis and I say, 'Goodbye, Lynda. Thanks for everything. Keep in touch.' Louis puts his arms out to her. He's crying, she's crying, I'm crying, Matthew's flicking through the cable channels for Brazilian beach football . . . this is as far as the lump in the throat allows me to get.

Matthew caught me at it the other evening. 'Why are you crying?' he asked.

'I've been watching a gerbil being put to sleep on *Animal Hospital*,' I said.

'I can see how devastating that would be,' he said. 'Shall I dial the Samaritans for you?'

Actually, this idea has occurred to me before. I probably would have done it by now, but for the fear of rejection.

'Hello, Samaritans. How can we help?'

'I'm suicidal.'

'I see; and why's that?'

'My nanny has resigned.'

'I'm sorry, but I have an alcoholic manic-depressive waiting on line three . . .'

'She's wonderful, you see. She's been with us since Louis was two days old.'

'And Jonathan Aitken on line four . . .'

'And she cooks him special lunches . . . Hello? Hello?'

No, they just wouldn't understand. Somehow, we have to find a way to stop her going. Appeal to her better nature. Emotional blackmail. Steal her passport. Anything.

•

But as much as we adore Lynda, it must be said that she has her selfish side. As if the resignation itself and the short notice period were not enough, she has now announced that she is taking a holiday. A holiday! – after just a year in the job!

'Before I go, I want to see as much of Britain as possible,' she explained.

'Shepherd's Bush is very nice in the spring,' I said.

She didn't reply. She said she was going on a tour – of the West Country – so I suggested she might like to take Louis with her. 'He loves coach travel.' Again, no answer. She just handed me a notebook with *Louis's Week* written on the front.

Inside she had listed the starting times and addresses for all the various playgroups, swimming lessons and music classes, and a day-by-day menu. 'You didn't have to do all this,' I said when I'd read it. 'I'm not totally incompetent, you know.' Lynda just sighed. That's one of the things I love most about her. She's a woman of so few words.

•

Some sociologists and child experts, foot soldiers in the army of the post-feminist backlash, now insist that babies and small children develop better when their mothers are with them all the time. I think there may be something in this. Lynda has been gone only a day, and already Louis has made an important breakthrough.

In the time it took me to wrestle the Postman Pat bubble bath from the dog's mouth, my brilliant child had mastered the safety lid on the Nurofen pot I had handed him as a diverting rattle. He even managed to put two pills in his mouth. 'An excellent toy,' said Matthew, sticking his fingers down poor Louis's throat. 'When I've finished doing this, why don't you settle him down with the carving knife?'

The duty officer at the Chelsea and Westminster Hospital Poisons Unit advised that the one thing not to do was stick fingers down the throat, and then incredulously asked, 'How on earth did he get the lid off?'

'He's a child genius,' I replied. 'Amazing, isn't it?'

He said that the pills were pretty harmless if he had only taken two. 'Just watch him carefully for twenty-four hours and make sure he drinks plenty of milk.'

I spent all of fifteen minutes watching Louis very carefully indeed as he demonstrated precisely how he had got the childproof lid off the Nurofen. It's all in the wrist action; a little pressure applied in the right place, two clicks, a half turn and it's away. Sheer genius. I tried it but Louis, as I proudly announced to my mother-in-law later that day, was the undisputed champion. Strangely for such a doting grandmother she didn't seem that impressed.

Neither did Lynda, when she rang to see how Louis was. Matthew muttered something about a deranged mind and suggested I book a temporary nanny for the rest of the week. I didn't dignify it with a reply. It's a trick I've picked up from Lynda.

•

The agency nanny arrived in time to give Louis his breakfast. I left her to it while I went upstairs to get dressed. When I returned ten minutes later she was gone. She'd taken Louis to the park.

Two hours later, they were still out, and I was reading and rereading her references, not quite sure what to look for. Some small clue, perhaps. 'Sandra is reliable, punctual and conscientious, and since her brief stretch in Broadmoor last year, she has restricted her baby-snatching to no more than one child a month.'

An hour after that, I was driving round Shepherd's Bush looking for them, sick to the stomach with panic. I eventually spotted them walking back towards the house, Louis fast asleep in his pushchair. I drove straight past, parked and was back inside to answer her knock on the door two minutes later.

'Hi-eee,' I said. 'Nice walk?'

'Yes, thanks,' she said. 'I just saw you drive past. You were in a hurry. Been crying?'

I told her I'd been listening to a talking tape of a hamster being put down on *Animal Hospital*.

•

Lynda has returned, full of what a lovely time she had away from London. I have offered to move to the country. I've offered her more money, clothes, a car. I've tried subtle emotional blackmail: DON'T GO, LYNDA written on the fridge in brightly coloured magnetic letters. I seriously considered stealing her passport and blaming it on the dog, but she caught me eyeing her bag. 'I see you're carrying your passport around with you,' I said. 'Why don't you give it to me for safe-keeping?' She just did that thing of not answering that she is so good at.

31 May 1998
A Journey to the Country

There is a moment in every car journey over six miles, and plenty under that, when Matthew becomes philosophical. This is the calm both before and after the storm, the sixty-second hiatus between the bout of map-flinging, horn-bashing, foul language and fist-waving just ended and the one about to begin. On a good day, the existential treatise comes in a traffic jam; on a bad day, a red traffic light is enough. But it always happens somewhere and it always takes exactly the same form.

It begins with rhythmic rocking. The head gently butts the steering wheel three times, then it goes into the hands and a low, melancholy moan is emitted. 'Would you please explain to me,' he says, finally, through parted fingers, 'exactly what the point of living might be? What is the point to being alive? What is the point?' He never gets an answer because I am always pretending to be asleep. Asleep I cannot be held accountable for the closure of Hammersmith Bridge. Awake I am Director of the Council Roadworks Division. Unconscious, I am innocent of formulating government policy on highway maintenance. Conscious, I am Minister for Transport with special responsibility for motorway cones.

Car journeys are torture for most couples, I know. I

am not, however, aware of anyone having used a roadside AA phone to ask for the number of a good divorce lawyer (London to Cornwall, 1992). I would also be intrigued to hear of any other incidents of a journey being made twice in order to settle a dispute over the quickest route. In our case it was a simple, much-frequented journey from Primrose Hill to Shepherd's Bush, a mere four or five miles. It was a Sunday evening and we were setting off home from Matthew's parents' house.

'Why,' I asked, as we turned the wrong way onto the main road, 'do you insist on going via Maida Vale?'

'Fine,' he said in his you've-really-blown-it-now tone. 'Let's settle this once and for all. We will drive home my way. We will then turn straight around, go back to my parents' house and start again with your route.'

'Can't you drop us off first so I can put Louis to bed?'

'No,' he said. 'Louis is my witness.'

•

In a bid to rescue the resurrection of our social life, after a sequence of disastrous dinner parties, I have taken the step – some would call it bold; others clinically insane (I'm with the others) – of wangling us an invitation to spend a bank holiday weekend with friends in Kent.

'You go on ahead with the car,' I said to Matthew. 'Louis and I will hitch a lift with an escaped serial killer, and meet you there.'

'You're neurosing about the driving, aren't you?' said Matthew. 'But there's no need. I've looked at the map, and it's quite simple. We just get onto the M25, head east, hit the M20 and Bob's your uncle.' He has promised to be calm throughout the journey, and to take full charge of navigation. In return, I have sworn an oath not to mention my father's funeral (London to Newmarket via Slough; arrival at cemetery with coffin halfway through descent).

'It's my father's funeral all over again,' I said, and this time it was me with my head in my hands. We were indeed on the M25, but heading west, and after a particularly vivid display of fist-shaking at a Vauxhall Cavalier, Matthew had just asked me to explain to him precisely the point of being on this planet.

I said, 'You assured me you'd studied the map.'

He said, 'You know I suffer from cartographical dyslexia.'

I said, 'I'm not getting involved, and besides, there is no such thing as "cartographical dyslexia".'

He said, 'I'm Jewish.' We turned round and the journey, astonishingly, proceeded without further incident. Louis slept, the roads were fine, the route was good, and we arrived punctually at 1 p.m., in time for lunch.

Perhaps it was the shock of the relatively incident-free journey or perhaps Matthew is having difficulty with our gradual re-entry into society. Whatever. It was at this point that things took a dramatic turn for the worse. My husband mutated from Victor Meldrew into the Harry Enfield character with the flat cap, who tells people that they did not, under any circumstances, want to do that.

A fellow guest arrived late, tired, crumpled and moaning after a delayed train journey. 'You shouldn't have come by train,' said Matthew with nauseating sprightliness. 'You should have come by car. Honestly, it took us no time at all, M3, M25, A21 . . .' He had to be dissuaded, almost physically (actually, physically, to be honest, with a kick on the shin), from fetching the map from the car.

The weekend got underway, other people arrived from various parts of London and the Home Counties and by Sunday evening Matthew had become The Man Who Mistook Himself for Someone Other than the Most Boring Man on Earth. At lunch on Monday, he tried to engage a newcomer in a debate about the best way to the house from a village two miles down the road. ('But wouldn't it have saved you a minute or so if you had turned left at the pub, and approached from the east?')

•

'Right, I've looked at the map,' said Matthew, 'and I think the best way home is A21, M20 into London, Lewisham, Vauxhall Bridge. You don't want to go on the M25, not on a bank holiday Monday.'

An hour later, as we sat motionless on the M25, he asked me what I thought the point to human existence might be. 'What is the point?' he said as he took his head from his hands to scowl at a Ford Mondeo.

Meldrew was back, unbearable of course, but marginally less so than Harry Enfield. 'Never again,' he fumed.

'Never,' I sighed, letting out a gentle snore.

7 June 1998
List of Chores

I have often marvelled at the way Lynda the nanny is capable of stopping Louis dead in his tracks. 'No, Louis,' she says firmly and then she repeats it: 'No.' The effect is immediate. He removes his hand from the internal workings of the video and throws her an 'I am so sorry, what was I thinking of?' look that is surprising – precocious, even – in a person of one.

It's all in the tone. There is no panic or anger in Lynda's voice, just firmness. I don't know if she has deliberately modelled it on anybody, but if she has, it could be Arnold Schwarzenegger – 'Don't even think it, bay-bee,' – in *The Terminator*.

I have, as I say, admired this tone for a long time, but until this morning I was not sure whether its effect was limited to very small children. I can now confirm that it is just as effective on other age groups.

Normally the most placid, easy-going person you could wish to meet, Lynda strode purposefully across the room, grabbed the phone from my hand and said, 'No, Rebecca. No.'

I was on the verge of handing my life back to that stroppy, fag-raddled hellcat, our former cleaning lady, Trish. I was in the process of calling her to say, 'I can't cope. I am drowning in dust and dirt. Come back. All is forgiven.'

'Sit down,' said Lynda, taking my arm, and leading me – with the kindly authority of a geriatric nurse – towards the sofa. 'It can't be that bad. Nothing is so bad you have to call Trish. We'll make a list of chores and we can do them together.'

Lynda has missed the point here, though. Because I already have a list, but it goes back decades. A few things have been ticked off over the years, but hundreds, possibly thousands, remain hanging over me. 'Do English project (Turtles)', for instance, from 1971; 'Tidy bedroom' and 'Join Pony Club' (1968). The list is not just endless, it has no definable beginning. My mother can confirm that it dates back to somewhere in the 1960s, but cannot be more precise than that. 'Clean out ferrets' is still outstanding, as is 'Remove half-eaten sandwich from duffel bag'.

The trouble is, I am a compulsively methodical person. Everything must be done in sequence so it is impossible for me to tackle chore number 10,978 – 'Fix baby gate' – when I know that chore number 129 – 'Darn Bay City Rollers scarf' – has yet to be attended to. Mrs Drink, my maths teacher, said that if I hadn't been so busy attending to chore number 245 – 'Get boyfriend' – I might have paid more attention to chore number 267 – 'Pass maths exam'. Mrs Drink didn't understand that I was a victim of my own scrupulous standards of chronological chore-completion. Just as Lynda fails to understand now.

•

This morning's 'Right. That's it, my life is chaos, I am worthless and good for nothing. I am calling Trish' outburst was provoked by Matthew asking if I had bothered to arrange a weekly delivery of organic fruit and vegetables yet. He is going through one of his biannual healthy living phases and this one has so far involved the purchase of three books on transcendental meditation, which currently lie, unopened, on the bedside table alongside half a bottle of whisky, a full ashtray and a copy of the *Racing Post*. He has also bought a video, *Qi-netics Holistic Exercises*, which he has watched once, from an armchair, smoking a large cigar.

Although I can hardly be blamed for treating this campaign with a certain detachment (he has just returned from Tesco's with a family-sized pack of Toffee Crisps and two giant Whole Nuts), it is true that six weeks have passed since he announced his intention to cleanse his body and aura. My part in this project, he told me, was to organize the delivery of organic produce. Thus it was that 'Matthew's aura food' was added to my list under 'Renew residents' parking permit'.

•

The parking permit is, in fact, at the root of all my current problems. Without one I am forced to leave the house every morning to buy a daily parking ticket, thus breaking the sequence of chores on the list. Instead of embarking on 'Do housework', which is about ten entries above 'Advertise for new cleaning lady', I begin the day with a frantic search for spare change for the ticket machine, followed by a trip into the road wearing a dressing gown and wellingtons. Then, just as I walk back into the house, Matthew goes and asks after the arrival time of his organic veg.

The paralysis born of frustration and guilt that this induces puts the entire day out of kilter. When, at 6.30 p.m., Matthew begins his ironic search for organic carrots – looking under the sofa cushions, opening the tumble-dryer door – a row ensues along the lines of 'get your own bloody vegetables'. A row, though, is preferable to asking for 275,198 other chores to be taken into consideration. Even in this marriage, I cannot explain that I failed to ring the fruit and veg company because of a half-eaten twenty-seven-year-old sandwich in a duffel bag in Dorset.

•

Lynda originally suggested that, for psychiatric reasons, we draw up a new list and make it circular, no beginning, no end. But the M25 would not be big enough to accommodate a list of my chores. So we have stuck to the traditional up-and-down method and listed things in order of urgency. Lynda has insisted I 'draw a line under' all chores pre-dating New Year's Day 1998.

The new list begins '(1) Buy parking permit' and Lynda has suggested that to avoid buying a daily ticket before leaving for the council building I set off, in the car, before 9 a.m. 'On the way back you can stop off at Sainsbury's Homebase and buy weed killer and a spade.'

'"Buy weed killer" is number nine on the list, and "spade" is twenty-two,' I whine. 'I'll be breaking the order of the chores.' Lynda said nothing, picked up her pen and taking one long, deep breath amended the list. It now reads as follows: '(1) Parking Permit; (2) Weed killer; (3) Spade; (4) Psychiatrist.'

14 June 1998

We Have Decided to Move to the Country

There are moments, more and more often now, when I truly believe I'm living in a medley of sitcoms. One day I might be Margaret Meldrew, the next I might be Wendy Craig (actually I am permanently Wendy Craig and will remain so until I dye my hair and stop burning the dinner). There was a particularly disturbing moment last week, on the other hand, when I looked in the mirror and saw Olive from *On The Buses* staring back at me.

Today, though, thanks to Matthew's latest obsession with moving to the country and starting a smallholding, I am poised to become Felicity Kendal in *The Good Life*. (There are, it must be said, clear distinctions to be drawn between Felicity and me. She is the former Rear of the Year, for example, a title I might have won fifteen years ago had the contest been held in a fairground hall of mirrors.)

Veering slightly from the original *Good Life* concept, Matthew has decided to set his organic smallholding in the country rather than a suburban back garden. The irony here is so obvious and predictable I imagine we will be tripping over it on a daily basis as we set out to feed the pigs. I am the one who was brought up in the countryside. Matthew is the North London boy who until now suffered panic attacks at the prospect of anything one degree more rural than Shepherd's Bush Green. I am the one who once gave up a perfectly good job in London to move to Dorset with a Jersey cow and a lurcher. Matthew is the one who lived on the edge of Hampstead Heath for twenty years and can still remember every one of his four walks.

•

Nevertheless, one weekend in Kent, walking in bluebell woods – hurrying through bluebell woods, in fact (trampling over the things, in strict truth), to get back in time for the racing on the telly – and now he's up at 5.00 a.m. every morning listening to *Farming Today*.

'We've got to do something about the oil-seed rape problem,' he'll say. 'It's ruining our countryside.'

'But that's just the point,' I tell him. 'It's not our countryside. We'd hate it. Or at least you'd hate it.' He ignores me and flicks through his Barbour catalogue.

It is true that two months ago, after a short Matthew-less holiday in the countryside, I conceived a pie-in-the-sky, get-rich-quick-plan that would enable us to live in rural Devon, with servants. It is true that Louis's childhood years would be vastly improved by breathing clean air, and that the dog would be happy. It is also true that if I were married to someone else, someone who could go on a picnic, for instance, without taking a radio to check the football results, I would also love to be in the country. And, in my defence, it was always stipulated that, in order to accommodate Matthew's needs, my Devon plan revolved around the sudden injection into the joint account of £22 million.

We would have to be rich so that we could create our own skewed version of CenterParcs – a pleasure dome in a rural setting but with Ladbrokes, slot machines, take-aways and a multiplex cinema.

Without these things Matthew would be bored. He can't ride, he hates walking, he loathes Janet Street Porter, he doesn't shoot, thank God, and the one time he attempted a round of golf he was chased back to the clubhouse from the second hole by a wasp.

Matthew is phobic about wasps. He has never been stung, and is certain that if he ever were to be he would suffer a violent allergic reaction – 'anaphylactic shock', he calls it – and die within three minutes. I have tried explaining that the countryside is full of bees, hornets, even adders, but most of all wasps. It doesn't matter, he says. He'll carry a phial of adrenaline (the antidote) and a small syringe.

'I bet Coombe Bisset doesn't have a betting shop,' I said as Matthew reached for the appropriate Ordnance Survey map. He's bought dozens of them, from Worksop to Dungeness. 'I bet Chew Magna doesn't have cable TV,' I continued. I was reading from his list of requirements. The one he recites to estate agents down the phone – 'Four bedrooms, anything with a bluebell wood and a bit of land. Is there a casino in Salisbury?'

His plan is to spend a week next month viewing properties. He has narrowed his search down to three counties, Wiltshire, Hampshire and Kent, and I have twenty-one days to convince him that he has never been so wrong about anything in his life.

•

He has agreed to drop the smallholding idea. I told him that I would refuse to take part in any animal husbandry and that goatherds in the Winchester and Tunbridge Wells areas are at a premium these days, charging anything up to £50 an hour. Forcing him to watch an episode of *Emmerdale Farm* helped a little and the simple suggestion that he should mow our lawn introduced him to the idea of manual labour. It was the first time since we bought this house that he had ventured into the shed, which he pronounced 'filthy'. 'Don't you ever dust in here?' A bee chased him back inside after ten minutes and he left the mower precariously balanced over the fishpond at full throttle.

By the end of the week it was all pretty much over. 'I cannot deal with these people,' said Matthew, slamming down the phone and hurling a three-bedroomed semi on the outskirts of Devizes into the bin.

'Perhaps your specifications are a bit narrow,' I venture. 'The chances are the MGM Leisure Group is consciously avoiding bluebell woods when they plan their sites.'

With any luck the rural dream will be finally dished by Matthew's obsession with organic produce, which promises him the 'body and aura cleansing' he so craves. 'Pathetic,' he sneers, picking over our latest consignment of wilted, shrivelled, miniature vegetables and blight-spotted and bruised fruit, including a mango he believes is a scale-model of his own liver, sent to taunt him.

'It's a metaphor for the country,' I tell him. 'Shiny red apples do exist, but only in Tesco's in Shepherd's Bush.'

21 June 1998
Waiting for Joe

Joe is a carpenter, a very good carpenter. He is utterly charming; we all love him. He's like the Pied Piper. Louis's face lights up when he walks in, Steptoe rolls over with his legs in the air, I put the kettle on and Matthew stands about and chats. Joe is southern Irish, tall, thin and really, really nice. Late last November he agreed to build us some shelves in the sitting room. The job, he said, would take him two, three days, maybe four at the outside, and would be completed by Christmas.

In December he came to measure up and give us a quote. Then he came again, three times, and each time it was lovely to see him. On 2 January he did actually give us the quote, and on 9 January he remeasured up for the fourth time and gave us another quote. On 15 January he rang to say he wouldn't be coming that day after all, but he'd definitely be round the next, to measure up and give us a quote.

He didn't come the next day, but he did ring the day after that to say sorry he hadn't been able to make it the day before, but would there be anyone in if he came tomorrow? I'll be in, I said. I'll wait.

He arrived last Friday with some timber but said he wouldn't be able to get started until he'd measured up.

Never mind. The house is full of the promising aroma of freshly sawn wood.

Scientists and anthropologists are always doing research into how the span of our lives breaks down into various activities. We spend so many years asleep in bed, so many months watching telly, in the bath, on the phone . . . But they never tell us how long we spend waiting for workmen. Perhaps they're still waiting for the pollsters to turn up with the results?

Over the past two years, since we bought this house, 68 per cent of my time has been given up to waiting for a workman. I wasn't patient with all the others. They were cowboys, out to get us. Joe's just disorganized.

There was Paul, for instance, a plumber with a filthy temper. He rang from his mobile in March 1997 to check we were in because he had the chrome pipe (£175; parts and labour) for the bottom of the bath. It was a mean trick, though, because he said he was passing the end of our road at that very moment but that was the last we heard of him. The Shepherd's Bush Triangle must have got him.

Then there was Mike the electrician, who came complete with his own stereophonic music system, a four-foot-wide ghetto-blaster which sat at his feet like a well-trained dog while he worked. Mike charged £200 for some of the most expertly exposed wiring I have ever seen and then left. The last we heard was the bass thump of his blaster fading into the distance as he turned the corner into the Uxbridge Road.

And then there was Bob, another plumber, who sucked his teeth and charged £350 for his diagnosis that all our radiators had been installed upside down. 'I've got a hiatus hernia operation tomorrow,' he told me, 'but I'll be on my feet by Thursday to sort you out. See you then.' We must assume the worst, that he never pulled through.

The purpose of my life now, though, is to find something to do while I wait for Joe. Should anyone enquire what it is, for example, that I like about gardening, I will reply that I love planting and nurturing, I love being outside, but most of all, it gives me something to do while I'm waiting for Joe. I am waiting for Joe at this moment. I've been waiting for him since 9 a.m., it's now 3.45 p.m. and I'll still be waiting for him when the sun goes down. Just as I waited for Joe all yesterday, and the day before that, and just as I'll be waiting for him again this time tomorrow.

It is what I do. It's my life. I am Louis's mother, Matthew's wife. I am columnist, friend, daughter, frequent visitor to Tesco's, charwoman, gardener, feeder of Steptoe . . . I am all these things, and yet they are sidelines. What I really do, the real purpose of my presence on this planet, is to wait, very patiently, for Joe.

'Joe's left his tools here,' said Matthew, stubbing his toe on a Black & Decker Workmate, 'that's a good sign.'

Only it isn't. Joe's tools have been in the cupboard under the stairs since Christmas, he just got them out on Friday.

'Why don't you ring and ask if he's coming?'

'No,' I said. 'Then I'd know for sure. I couldn't cope with the finality.'

The sun has set, and I'm still writing, still finding

things to do while I wait for Joe, even though today's vigil is now officially at an end because he rang five minutes ago.

'Hello, Rebecca,' he said, 'it's Joe. Just to let you know I can definitely come on Sunday.'

'Are you sure? You don't mind working on the weekend?'

'No, I don't mind. Better crack on. Get the job done.'

'Joe, are you really coming on Sunday?

'No, Rebecca,' said Joe quietly. 'It's not very likely at all.'

28 June 1998
Computer Games

I knew there was something seriously wrong. Matthew was being furtive. He was pale, tired and withdrawn, and there were nights – more and more frequent – when he was staying up until three or four in the morning.

As for his body language, it spoke for itself: his refusal to look me in the eye, the way his hand covered his mouth whenever I asked him how he was getting on with what I hoped was nothing more sinister than a particularly heavy workload, shut in his office – his lair, as it has become – all day and into the night.

If I disturbed him to ask if he needed feeding or watering, there would be a sudden flurry of activity, like a schoolboy hiding his catapult under his desk. He would turn round in his chair to face me and deliver a fake but cheery 'Hi!', shiftily glancing over his shoulder in case he'd left any evidence – an open address book, a photograph. As I spoke I would scan the room, neither of us concentrating on what the other was saying.

I discovered the awful truth by sneaking up on him, creeping one night in stockinged feet along the hall to the door of his office, where I stood, not breathing, just listening. I don't know what I expected to hear; the faint murmur of an illicit telephone conversation, perhaps: 'I'll try to get out tomorrow afternoon. I'll tell her I'm going to the betting shop. That should give us five hours clear. I'll book us a room at the Hammersmith Novotel.' It took me a while to decipher the sounds I did hear – a faint but regular bleep, the click of a computer mouse and then, every minute or so, the synthesized roar of a crowd followed by the congratulatory slap of a thigh. And then it dawned: Matthew was playing computer golf, and he was obviously winning.

The discovery that her husband is having an affair is one thing. But this. *This.*

•

It could have been worse, I suppose. I might have unearthed a limited-edition scale model of the Starship *Enterprise*, or found him watching repeat episodes of *Crossroads* on UK Gold, or I might have walked in on Matthew and Frank Bough browsing through a copy of *Skin Two* magazine. At least I could have been big about Frank, sought counselling, told myself it was my problem if I had a problem with it.

Initially Matthew was horrified at being discovered. He was embarrassed, obviously ashamed. But then came the bragging, the self-justification: his putting skills, his 'shot game' and his length off the tee. 'I've just hit a four iron from 163 yards to within six inches of the pin,' he would tell me. 'I've stored the action replay. Would you like a look?'

Sometimes sarcasm is inadequate and only silence will do.

'Oh, come on,' he'd say. 'It's great fun, don't you think, shooting under sixty round the very difficult course at Sawgrass?'

'Is it fun, Matthew?' I asked. 'Or is it merely very sad?

I wandered around for a few days looking depressed and sighing, phoning my mother at hourly intervals, and eventually Matthew agreed to remove all his games from his Apple Mac and throw them away – the golf, the patience, the backgammon, the one with fighter pilots and tubes of napalm, something called Aqua Blooper Piper! The cold turkey was hell. He paced, he rocked, and his head rarely emerged from his hands. But we got through it. It was a nasty moment for the marriage, but we pulled through. We survived.

•

Except that Matthew didn't throw those games away. Having removed them from his Apple Mac upstairs, he hid them in my Apple Mac downstairs. It was a devious move. He was relying on my computer illiteracy – the very thing, it turned out, that was to prove his undoing.

One evening, while attempting a spell-check on my latest list of 'Things to do', I hit two wrong buttons together and unwittingly summoned the forces of evil lurking within my computer. Up it flashed on the screen – a little square folder called simply 'Matthew's games'. I double-clicked on the mouse, double-clicked again and I was in.

I determined to destroy them for ever, these mindless,

pathetic, infantile time-wasters. These accoutrements of the sad and lonely which had kept Matthew up until dawn night after night, monopolized our lives, threatened our marriage . . .

•

Aqua Blooper Piper! It's a game in which you have to join two pipes, picking up a series of differently shaped plumber's joints from a constantly moving conveyor belt and clicking them into place with the mouse.

It is 4.35 a.m., and I have just completed level three. It's not easy, not easy at all. Sometimes you think you've done it – the pipes look nice and secure – so you click the mouse to turn on the tap. But no! You've left one tiny joint open, the pipes spring a leak and you are right back where you started, back with the apprentice plumbers. All those hours wasted, but you don't give in. You keep on going.

There is a pause option that means if Louis wakes, the phone rings or the dog asks to go out, I don't have to waste a game. There is also a facility called 'The boss is coming', which enables you to blank the screen in seconds if someone should be approaching. Just one more game, I think, before I consign it to cyber-oblivion . . .

•

Lynda the nanny knows my secret. I don't know how she knows, she just does. The atmosphere is awful; she makes no attempt to hide her disapproval. She says nothing, but I know what she is thinking: How can you live with yourself, wasting precious time when you should be with your child? I sometimes think the sooner she leaves for Australia the better.

Matthew, on the other hand, has no idea. He thinks I am having an affair.

12 July 1998

The Hypochondriac

The thing about living with a hypochondriac is that you just can't win. If you show too little sympathy, you are heartless and inhuman. If you show too much, he thinks you 'know something' – that you are in league with a host of imaginary specialists who are baffled that he is still alive.

In the seven and a half years we have been married, Matthew has suffered the following: eleven heart attacks (or myocardial infarctions, as he calls them); six strokes ('cerebral haemorrhages', or 'transient ischaemic attacks'); nine skin cancers ('malignant melanomas'); thirteen brain tumours ('brain tumours' – he has yet to discover a more impressive technical name for them); three motor neurone diseases ('lupus'); bowel, colonic and testicular cancers beyond counting; constant high blood pressure ('hypertension'); renal failure; an enlarged liver; flesh-eating bug ('necrotizing fasciitis'); bacterial meningitis; brittle-bone disease; rheumatoid arthritis; ordinary arthritis; and scurvy.

These are the ones I know about. I can only begin to guess at the rest of his imagined ailments, though a flick through the leaflets he keeps tucked inside his copy of

Black's Medical Dictionary gives a horrifying insight, particularly the one on pre-eclampsia.

•

This week, Matthew has multiple sclerosis. There is, he says, a strange tingling sensation in his fingertips, and his teeth are 'permanently and unnaturally on edge'. I resist the urge to suggest that he might just be suffering from overexcitement at the prospect of the World Cup final and remind myself of what happened on New Year's Eve four and half years ago when I failed to take him seriously after he started behaving like a romantic poet with tuberculosis – shivering, chattering his teeth together and wiping his brow.

'Feel my forehead,' he had said. 'I'm very, very ill.'

Well, I am sorry, but there are times when a hypochondriac's carer just can't be doing with it and this was one of them. I was tired, we'd just come through a two-week 'I am diabetic' phase and I wanted to sleep. I felt the forehead as requested, and pronounced his temperature normal. When I awoke, I found him ushering in 1994 in his duffel coat and my sheepskin mittens. He was shaking and the thermometer was rattling against his teeth. He had a temperature of 103 (103.7, as he insists). The virus kept him bedridden for two weeks.

He still reminds me of it now. He'll simply say, apropos of nothing at all, 'Do you remember that time I nearly died and you ignored me?'

•

'So what's it like, then, this tingling?' I ask him.

'It's tingling,' he replies, 'very, very serious tingling.'

He is now jabbing his fingertips with a darning needle, a procedure he saw being performed on *Casualty*, only on *Casualty* it wasn't with a darning needle and the patient had a spinal injury. If Matthew knew the name of the instrument that was being used, he'd be straight off to the surgical appliances shop in New Cavendish Street to buy one. He'd add it to his collection – the stethoscope I bought him last Valentine's Day, the blood-pressure kit (wedding anniversary) and a cholesterol-testing machine (impulse purchase). Now he's jabbing his gums with the darning needle.

'My only concern is for your state of mind.' I tell him. 'Stop pacing or you'll bring on another bout of Marcher's haematuria.' This is an ailment he was particularly proud of (symptom: peeing blood, which I put down to a bowl of borscht, but which proved to be the result of a sudden keep-fit regime).

He wants me to phone the doctor. Hypochondriacs can never phone the doctor themselves, they are too debilitated by the hypochondria to do anything but pace with their heads in their hands.

•

When Matthew returns from his doctor's appointment that evening he has the same look he had last time (reprieve from bowel cancer) and the time before that (elbow joint not noticeably enlarged) and the time before that (we all have pronounced veins around our ankles). It's an evangelical look, a beaming, beatific, glad-to-be-alive twinkle-eyed gleam. 'The doctor says there is nothing wrong with me,' he says. 'It's not multiple sclerosis, apparently, because the tingling doesn't get worse when I am in the bath.'

And then before skipping upstairs for his daily upper body, face and neck examination, Matthew grabs Louis, lifts him high in the air and gives him the kind of hug soldiers would give their little ones as they disembarked at Southampton docks after four years fighting for their country. It's a hug that says, 'I am going to live to see my child grow up after all.'

Later that evening he appears, white-faced, in the doorway He has found a lump. He takes my finger and guides it to just behind his right earlobe. 'It's like a pea,' he says, pressing my finger hard into the edge of his jawbone.

'I can't feel anything.'

'Do you think it's serious?' he asks.

26 July 1998

Prince Charles Comes to Devon

The monstrous good-luck beard was what finally did it. The screaming at his Wembley-sized television screen I could handle after seven years' training. The solitude – match after match, day after day, week after week – was water off a football widow's back, and as for the suicidal gloom after the Argentinean game, this had its compensation: at least he wasn't screaming any more.

But the superstitious beard, which he grows for all major footballing events involving Spurs or England, was too much. In the opening stages, during the qualifying matches, the early growth made him look quite handsome, almost Christlike, but by the time they'd battened down the hatches in Toulouse, he'd metamorphosed into Dave Lee Travis. He promised to wear the monstrosity, no trimming, for one calendar year, if England won, but he would shave it off the moment they went out. God bless you, David Beckham.

My mistake was to join him in front of the television for the penalty shoot-out. As Batty missed his kick, Matthew's head crashed despairingly into those ever-waiting hands, I stood up to perform a one-woman Mexican wave while crooning, 'It's coming off, it's coming off. His beard is coming off,' to the tune of 'Three Lions'.

He didn't say anything at the time, just looked at me like a wounded fawn. 'So do you want a lift to Trumper's in the morning, then? I'm going near Mayfair,' I said a little later.

'Oh, no, I'm not going to the barber,' he replied. 'Not now that you've gloated.' That was it. That's when I finally cracked, and booked my second escape to Devon in the space of four months. Same cottage on same remote country estate.

•

My mother and her lurcher Sam have joined us – Louis, Lynda, Steptoe and me. My stepmother is popping down for a day or two en route to her aunt in Truro.

Everyone is happier. I called Matthew from the phone box, and he sounded more content, on his own at home with his new Sony PlayStation – the one he bought as 'post-penalty shoot-out solace'; the one he insisted he had every right to buy, on the grounds that 'my friend Giles has one'. He has even consented to an appointment with his barber.

Devon is glorious, occasionally sunny, mostly wet, but lush, green and silent except for the sound of rain on the pond and the whirr-plop as the anglers staying at the big house reel in and out. It is bliss. There is no telephone or television, no football, no constant questioning of Jimmy Hill's sanity. Nothing happens here to ruin the tranquillity.

•

A security man was hiding in the undergrowth by the stream. Louis found him as we returned from a walk this morning – a walk on which we had to negotiate a Range Rover parked across the cattle grid, and came across an entire army of gardeners, each wielding a noisy motorized tidying implement: strimmers, saws, mowers. Everywhere now, busy, busy people are bustling.

The security man was a fat-necked fellow in a black suit with a walkie-talkie. He looked like Special Branch or MI5 and he retreated into the undergrowth when he saw us, his crackling walkie-talkie mingling tunefully with the incessant whirr of mowers and the helicopter now circling over the estate, which caused Sam, the lurcher, to take fright and disappear across the fields, my shrieking mother in hot pursuit. Oxford Circus Tube in the evening rush hour would seem like the quietest corner of the desert compared to this Devon scene that has come to resemble the opening credits of *Apocalypse Now*.

•

Returning with Sam, my mother looks flushed, but not from the chase. The head gardener, after being threatened, I imagine, with his own Paraquat, has tipped her off. 'He says we should be outside the front of the cottage at 3 p.m. if we want to see what all the fuss is about. He wouldn't say any more except that it's to be a private visit and HRH's helicopter will be landing in the bottom field.' With that, my mother rushes upstairs to change and practise her curtsey. I have a terrible feeling that, when I next set eyes on her, she will be wearing a hat.

Meanwhile, my stepmother, with the feeble excuse that she is meeting her aunt in Truro that evening and going straight to the theatre, is now wearing something in which Joan Collins would look absurdly overdressed at a palace garden party.

Lynda has scrubbed poor Louis's face pink, and after two hours of speculation as to the identity of this particular HRH and how he or she should be greeted (Should we take pictures? Should we search for bunting?) I declare that I am going for a siesta, and if the royal chopper landing a mere hundred yards from my bedroom window fails to wake me, I couldn't care one iota less. In fact, should the entire Royal Family turn up en masse and express a desire to stage a post-Diana public-relations photo-opportunity for the world's media at the foot of my bed, I am not to be woken. I just want peace.

I wake at 3 p.m. precisely. It wasn't the helicopter; it was the shrieks of girlish laughter coming from outside my window. Lined up, as if on parade and waiting inspection from their colonel-in-chief, are my mother, thankfully not in a hat (although only because she didn't pack one, and didn't have the time or the materials to run one up), my stepmother, Louis, Lynda and the two dogs.

The giant hogweed is now bristling as the security guard has been joined by three of the gardeners' wives, all loitering furtively with a we-always-spend-Monday-afternoons-in-the-undergrowth-hung-about-with-Kodak-Instamatics air about them.

•

Prince Charles was half an hour late, and we were getting very twitchy and taking it personally. The helicopter landed and a few minutes later the royal head appeared over the bank of cow parsley the other side of the water. As he and his entourage walked around the pool he looked across at us, took one hand from behind his back and waved. Someone – and it was inevitable, I suppose, that one of our party would disgrace us – took a picture, with flash, and shouted, 'Hello, sir!'

It was me of course. I let the side down. My mother, stepmother, Lynda, Louis and the gardeners' wives stood in well-behaved silence, watching. Even Steptoe, who charged towards the pond barking hysterically, showed greater decorum.

And an hour later, it was I who was casually wandering about in the bottom field when Prince Charles and his men made their way back to the helicopter. He stopped to talk to me, and fondle Steptoe's ears, or perhaps it was the other way round – perhaps I stopped to talk to him. I couldn't possibly reveal our entire conversation, but he did apologize for disturbing our peace. 'Not at all, it was a lovely surprise,' I said. 'And anyway, sir, who wants peace?'

•

Back in London, I am so proud. The World Cup is four glorious years away. Matthew's monstrous facial growth has gone, and Louis has taken to walking about in the garden with his hands behind his back.

2 August 1998
Postman Pat and the Road Rage Incident

A large pyramid of uncooked basmati rice sits in the middle of the kitchen floor, and a terrible silence – a silence that crackles with resentment, accusation and counter-accusation – permeates the house tonight. We are in the midst of a row, and for the first time since the earliest days of our marriage, I have used physical violence against my husband.

The last time was on New Year's Eve 1991, following a dispute about my method of cooking carrots. I was frying them in butter and lemon juice, to Matthew's own recipe, and to what I insist to this day would, had history taken a more tranquil course, have been a perfect, golden-brown conclusion. Disputing this, Matthew predicted a charred, black and inedible outcome. I held my ground. He held his. Defiantly, I turned the flame up. He turned it down to a gentle simmer. I turned it up to maximum. He turned it off. Then, as he stormed out of the kitchen, I took hold of a bottle of beer, aimed and threw it, catching him, from a distance of fifteen feet, flush on the back of the neck. So impressed was he with my William Tell accuracy that he rushed back to congratulate me and there the row ended.

How and when this current row will end I am not

sure, because the subject matter is so much more serious. It began when, after witnessing a road-rage incident, Matthew took the side of an enraged cyclist whom we now know to be Miss Hubbard, and I took the side of the driver, Alf Thompson, who was causing an obstruction. I defended Mr Thompson on the grounds that we didn't know the reasons behind his decision to stop in the middle of the road, it was pointless to get cross since he would doubtless be moving on shortly, etc., etc. And so the row rumbled on, until eventually, back in the kitchen, the one-kilogram packet of Tesco's basmati I was opening found its way not into the saucepan but thwack against Matthew's lower back.

Muttering something about ringing Erin Pizzey, he has withdrawn to his study to play computer golf and I to my desk downstairs. The rice can stay where it is.

•

Whatever the subject, the rows between Matthew and me follow a five-stage formula as rigid in its way as the rules governing a sonnet or a Japanese haiku.

Stage one is the Disputatious Question. In this case, it was me asking him when he was going to stop rambling on like Percy Sugden over a pint of stout in the Rover's about folk having the good grace to observe the common courtesies of Her Majesty's highways. On other previous, and no doubt future, occasions the Disputatious Question might be me asking whether Matthew has any plans to remove the damp towels from the bed, or Matthew wondering if I have any plans to complete the tax form he put on my desk last October.

Stage two of the row is the Tonal Riposte, in which

the person sarcastically questioned replies by attacking the questioner's tone of voice. 'I'd be happy to stop going on about Miss Hubbard's impatience/pick up the towels and put them, neatly folded, on the heated towel rail/fill out the tax form – if only you'd ask in a less aggressive tone.'

Stage three is the Tonal Counter-Strike, which sees the person accused of using the aggressive tone levelling exactly the same charge at the accuser. 'There was nothing aggressive about my tone. My tone was perfectly sweet. You're the one with an aggressive tone.'

Stage four is the Muttered Departure, in which the person most recently accused of using the aggressive tone (the one who originally asked the sarcastic question) leaves the room, murmuring something melodramatic about the sheer impossibility of sharing a roof with the other person, or about calling Erin Pizzey.

Stage five is the Reciprocal Apology, when each side strives to outdo the other with wildly exaggerated acceptances of the blame. Right now it is impossible to predict when or even if we will reach stage five.

•

It is now midnight and it looks like I am going to be the one to apologize. I have been going over the argument in my head. There is no doubt that he started it but it was I who lost my temper. I am in the wrong because I threw the rice. I must apologize.

I can hear the television on upstairs. He's finished playing computer golf. I am not even to be granted the satisfaction of interrupting him mid-swing.

'I am sorry I threw the rice at you,' I say.

'Forget it,' he says, 'it was entirely my fault. But I still think you were wrong. Miss Hubbard had every right to be furious with Mr Thompson.' And with that he rewinds Louis's *Postman Pat* video, invites me to sit down next to him and we go through the opening scenes of the Greendale road-rage incident frame by frame.

Matthew: 'See, Alf Thompson was on the defensive. He was aggressive and very rude.'

Me: 'But Miss Hubbard was being ridiculous. She can see with her own eyes that there is no way Alf can move his tractor until Pat has moved his van. It's not as if she's got anything to do with her time but cycle round Greendale all day. It wouldn't have hurt her to have waited two minutes.'

We finally agree to disagree and continue watching the video until Alf, in an attempt at a U-turn, bumps into the wheel arch of Pat's van. 'Which reminds me,' I say. 'You've done absolutely nothing to get the car fixed.'

'It's your car,' says Matthew. 'You get it fixed.'

'You were driving it,' I say. 'It was you who crashed into the barrier . . . in an *empty* NCP.'

'There you go again with that aggressive, sarcastic tone,' says Matthew, heading for the door. 'Why can't you just ask nicely?'

I did ask nicely. There is nothing wrong with my tone. My tone is perfectly sweet. It's his tone that's the problem.

6 September 1998
Perfect Georgina

Georgina is a terrible driver. From the passenger seat of her Peugeot 205 – 'the death seat', to give it its official name – I have experienced what it is like to be hurtled around the tiny, double-parked streets of Trouville-sur-Mer, thrust back by the kind of G-force that would frighten Damon Hill, feet frantically pumping at an imaginary brake pedal. Her parking technique, the ramming method, has long since pulverized her own bumpers and is now systemically rearranging those of countless numbers of innocent French motorists. I mention this with glee, because Georgina's driving is her one and only fault, and I am clinging desperately to it.

Since embarking on our summer holiday, sharing a house by the sea with Georgina and her husband John and their two-year-old son Oscar, I have had little to occupy my time but line up my own faults and inadequacies, one by one, against her talents and attributes.

Georgina is twenty-eight, with a perfect figure interrupted only by a tiny, compact four-month pregnancy. I am nearly thirty-eight with irreversible body flaws that were fully matured long before my own pregnancy. Georgina is dark-skinned with a head of brown curls which just fall. They don't even have to try, they just tumble perfectly around her angel face. I am fair-skinned – orange skewbald, in fact, owing to shoddily applied fake tan – and like all dumb blondes I wish I was a clever brunette with hidden depths.

It would be unfair on myself to deny that we do have things in common. We both, for example, love horses. Georgina during her days as a professional jockey in America rode 150 winners. I have one clear-round gymkhana rosette, the result of a swap for a copy of 'All Kinds of Everything' by Dana in 1970.

Sitting out on the veranda giving Louis his bottle, I ask Matthew if he considers my driving to be enough of an asset. Does it compensate at all for the fact that Georgina has for the third consecutive night provided not just supper (night one, chicken roasted with lemon and rosemary; night two, roast lamb with couscous and an aubergine bake; night three, a pasta dish, far too subtle for me to attempt to describe it), she also made, by way of an amuse-gueule, the scallop fishcake with coriander and chilli which he was about to pop into his mouth?

'Do you think that my ability to parallel-park is enough?' I ask, dipping into a bowl of peanuts, peanuts which Georgina has shelled, marinated in soy sauce and then oven-roasted. 'Given, that is, that I have never and am not ever likely to bring you an ice-cold glass of rosé and a plate of foie gras toast while you lie on the beach of an evening?' (as Georgina did a couple of hours ago).

'You can't parallel-park,' says Matthew, gazing distractedly in the direction of the sea from which Georgina, all dripping curls and brown limbs, is emerging after an evening swim. And then he reminds me of the times when I have parked so badly that he has been moved to suggest wittily that we take a taxi to the pavement.

Georgina and I pass as I take Louis up to bed. 'I've put a mosquito repellent in his room for you,' she says. 'The instructions are in French so if you have a problem, let me know.' This is just one of the many kindnesses Georgina has performed since we arrived here. It was Georgina who made the appointment for Louis to see a doctor when he came down with mild laryngitis the day after we arrived; Georgina who translated the dosages for the antibiotics, the cough mixture, the cortisone and the Calpol; and Georgina who then produced three phials of homeopathic remedies in case I was worried about continuing with the cortisone. Yesterday, when she returned from a quick trip back to her home near Paris, she brought a towelling robe for Louis; I had mentioned offhand that you cannot buy them in England for children under three.

The woman is killing me with kindness. I don't know how much more I can take.

•

God be praised, Georgina has made a mistake! On my way downstairs this morning, I stopped off for a loiter in the laundry room, vaguely wondering whether a spot of ironing might help me regain self-esteem, and found in the washing machine, with John's shirts, a paperback novel, thoroughly pulped after a full, fast-coloureds 60° cycle. The washing machine is blocked and flooded and the shirts are coated in soggy papier mâché.

Here, after five days full of countless examples of Georgina being funnier, cleverer and generally so much more of a perfect human being than me, is an opportunity for me to shine. I will quietly put it right. I won't say anything, I will simply clear up the mess, sort out the shirts and unblock the washing machine. Georgina need never know.

It says a great deal about me, however, that I cannot resist the temptation, as I hear John coming up the stairs, to show him the pulped book and his paper-coated shirts. 'Don't worry,' I say. 'I'm good with washing machines, they're a bit like cars. I'm good with cars. I'm an excellent driver. Poor Georgina, she's so tired, she does so much.'

•

The laundry room is flooded, the caretaker of the house had to be summoned, by Georgina in her perfect French, to put the washing machine back together. The shirts are now rock-solid and look like art installations because I put them in the tumble-dryer. The least I can do is pick off every single flake of hardened paper, rewash the shirts and iron them.

I am on to the third shirt in as many hours when I look up to check on Louis. He is on his way to the laundry room with a paperback book in his hand. I follow him. Into the washing machine goes the book, back to the bookshelf totters Louis and another paperback, this time a copy of *Verlaine et les poètes symbolistes*, which must have belonged to the poet who once lived in this house and is probably of huge historical significance, is thrust into the drum.

I am not saying anything. She still can't drive.

27 September 1998
Making a Will

Our new 'We must make a will' conversation made its debut on a recent journey to Normandy, five minutes after emerging from the Channel Tunnel at Calais. Matthew had asked for the fifth or sixth time that day, 'What is the point of being alive?' and on this particular occasion I replied, 'If you do not stop wagging your finger and shaking your head at that juggernaut, we won't actually be alive for much longer. We will be bludgeoned to death with a wheel jack. Louis will be an orphan and we haven't made a will yet.' I had been saving this thought up for some time, waiting for just the right occasion to use it. I could have posed it the week before on the Marylebone Road (Audi A3: simultaneous finger-wagging accompanied by supercilious false laughter), or the following day on the M4 outside Didcot (Vauxhall Astra: simultaneous fist- and head-shaking). But in the event I was glad I had waited for the Giant Haystacks of the French trucking fraternity whom Matthew was racing, in the slow lane along the A29 towards Le Havre. Mathew, feeling more energetic on foreign soil, gave Haystacks the full repertoire: speeding alongside him, he shook his fist, wagged his finger, shook his head, wound down the window and banged the side of the car door. Quite which gesture would have got us murdered had Haystacks not been in such a hurry to get home for his tea is hard to say, but at the moment my money is on the head-shaking. If someone did that to me I would most definitely want to kill them.

•

I have rung the solicitor three times now about the will. My conversations with him are similar to the ones I have with our accountant, only our accountant understands that I do not comprehend a word he is saying to me, says it anyway to cover himself and then sends me bits of paper to sign. The solicitor, though equally solicitous, seems to think that if I am to make a will I should take more active a part in it than that of mere signatory. We have reached an impasse.

Now my mother-in-law, keen that Louis should not be taken into care because his parents died intestate, has come up with a solution. She has sent me a cutting from the *Daily Telegraph* advertising the 'Telegraph Will-maker'.

I sent off for a kit, which duly arrived and then sat on my desk unexamined for a week until my mother-in-law rang to ask if I would be so kind as to bequeath her my velvet Prada evening bag.

And so I sat myself down with the Telegraph Will-maker, a gin and tonic and twenty Marlboro Lights to decide the disposition, as Matthew calls it (he failed some law exams very badly once, and is always keen to show off what little he did learn), of all my worldly goods.

The problem is, and this is something not even the

Telegraph Willmaker can solve, I do not have any worldly goods to leave. I discovered this when Matthew consented to answer various questions (only sensible ones and only at half-time).

The first category of bequests dealt with by the Willmaker is gifts. There are several gift options, including money (not main estate), personal belongings and pets. Foolishly wasting one of my questions to Matthew by asking whether he thinks Steptoe could seriously be considered by any recipient to be a gift, I bequeathed the dog to my mother and moved on to main estate. 'Who should get all the money?' I asked Matthew.

'The money!' he snorted. 'What are you talking about? The money? We haven't got any money. Not a bean.'

'Well, what about my half of the house?'

'Your half of the house?' and this time he snorted so violently he had to fetch a Kleenex. We are apparently mortgaged up to and beyond the hilt, and our pension, he now tells me, is invested in the stock markets of the Pacific Rim.

'Well, what about the car?' I asked. This time Matthew just arched his eyebrows and reminded me of the sensible questions only rule. My old Mercedes with 150,000 miles on the clock is apparently worth less than the petrol in the tank, which isn't much since we drove back from France.

The sixteen million television sets in the house are all on interest-free credit and we have no silver. I have nothing to leave anyone. Nothing but a Prada bag, a collection of ten-year-old *Vogue*s, one pearl earring and a bottle of Body Shop passion-fruit face-wash. Oh, and one framed photograph of me and Louis together in which I have five chins and what appears to be a Noel Edmonds hairstyle circa *Swap Shop*. I can just imagine what they'll tell Louis when he comes into his inheritance. 'Look, there you are, such a sweet baby, and that's your mother just a few months before the Shepherd's Bush Road Rage slaughter. Nice woman. Didn't leave you anything. Terrible haircut.'

•

The will is never to be completed for the simple reason that Matthew and I cannot agree on who Louis's legal guardians should be. If we died tomorrow, of course, he'd go to his grandparents, but what if we were on a family outing, all of us except Louis, and Matthew decided to take on a posse of Hell's Angels over a tailback on Chelsea Bridge? We'd all be slaughtered and then who would have our only child?

Matthew has rather eccentrically and with neither explanation, apology or hint of irony suggested that Louis go to Peter Mandelson. I said that if we were going down the celebrity route, I would rather opt for Jeremy Paxman.

Once again an impasse in the will-making process has been reached. The Telegraph Willmaker sits on my desk, almost complete but not quite. I have even filled in my instructions for cremation – ashes to be scattered in Tesco's parent with child parking space on the basis that I never managed to bag it when alive so would like to make the most of it in death.

4 October 1998
Lynda Leaves

There are many times over the past seventeen months when Lynda the nanny has found me in the shed. In the beginning, just after Louis was born, I would hide in there to escape the cleaning lady. Then there was the period when I took to smoking in the shed, before I discovered that Lynda knew about my three-a-day habit.

It is rare that she ever finds me there on legitimate business, the urge to pot and propagate coming seldom, so she knows the general rule is that if I am in the shed something is afoot; something is wrong, something is to be avoided.

Today, though, as I sat in the shed, on and off throughout the morning, I knew she wouldn't come and find me. Lynda is in hiding, too. We are all avoiding each other. Matthew is reading a book, his PlayStation momentarily switched off. As far as I know he hasn't so much as glanced at his *Racing Post*, and the television is enjoying a rare moment of darkness, even though there is almost certainly a live football match from Papua New Guinea, or even Chad, on Sky Sports 231. Even Steptoe has sensed the atmosphere and has, out of respect, decided not to chase next-door's cat, which he has been baiting since breakfast time.

•

This is all because today is Lynda's last day, and we can't look each other in the eye. It's one of those days when I wonder how the rest of the world can carry on as if everything is normal while I have a permanent, headache-inducing lump in my throat. The shed is where I come when I lose it; when the lump rises too quickly and before I know it I am incoherent with tears. I wait in the shed until my face and eyes return to their normal colour, compose myself, blow my nose, rearrange my expression and return to the house to perform some needless task that will keep me busy.

But it doesn't work. The decision to launder the cover of Louis's car seat, for instance, provoked another bout of sobbing when I remembered how for the first three months of Louis's life Lynda was the only one competent enough to strap him into it. This in turn reminded me of how I insisted that she came with Matthew to collect Louis and me from hospital the day after he was born. 'Do you know how to install the baby seat?' I'd said to Matthew minutes after the birth.

'No,' he replied.

'Lynda will know,' I said, 'you must make sure she comes with you.'

'Lynda will know' is a phrase we have both used hundreds, thousands, of times since. Lynda will know why Louis has a temperature, Lynda will know how much Calpol to give, Lynda will know how to turn the central heating off, fix the pump in the fish-pond, sack the cleaning lady.

•

At 1.30 p.m. Lynda's friend Jim will knock on the door. He is to drive her to Victoria station, from where she will travel to Gatwick.

By 7.30 this evening she will be leaving the country. Her rucksack is sitting by the back door where she left it, packed and ready to go, at 9 a.m. this morning. This is just dead time now.

She's playing with Louis in the garden, crawling around on all fours; Louis is the only one unaffected by this funereal atmosphere. I'm going to have to make it past them, back to the house, without breaking down. Lynda sees me coming, rears up, deposits Louis in the wheelbarrow and bolts through the back door into the boiler cupboard. She is in there for ages so I eventually knock on the door. 'Are you all right? Not too hot in there?'

'No. I'm fine,' she replies in a wobbly voice. 'Just checking the thermostat.'

'Right,' I say. Then off I go again. Wobble-wobble goes the chin; throb-throb goes the throat lump; back to the shed I go.

•

It was awful. As the dreaded hour approached we found ourselves gathered silently around Lynda's rucksack. 'Well, this is it,' I said with mock cheer, handing Louis to her for a kiss goodbye. 'Take care of yourself. Thanks for everything.'

'No worries,' she said.

And then I lost it again. Along came the tears, the contorted face and the inability to utter another comprehensible word. Then Lynda started and Louis stuck his finger up her nose. Matthew wandered off, shoulders hunched, hands in pockets, and switched on the television. He sat in front of it, hands cradling head. Jim knocked on the door. I took Louis from Lynda, handed her the rucksack and off she went.

That night Matthew and I both dreamt about her. In Matthew's dream she made it to the final of the US Open tennis tournament, where she lost quickly – in twenty-five seconds, apparently – straight sets (6–2, 6–2) to Jana Novotna. Then she broke down, Matthew said, and cried on the Duchess of Kent's shoulder. In mine she was crawling on all fours through the Serengeti, with Louis on her back.

This morning I rang Jim. 'Did she get off all right? How was she?' I asked.

'Bit tearful,' he said, and I was glad.

11 October 1998

Feng Shui

As I have just explained to Mathew, feng shui is all about harmony, and we could use a little harmony at the moment because Matthew is unusually irritable, even by his own standards. I have just spent £300 consulting a feng shui expert.

What seems to annoy him particularly is that it was him who put the idea into my head. In response to a mild complaint about the fact that each time I dismount my executive swivel chair (second-hand shop, Shepherd's Bush Road) I bash my ankle, he said, 'Next thing, you'll be complaining about the feng shui.'

It's easy for him to say that. Matthew works from a lovely old refectory table upstairs, overlooking the garden, surrounded by comfy sofas, family photographs, polished wooden floorboards, expensive Liberty rug. My 'work station', as I attempt to glamorize it, is a plywood bench, facing an exposed brick wall in an annex just off the kitchen. I have asked Matthew occasionally (three times a week, in fact, for two years) to let me work at his desk, but he will not countenance it.

'Of course the feng shui's all wrong.' I replied. 'Why didn't I think of that. I'll call a consultant in the morning.' Matthew's head went into his hands. The *One Flew*

Over the Cuckoo's Nest rocking to and fro began, and then, releasing the head, he unleashed a new gesture – the demented screwing-up of his eyes as though blinded by the glare from a thermonuclear detonation.

•

Matthew was out when Sarah Shurety from the feng shui company paid me a visit. In his absence I was free to be as disloyal as I wished without interruption, and proceeded to make it clear from the start that anything that was wrong with the house was Matthew's fault. 'For example, you'll find that every room, with the exception of Louis's bedroom, the downstairs loo and the bathroom, has a television set in it,' I said. 'Now I'm no expert, but that can hardly be good feng shui, can it?'

While Sarah, whom I grew to love deeply over the next few hours, was agreeing that indeed it couldn't, I led the way into our bedroom and introduced her to the twenty-three-inch screen Sony monopolizing the foot of the bed. I also showed her the video, the stereo, the unspeakably hideous speakers, the 5,678 feet of exposed wiring and the five remote controls (one for terrestrial TV, one for cable, one for the video, one for the stereo and one for turning the lights on and off) infesting Matthew's pillow.

Lovely Sarah looked slightly shocked. 'The television will definitely be affecting Matthew's health because it sucks energy. He is susceptible because he is a Rabbit,' she said, and in its place she has suggested we hang a picture portraying a loving scene between a man and a woman so that 'When you look at it, it makes you think, "You are my bestest friend. I'm really pleased to be waking up with you and I love you lots." If you can't afford a painting immediately, you could always hang an Athena poster instead.'

I can imagine precisely what Matthew will say if he wakes up one morning to find an Athena poster in place of the Teletext racing results, and it won't have anything to do with being 'bestest friends'.

•

By the time we had finished our tour of the house I had calculated that by selling five of our six televisions and video recorders I could raise enough money to buy the three fish tanks Sarah has prescribed, the goldfish, which will bring 'money luck', the dark-coloured fish, which will ensure a happy marriage and good health, and the following not-so-urgent extras: a picture of Oxford University for Louis's room to encourage him to great things; a stencilled border for Louis's room which is to bear the inscription A YOUNG KING LOUIS WHO WAS KIND AND HAPPY LIVED IN A ROOM AS BLUE AS THE SEA AND EVERY NIGHT THE MOON AND THE STARS LOOKED DOWN AND FILLED HIS DREAMS WITH HAPPINESS AND LAUGHTER; the repainting of Louis's room so that it is as blue as the sea; and a professional photography session so that we have enough happy-family, kite-flying, hugging photographs to promote familial harmony.

If there is any money left over, I will rehang all the doors, which Sarah says open the wrong way, and put a bell on the front gate, which will promote, from what I can make of her notes, squeamishness.

•

Matthew has just asked me precisely which Athena poster my 'feng shui friend' is suggesting. 'Perhaps the one of the tennis player scratching her bum?' This is not going well.

He says that if I wish to wind artificial flowers round the security bars on the kitchen window, if I wish to take out an annual subscription to *Fish Keeper's Monthly*, if I wish to hang mirrored balls from every available extremity, it is up to me but the televisions, the videos, the PlayStation, the wiring are staying. We have reached an impasse.

'Let me work at your desk,' I pleaded.

'I will not let you work at my desk,' he replied, 'because you will move the telephone, the pictures, the mouse mat and the ashtrays. You will derange the cushions on my chair, and you know I cannot concentrate properly unless they are all in their correct positions.'

'You mean I will destroy the feng shui of the desk?' I asked.

'That's precisely what I . . .' He stopped, the victim of a rare moment of self-irony. 'Use the desk,' he said. 'You are more than welcome to my desk.'

18 October 1998
The Tandoori Diet

Autumn has arrived, and while others will be aware of the nights drawing in, crispness in the air and the turning of the leaves, for me it is different. I first know autumn by the scent of cardamom pods, and the sight on the kitchen table of murky green boiled spinach, orangey-yellow pilau rice and, above all, the rich russet red of takeaway tandoori chicken. Matthew is dieting again and he will continue to do so until Christmas.

In a world full of fad diets, from cabbage soup to nothing but chocolate, Matthew's weight-loss regime is, by any standards, deeply eccentric. The general consensus of health experts is that one should eat well-balanced meals regularly throughout the day. Courageously ploughing a lone nutritional furrow, Matthew disagrees. He believes that the way to lose weight is to eat nothing, except perhaps a small piece of fruit, from dawn until dusk. He says he enjoys it, that he relishes the gnawing sensation, his body eating away at his hunger.

That, at least, is what he says when he has just eaten. What he says in the hour leading up to his daily repast, if he is speaking at all, generally revolves around his hypochondria. 'I'm feeling very tired, so tired, unnaturally tired. Do you think I am very ill?'

'What have you eaten today?'

'Six seedless grapes and a plum.'

Then, at dusk, he will open the fridge, survey the vast range of salads and health-giving soups, decide he is by now too weak from the gnawing hunger to slice and steam so much as a courgette, and head for the telephone.

Every fourth or fifth night it occurs to him that the owners of the tandoori restaurant in the Uxbridge Road must think he is mad, so he prevails upon me to order his food for him. I am, he insists, to use my maiden name and affect one of several regional accents, deployed on a rota basis: Dorset, Birmingham, Dublin, Glasgow and then Liverpool – and collect the food rather than have it delivered. Thus, he believes, they will not be able to connect me with him.

What he doesn't know is that halfway through placing the order, just as I have requested 'one full tandoori chicken, please, and a portion of pilau rice', and Matthew has barked, 'No drumsticks,' from the other side of the room, the man on the end of the phone says, 'Would this be for Matthew?'

'Yes,' I reply, 'and I'll be along in thirty minutes to collect it.'

Occasionally, aware that he is a valued customer to be nurtured, the restaurant puts in a complimentary nan bread. 'What are they trying to do? Kill me?' Matthew wails. 'Can you imagine what the calorific content of a nan must be?' Then he will consult his baby-pink plastic calorie counter before ripping the bread in two and flinging it in the bin.

By the time we reach week three of the diet a new phase has been reached. The 'This may be hell, but it will be worth it' phase is well and truly behind us and we have progressed to the 'What is the point, what is the bloody point?' phase. Our bathroom scales have made their annual appearance in the kitchen. Matthew checks his weight throughout the evening, between mouthfuls of chicken. The pound he lost in the first week, along with the half-pound he lost in the second week, have now returned to taunt him. He has taken to carrying out body searches on himself, clutching at his waist – presumably in the hope that he will be able to locate the recalcitrant twenty-four ounces and send them packing with a shaking fist.

I have tried explaining to him, very slowly, that instead of gnawing away at his hunger, his body will now be gnawing away at the chicken and clinging on to it for dear life. 'There is no way it's going to give it up,' I say. 'That chicken is all it's got in the world.'

'This diet has worked before,' says Matthew, 'and it will work this time. I will be patient and vigilant.' And with that he mounts the scales twice more, once with the by now empty tandoori carton in his hand, once without. For verification he places just the carton on the scales. And then he takes some notes.

•

By week four things are looking up. The demise of his calorie counter (an incident involving a complimentary popadom) has made Matthew even more determined not to risk ingesting anything other than the chicken and rice, but the good news is that the pound and a half have fled once more, taking with them another five ounces. To celebrate, Matthew has splashed out on a second pair of scales for the bedroom, so he can weigh himself in privacy with or without clothes and avoid frightening the new nanny. He has also had a haircut (weighing himself before and after the barber's).

We may still have more than two months to go but I can sense we're on the home straight. He has even agreed that we should eat out on our wedding anniversary. In previous years I have had to make do with ordering an extra portion of chicken and rice for myself and insisting that we at least sit down together to eat it. One year I was tempted to suggest he might, just for the occasion, like to use a plate rather than the carton but held back on the basis that he would probably want to weigh the plate before, after and during the meal.

I would rather not spend my wedding anniversary in the Uxbridge Road tandoori, where the carpet smells of tomcat and the background music would lead you to believe that the same tomcat is being prepared for inclusion in one of those mysterious 'meat' dishes which crop up on the menus of Indian restaurants. Matthew, however, is insisting that he cannot possibly risk going anywhere else because calorific content can be so variable. He is also insisting that we arrive separately and greet each other in the manner of surprised old friends. I am to affect a Swedish accent.

25 October 1998
Competitive Parenting

I have no resistance whatsoever to any compliment, genuine or insincere, that is paid to my son. It has been that way since the day he was born. A friend tells a story about a new mother of his acquaintance who started weeping in the maternity ward an hour after giving birth. Her husband, not entirely sure whether post-natal depression was supposed to kick in quite so soon, asked her what was wrong. She said she was crying out of pity for all the other mothers. If Pol Pot was to knock on our door of an afternoon and start raving about Louis's prodigious intellect, noting his frequent use of the word 'helicopter', I would have overlooked the killing fields, asked him if he'd eaten yet and invited him to stay the night. And if Noel Edmonds were to drop by and marvel at Louis's sophisticated taste in food, pointing out how few eighteen-month-old children have a passion for black olives, I would . . . well, no, perhaps not. I have some resistance. But very little.

The problem with the day nursery Louis attends two days a week is that the staff don't seem to realize quite what they're dealing with. It is in every other way an excellent day nursery, certainly the very best in the area. But for some reason, when I ring, as I tend to do twice a day, just to see how he is, they say, 'He is fine. A bit teary after you left but he's fine now.' Fine? Are they mad? Fine means he's not ill or miserable, but it does not convey remotely the fact that Louis is not just adorable but also a genius. There is, for instance, never any mention of the fact that he is now saying 'parachute' intelligibly or that he is obviously very musical and can dance the 'Hokey-Cokey', correctly putting his left leg in, and then his left leg out, shaking it all about, and turning.

'He's fine,' says Matthew. 'Stop ringing them, they'll call you if there is anything wrong. If every parent rang twice a day in the hope of being told that their child had just split the atom, they'd never be off the phone.' He says all parents think their children are more beautiful, clever, amusing than anybody else's. He said I was like this when Steptoe was a puppy.

•

Louis and I have just been to a fund-raising 'fun day' at the nursery. Louis was looking particularly lovely in his new Baby Gap corduroys and Osh Kosh polo shirt. When some Irish dancers appeared he jiggled around enchantingly to the music, clapped his hands in time to the beat of the limbo dancers who were on next and said both 'parachute' and 'helicopter' to the woman next to us in the queue for the loo. Nobody noticed. Nobody said, 'Isn't he sweet, isn't he brilliant?' They were all too busy gazing at their own children, wearing on their faces the same sickly sweet smile of parental pride that I wear if Louis so much as sticks his finger up his nose.

Other parents look at you but they don't acknowledge you. They are only checking to see if you are noticing and admiring their offspring. And of course you aren't. You're too busy gawping stupidly at your own.

When a two-year-old boy took off across the dance floor and danced his own version of an Irish jig, a genuinely funny moment, the impartial nursery workers all cheered and clapped. The parents of all the other children, me included, remained stony-faced. And the woman behind me whispered 'hyperactive' in her husband's ear.

8 November 1998
Huge Tax Bill

The first sign that something was horribly wrong with our finances came when I returned home one evening last week to find that entry to the house was impossible. The path was blocked by a phalanx of staff from Majestic Wine Warehouse bearing cases of wine and other assorted off-licence goods. I squeezed my way past one man going in with two cases of Sancerre, and another coming out to collect three of Bourgogne. But only when I had slalomed around five boxes of Czech Budweiser, eight twelve-packs of Evian and a case of malt whisky did I find Matthew. He was staring with mad eyes at a clipboard. He looked up at me and shook his head silently.

'How much?' I asked him.

'Don't ask.'

'More than £500?'

'*Do not ask*.' He lapsed again into silence as he scrawled his signature on the invoice and handed the clipboard back to a young man who left after wishing us, in a decidedly nudge-nudge, wink-wink tone, a 'very good evening'.

'You've had bad news from the accountant, then,' I said sympathetically when we were finally alone.

'Terrible,' replied Matthew. 'Simply disastrous.'

In most houses the sudden arrival of this much alcohol would point to a piece of good fortune . . . five balls plus the bonus on the Lottery, perhaps, or a nice legacy from a great-aunt in Shropshire. In our house, the precise reverse is true. Matthew only ever bulk-buys alcohol like this, in fact only ever spends money at all, when we are broke. Then it's as if he's been given a week to live; it's spend, spend, spend.

Generally, during periods of fiscal tranquillity, he is Scrooge himself. The odd bottle of cheapish claret sneaks in, and the vinegarized remains of a mediocre Chardonnay can usually be found in the fridge. But the moment one of those portentous yellow envelopes from Barry the accountant hits the doormat Matthew is in the car and off on that sixty-second drive to the Majestic Wine Warehouse in the Goldhawk Road which usually results, later in the day, in a delivery of four cases – two white and two red, at about £10 a bottle.

This time, having completed an inventory of his purchases, which mysteriously includes three pairs of identical brown lace-up shoes from Marks & Spencer, I can only imagine that the accountant's yellow envelope must have contained very grave news indeed. Along with the above-mentioned claret, Sancerre, beer, whisky, still water and brown lace-ups we have four dozen bottles of Perrier, a case of champagne, a case of rosé, three bottles of dark rum, three bottles of white rum, five bottles of Stolichnaya vodka, four of gin and four of Courvoisier, twenty-four tubes of barbecue-flavour Pringles, twenty bags of salted cashews, three corkscrews, two extra twenty-four-bottle wine racks and a bottle of Cointreau.

'We hate Cointreau,' I say, directing my dissent at something small and manageable.

•

After a prolonged and relentless period of interrogation, Matthew has finally cracked and specified what for five and a half hours he would only refer to as 'our impending financial perdition'. It is the tax bill he must pay on 31 January next year. When he finally told me precisely how much we owe I poured us both an enormous Cointreau. We then had three more each, and midway through the fourth began running through the options.

Suicide is quite appealing, but seems a little unfair to Louis, especially as we have still not decided who should become his legal guardians in the event of his being orphaned. Matthew argued strongly for fleeing the country. I proposed selling the house and putting ourselves on the waiting list for a council maisonette. Matthew insisted that if we must stay in the country it should be in this house, where we can at the very least offer the bailiffs something decent to drink.

Eventually, after a fifth Cointreau, we agreed to continue spending money insanely, on the grounds that it is not our problem any more, but the Inland Revenue's. He is going back to Majestic, he says, to pick up some cases of rare vintage port and then, handing me a considerable-sized wad of £20 notes, suggests I take myself off to Harvey Nichols in the morning. Then we are to meet up in the glassware department of Peter Jones which, the Majestic Wine Warehouse aside, is the only place Matthew is happy shopping – we have a magnificent and never used collection of brandy balloons. For the coup de grâce, Matthew has booked us into Le Gavroche, possibly the most expensive restaurant in London, for my birthday . . .

•

The Majestic Wine Warehouse van has returned, and taken everything (except the Cointreau) away. We are, I am informed, to resume normal expenditure.

Matthew has spoken to Barry (it took three days and two pre-phone-call Cointreaus) and we have been given a reprieve. The tax bill is to be spread, from January, over a two-year period in four six-monthly instalments.

Le Gavroche has been cancelled. Matthew says we cannot possibly afford it and, employing a particularly nauseating holier-than-thou tone, has given me instructions to return my grey flannel Nicole Farhi trousers and cashmere Joseph sweaters (four) to Harvey Nichols. Only I won't. I will be keeping them and I will say they were a birthday present from my reckless spendthrift of a husband.

29 November 1998
Shopping

Shopping trips with Matthew, which are kept to a bare minimum of two or three each year, can be divided into three distinct phases, and it is vital that I am prepared both mentally and physically for each. First there is the 'Right, are you ready? Off we go' display of bullish enthusiasm, which demands that I am indeed ready to go, and will not breach his strict 'no dawdling' rule by being unable to locate the car keys for a full fifteen seconds. (By not being absolutely ready I put the entire outing in jeopardy; there is always the chance he could call the whole thing off and while there are times when I would deem this a reprieve, in the case of the birthday-present expedition we are now embarking upon avarice gets the better of dread and I am determined that nothing will prevent us from going.)

Phase two is the car journey. For this I must be equipped with an *A–Z* in order to find routes that circumnavigate any roadworks, accidents or the twenty-second wait by the pedestrian crossing outside Tesco's. For a trip to the Fulham Road, a mere three miles from home, I have been known to call the AA on the morning of departure for a traffic report.

Phase three is the shopping process itself. Most outings

would be too painful to go into in detail so I will relate what happened on our last one, which went comparatively smoothly. Earlier this year we went to Sainsbury's Homebase to buy some deckchairs. As always in any retail environment, Matthew became seriously ill and began taking his pulse and thumping his chest shortly after entering the store. So I wandered off into a Laura Ashley concession (breaking the no-dawdling rule) to give him time to recover. By the time I came out he had vanished. I found him ten aisles away wrestling with a deckchair in the manner of Mick McManus. The deckchair was winning and had Matthew in a Boston crab. A young assistant in green dungarees attempted to intervene and between the two of them they grappled the deckchair into what looked like submission. Matthew sat on it and it collapsed under him. I picked him up and drove him to Charing Cross Hospital where he insisted on having his coccyx X-rayed. There was no damage done but we failed to buy any deckchairs.

•

We have just returned from Joseph in the Fulham Road, where we failed to buy me a sheepskin coat. Phases one and two went well, but phase three cannot be considered an unqualified success. During the walk from car to shop Matthew succumbed to illness – not to a violent migraine (Harvey Nichols, winter 1987) or to uncontrollable shaking (Harrods, spring 1995) or dizzy spells (Fenwick, Christmas 1992); this time out he appeared to have discovered a shrapnel wound in his left knee and he had developed an exaggerated, embarrassing limp.

Upon reaching the shop, before we were through the

doors he started banging his head on the plate-glass window through which he had spotted, and taken offence at, a young male shop assistant in a Jean-Paul Gaultier latex kilt. Once in the shop the pain from the shrapnel apparently worsened and he staggered, now dragging his left leg, to a chair and asked for a glass of water.

His head then went into his hands and he started gasping for air. 'I don't care how much they are. I don't care how many you want in what colour. I don't care if we have to remortgage the house and sell the car.' He was now hyperventilating. 'Just choose one. Choose two. Anything to get us out of here.'

Grabbing the first thing to hand – a grey sweater, not dissimilar to last year's – I handed it to Matthew, saying, 'This is just what I want. I love it more than I could ever love a sheepskin coat. Please let me have this perfect grey sweater.' Matthew made his way to the till where there was a queue. It was a very small queue; just two people, who were quickly informed by Matthew that he had gone blind and deaf. Leaving the sweater unpurchased on the counter, I took him by the arm and led him to the door.

By the time we were halfway to the car his hearing and eyesight had returned and the shuffling gait was gone. Striding out several paces in front of me he embarked on a long and impassioned critique of a) the absurd narrowness of West London streets, and b) the sheer 'quasi-fascistic insanity' of residents' parking restrictions on weekends.

•

And so, one hour after setting off, we returned home to a new, fourth phase; the 'That was fun, we must do that again' phase. 'Shopping isn't so bad, really,' he said, kicking off his shoes. 'What do you want for Christmas? We could go to one of those new malls outside London. Make a day of it, why don't we?'

1999

17 January 1999
The Beef Temptation

Within ten feet of me, as I sit here writing, there is a large, barely touched joint of cold rare roast beef – organic beef; finest sirloin – swaddled happily in its tinfoil on the second shelf of the fridge, in between a tub of Olivio margarine and a jar of horseradish. I can be so specific about its whereabouts and the identity of its neighbours because I have, in the past hour and a quarter, been to visit it seven times. On three of those occasions, I have lifted it out of the fridge, unwrapped it, stared at it, counted the number of times the butcher's string encircles it, rewrapped it and replaced it.

Why that beef is in the fridge has already been the subject of some discussion. Matthew insists he wanted to cook me a really good supper last night, by way of a fitting launch for the diet I began this morning. In a normal household, it would be easy to accept this as a sweet spousal gesture. In this household, though, the motive requires closer examination – and having examined it with a mental microscope, I conclude that he has done it out of nothing more or less than mischief. Why else did he buy such a large joint (from the most expensive butcher in the history of the world) for two people, if not to be sure that there would be four or five pounds of it left over, in the fridge, in tin foil, to tempt me the morning my diet began?

He is trying to break my spirit, to prove to himself and to me that I have, as he maintains, 'not one iota of willpower'.

•

The 'Zero Willpower' debate is one we have two or three times a year, every time I announce a plan for any kind of self-improvement. Whenever, for example, I say that I am going to give up smoking, he replies, 'No, you aren't. You have absolutely no willpower.'

I say, 'Yes, I do.'

He says, 'No, you don't.'

I say, 'Yes, I bloody well do,' and he ends the pantomime exchange with a question:

'The last time you gave up smoking, how long did you last?'

Identical conversations ensue whenever the spectre of a summer holiday near a beach turns my mind to getting fit, and I mention that I will start going regularly to the gym; or when the stack of unopened yellow envelopes from Barry the accountant terrifies me into expecting a dawn raid from the Inland Revenue, and I hint at sorting out my taxes.

The tragedy is that he is completely wrong – I have endless willpower, but the circumstantial evidence is against me. The answer to the smoking question has ranged from six to nine minutes. I did join a gym a year ago, paying the £600 membership fee upfront, and have since made a total of three twenty-minute visits (Matthew enjoys calculating the cost of each visit, he works it out at just over £10 a minute); and since I last moaned about the income tax, the pile of unopened yellow envelopes has tripled.

Yesterday morning's conversation followed the usual, rigid form. I said I was going on the cabbage-soup diet. He said I wasn't because I have no willpower. I said I was because I have. He asked how long the nothing-but-apples detoxification diet lasted in the summer. I didn't answer. He did. 'You began it at seven fifteen, one morning in June. You had a *pain au chocolate* at 8.28 a.m. Before your first apple.'

Then he drove to the butcher to buy the beef that is now taunting me. On the way back he stopped off at a baker, so that instead of the usual one egg (an egg so old that if it were discovered in Iraq, it would be classified as an agent of biological warfare) we have proper, edible food in the fridge for once. There is no question he has done it on purpose. If I fail in my diet, it will be Matthew's fault. Without him I would succeed. It's the story of my life. I'd have succeeded in passing my maths exam if I hadn't left my rough book on the bus; I could have kept that Saturday job in the ladies' underwear department of Cherry's in Blandford if my alarm clock hadn't broken. But as everyone, from my mother to my husband, constantly reminds me, there is always an if.

If, for instance, there was a way of retrussing the beef in the fridge, so that Matthew would not notice any missing slices, I could have a sandwich. I could keep the bread in the shed along with a jar of horseradish.

•

The retrussing was surprisingly easy, although the string is a different colour from the original, being yellow parcel string, all that was available from the shop at the end of the road where I bought my loaf. If Matthew notices it I shall tell him the beef must have gone septic and should be thrown out.

He has just returned. He's opening the fridge. He's taken out the beef. He's examining it. He's just come over and asked to borrow my ruler.

24 January 1999
Early Retirement

There was a time, pre-1999, when Chris Tarrant was not well liked in this house. If never quite a serious rival to Eammon Holmes and Danny Baker for the top slots, he certainly ranked in my top-ten celebrity hate figures. Now, though, I love Chris Tarrant. I worship him as a saviour, for he will always symbolize a turning point in my life. He is the Messiah who gave shape and meaning to my future with Matthew. Chris Tarrant has inspired in us both an ambition to enter an old-age home – one of the most elegant and genteel kind – as soon as possible.

Matthew keeps repeating that there is a delightful irony in the idea that Chris, a middle-aged man so obviously and desperately obsessed with clinging on to his youth, should be the one to point us in the other direction. But then Matthew is a man who can find delightful ironies in a tube of Pringles, and I don't take much notice. Whatever the differing natures of our mid-life crises, Chris has given us the focus we lacked, and for that I thank him from the bottom of my heart.

•

Initially, *Who Wants to be a Millionaire?* was the cause of disharmony because it was on every night at 8 p.m., and clashed with Louis's bedtime. So Matthew would come upstairs as usual to put Louis to bed, only instead of putting Louis to bed he would put Louis on his knee and with a flourish of the remote control begin his nightly half-hour vigil, shattering my carefully contrived air of sleepy, post-bath, bedtime story contentment with yells of, 'Don't ask the audience, you cretin,' and 'Where do they find these people? The Royal Society for the Protection of Village Idiots?'

There were even times when both Louis's and Matthew's heads would disappear into their hands in unison as some 'poncing halfwit' contestant would opt to take the £32,000 rather than continue and risk going home with just £1,000.

Then, as the weeks progressed, I too became hooked. Our half-hour in front of Chris Tarrant became a nightly ritual, and before long we could talk of nothing else. Last Monday at 9 p.m., as we reviewed that night's show in the minutest detail, Matthew asked what we should do if somehow we won the million, and it came to me in a flash.

'Buy an annuity,' I said, 'and go and live in an old-age home.'

Mathew nodded. 'Brilliant,' he said.

The point, as Matthew immediately understood, is that in an old-age home, our lives will in essence be exactly as they are now, only better and free from guilt. My hours, for example, will be unchanged. I will be woken at 6 a.m., just as I am now, only not by a twenty-one-month-old demanding pasta for breakfast but by a young woman insisting I have a cup of milky tea. And I will retire at 9.30 p.m. as I do now, although not in order to be able to rise again at 6 a.m. but because that's what happens in old people's homes.

Matthew will find a soulmate among the other residents, someone with whom he can stay up till the early hours watching obscure football matches on cable television until a starched white nurse fetches him, wheels him along the corridor in a Lloyd Loom wheelchair and tips him into bed. He will rise at midday to find me reading under a pergola in dappled sunshine and a hat. A quick peck on the cheek and a cheery, 'I'll see you at teatime,' and he'll be off to the betting shop in Chichester or possibly one of the racier suburbs of Tunbridge Wells.

In this retirement home our much-loved ritualistic debate about having no friends will fit in effortlessly over the Battenburg cake, since none of the other residents will have any friends either (albeit through death rather than unpopularity). Nor will my constant moaning about being exhausted fall on deaf ears. Far from it; instead of provoking scornful looks, it will elicit a kindly, 'Of course you are, dear. Why don't you take a little nap?' With nurses and a doctor on constant call, Matthew will be in hypochondriacal heaven.

As for our cultural life, this too will be unaltered. We will do what we do now, only more so: we will watch a great deal of television and then deconstruct what we have seen until bedtime.

•

We have worked out some of the fine detail – a great bonus for me will be the chance to indulge my passion for jigsaw puzzles, and Matthew insists on bringing his PlayStation. We agree that once a month we will travel to London on the train, and have lunch at the Basil Street Hotel in Knightsbridge. There is plenty of time to finalize the rest, since we will not be able to enter the nursing home until 2015, when Louis is eighteen.

I will be fifty-six then, and Matthew, who is thinking of writing to Norris McWhirter to enquire about an entry in the *Guinness Book of Records* (youngest old people's home inmates), will be fifty-three.

'Well, that's sorted, then,' he said as he settled down for the night in front of his new collection of *Steptoe and Son* videos. 'We needn't worry about being too youthful. If youth is wasted on the young, then old age is most certainly wasted on the old.'

21 February 1999
A Day at the Doctor's

This is how Mrs Hill must have felt after seeing Graham and little Damon off to the racetrack on a Saturday afternoon. She would have made herself a cuppa, sat back and sighed, 'Aaah, bless 'em, boys will be boys.' And perhaps Mrs Kray relished these moments of tranquillity as she settled down to remove the bloodstains from Ronnie's and Reggie's shirts, having happily packed the twins off for a spot of early morning ear-nailing.

I have just seen Matthew and Louis off to the doctor's surgery. Both were up bright and early this morning in readiness for their eight thirty (Louis) and eight forty-five (Matthew) appointments. Louis rubbed happily away at his conjunctivitis as Matthew settled him proudly into his pushchair, while wincing gaily at the stabs of pain ('excruciation' as he prefers it) in his right shoulder . . . pain that has had him hunched and immobile for three days now. And as they set off down the street together, waving cheerily back at me, I imagined I could read their thoughts.

'This is the life,' they were saying to themselves. 'This is how it should be. A father-and-son bonding session in the waiting room of the Grove Medical Practice.'

So I sit with my cup of tea, the house silent around

me, thinking, Aaah, bless 'em, wondering if I should take Steptoe to the vet (slight limp in front left paw) and reflecting that our lives these days are almost entirely preoccupied with health.

•

We seem to have skipped a generation, Matthew and I. Our conversations are not the ones our parents had. Instead, they mirror those of our grandparents. I vividly remember mine comparing nights (troubled or fitful), glands (swollen) and temples (throbbing) over their breakfast prunes, the wholemeal high-fibre toast neatly propped between a tin of Andrew's liver salts and a bottle of aspirin. Yet there was an unmistakable competitiveness to my grandparents' conversations (my grandmother's 'old tum' complaint usually trumping my grandfather's hammer toe), while ours are mutually congratulatory.

For my part, I have learnt through experience that this is the only way to live with a hypochondriac of Matthew's class and distinction. By highlighting my own ailments, no matter how slight (a broken fingernail will do), I am able to deflect his attention from his own. Louis has grasped the rules of our game at a frighteningly early stage of his development.

Only last week, suffering from a slight ear infection, he took hold of my index finger and led me to the front door, repeating over and over, 'Doctor, doctor.' He also insists that he will take medication (usually Tixylix cough mixture) only in the supine position, hand on brow, which pleases Matthew enormously.

This is hardly surprising, given the conversations he

is privy to – and now part of – each and every day of his young life. 'How are you?' I will ask Matthew on waking, and his answer will follow seamlessly on from the night before, when it was decided he would wait until morning before calling the doctor for an appointment. His reply will either be a morose, 'A little better, I think, but it still aches,' or an optimistic, 'Worse, much worse, and now it's gone to my ear/chest/right thumb.' Then, in the manner of someone chancing upon a happy coincidence, I will say, 'My sinuses are no better and Louis has been up all night teething!'

This morning's ailments would have produced a perfect three-card trick down at the Grove Medical Practice – Matthew's shoulder, Louis's eyes and my own marvellous new ailment, a jaw that is so out of alignment my teeth no longer meet – had it not been for the fact that the doctor couldn't fit me in until late morning.

Perhaps it's better this way, I think, sipping my tea and wondering if my jaw can cope with toast; a family outing would have been nice, but this way Matthew and Louis can spend some special time together. I've decided I will take Steptoe to the vet, and spend some time bonding with my dog.

•

All in all, it has been a hugely successful day for each of us, although it should be admitted that by mid-afternoon the usual air of mutual congratulation had turned to one of ruthless competition. I am outright winner with my referral to the hugely impressive-sounding maxillofacial surgeon, who happens to have a consulting room in the equally impressive-sounding Princess Grace Hospital.

Steptoe's limp, the result of a grass seed embedded in his paw, is now being treated with regular salt-water baths and antibiotics, and the boys returned from the doctor with a tube of eye cream for Louis, and for Matthew an instruction from the doctor – who he claims, said he had a 'very severely damaged trapezius muscle' – to see an osteopath.

Matthew has taken my clear trumping of him well, and is not being too ungracious in defeat. He is simply refusing to talk about it. I don't mind at all. I am savouring a rare victory, and save for the fact that it would look like gloating – and the other fact that my winning condition makes it physically impossible – I would now be smiling broadly.

7 March 1999
Just a Short Break

The discussion that Matthew and I have whenever a holiday or short break looms could be staged at the Donmar Warehouse. It would be a tense two-hander starring Sir Ian McKellen and Sinead Cusack. There would be no scenery, just bare brick, damp from condensation, a table, two chairs and an ashtray. The tone would echo one of those episodes of *EastEnders* when the scriptwriters come over all Pinteresque, and decide to have just Dot and Ethel, or more recently Peggy and Pat, baring their souls to each other. Glimpses of the curtained windows reveal the sun coming up or going down. The distant chink of milk bottles being delivered or the chatter of children returning home from school hint at time dragging remorselessly by while two people, closeted together by circumstance, uncover the gritty reality behind the charade of their daily lives.

The author would not, despite the frequent lengthy pauses in these deliberations, be a follower of Pinter, but of Kafka, because this is a nightmare . . . a repetitive, circuitous nightmare with no end, no resolution in sight.

'I've had it. I've just about had it,' is the traditional opening line. 'We've got to get away for the weekend at the very least, for a change of scene.' Matthew then stops pacing, lights a cigarette and sits down.

I join him. 'Hot or cold, beach or country?' I ask.

'Please be sensible,' he says.

The script will vary from here on in, the winter version usually running along the following lines: 'There's no point going anywhere hot at this time of year. It would take too long to go somewhere hot.'

'Cold, then. How about skiing?' I might ask, provoking a little earlier than usual the request for 'sane and sensible suggestions only, please'.

Matthew has always said that while he'd be happy to go on an après-skiing holiday, it isn't fair to ask a Jewish man to take part in a sport that requires coordination.

Over the next few hours all my suggestions are similarly rejected (Matthew seldom makes any suggestions himself). The British countryside fails the 'sane and sensible' rule (lack of gambling facilities), and of the only provincial cities he seems to have any time for, Bath strikes him as 'too twee' for a period of anything more than sixteen hours, and the others (Bristol, York, Durham and – for reasons I have never been able to fathom – Plymouth) are ruled out due to lack of good restaurants.

'So it's definitely abroad, then?' I say, when we've exhausted the domestic possibilities.

'Abroad? Do you seriously think it's worth going abroad for just two days?' asks Matthew.

'So you'd rather stay in Britain?'

'No! We've just been through Britain. There is nowhere in Britain we want to go.'

'So not Britain, then?'

'No, let's go abroad.' And so it goes on, brain-aching circular arguments spiralling on and on into infinity or at least until the cigarettes run out and I decide to proceed to Act Two.

•

In Act Two (the dictation of the shortlist), I play the part of a secretary. Matthew plays himself. At the top of the shortlist I have written, according to Matthew's instructions, 'Eurostar to Paris'. Then comes 'Weekend in Venice'. Third is 'Trip to Rome', and next is 'Two days eating roast goose in Budapest'. But for the unexpected addition of a fifth option I could have saved myself the writing and fished out the list made exactly six months ago, but Matthew has dreamt up a new alternative: 'Go to grand West End hotel (Ritz or Connaught)'.

I ask him if he really thinks that being in central London will be relaxing. Doesn't he want a change of scene? He says he thinks it would be marvellous; he is flushed with his own brilliance, completely sold on the idea. The West End, he points out, offers superb gambling facilities, he can take his Sony PlayStation without running the risk of it being irradiated in a customs X-ray machine and he won't have to miss Channel 4 racing's *Morning Line* programme or *Grandstand*.

•

'London it is, then,' says Matthew.

'Ritz or Connaught?' I ask.

He can't decide, so our final deliberations, the very last run through the shortlist before ruling anything out, take place in the very early hours. I can't hear the distant chink of milk bottles because they don't deliver in our part of Shepherd's Bush, but I can hear the unmistakable throb of our neighbour the boy racer's car stereo as he returns home from a great night out. The streets are otherwise empty and suitably atmospheric, as I discover during a bleak trip to the twenty-four-hour garage at the top of the road for more cigarettes.

I get back to find that Matthew has been making his own annotations to the list. London has been ruled out and so is Paris because we've been there so often before. Venice would be nice, but is winter the best time to see it? In Rome there is too much to see in a weekend. And Budapest . . . well, he's been feeling a little dyspeptic lately and thinks the geese might be too rich.

'London hotel it is, then,' I say.

'No,' says Matthew. 'We can't do that. We'd get depressed. It is vital we have a change of scene.'

We finally make a decision. We're going to Paris because we know Paris.

Which is probably why we've been there so often before.

21 March 1999
The Lost Weekend

No matter how old, accomplished, worldly or rich Matthew and I might one day become, we will never feel grown-up enough for a hotel like Le Bristol in Paris. We agreed on this when the bell-boy took our bags – mine too full to be zipped, with socks and winceyette pyjamas spilling out of the top. And we agreed on it again as we stood in the foyer checking in, trying to look blasé, as though we stay in grand hotels every weekend and that if anything the rococo gildings of the Bristol were a bit of a come-down.

Still there was no question that all of them – bell-boy, receptionist, concierge, the man who came to fix the broken handle on the bathroom door – knew we were impostors and, while we were checking out the complimentary soaps, they were undoubtedly convening in the staff room to speculate as to whether we were the lucky winners of a luxury weekend break for two off the back of a packet of Kleenex.

•

They are half right. We should not be here at all, and but for a piece of disastrous financial news we wouldn't be. Negotiations about the destination of our weekend break had stagnated after 110 hours of tense talks. It seemed we would be going nowhere until, at the eleventh hour, a surprise diplomatic breakthrough came in the form of one of those much-feared yellow letters to Matthew from Barry, our accountant. Matthew opened it gingerly, blanched, sat down, read it, read it again, blanched some more, poured himself a huge whisky, reread it, drank the whisky, read it twice more, refilled his glass, read it a sixth time, knocked back the refill, read it again, scrunched it up, lit a cigarette, unscrunched it, read it for what was to prove the eighth and final time, gave out a howl, put his head in his hands and began rocking to and fro on the sofa.

'Is it bad news?' I asked. He released the head, and turned it towards me, staring for a very long time into what was clearly an abyss, and weighing up whether 'Is it bad news?' was too stupid a question to warrant even sarcasm. Concluding that it was, he rose to his feet.

'Right, that's it,' he said. 'We're finished. I'm going to Majestic Wines to buy five cases of vintage port – ' his Pavlovian response to any bad news is wine-purchasing – 'and when I get back I'm booking us into the most obscenely expensive hotel we can think of.'

•

That was how we came, this Friday afternoon, to be in the Bristol, and although I cannot be sure it is worth the money (Matthew refuses to discuss the cost, preferring simply to reiterate the mantra 'we are damn well going to get our money's worth' every four minutes), it is a magnificent hotel, and the room is large and very comfortable.

While I am unpacking Matthew flicks through the room-service menu, suggesting we 'continue the madness with some food and a bottle of champ— Oh my God. Oh my good God.' Then he drops the menu.

I pick it up. There is no champagne under £80. A steak is £40. A club sandwich is almost £20. A cup of tea is a fiver. An egg – a humble boiled egg, for heaven's sake – is £3. I suggest we drink water from the bathroom tap out of a tooth mug and order one egg with two teaspoons. Matthew doesn't hear me, all his concentration being directed towards siphoning his glass of Johnny Walker Black Label back into its miniature bottle. He has just caught sight of the minibar tariff.

•

And so we ventured into the streets of Paris and had supper in a quiet little restaurant – a quick supper, since Matthew insisted we should return to the hotel in time for an early night so that 'we damn well get our money's worth'.

I wake at three o'clock in the morning, the victim of something – probably one of the three oysters allocated from the shared half-dozen in our quick supper – and proceed to get my money's worth from Le Bristol's capacious bathroom until 6 a.m., when I fall into a deep sleep.

It is midday on Saturday when I wake and Matthew has gone out, leaving on his pillow Barry's un-scrunched letter. Attached to it is a note which says, 'Have gone out in hope of finding cup of coffee and croissant for less than the price of a 1947 Bugatti. Hope you are feeling better. Don't give a thought to imminent bankruptcy. Order anything you want from room service.'

I notice the telephone has, intriguingly, been removed from its socket, and has completely vanished. I am not at all hungry. The pale yellow of Barry's writing paper makes me feel ill again. After two more trips to the bathroom, a chance to inspect once again some of Le Bristol's fine porcelain, I desperately need water. I drag my racked and aching body to the minibar. A minute bottle of Evian is priced at a fiver. I drink one, and hide the empty bottle in my luggage.

•

Sunday morning has arrived and now that I am finally feeling better it is of course time to check out. By leaving the room ahead of Matthew I reach the lobby in time to pay for the Evian and persuade the nice receptionist to keep quiet about it. 'My husband will be along in a minute to pay the rest of the bill,' I explain.

Matthew is taking ages. Although we were on the first floor, and although our luggage has already been collected, he insists on taking the lift – a giant, overwrought, gilded monster of a thing, which whirrs and cranks its way slowly, very slowly, through the building.

When it finally arrives, Matthew steps out and apologizes for keeping me waiting, loudly explaining, for all to hear, that he 'was damn well going to get his money's worth'. The concierge glances at the bell-boy. They both nod, smiling the tiniest but most knowing of smiles.

28 March 1999
Matthew and Wasps

The still life that Matthew assembled on the kitchen table this morning brought to mind those police photos of what lurked beneath the serial killer's bed . . . assorted automatic rifles, machetes, a blunt instrument, newspaper cuttings, a balaclava and an anorak. Or, in Matthew's case, three aerosol cans of insecticide (assorted brands), newspaper cuttings from last year on the Eurowasp, a fencing mask and a rolled-up copy of the *Sunday Telegraph* tightly taped around the cardboard inner tube from a roll of Bacofoil. Lying a few inches to the right of this arsenal, meanwhile, resplendently furled around itself, was my late father's legacy to Matthew – an antique horsehair-and-leather fly swat. He too had wasp-phobia. They bonded over a can of Raid.

When I mentioned the serial killer analogy to Matthew, he smiled horribly and said, 'I am indeed a serial killer. I intend to kill as many as I can.' And then he lovingly placed each item on the kitchen table into a plastic stack-a-box, which he then carried upstairs to where it will reside, under his desk, until late autumn.

Although this is, by and large, the same ritual we go through every year within fifteen minutes of Matthew hearing the first buzz, the fencing mask is new. He claims it as his own idea, but as Louis could tell him, Winnie the Pooh thought of it first.

The fencing mask comes from a charity shop in the Shepherd's Bush Road and Matthew says it is 'only to be worn in the event of swarming', but since Matthew's definition of 'swarming' is two wasps in the same room, I suspect we may be seeing rather a lot of it. I do not like the fencing mask. To me, the fencing mask suggests that this year the wasp madness may have intensified.

The root of the wasp madness lies in the fact that Matthew has never actually been stung and he says he cannot rule out the possibility that he may have an allergy to wasp stings that would cause 'anaphylactic shock' (to which adrenaline is the antidote), closing his throat and killing him within seconds. And since the doctor won't supply him with a phial of adrenaline to carry around at all times he is now looking in *Thomson's* local directory. He appears to think there is a black market in adrenaline and that those black-marketeers are advertising in *Thomson's*. He is clearly demented.

•

Today, it really began. The first sign that a wasp has invaded Matthew's airspace comes when he puts up the traditional cry of '*Waaaasp!*' He sounds like a Master of Foxhounds hollering or a golfer shouting 'Fore!' when a ball is set in the direction of a passing rambler's head.

The first cry of the season went up this morning. While I have never actually witnessed a wasp-kill – to share airspace with the wasp would be to run the risk of inhaling several fluid ounces of wasp-killer – I have eavesdropped on a few. I am familiar with the ritual.

'*Waaaasp!*' is followed by frantic scraping on the floorboards as Matthew rears back in his office chair and scrabbles about for the deadly stack-a-box. Then comes a sound similar to a snare drum; the sound of my father's horsehair swat landing on random surfaces. The 'pssst' of the aerosol comes next, followed by the dull thud of death as the rolled-up *Sunday Telegraph* is brought in for the final blow.

This year I happened to be passing his office door when the cry went up, and decided to stay and watch from a safe distance. As I stood in the doorway, a second wasp flew in, and on went the fencing mask. Then, after flailing about pointlessly with the fly swat, Matthew dove under his desk and emerged with a can of Pledge.

'What on earth are you doing?' I asked him.

'Composing a baroque concerto for harpsichord and lute,' he screamed, 'what do you think I am doing?'

I retreated to the safety of the kitchen and ten minutes later Matthew came downstairs flushed and sweating, but elated enough from the first kill of the season – for him, it's like being 'blooded' after killing your first deer – to propound his new theory that whereas the wasps might have developed a resistance to well-known brands of insecticide, he doubts that they've had enough exposure to Pledge 'to develop the antibodies'.

'This year, I'm not taking any nonsense,' he said, making himself a mid-morning snack of toast and honey, a little amuse-gueule for the wasp, perhaps. 'This year, I'm going to give them something new, something they won't quickly forget.'

•

Louis and I were in the garden when we first became aware of the latest development in the wasp war. We heard movement above our heads so we both hid behind a shrub and peered up through the foliage. Above us on the veranda stood Matthew, wearing rubber gloves and fumbling about with a screwdriver. He was making holes through the middles of the two dead wasps, and through these he threaded a long piece of string, which he then stretched across the frame of his office window, before fixing each end with a piece of Blu-Tack.

'Now then, you wasps,' he said, addressing the air outside the window, and giving the string a final coating of Pledge, 'see what happened to your friends. Let this be a warning to you all.'

4 April 1999

Louis's Hoover Obsession

Ebenezer Scrooge was warned of impending terror by the jangling of Jacob Marley's chains. For my dreaming self, it is the jangling of Jimmy Savile's bracelets. They jangled again this morning, just before 4 a.m., ushering in my recurring nightmare. Clink, clank, clank, they went, and Sir Jimmy was with me once more. If the dream were not so easily interpreted, I would now be consulting a Jungian psychoanalyst to help me decide whether I require more intensive therapy. Not because it might mean that I am in love with Sir Jimmy, or that I want him to be my real father (if there were any paternity yearnings, I think I'd rather go for Michael Winner), but because it highlights the extent of my need to be a good mother. The reason I keep dragging Sir Jimmy away from Stoke Mandeville for a cameo in my subconscious is my desire to please Louis.

'Now, then,' says Jimmy, lolling in his high-tech *Fix-It* chair, 'a lovely lady called Rebecca has written to me, goodness gracious, to say that her little boy is very fond of household appliances. Would I fix it for him to meet Mr James Dyson, a very clever man, who invented the bagless vacuum cleaner?'

James Dyson, who is played by Nigel Havers, then

descends into the studio, pausing in front of Jimmy's sofa to rapturous applause, and we are shown a short film in which Louis is taken around the Dyson bagless-vacuum-cleaner factory, followed by a clip of Louis vacuuming the corridors at Buckingham Palace. The Queen pats him on the head and thanks him for his sterling work. Finally we cut back to the studio, where Louis is now on the sofa with Sir Jimmy, Nigel Havers, the Queen and me to receive his *Jim'll Fix It* medal from Her Majesty. In front of him is a Dyson cylindrical and a corgi . . . his souvenirs to take home.

•

The nightmare woke me at 3.57 a.m., and an hour later, I was woken again.

'Ooooerrr,' went Louis. 'Oooooerrrrr-oooooeeeeee-rrrrrr.' This is his vacuum impersonation, Shepherd's Bush's nearest equivalent to the dawn chorus.

At 6.30 a.m., having seen to three carpets with the Dyson, he shut himself in his bedroom, shouting his new catchphrase, 'Go away!' Through the keyhole I could see he was ironing Tinky Winky. Ironing takes a close second to vacuuming in his list of hobbies. (The only other, a distant third, is pulling snails out of their shells.)

A friend tells us not to worry about the housework fixation. Her son, now eight and happily preoccupied with computer games and hitting his sister, was taken to a child therapist at three because of his close relationship with a mop. 'We were desperately worried at the time,' she says. 'But they grow out of it.' The health visitor says the same. 'He's just copying his parents,' she said, an unwittingly provocative remark which started me off on the fact that Matthew couldn't tell the difference between a vacuum cleaner and a garden fork. The health visitor changed the subject by asking Louis to show her his favourite toy. He took her to the cupboard under the stairs and showed her the Dyson.

•

This weekend Louis and I are staying at a hotel in Dorset, where my family are gathering to celebrate my grandmother's ninetieth birthday. We arrived to find my mother and grandmother in the lobby. Unfortunately, they had chosen to position themselves right next to a Hoover, abandoned temporarily by one of the hotel cleaners. Both mother and grandmother took the snub quite well ('I'm sure he'll say hello in his own good time'), and the cleaner – having lifted Louis on to her shoulders so that he could dust the picture rails – then demonstrated the attachment used for cleaning round the skirting boards. He was thrilled. Even an expert likes to learn new tricks.

It took twenty-five minutes to make the journey from the lobby to our room. It would have taken an hour had I not blindfolded Louis with his scarf in order to avoid the Black & Decker Dust Buster at the top of the stairs. I thought of complaining to the management, but what would I say? 'You knew I was coming with a two-year-old boy, so what on earth possessed you to leave that ironing board propped up outside room number 31?'

In our own room, which I had naively imagined would be a sanctuary of appliance-free tranquillity, we have so far discovered a two-speed hairdryer in the bathroom and a radio by the bed, both of which I put on the top shelf of a cupboard while Louis wasn't looking. Not that he was that interested, being occupied in unpacking his own toy vacuum cleaner (a miniature, battery-operated Dyson, with brightly coloured foam beads which whirr around the cylinder), his iron and his ironing board. Louis is not fooled by these toys, of course, but has been known to play with them for quite long periods when real ones are not available.

It was while I was on the phone to Matthew ('We've arrived safely, bit of a drama with a condom machine at the motorway service station but otherwise we're fine') that the crash came, followed by the inevitable wail. I knew what it was the second I heard it. There was only one thing it could have been . . . the one thing, besides a Gideon Bible, which inhabits every hotel room in Britain. In this case it was hidden in the cupboard whose door I left open after hiding the hairdryer and the radio.

•

Louis was lying underneath the trouser-press when I found him – not hurt, just shocked that a member of the gadget family should have turned on him in this way. Twenty minutes with the broken kettle outside room 25 calmed him down.

In the dream that woke me this morning, long before the hotel came to life, Louis received a Blue Peter badge from Valerie Singleton for saving a Corby trouser-press from drowning in Poole Harbour.

25 April 1999
Gaslight

The lights fused last night, as I was going to bed early with a book. Matthew had just gone out. He has always gone out when the lights go – this was the fifth time in a fortnight – and I don't know how to put the fuses back in, or on, or through, or whatever you do to broken fuses. Come to that, I'm not sure where the fuse box is, although it might well be by the front door – the one Matthew walked through on his way out.

I read with a torch until the lights came on again, which was also when Matthew must have come home. I could hear him moving downstairs. Then the lights went off again. Then on again. Then off. On, off, on.

It's all very strange, this lights business. It reminded me of something I've read, or perhaps it was a film, in which a husband tries to drive his wife mad. I am sure flickering lights come into it somewhere.

The more I thought about it, as I sat there in the dark (the lights went off again) listening to Matthew moving about downstairs, the more I convinced myself that my husband too had read this book or seen this film. Inspired by it, he is trying to make me think I have gone mad. He obviously wants to have me sectioned and sent to the Priory, or possibly a nursing home for the mentally frail in Godalming. I haven't worked out why yet, but I am sure that is what he is trying to do.

•

Matthew's moved on from the lights now. We're onto stage two: the 'make her think she's got amnesia' stage. He keeps 'reminding' me of things he has apparently told me, things I know nothing about, such as having some friends round for supper on Thursday when I have arranged to go out with a girlfriend. 'You must remember,' said Matthew, 'I told you last week they were coming.' But I know he didn't.

'Matthew,' I asked him, 'is there a book or a film in which the husband tries to make the wife think she's lost her mind so he can get her out of the way?'

'Yes, *Gaslight*. It's a film,' he answered, suspiciously quickly.

And now it all makes sense. Charles Boyer wanted Ingrid Bergman out of the way so he could search for the missing jewels belonging to her murdered aunt. We have no missing jewels in this house. But Matthew's motive, as he sits there flicking through Teletext, his Sony PlayStation at his feet, listening to the cricket on his short-wave radio, a Dixons catalogue on the table in front of him, is all too plain. He wants me exiled to Bedlam so he can turn our house into an unstately pleasure dome. He wants to take over every room with giant television screens, slot machines, joysticks and table football.

•

'We've got *Gaslight* on video, haven't we?' I said.

'Yes,' he said. 'But now I come to think of it it's probably one of the ones we lent to Suzie.'

Despite Matthew's use of the word 'we' I have no recollection of lending videos to Suzie, our next-door neighbour. I don't remember doing any such thing, and now she's on holiday in France so I can't check with her.

'I don't remember lending Suzie any videos,' I said.

'Well, you weren't here when she came round but I definitely told you,' said Matthew. 'You have been very forgetful lately,' he continued, 'you can't even remember the PIN number you've had for ten years, can you?'

'Can't I? I don't remember forgetting it.'

'No,' said Matthew, 'I don't suppose you do. You look a little tired. Why don't you go and lie down for a while.' I vaguely remember Charles saying something very similar to Ingrid.

And then Matthew came home with a copy of *Gaslight*. He said had bought it to replace the one I couldn't remember lending to Suzie.

'Why don't we watch it together this evening when Joe has gone?' says Matthew. 'You do remember Joe is coming round to have a look at the fuse box?'

'No,' I said, 'I don't just not remember it, I never knew in the first place. I promise you. You never told me Joe was coming.'

'But it was you who left the message on his answerphone,' said Matthew. Did I? Perhaps Joe is in on this too.

Now Matthew's mother has phoned to 'remind' me that she can't look after Louis on Wednesday as she usually does. 'You are a bit forgetful sometimes,' she said. 'So I thought I had better phone.' It's as well she did. I have no memory of her ever mentioning this at all. Consequently I have failed to ask Tanja to come and look after Louis on Wednesday.

Tanja is here now. She is downstairs talking to Joe and Matthew. I must be careful. They are all in on it. Or perhaps I am going mad. But I mustn't think this way. When Ingrid Bergman thought this way she almost did go mad.

•

Joe and Tanja have both left. Tanja apologized for not giving me the message from Matthew's mother, and Joe discovered a short circuit which blew the fuses every time the burglar light outside the front door was activated – every time, for instance, that someone (apparently not just Matthew) entered or left the house in the dark. He seems to have fixed it, because when Flo, Suzie's daughter, came round a little later to return the videos Suzie had borrowed, the lights all stayed on. Of course all this means is that Flo, and probably Suzie, are in on it too.

16 May 1999
Defending Blondie

There is a well-known syndrome whereby married couples find that they are able to finish off each other's sentences. Matthew and I are not remotely affected by this syndrome because, although we talk to teach other, we don't often listen, so if we were to attempt finishing each other's sentences we would get it wrong. Some recent attempts demonstrate this.

R: 'Do you want a mushroom omelette or a . . .'

M: 'Left kidney. I've got an infection in my left kidney.'

R: 'When you pick Louis up from nursery, please remember to ask them . . .'

M: (reading *Daily Mail*): 'What is the point of Paul Johnson?'

R: 'If you are going upstairs, please could you bring down . . .'

M (reading *Daily Telegraph*): 'The Serbian government.'

Tim the car mechanic and I, on the other hand, can always, without fail, finish each other's sentences. He knows exactly what I am going to say; he probably knows it's me before he picks up the phone. Tim looks after the Y-reg, seventeen-year-old Mercedes 280SE with

160,000 miles on the clock that I bought for £2,100 a little over a year ago.

R: 'I'm leaving early today because I have to take the car to the . . .'

M (animatedly): 'Scrap yard.'

R: 'No, to Tim. He's going to fix her up again.'

Before I bought this car, the car that Tim and I love but which Matthew hates and wishes to scrap, I had little time for the kind of person who anthropomorphizes inanimate objects. But on that spring day, a little over a year ago, as Matthew paced up and down in the road outside our house with his head in his hands, I carried Louis (who was then just one year old) to the sitting-room window to show him our new car. 'Isn't she lovely,' I said, 'with her shiny chrome and her original hubcaps?'

Since then Tim and I have always referred to the car as 'she', and I have (unbeknown to Matthew) named her 'Blondie' for her clotted-cream-coloured paintwork.

•

I have been tending to Blondie as if she were my first-born, largely because she is quite magnificent to look at and people give way to me on the Shepherd's Bush roundabout, but also because I am determined to prove Matthew wrong. She may have 160,000 miles on the clock and a recurring radiator leak, but she is not yet ready for the scrap heap.

Every day I have checked the water and once a month I have checked the oil and the tyres. Each time it has rained I have applied towels to sop the Lake Windermere that forms behind the driver's seat so that Matthew might never know the sensation of driving a portable swimming pool.

And once every fortnight I have had long, involved telepathic chats with Tim as to how she might somehow be kept alive: 'She keeps cutting out towards . . .'

'The end of long journeys,' finishes Tim.

Or: 'The back windscreen wiper . . .'

'Gets stuck and smells of burning,' concludes Tim.

And then came the fateful day, the day when Matthew came home with the leaflet which said that leaded petrol will not be available after 1 January 2000. He was waving it about his head, like a football rattle. It reminded me of a scene from *The Six Wives of Henry VIII*. The car was Anne Boleyn, Matthew was Thomas Cromwell, the leaflet was the death sentence bearing the King's signature: 'It'll have to go,' he said. 'It would be a false economy to convert it.'

'How do you know?' I asked. 'I'm sure Tim can do it quite cheaply.'

'Fifty pence spent on that car would be a false economy,' said Matthew, and then he started with the 'worthless' rant. 'That car of yours is worthless. It's a disaster. It pollutes the environment. It sounds like a combine harvester and the inside smells like a wet dog basket. There are 747s that do twice as many miles to the gallon as your car.'

•

I don't know how much longer I can defend her. She's on her final warning. One more mistake and Blondie's history.

'Tim. It's Rebecca. We've just been to Sussex for the weekend and . . .'

'The engine kept cutting out and Matthew says it's got to go,' finishes Tim.

Matthew has been saying the car has got to go repeatedly since 10.02 on Saturday morning, when she started her habitual stalling, not towards the end of a long journey but pretty much at the beginning of one.

The first stall came at the speed hump not twenty yards from our house. Matthew shook his head as he turned the key in the ignition and said: 'It's got to go. I tell you, this car has got to go.' He said much the same thing at the mini-roundabout and again at the traffic lights. By the time we hit the M25 it had been raining for half an hour and Lake Windermere was swishing away behind Matthew, causing little waves to lap at his heels. We stopped on the A21 in a lay-by to allow the radiator to cool down sufficiently for a top-up, and Matthew draped his socks over her bonnet to dry while he leant against a rubbish bin, scowling and repeating, 'It has to go,' over and over, rocking to and fro, his head buried in his hands.

•

Tim has sorted out the stalling for the time being and he is tackling the radiator leak with renewed vigour. He says everything will be fine for a while: 'I don't suppose you've had time to . . .'

'Find out how much she'll cost to convert? About £500, I reckon.'

'Oh,' I say. 'That much? Well, that's it, then . . .'

'Book her in for Thursday?' asks Tim.

'Yes, please.'

23 May 1999

What to Do for the Millennium

The Tesco's Millennium wall chart in Louis's bedroom has been troubling me ever since I pinned it up a week ago. In itself, it is harmless enough and even educational (I had no idea that 'in 1750 end-over churns quickly turned cream into butter'). And Louis enjoys putting the stickers against the names of various heroes and heroines of the past thousand years, although not necessarily the correct ones. What worries me far more than the possibility that he grows up believing Nelson Mandela was a white woman in a prototype nurse's uniform with a thing about lamps is the nagging premonition that in about ten years' time he will come upon this wall chart, yellowing and dusty, in a box, in the attic. After asking how come Florence Nightingale has been depicted as a white-haired black man in a garish shirt, he will turn to me and ask, 'What did we do for the Millennium, besides collecting stickers for a wall chart?' And unless there are dramatic developments in the coming months, I will have to say, 'Nothing.'

Louis will be distraught and will want to know why we didn't do anything when all the other children in his class at school will speak of little but their parents' exotic Millennium activities. 'Jack's parents hired Gugulu

Island in the South Pacific so that they were the first people on the planet to see in 2000, Wilf's mum and dad went to Stonehenge and held him above the head of a chanting druid and Ellie's family took the space shuttle to the moon to watch the day break over Hammersmith. But you,' he will scream, pointing accusingly, 'you stayed in, put me to bed at 8.30 p.m. as usual with a Winnie the Pooh talking tape, and retired to mark this uniquely significant date by watching your sad videos of sad old films over a sad half-bottle of champagne and some Nurofen! I am ashamed to call you my parents. What kind of people are you?'

•

'What kind of people are we?' I asked Matthew last night, explaining my premonition while Louis attempted to stick Winston Churchill where Neil Armstrong should be.

'We are the kind of people who stay in for the Millennium,' he replied. 'Because no one wants to spend it with us. Everyone hates us.'

A few months ago, if I had asked him this, he would not have recycled the old 'we have no friends' argument, he would have said that we were staying in on the night of 31 December because of the Millennium Bug. We – Matthew – were convinced that computer failure would lead to the instant and irrevocable breakdown of society, and therefore we would be barricading ourselves against looters, locking ourselves in the garden shed with a stockpile of logs, an electricity generator and several hundred tins of food. But all recent reports insist that the bug has been greatly exaggerated, and that apart from the odd malfunctioning microwave or misbehaving traffic light, life on 1 January 2000 will be much as it was on 31 December 1999. So now our Millennial activity must be explained instead by the ancient and well-worn thesis that 'we have no friends'. Except that I am not prepared to accept this. 'We do have friends,' I argue, 'and I bet they are doing nothing as well.'

'Ring them and ask,' says Matthew, 'and I bet you twice as much they are all going away somewhere, probably Norfolk and probably together. Go on. Ring them.'

•

The recipient of the first phone call is, to her credit, a little embarrassed to admit that she and her family are spending Millennium night with a disgraced former high-court judge in the Buckinghamshire home of a millionaire industrialist, and, I gather from the ease with which I manage to slip the Millennium question in, that the subject of how to spend it has temporarily replaced those other middle-class dinner-party topics, children and house prices.

'What are you and Matthew doing?' she eventually asks.

'Oh, not much,' I say. 'Probably nothing. You know us.'

The second recipient says that he, his wife and their four children (one on the way) are going to Norfolk.

'Norfolk?' I say in a ridiculously high octave.

'Yes,' he says, 'Diss. And you?'

I tell him we are going to a small village not too far away from Diss called Datt, but it is a very old joke and he quite understandably doesn't laugh. So I break the meaningful silence by saying, 'I don't know what we are doing. Matthew's planning a surprise.'

The third friend to be called says that she and her boyfriend have made plans to rent in Norfolk. 'Norfolk?' I say. 'How lovely. How imaginative.'

•

'I bet everyone we know is going. I bet they are all renting the same Grade II listed manor house,' I whine to Matthew. 'I bet they are all staying together and they'll sing "Auld Lang Syne" and keep the children up and in the morning on New Millennium Day they will have a huge breakfast and go for a walk and stop off for a pub lunch. They might even do some wife-swapping or play charades and we'll be sitting here in W12 with our turkey leftovers and a packet of Nurofen watching *Casablanca*.'

Matthew says that he is becoming tired of my increasingly frequent outbursts of paranoia (he seems to have forgotten that 'we have no friends' is his theory, not mine).

And then the phone rang and Matthew answered it. It was a 'friend' asking him to the football on Saturday. 'By the way,' said Matthew, 'what are you doing for the Millennium . . . Diss? . . . Really? . . . Us? Oh, I don't know. Rebecca's planning a surprise.'

6 June 1999
We Have Decided to Move to the Country Again

Bluebells do strange things to Matthew's mind. They may have come and gone for the year but the effects still linger. Matthew may not be able to tell the difference between a rhododendron and a pansy, but he is always affected by bluebells. It is almost as if, like poppies, they contained an opiate capable of turning his mind away from all its usual urban preoccupations like tandoori takeaways and betting shops, transporting it to country lanes.

Matthew does not quite clasp his hands in front of him in awe when he thinks of a bluebell wood, but there is definitely something of the John Boy Walton about him from April to May.

'That tree in the front garden, the one with the nice pink blossom,' he'll say, his grasp of the subject falling tantalizingly short of the word 'magnolia', 'it's about to bloom. That must mean the bluebells will be out soon.' Then, with a faraway look in his eyes, he suggests that we visit them, as if the bluebells were a sad, lonely old couple in need of cheering up: as if all around Britain there are clusters of depressed bluebells waiting for their annual visit from Matthew.

So we do visit them. This year, we have been to see

the Sussex bluebells and the Wiltshire bluebells. On both occasions we stayed with friends who happened to have access to particularly (for Matthew anyway) intoxicating bluebell woods and who live in lovely houses with beautiful gardens. On both occasions the sun shone and the countryside looked its best, and on both occasions Matthew introduced the sole topic of conversation for our return journey to London with the words, 'We are definitely moving to the country.'

•

It all seems so familiar. Even as I write I feel as if I have written of it before – perhaps because I did, last year, when Matthew went as far as having property details faxed from every estate agent within a hundred-mile radius of Greater London. Like the bluebells, Matthew's fixations are locked in an annual cycle, and so inevitably are the subjects for these column, and so are you.

What makes it all the harder for me is that there is nothing I would love more than to live in the country. It would be so easy for me now, such fun indeed, to join in with the knee-jerk enthusiasm, to help compile the list of reasons not to stay in London, to plan our finances for a future which promised a bit of land and perhaps a few chickens. But I must remain silent, not allow myself so much as a flicker of hope, because I know that all too soon the demented country ramblings of a man who has temporarily mistaken himself for Tess of the D'Urbervilles will cease.

For in reality Matthew hates the country. His idea of a bracing walk is the journey from our front door to the mini-cab he orders to take him to the Tube station each morning. And so instead of excitement at the promise of moving to the country I experience a torpor, a heaviness, an unwillingness to participate. The bluebells' mysterious, drug-like effect is pervasive and all I can do is bite my lip and wait for it to pass.

•

As we drove away from our Wiltshire weekend this year and pointed the car in the direction of the M3, I estimated that Fleet Services would just about mark the point at which he would once again be extolling the virtues of London life. 'Anonymity. That's the great thing about London,' he'll say, without warning or conversational segue from the weeping willow he had just mentally planted along his imaginary stretch of river, complete with fishing rights and a boat. 'Nobody cares if you live or die in London, that's what I love about it. Nobody's going to stick their nose in your business. Not like the country with its WI and sherry and interfering busybodies trying to ramble across each others' back gardens.'

'Leave the country to the country folk,' he'll say finally, and I will resign myself to a life in London, to finally walking the Thames Path to Docklands and spending more time in the garden. But this time I was wrong about Fleet Services. That journey back from Wiltshire was two months ago and Matthew has since then been making important strides towards sanity. He appears to have come up with a plan so apparently rational that I am in danger of allowing myself a smidgen of excitement. We may well be moving to the country ... in 2002. 'I have had a word with Barry,' said

Matthew, and surprisingly he was not holding a bottle of Famous Grouse, the norm after any communication with the accountant, 'and I have worked out that we can have the best of both worlds: a house in the country and a tiny flat in London. If we save, we could move in time for Louis to start school.'

Dare I get excited? Dare I mentally plan the house, the garden, the bucolic existence, a happy, healthy, country childhood for Louis? Should I give voice to my longing to live in a converted water mill and keep rare breeds of duck? Or should I call his bluff and remain silent, as I have until now, even when he shared last week his belief that 'eggs are the new radicchio. We must go into the chicken business'? Even when for no rational reason he suddenly proffered, 'We must try and move before the lambing season'? This evening though, the doorbell rang at 10.30 p.m., and Matthew was handed his takeaway order: tandoori chicken, pilau rice and keema naan. 'Twenty minutes, that took,' he said, spooning aubergine pickle onto his plate. 'Twenty minutes from phone to first mouthful. You won't get service like that in Wootton Bassett.' And it was then that I knew that it was all over for another year.

25 July 1999
Mr Beaumont

Mr Alan Beaumont of Beaumont Plumtree Simmons Registered Insurance Brokers and Independent Financial Advisors is arriving here in one hour, and I have just lit my first cigarette for two months. I do not, however, feel as guilty as I might: Mr Beaumont is the nicest of registered insurance brokers, and I doubt a gentler or more patient person ever gave independent financial advice – nevertheless the prospect of what lies ahead, what will be unearthed from the quagmire of my financial affairs fills me with such dread that a Marlboro Light is the least damaging drug I deserve.

The subject of Mr Beaumont's visit today is my pension plan, or possibly non-plan. I do not know which, because for the past year, since we last met, I have been doing with Mr Beaumont's letters what I do with all financial communications, be they from him, Barry the accountant or the bank. I have filed them away, with care but unopened.

Mr Beaumont is coming to Shepherd's Bush from Ilford, a hideous journey especially in the current heatwave, but he is making this sacrifice for a very good reason. If we met again in a restaurant, as I suggested, when he asked me for Form 121C, about contracting out of something or other, or Form 321(c), concerning contracting into something else, I would clap my hand to my forehead and say: 'You won't believe this, Mr Beaumont, I am sure I had it when I left the house but it's just not here now.'

Here, at home, there is no excuse. I am cornered. There is no escape.

•

Mr Beaumont has arrived, and I have shown him out to the garden, where, in the nicest way, he gives the impression of being eager to attend to the matters at hand. I am even more keen that we make the most of the fine weather, and have draped the garden table with a sunny yellow Provençal-print cloth upon which I have placed a bowl of roses. Mr Beaumont is settling himself down, removing various documents and a fountain pen from his briefcase, and is now waiting for me to return with the glass of water he requested. I had rather hoped he would ask for coffee, which would have taken so much longer to prepare.

I have, however, overridden his polite refusal of the offer of ice, although I was unable to convince him that I really ought to nip out to the shop to buy a lemon. The poor man is obviously gasping after his hot car journey in rush-hour traffic and has now removed his jacket and asked if he might move his chair a little into the shade. Despite my attempts to interest Mr Beaumont in the hollyhocks and the suggestion that we move the chairs and table next to the shed at the other end of the garden where it is really shady, all avenues of procrastination have been exhausted.

Once I have delivered a short anecdote on the provenance of the file which contains his unopened letters – it is covered in novelty fake fur ('So much less daunting than the common-or-garden ring binder, don't you agree?' 'Oh, yes, I can quite see that now you mention it.') – Mr Beaumont clears his throat and begins.

'Now, then, let's have a look,' he says, opening his own common-or-garden ring binder. 'Let's get the ball rolling.'

I interrupt him to thank him for coming all the way to Shepherd's Bush and ask if it is normal for independent financial advisors to visit clients in this way. He side-steps the question, which is a shame because it could have led to some excellent diversionary conversation, and simply says: 'Oh, well, it's nice to get out of the office from time to time and this is certainly very pleasant. Now then, when we last met, exactly a year ago, we agreed that you should look into all the staff pension schemes you may or may not have joined since you started working in 1981.'

'Yes,' I say.

Mr Beaumont waits for me to continue but when I offer an utterly vacant stare instead he says: 'However, I never heard from you.' He pauses again. I stare. 'And subsequently,' he says, 'I sent you some letters of authority to forward to the various companies you have worked for, enabling them to deal directly with me and save you a lot of bother.'

'Oh, yes, I've got those,' I reply enthusiastically, opening my novelty file to produce them with a self-satisfied flourish.

'Well, not to worry,' says Mr Beaumont kindly, with

barely discernible undertones of exasperation. 'We can do you some new ones with this year's date on. All you have to do is send them off this time and then we can get the ball rolling.'

'Excellent,' I say.

'You could make an AVC on your existing staff pension plan or you could do it on a free-standing basis. Which would you prefer?' says Mr Beaumont.

'Yes,' I reply, confidently, 'I think that's probably best.'

It is now Mr Beaumont's turn to stare and then he says, 'If I might have a look at a payslip, I could check exactly how much is already coming out of your monthly salary. Do you have a payslip?'

'Oh, yes,' I say.

•

It has become a game of poker, a question of who will blink first.

'Might I have a look at a payslip?' asks Mr Beaumont. I forage about in my novelty file and Mr Beaumont wipes his brow and moves his chair a little further into the shade.

It's 12.30 and Mr Beaumont has been talking for thirty minutes about occupational pension schemes and voluntary contributions, top-rate tax relief and statements of benefits, dependants and private medical insurance. I have been nodding in what I imagine to be a knowing and encouraging manner. He knows that I don't have a clue what he is talking about, and I know that he knows. But he is a very sweet man, and seems happy to go through the ritual in exchange for a little mild sunstroke.

'So, then,' says Mr Beaumont, in what sounds enticingly like a conclusion, 'it's acquittable life, then?'

'Yes, that sounds excellent,' I say, hoping that I heard him correctly. 'Give me acquittable life any day.'

He sighs then smiles, returns his papers and fountain pen to his briefcase and I show him to the door.

19 September 1999
Barbecue

Every year Matthew holds a barbecue at which I am his only guest. Each time he announces this event he says that it is to be a trial run because he wants to perfect his technique before asking anyone round to share it with us. The memory of last year's fiasco, which after nearly two hours of barbecuing produced no cooked food, two still unrecovered blackened patches of lawn and several complaints from the neighbours, would, I had thought, put him off this year. In my naivety I imagined that 1999 would pass without incident on the charcoal and fire-lighter front.

But no. Today he announced that he is holding his barbecue this evening and then he left the house, returning two hours later with the following: three two-kilogram sacks of charcoal, two boxes of hickory chips, a pair of barbecue tongs, a barbecue spatula, barbecue gauntlets, a bottle of Ass Kickin' Chicken Wing Sauce, the label on which boasts that it is able to 'Kick Yo' Ass Hot!', and one bottle of Dante's Inferno Tandoori Grilling and Baking Sauce.

He also bought sixteen chicken wings, two large steaks, twelve Merguez sausages and twelve giant prawns, three bags of salad and two punnets of cherry tomatoes. He is not, he has reiterated, although the bulk purchasing would suggest otherwise, planning to invite anybody.

•

It is a sound that will haunt me all my life. It will never go away. I heard it in my dreams last night, and as I looked out over the garden this morning it was still echoing in my head. One by one, at approximately 8.30 p.m. yesterday, the residents of our road in Shepherd's Bush could be heard shutting their windows. With no wind to direct it, the acrid grey-brown cloud of smoke (hickory chips mixed with firelighters and paraffin) was rising up in a straight line. Just as it reached the level at which it could cause the most damage, and apparently of its own volition, it took a sharp right turn into windows which had been left open on what was the hottest, stickiest, most airless night of this millennium.

'It's quite all right,' Matthew was yelling at the windows as they closed. 'Once the preliminary smoke has burnt off, everything will be fine.'

From the back step where I was standing – such is the humiliation that this is as far outside the house that I will ever again venture – it was difficult to see Matthew. He was shrouded in smoke to his waist. 'Please, just put it out,' I shouted. 'Pour a bucket of water over it or something. There's a man at the door who says his smoke alarm has just gone off.' This wasn't entirely true. There had been a man at the door a few minutes earlier who was collecting for Shelter. 'You can smell it right down on the Goldhawk Road,' he said. 'I thought there was a fire along here.'

'Don't worry,' shouted Matthew. 'It's all under control.'

I closed the back door to stop any more smoke coming in, and groped my way to opening the front door to release the cloud which had formed inside the house.

'What's going on?' I heard someone on the pavement ask. 'Some idiot's having a barbecue,' answered the man from Shelter.

'Please, Matthew,' I shouted from the back step, 'there's a man at the door who says he's having an asthma attack.'

'All under control,' shouted Matthew.

Visibility was now reduced to four feet. Had a hansom cab come racing out of the pea-souper fog that had whorled its way around our house I would have hurled myself in front of it just to end the embarrassment.

•

'Why on earth are you embarrassed?' said Matthew this morning as I threw a bucket of water over the still-glowing embers. 'People have barbecues all the time. It's all part of city life. Nobody minds.' Then he waved cheerily to a neighbour who was not, as I first thought, waving back. He was making angry, possibly obscene, wafting gestures from an open window.

Matthew is now lining up his marinades in preparation for a second attempt this evening. He never got round to actually barbecuing anything last night – 'Bit of a smoke problem,' he said, 'I think I overdid it with the hickory chips' – and by 9 p.m. Shepherd's Bush is once again shrouded in smoke.

It's not as still and airless as last night. There is a

whippy little breeze, so that's an improvement. Only those in the houses to our right are badly affected. The ones who live in the houses to our left are leaning out of their windows laughing at us.

'Matthew, there is a man at the door with an oxygen mask,' I shout from the back doorstep. 'He says his wife and three children are in hospital suffering from smoke inhalation.'

'Can't hear you,' Matthew shouts back.

There *had* actually been a man at the door a few moments ago – a Jehovah's Witness. 'Having a barbecue?' he asked. He said everyone in the road was talking about it, and he could smell it right up by the Tube station. I thanked him for letting me know and shut the door before he remembered to ask me if I'd thought about God lately.

'Matthew, the police have been on. They say you are causing a disturbance and behaving in an antisocial manner.'

'All under control,' Matthew shouts back. 'I've finally cracked it,' he says, thrusting a chicken wing at me. 'We'll invite people round tomorrow night.'

•

'. . . heavy rain and thunderstorms,' says the weatherman on the telly. I feel a bit sorry for Matthew until I remember it is only a matter of weeks before the beginning of autumn when he begins his obsession with having a log fire. He's already bought the toasting fork, and the crumpets – ten packs of eight – are waiting in the freezer.

26 September 1999
Matthew's Meshugas

The catalyst for Matthew's latest obsession was *Songs of Praise*. Although neither Matthew nor I are ardent fans, this is one of our son Louis's particular favourites. Matthew says this is because the banality of the songs and the infantile certainty of the praise remind him subliminally of *Sesame Street*.

After a miserable day inside with a sore throat, Louis had declined to dine at the table, and was sitting on the sofa with a cold collation. It was, I admit, a rather eccentric mixture of foodstuffs: gefilte fish balls, baby prawns, diced bacon and Thomas the Tank Engine Dairylea cheese triangles spread on a matzo cracker.

Matthew, who had just made himself a bacon and pickled cucumber sandwich, came and sat down next to Louis. I knew he was working up to something. He looked at the prawns, then at the telly, then at the bacon, then back at the telly. The congregation was halfway through the second verse of 'Stand Up, Stand Up for Jesus'.

Prawns, telly, bacon, prawns, telly, bacon, telly. Finally he looked at me and out it came: 'Prawns with bacon. Gefilte fish and "Stand Up, Stand Up for Jesus". Very kosher, I must say.'

I ignored him, thinking that this was just a ruse to enable Matthew to change channels to Sky Sport, but I was wrong.

'Don't you ever worry,' he said, 'that Louis is going to grow up without a clue about the half of him that is Jewish? Don't you think he ought to learn something about the Jewish religion?'

With most people this would be a sensible suggestion. I believe that Louis should be brought up to know about Judaism, just as he should know about Anglicanism, and that he should have the chance, to use the usual phrase heard in interdenominational marriages, to decide for himself which, if either, he wants to embrace.

Matthew, however, is not most people. And though I am no expert on Judaism I am an expert on Matthew. I also know a little Yiddish, so I can state confidently that this is nothing but another of his meshugas. A meshuga is a minor lunacy or obsession, and if *Mastermind* was still going, and I was on it, my specialist subject would be 'The Meshugas of Matthew'.

Until now Matthew has always said that he is opposed to all religions, including the one he was born into. This, however, is no guarantee that he will not come home this evening in a wide-brimmed hat, with his hair hanging down either side of his forehead in ringlets, announcing that he is giving up journalism in order to train for the rabbinate.

•

The matter (or problem, as Matthew has decided it now is) of Louis being given the chance to embrace his Jewishness is raised several times over the next few days. I point out to him quite early on that he is worrying unnecessarily. Because my family lives more than a hundred miles away in the West Country and Matthew's lives only five miles away in North London, it is geographically dictated that Louis is likely to attend far more bar mitzvahs than Church of England bring-and-buy sales. If, however, I suggest, Matthew wishes to put the arrangement on a more formal footing, we could keep a rota – one smoked-salmon bagel for one Victoria sponge, for example.

Then a few days later Matthew cancelled a weekend in the country at the last minute because we were invited to a Rosh Hashanah (Jewish New Year) dinner. We were asked for nine o'clock, which Matthew thought a bit late for a dinner invitation but only because it didn't occur to him that everyone else present would have prefaced the social aspect of the occasion with a trip to the synagogue.

At dinner, from the other end of the table, I could hear him lecturing a young wife who had recently converted, and whose knowledge of Judaism therefore dwarfs his own, about the significance of Rosh Hashanah: 'One of the most solemn occasions,' he told her as he lit a cigarette from a sacred candle.

•

'Wasn't that marvellous?' Matthew said as people began to leave at 1 a.m. 'One of the things I must impress upon Louis is that, whatever else happens during the rest of the year, one must respect and sanctify the High Holy Days.'

As we headed towards the front door our host approached. He knew this wasn't exactly in the Talmudic mainstream, he said, but he'd been thinking about Matthew's suggestion of ending the evening with a visit to a casino and decided that it was an excellent idea. Matthew looked pained, confused and guilty. Clearly some ferocious internal battle was being waged and it lasted for perhaps two seconds.

As I made my way home on my own in a taxi I pondered the sanctity of High Holy Days and wondered which bit of this evening I should describe to Louis. I decided to tell him about the delicious gefilte fish balls, the candlelit dinner in the garden, how pretty it all was, the meaning of the word meshugas and how his father would be having a lie-in in the morning after a very late night. Next weekend we are going to Dorset, where there is a car-boot sale to raise money for the church roof.

14 November 1999
Making a Crumble

Matthew has a degree in classics and is not a man to wear his learning lightly. Which is why, when I told him I was panicking about the pudding I have volunteered to make for our dinner-party on Friday night, he said, 'It's hardly a labour of Hercules, is it? I mean, it's not as if Zeus ever said to Hercules, "My son, now you have slain Cerberus, the hound of the underworld, and cleaned out the Augean stables, you shall bake a fruit crumble." '

What Matthew doesn't understand is that the crumble has been dominating my thoughts, dreams and behaviour patterns for days now. In fact I have just woken from a dream in which Delia Smith and Ainsley Harriot were standing over me, shouting, 'Mix, two three four! Blend, two three four! Crumble, two three four!' I was crouched on an exercise mat with a mixing bowl in front of me. 'Feel the burn!' shouted Ainsley. 'Feel the flour between your fingertips!' shouted Delia.

Matthew is right. Making a crumble is not a Herculean task but it is, for me at least, a worrying one. I never normally cook because I am not very good at it. Matthew, who is a brilliant cook, puts my culinary ineptitude down to the fact that I can't do maths. My numerical dyslexia, he says, creates a mental block which renders me unable to weigh or measure foodstuffs or cook them for the correct length of time at the right temperature. He regularly reminds me of the McDonald's Happy Meal which I microwaved for Louis recently. After three minutes (apparently only thirty seconds were required) the plastic toy and its wrapper had melted and melded with the cheese from the burger, and Matthew said he was going to put the end result up for entry in this year's Turner Prize.

•

I have three days left to worry about the crumble. I thought I had four but Matthew has drawn a little diagram on Louis's blackboard which shows that if today is Wednesday and the crumble is required on Friday, that makes three days. I didn't *have* to volunteer to make a crumble. Matthew, who always cooks but never does puddings, would have been happy with the patisserie-bought tart we always have whenever anyone comes to dinner. But, and it must be something to do with the time of year, I suddenly I feel the need to cook. Last winter I volunteered to do the roast potatoes, and although the end result was good (crispy on the outside, fluffy on the inside) they did not reach this state of perfection until long after our guests had departed.

So there we were two evenings ago, sitting in front of the fire, when my thoughts turned to stews, casseroles, dumplings and crumble. 'I'll make a crumble,' I said.

Matthew was silent for a while until, getting up from the sofa and taking my hand, he led me to the kitchen. 'Let me introduce you to the oven,' he said.

And so it has become a matter of principle now. A crumble I shall make.

•

'I am not goading you,' said Matthew, scraping the uneaten, burnt chicken nuggets I had prepared for Louis's supper into the bin, 'I am simply asking, since you only have one evening left for your practice crumble, whether or not you have decided on your fruit.'

The truth was that I had decided on my fruit but Tesco's didn't have blueberries. They didn't have cooking apples either, as I discovered only after a wasted round-trip home to consult the cookery book for alternative crumble fillings.

Matthew then disappeared upstairs to make a phone call. An hour later Rachel, who is among those coming to dinner on Friday night, telephoned. She said she was returning Matthew's call. Matthew, rather mysteriously, said he would take it upstairs. While he was gone I consulted another cookery book and found a recipe for apple and plum crumble. Tesco's do have plums. It will require a certain amount of maths to replace the apple and plum combo with just plums but, with concentration and a calculator, I should be able to do it.

•

It is now Thursday evening and I am not making a practice crumble.

Tesco's did not have the muscovado sugar the recipe requires. They said they would have some in by tomorrow. Matthew, who is taking an irritatingly close interest in this whole crumble business, has disappeared upstairs to make another phone call. That night I have a dream in which Matthew and Marco Pierre White show me how to use an abacus which is strung with plums and apples instead of beads.

Dateline: Friday morning. Following a recipe from Annabel Karmel's *Family Meal Planner* and Nigella Lawson's crumbling technique, I make the crumble and put it in the fridge. I have partially cooked the plums and they too are now in the fridge. At around eight thirty, just as we are sitting down to Matthew's beef stew, I shall unite the fruit with the crumble and cook in a medium oven for 25–30 minutes.

Rachel has just phoned again and asked to speak to Matthew. He has taken the call upstairs.

•

The crumble is on the table – only slightly burnt, and if I were making it again I'd change the crumble to plum ratio to favour the plum. Next to it is a jug of cream and next to that is the *tarte au citron* which Rachel, very sweetly, bought from a patisserie in Islington as a dinner-party gift.

I offer them a choice. 'Tart or crumble?' I say, serving spoon hovering in readiness over the crumble.

'The crumble looks delicious but I'm just too full,' they say.

They say they'd love a tiny slice of tart, though. 'Just a taste. Not too much.'

12 December 1999
Superstitions

As I eat my lunch – a Tesco's Caesar salad – it does not surprise me that there is a magpie sitting in the tree outside and staring at me. Magpies, ladders, black cats are plaguing me at the moment. I can hardly take a bath without finding a solitary magpie, harbinger of doom, nesting in the soap dish or stealing the cap off the hair conditioner. As a result of recent events, however, I am not going to raise my right arm in salute and recite, 'Four, three, two, one,' the tactic I have always employed as an antidote to the bad luck which superstition says a single magpie can bring. I am in fact so determined not to do this that I am now sitting on my left hand, while eating with my right, in order to eliminate any chance of either of my hands flying into involuntary salute. I am determined to wean myself off superstitions altogether.

Two minutes later I am choking almost to death on a crouton.

•

It started with a simple mission. I was to collect Louis from Matthew's parents in Primrose Hill. 'Please don't put your keys on the table,' said Matthew's mother as I walked in and did just that. 'It's terrible luck. Take them off the table.' I'd never heard this one before (new shoes on the table, yes, but not car keys) and, knowing Matthew's mother, it is probable that no one else ever has either.

So, ignoring her request, I reached out for the cup of coffee she was passing me and spilt its contents on my new suede shoes, which, ironically enough, would have been safer if I had put them on the table. The coffee would have scalded my feet and I would have spent the rest of the day in Casualty, but at least my new shoes wouldn't have been ruined. As it was, I spent the next two hours waiting for the AA and listening to Matthew's mother as she told me repeatedly that if I had removed the keys from the table as requested, there is no question my car would have started.

Perhaps it was because of this that I felt the need to observe so strictly the 'one for sorrow, two for joy' magpie rule the following day when Matthew, Louis, Steptoe and I went for a walk. 'This is getting ridiculous,' said Matthew as my arm jerked into the air for the twentieth time. 'You cannot go round in public doing what, to the innocent passer-by, must look like a Nazi salute. Louis will be taken into care.'

There were, it has to be said, a great number of magpies in the park that day, and they were all going about their business on their own. Not a single bird in the entire West London magpie community had seen fit to fraternize with a fellow magpie.

'There must be another way,' said Matthew.

'Four, three, two, one,' I said.

'This is madness,' said Matthew. 'It is impossible to hold a normal conversation with you.'

'Four, three, two, one,' I said. 'If I don't observe this

ritual, terrible bad luck will befall me and, possibly, you, and Louis, and our entire extended family. Magpies are particularly malevolent birds.' Before I had finished speaking Matthew had hurried off in the direction of a large cedar tree. Once there he began tapping on it. He tapped forty-nine times. He always does this, at the very mention of anything that could, in any way, tempt providence (for minor matters he only touches wood seven times, for anything more serious it is the square of seven).

Two minutes later Steptoe got into a fight with another dog, came off worse and ended up with a cut behind his ear. 'It's the magpies,' I said. 'I missed at least three while I was watching you tap that tree. That leaves us with two more disasters yet to befall us.'

Matthew ran back to the cedar tree. He said he was going to tap fifty-six times in an attempt to counteract the influence of the two unacknowledged magpies.

Another magpie flew in front of us. I raised my right hand and counted, 'Four, three, two, one.' Louis fell in a puddle and started crying. I saw a blonde woman about fifty yards away staring at us. She was the image of Esther Rantzen – coming, no doubt, to take Louis into a Childline care home.

•

That evening Matthew and I started watching *I, Claudius* on video. It begins with the young Claudius going to see the Sibyl.

'I'm like the Sibyl,' I said. 'I'm plagued by omens.' The previous evening we had watched *Blade Runner*, in which the first 'replicant' to appear was, according to its database, created on 10/4/2017, the day Louis will reach twenty years of age. Added to that, the replicants are created by the Tyrell Corporation, different spelling, different pronunciation but unquestionably the same name as mine. Unquestionably an omen.

'You are not like the Sibyl,' said Matthew. 'The Sibyl predicted the future in gnomic verse' – 'gnomic' is one of Matthew's favourite words; he uses it to tell the world he has a classical education – 'whereas you make Nazi salutes at magpies. You are not the Sibylline Grace. Sybil Fawlty, perhaps . . .'

•

This morning Matthew's mother dropped in to see Louis. Just before leaving she asked if I had a stamp she could buy. I found her a stamp and she started rootling about in her bag for change. 'Please don't worry,' I said, 'you really don't need to pay me,' and she looked at me as if I was mad.

'You must always pay for stamps,' she said. 'You must pay for stamps at once, and with the right amount, to the penny. It is terrible bad luck not to pay for stamps.'

I was tempted to ask if she was making it up as she went along but waited instead for her to find exactly 26p in her bag.

Louis and I walked her to the car. She had a parking ticket. The traffic warden was just snapping his notebook shut and crossing the road. 'That wouldn't have happened if you hadn't spent five minutes looking for 26p,' I said. She gave me another look, not unlike that of a magpie, and I went back inside to tap on wood forty-nine times.

19 December 1999
The Soda Siphon and the Dartboard

Matthew says it's the soda siphon all over again. The soda siphon was my birthday present to him in 1996. It didn't work when he opened it, and it still doesn't work now, except as a pleasing ornament. He mentions it occasionally, and I am aware that my defence does not hold water, unlike the soda siphon (holding water is all it does do). 'It's your soda siphon now,' I say whenever the subject is raised, 'you deal with it.'

'It is not my soda siphon,' asserts Matthew, 'I never formally accepted it because it was faulty. You owe me a soda siphon . . . a fully functioning soda siphon. Where's my soda siphon?'

This year I bought him a dartboard. He was thrilled with it. Never before, with the possible exception of the blood-pressure testing kit I gave him (on Valentine's Day), have I seen him so ecstatic about a present. He paced about the room looking for the perfect spot to hang it, shading his eyes with his hands, screwing up his face, doing that thing that artists do with their out-stretched thumbs in front of easels. 'You must get it hung by the end of the week,' he said. 'This dartboard must not become another soda siphon.'

A week has passed and Matthew's dartboard has yet

to make contact with the wall. Matthew says it really is the soda siphon all over again and before leaving the house this morning he took the trouble to prop the dartboard up against a pile of magazines on a table, next to the soda siphon. Tracey Emin could not have come up with a still life as laden with gritty realistic pathos as this.

I am not, however, allowed to ring the odd-job man who came two weeks ago to move an upside-down radiator to the opposite wall and reinstalled it in its new position still upside down. I had pleaded on his behalf, on the grounds that we don't know anyone else, that the same man had successfully hung two mirrors the right way up and I couldn't see much room for error in a dartboard but Matthew said, 'I will not have that man in my house' – a phrase he has taken to using often. It must be something to do with reaching the wrong side of thirty-five – he's come over all territorial. He said it last week when, not for the first time, he found my tame Jehovah's Witness, a Leonardo diCaprio lookalike, sitting on the sofa, drinking tea and reading pamphlets out loud to Louis. He came very close to saying it about Steptoe the other day. It just seems to trip off his tongue lately.

•

After several phone calls to friends and acquaintances in the area asking if they know of a good odd-job man, only to hear repeatedly the phrase 'no, but if you hear of one, please let us know', I gave up and went to Tesco's, where there is a notice board advertising local services – ironing ladies, babysitters and one odd-job man, called Derek.

Derek, who would doubtless describe himself as a 'chirpy chappy', arrived on the doorstep within an hour of my phoning. I made him a cup of tea ('no sugar, thanks. I'm sweet enough already') and he told me that I'd picked the right person to put up a dartboard because he had once met Jocky Wilson. Derek then commented on Matthew's stockpile of logs – which has overflowed from the shed into the kitchen; said he used to clean chimneys ('lonely business'); and then, on seeing Louis's toy box, told me his own children were grown up now (his daughter is apparently living in Canada with an orthodontist, and his son is a chemist – 'does a lot of celebrity work').

Then Derek made a fuss of Steptoe and said his late sister used to breed West Highland terriers. 'She had her champion stuffed when he died. We've got it in our garage now.'

'I'll leave you to it, then. I've got some work to be going on with myself,' I said, but Derek wasn't listening.

The phone rang. It was Matthew. 'Have you done anything about the dartboard?'

'I'm doing it right now!' I said, and, remembering the *Fawlty Towers* episode in which Sybil rings to ask Basil if he has yet hung the moose head while he is in the middle of trying to do that very thing, I slammed the phone down.

•

Derek never did hang the dartboard that day. He did, however, spot the upside-down radiator over which it was to hang, and volunteered to install it the right way up. If I could have got a word in edgeways, I would have told him the dartboard was the priority. But I gave up in the end, after hearing about his wife's hobby – she writes poems and sends them off to greetings card companies – and a surprisingly technical account of his brother's stomach ulcer. Then Derek looked at his watch, asked if that was the time (it was), and left.

'It's not a total disaster,' I told Matthew that evening as he stood in front of the un-hung dartboard shaking his head and muttering, 'It's the soda siphon all over again.' 'He's rehung the radiator and he's coming back in the morning.'

•

Derek is here now; he's been here all day. It's 6 p.m. and he's downstairs playing darts on his own. Matthew has just come upstairs. 'Get rid of him,' he says to me. 'I'm never having that man in my house again. I've just had twenty minutes on his brother's stomach ulcer, and he's hung the dartboard upside down.'

I am surprised at Matthew; there is nothing he enjoys more than medical details. I go downstairs to pay Derek off, and he is scrutinizing the soda siphon. He says he's coming back tomorrow to see if he can fix it.

9 January 2000
The Lie Detector

A combination of the cold weather and Matthew's log stockpile has driven my imaginary psychotherapist, Mr George Sanders, out of the shed and into the spare bedroom. The arrangement suits me very well as I need to consult him on a pretty regular basis right now. 'What seems to be the problem, dear lady?' he asks, shooting his cuffs from the sleeves of his salmon-pink velvet smoking jacket with navy blue quilted moiré collar, and tweaking his maroon and ochre paisley-print cravat. 'Calm yourself down and do try to stop rocking backwards and forwards.'

The problem is that I am surrounded by doubters and gainsayers. Until very recently I had a different problem, in that no one seemed able to hear a word I said. I would make a joke, silence would greet it, someone else would make the identical joke thirty seconds later and the room would combust with laughter. I didn't like it at the time, but I think I disliked it less than always being accused of lying, which is what is happening now. I am being heard in crystal clarity by people who mistake me for Pinocchio. It makes me feel like Jeffrey Archer in drag, and, needless to say, Matthew is the prime culprit.

The latest is just one in a long line of similar incidents:

Matthew refuses to believe that the car was locked when his shoes, which I had collected from the menders, were stolen from it. 'I'm not bothered about the shoes,' he said after I had spent a frustrating forty minutes repeating over and over again, 'I locked the car. I know I locked the car. Please believe me. I locked the car,' and finally storming upstairs to the spare room.

•

Matthew thinks I should at least admit to the possibility that I might have forgotten to lock the car, given that there is no sign of a break-in. He knows this because he paced up and down outside on the pavement next to the car for ten minutes, trying to get inside the mind of the shoe thief.

'I know I locked the car,' I said to George Sanders.

'You're rocking again,' said George, crossing his right leg over his left knee and toying with the top of his amethyst and cobalt Sea Island cotton sock.

'I'm going to get a lie detector,' I announced to Matthew this afternoon. We were driving to lunch at a friend's house.

'Now you're being silly,' he said.

'You might think it's silly,' I said, 'but there is a principle at stake. I am determined to prove my innocence.'

'I am not saying you are lying,' said Matthew, 'I am simply saying that you are mistaken.'

•

'Oh, I'm always forgetting to lock the car,' said our friend Penny in a placatory fashion halfway through lunch, after Matthew had asked repeatedly that I drop the subject of whether or not I locked the car. 'It's so easy to do when you've got a small child, a dog and shopping to deal with.'

'It's precisely because I've got a small child and a dog and shopping that I know absolutely that I locked the car,' I said, rather too aggressively. 'I remember locking it because it was so difficult. That's why I left the shoes in the car, because I couldn't manage to carry them along with everything else I had to hold on to and lock the car at the same time.'

Matthew gave me a look and changed the subject: 'Rebecca said she saw you in a Sugar Puffs advert the other day,' he said to Penny's husband, Mark, who is an actor.

'She couldn't have done,' said Mark. 'I haven't made a Sugar Puffs advert,' and Matthew gave me another look, a look which said: 'Go on, get yourself out of this one.'

'I did see you in a Sugar Puffs advert,' I said. 'It was two mornings ago on Channel 4 at seven o'clock in between *Sesame Street* and *The Big Breakfast*.'

Mark shook his head. 'Wasn't me,' he said.

'It was you,' I insisted.

Matthew sighed as if to say, 'Here we go again with the lies, lies, lies.'

'It was you and the Honey Monster,' I said.

'Oh, the Honey Monster. Is that Sugar Puffs? In that case you're right. About a year ago I made an advert with the Honey Monster.'

'You thought I was lying, didn't you,' I said to Matthew. 'It happens all the time,' I then told everybody around the lunch table, 'so much so that I have arranged to get a lie detector.'

'You haven't arranged to get a lie detector,' said Matthew. 'You only thought of it on the way here.'

•

The car radio has now been stolen. Matthew says he is surprised it hasn't happened before and that this time there is no question I must have forgotten to lock the car. 'I know I locked the car,' I said. 'Do you really think that after last week's shoe incident I'd have forgotten to lock the car?'

'In that case,' said Matthew, 'if you are quite sure you locked the car, you can deal with the insurance people. They will ask you whether the car was locked and if so whether there was any sign of a break-in.'

'Fine,' I said. 'Leave it with me.'

It's been three days now and I still haven't rung the insurance people. 'Perhaps I didn't lock the car,' I said to George Sanders. 'Perhaps I am going mad.'

'You are getting this all out of proportion, dear lady,' said George. 'We all make mistakes. We are only human, after all. Go and tell Matthew that you are not absolutely sure that you did lock the car. He will understand.'

'No, George,' I said, 'I cannot do that. It is too late to go back. I must maintain innocence at all costs.'

•

'Perhaps you should get that lie detector after all,' said Matthew later that evening when I told him the insurance people had been permanently engaged for three days. 'Have you made any enquiries about how to get hold of one?'

'Yes, I have,' I said. 'But all the lie detectors in London are out with MI6. They made a block booking several months ago.'

'Of course they did,' said Matthew, 'and of course you did. Now go and sit down and I'll make you a nice cup of tea.'

16 January 2000
Depression in a Dressing Gown

Tradition has it that at this time of year, from January to early February, Matthew lives in his dressing gown. There is a film about a depressed woman called *Woman in a Dressing Gown* (1957), which I just know he has seen and been inspired by: the dressing gown is a metaphor for his own depression. During this depressed period Matthew elects to work from home and having put on the dressing gown, which is a particularly lowering shade of bottle-green, he affects a slow hunched shuffle, doesn't shave, makes himself milky drinks which he spills on the stairs and repeats the same few phrases over and over again:

1. 'What is the point? Tell me: what is the point?'
2. 'I have never – ' slow, low-slung head shake – 'in all my life, I have never . . .' more low head shaking . . . 'felt worse.'
3. 'Why in God's name do we stay in this country? Look at it! Just look out there!' (Said while standing in hunched position by window with milky drink in hand.)

This year the dressing gown went on early, between Christmas and New Year. It came off fleetingly when Matthew accompanied Louis and me on a family outing to Legoland. Matthew was briefly cheered when it became apparent that Louis had conceived a hatred of the place only marginally less irrational and intense than his own. He and Louis sat miserably in a fairy pod on a very small Ferris wheel. Matthew's head was in his hands as he repeated phrase number two over and over again, each repetition taking roughly one revolution of the wheel.

Throughout our train ride on the Snowball Express he emitted low, slow animal moans, and while we queued for Santa's Toy Factory he shouted, like a Tourette's syndrome sufferer, phrase number one at two-minute intervals.

We stayed at Legoland, at Matthew's insistence, for just one hour, and when we got home I changed. I put on my dressing gown (attractive blue and white fleck from the Conran Shop), and I have remained in it ever since.

Matthew, I have decided, does not have a monopoly on melodramatic, attention-seeking behaviour. Before the month is out, I will have proved that when it comes to depression in a dressing gown I leave him standing. Or slouching. Or rocking to and fro on the sofa. Wherever he is, I will outmope him.

•

It isn't working, though. Instead of interpreting the appearance of my dressing gown as a challenge, Matthew regards it as a wifely gesture of unity and has come over all team-spirited about the whole thing.

We say very little to each other during the course of the day. A typical piece of dialogue runs thus.

Matthew: 'How are you feeling?'

Me: 'Awful. Miserable. Utterly miserable.'

Matthew then pats me on the head in a 'that's my girl' fashion while saying, 'I've never felt worse myself . . . Never felt worse!' The unspoken sentiment here is 'Isn't this jolly good fun?'

Then, without even trying, I catch a head cold and it changes everything, because if there is one thing Matthew has never been team-spirited about it is his health. He makes it clear, within minutes of my reaching for the Nurofen Cold & Flu tablets, that he is not short of ailments himself and that they have, in fact, been running concurrent with the depression all along.

After a series of feeble attempts – an imaginary pea-sized lump behind his left ear, a strange tingling in the hair follicles, a numbness around his Achilles' heel – Matthew has topped my head cold with an appalling hacking cough which ten days later is still with us. The coughing fits can last up to four or five minutes and are followed by desperate clutching movements around the heart and pathetic gasps for air. Matthew insists it must be bronchitis.

I can't compete. I have given up. My dressing gown is off. I have returned to traditional daywear.

•

Matthew has removed his dressing gown because he is too hot. An airless fug has developed around his sick bed, and he refuses to let any air in because of the effect it might have on his weak chest and fragile disposition.

Annoyingly, our GP has diagnosed a viral infection.

I have just taken the newspapers up. Matthew told me to take them away. Had I not considered, he asked, the effect any kind of news from the outside world could have on him at this crucial stage in his rehabilitation?

I offered him a milky drink.

'Have you gone mad?' he asked. 'A milky drink with a bronchial infection?'

'It's not bronchial,' I pointed out. 'The doctor said it wasn't bronchial.'

'Believe me,' said Matthew, 'with my genes it's bronchial.' Then he embarked on the coughing fit, which I could still hear as I loaded our dressing gowns into the washing machine and set the dial to 'intensive'. I cannot compete.

•

Matthew has won this time, but next year I'll win. I'm planning it now. At some point between Christmas and New Year I will spend the night on Hampstead Heath, in the rain, without a coat, perhaps just wearing my dressing gown – like a romantic heroine. Once home I will drift in and out of consciousness with a raging fever as Matthew sits in vigil at my bedside, coughing and clutching at his heart and wondering where he went wrong.

23 January 2000
Walnut Cakes and Consommé

It is only a question of time before Tanja, who unpacks the shopping after Matthew has been to Tesco's, stops bothering to ask what she should do with the walnut cakes. She says she cannot remember an occasion on which she did not find two family-size ones. Tanja further points out that, so far as she knows, not once has any of those walnut cakes – a vast number in the year and a bit she has worked here – been consumed. So it would seem sensible if, shortly, we reach the stage when she removes the walnut cakes from the carrier bags, and – without so much as a glance at their sell-by dates – pops them directly into the bin.

'I'll tell you what,' I said to Tanja recently, 'instead of chucking them out, I think we should keep them. This time next year Libby Purves will ask me on to Radio 4's *Midweek* programme to discuss the provenance of my quite awesome collection of Tesco's own-brand walnut cakes.'

•

In a bid to stop the flow of walnut cakes into this house I have taken to displaying all those still within their sell-by dates between a photograph of Louis and our

Christmas card from Michael Winner (which I still can't bring myself to throw away). Matthew will eventually have to react.

Everyone who comes to the house comments on the display: several have asked if Michael Winner and the walnut cakes are connected, one person insisted that Tracey Emin must be involved in some way.

Sometimes when Matthew has been watching television I have taken a lurid pink-and-orange-striped feather duster and dusted those cakes, sighed and said, 'Aah, don't these walnut cakes look good next to Michael Winner's Christmas card? What an excellent buy those cakes were. Such a sound investment.'

Matthew has always ignored me when I have done this, until last night, when, after extreme provocation (I built a walnut-cake tower in his line of vision during *Match of the Day*), he cracked. All he would say is that he cannot explain why he is physically incapable of passing the walnut cakes in Tesco's without slipping two into his trolley. He knows it is odd, especially since he is not particularly fond of walnut cake, but please could Tanja and I accept the cakes as a fact of life, however baffling or irritating, and lay off?

•

I have just thrown the cake display into the bin, calculating the cost as I did so. 'Eight times £1.35!' I said to Matthew. 'That's . . . that's . . .'

'£10.80,' said Matthew helpfully.

'Exactly,' I said. 'It's the sheer waste I find so hard to accept. £10.80, that's . . .'

'Nearly £11,' said Matthew.

My remarks about the waste of money were, I must with hindsight accept, a serious tactical error. Matthew immediately bounced back from what had been an unusually supine position, and for the past few days we have been engaged in furious debate as to who wastes the most money in this house.

I have just spent ten minutes on the phone to Cable & Wireless trying to find out how much it costs to call 192, after Matthew raised the question of my 'incessant calls to directory enquiries when there is a phone book on the shelf, eight inches from your head'. The cost of the call I am now making – I am still on hold listening to Wagner – will probably comprise most of next quarter's phone bill but I am determined to find out exactly how much it does cost to call directory enquiries. Matthew says it is 25p minimum, and for a difficult number which has to be searched for, or for multiple enquiries, they can charge much, much more.

Someone has just got back to me and it seems Matthew is right. 'One call to directory enquiries,' I tell him, 'depending on the call package you are signed up to, can cost up to three-quarters of a walnut cake.'

•

'If you had only bothered to pay within fourteen days you could have saved £40,' said Matthew. He has just discovered an unpaid parking ticket inside the *A–Z* in the glove compartment of my car.

I have no defence at the ready and so resort to pointing out that he would never have found the parking ticket if he hadn't needed the *A–Z*, and he would never have needed the *A–Z* if he hadn't decided to abandon

Tesco's in favour of Sainsbury's, which he didn't know how to get to.

Matthew hasn't said as much, but I wonder if changing to Sainsbury's is his way of weaning himself off the walnut cakes. So far no Sainsbury's own-brand cake of any type has been purchased, although he has returned from the last two trips with three jumbo bags of Werther's Originals, which he likes even less than walnut cakes.

At 89p for a 300g bag the Werther's are coming in considerably cheaper than the cakes, with the added bonus that Louis and I quite enjoy them. Even taking into account the petrol costs involved in driving the extra distance to Sainsbury's in Ladbroke Grove, it seems Matthew is on to a money-saver here.

•

Matthew has just overheard me asking directory enquiries for the number of Sainsbury's in Ladbroke Grove. He was so incensed that I hadn't bothered to look it up in the phone book that he failed to ask why I needed the number in the first place, which was annoying because I was looking forward to telling him. It was to find out how much one tin of consommé costs so that I could multiply it by seventy-two, the number of tins he has come home with in the past fortnight.

Consommé! Why consommé? And why seventy-two? That's £263.40 worth of tinned soup!

6 February 2000
Mice

It is nearly six months since Matthew bought his Citroën AX from his cousin Lynda, and he has yet to apply for a resident's parking permit. So at 9 a.m. every weekday a £4.80 ticket must be bought from the pay and display machine, usually by me since at that hour Matthew remains in his green dressing gown.

This morning, during the daily scrabble through my bag for change, I irritably cited this constant feeding of the pay and display machine as being the single worst instance of money-wasting in this house. Worse even than Matthew's insane obsession with buying walnut cakes that are never eaten (his consommé phase was all too brief).

'Mmmmm,' said Matthew, sounding remarkably sanguine given the ferocity of my attack, 'I accept your startlingly original parking permit point, which I don't think I've heard put so well since yesterday morning, but you're wrong about the walnut cakes – I believe they are being eaten.' There was something of the 'my dear Watson' in his tone and he appeared to be inviting me, somewhat coquettishly, to follow his gaze to a point beyond my right shoulder.

•

A mouse was cleaning its whiskers in the dog's water bowl, probably washing off some last remnants of butter icing. We both stared at it for quite a few seconds until, all but waving back at us, the mouse sauntered off under the fridge. If that mouse had been human, it would have had its hands in its pockets and been whistling 'Always Look on the Bright Side of Life'. It was an Ealing Comedy sort of mouse, the Alfie Bass of the mouse world, fat and happy on a diet of Tesco's own-brand walnut cake.

It has been agreed that before the day is out Matthew will ring the council about his parking permit, and I will ring the council about the mouse.

'Mice,' corrects Matthew, wagging his finger and shaking his head sagely. 'Do not be fooled into thinking there is just one mouse. Remember: there's always *meshpocha* around the corner.' This is a phrase he has picked up from his mother, who, as it happens, is phobic about mice, *meshpocha* being the Yiddish for family, particularly in-laws.

As Matthew disappears upstairs two of Alfie Bass's *meshpocha* scuttle out of the larder and into Louis's wooden railway tunnel. I stand still, silently waiting for them to emerge riding a train, waving flags and shouting, 'All aboard!' in little mousy voices.

The phone rings; it is Matthew's mother. I must not mention the mice. She is so phobic she claims she often has premonitions before encountering a mouse and always knows if she is in the presence of one. She says she can feel it in her bones. She is calling to say that she is coming round later today with some chicken soup for my 'not quite flu'. Under no circumstances must she encounter mice.

'If she so much as suspects we are harbouring mice, she will never set foot in this house again,' warns Matthew on his way out.

•

The mice seem particularly active today, but Louis has been briefed not to say the words 'mouse' or 'mice' in front of his grandmother. Steptoe, who spends most of his time these days with his nose pressed threateningly against the skirting board, has been banished to the car.

I am reminded of Princess Anne's wedding day, when my mother invited some elderly residents from the village round because we were the only ones in the area with a colour television. The farmer next door had put mouse poison down earlier that week, and in the time it took Princess Anne to walk up the aisle of Westminster Abbey, make her vows, sign the register and emerge with her husband before a cheering public, a total of twenty-five mice had fallen down our chimney. No one said a word. Occasionally the thud of a falling mouse would cause a head to turn, and my mother would say, 'Excuse me,' as she sidled past on her way to and from the fireplace to collect the mouse with a trowel, but no one screamed or squirmed or asked why there should be such an abundance of mice falling down the chimney during the marriage of our sovereign's only daughter.

•

'We've got mouse,' said Louis when his grandmother arrived. Five minutes later, after a glass of whisky (Famous Mouse, I suggested, but she didn't laugh), she was sitting on the sofa, more or less calm, more or less believing that Louis had been joking. The phone went but I let the machine get it.

Matthew's mother apologized for being so sensitive and embarked on a series of mouse stories, most of which involved emergency glasses of whisky. She told me how when Matthew was a boy he would bring dead mice, caught by the cats, in from the garden to frighten her, and how she refused to sign the contract on their house until she had it in writing that there was no sign of any mice infestation.

And then she stopped talking so we could both listen to the answerphone message Matthew had just left. I put it on speaker phone. He said he was stuck in traffic, that he'd sorted out the parking permit and I was to send his love to his mother. 'Above all,' he said, 'whatever happens, you must not mention the mice. I cannot stress this enough,' he said. 'She must not discover we have mice.'

20 February 2000
One-Lung Day

Having decided that this year I will definitely hide Matthew's chest X-rays, I am now stuck for a hiding place. I can't hide them just anywhere. I must factor in the possibility that he might find them. If, for instance, I were to hide them in the shed, and Matthew were to chance upon them while counting his logs, he would know immediately that only I could have put them there, reasoning that chest X-rays do not end up in garden sheds by accident. The finger of blame would inevitably point to me.

No, the hiding place must be exactly chosen. Down the back of a radiator would be ideal, it being somewhere they could have innocently fallen – except that the heat of the radiator might warp them, in which case I would have to destroy them altogether, leaving just a farewell note and a pile of clothes on Southend Pier. I would rather start a new life in Acapulco than live with the consequences of damaging Matthew's chest X-rays. I must simply make the X-rays disappear without implicating myself, and then make them safely reappear once we've got next Wednesday out of the way.

•

Next Wednesday is 'One-Lung Day', the anniversary of the day Matthew was stabbed in the lung by an intruder while staying with friends in Johannesburg, a genuinely horrifying and life-evaluating incident, the long-term consequence of which is the almost as horrifying and life-evaluating anniversary ritual. One-Lung Day is the only day of the year upon which Matthew initiates a social gathering, although those invited are not aware what it is that they are being called upon to commemorate. They believe they have been invited to a normal dinner-party. In this respect, it is like an Agatha Christie in which a group of people are invited to a mystery island on false pretences. Only when they are congregated around the dinner table do they discover that they are all murderers and have been brought together by another murderer who will go on to prove systematically his superiority at committing murder. The common denominator which bonds the guests at the One-Lung Day Dinner is that they are all hypochondriacs.

Tradition has it that Matthew will mention blithely during the soup course that nine years ago today he was being wheeled at top speed, barely conscious, on a hospital trolley with drips and tubes trailing from him like spaghetti. The hypochondriacs will prick up their ears and urge Matthew to tell all. Matthew will, at first, feign reluctance to relive his ordeal, but after a while (usually towards the end of the main course) he will succumb. 'Hang on,' he will say, resignedly, 'I wonder if I still have my chest X-rays?' Then he will casually saunter to the other side of the room and express surprised delight at finding them so easily after all this time.

The hypochondriacs will revel in the proceedings,

knowing that while they may be outranked at hypochondria by Matthew they will at the very least get their turn at telling their own near-death experiences. In this way One-Lung Day is like a hypochondriacs' convention – I have, in the past, considered serving the vegetables in stainless-steel kidney dishes and replacing the napkins with swabs.

Using a chopstick as a makeshift baton to point at the X-ray, Matthew will then show precisely where the intruder's knife entered his chest, the exact breadth of the hair by which the knife missed his heart and the distance it stopped short of rupturing his aorta. When I first heard the story, in March 1991, it was a quarter of an inch from the heart, and an eighth from the aorta. At the last One-Lung Day Dinner, it was an eighteenth of a centimetre from the heart, and a thirty-seventh from the aorta.

•

Today, finally, I hid the X-rays in Louis's pyjama case. It is not that I wish to deny the seriousness of Matthew's stabbing incident. At the time, although we were only slightly acquainted, I was extremely concerned for him. I even rang him in hospital in Johannesburg and remember him describing fighting off a number of intruders, a number since revised to one on the evidence of those also present.

I am aware that the choice of hiding place inevitably implicates Louis, and that some people might question the character of a mother prepared to involve her son in such a deceit against his father; but they are not people who have had to endure eight One-Lung Day anniversary dinners. It is no surprise at this time of year to find

Matthew in a tight-lipped grimace, banging the small of his back with his fist, complaining that the lung is giving him 'a bit of gyp' (the nerve endings of the lungs, as he will then point out, are in the back). But today is different. There is no grimace: in fact, there is barely any sign of human life. Twenty-four hours before the One-Lung Day Dinner Matthew has come down with a mystery virus and an outer-ear infection. He has a temperature of 101° and is deathly pale. He has been in his dressing gown all day.

Normally, despite feeling this terrible, Matthew would derive a certain amount of pleasure from being so ill. There is nothing a hypochondriac of his calibre likes more than a proper, officially diagnosed ailment. But not today, not when it means cancelling One-Lung.

'We don't have to cancel, we could just postpone until next Wednesday,' I suggest.

'Next Wednesday won't be One-Lung Day. What on earth would be the point?' asks Matthew, as if for the life of him he could not imagine a dinner-party that did not involve chest X-rays. And then, placing the thermometer in his mouth for the fifth time in half an hour, he says, 'Perhaps it's for the best after all.'

'Why?' I ask.

'Because I can't find my chest X-rays.'

•

It wasn't such a bad evening in the end. I ordered Matthew his favourite tandoori takeaway and, after holding out until half-past nine, I finally cracked and produced the X-rays, which I handed to him complete with chopstick/baton.

He seemed to enjoy himself. And though I noticed that in the retelling of One-Lung he exaggerated the nearness of knife-blade to aorta and heart, I resisted the temptation to correct him. It was the least I could do.

27 February 2000
Anxiety Dreams

If the yellow envelopes from Barry the accountant keep coming at the present rate, by mid-June I will need to have another shed built in which to hide them from Matthew, who refuses to sympathize with my numerical dyslexia, the condition which renders me unable to add up and therefore unable to cope with my financial affairs. Raising the money to build the second shed, though, will lead to even greater financial chaos, and this will result in even more unopened yellow envelopes, which will eventually necessitate buying a larger house, or a football stadium . . . and so on.

This morning I woke in the early hours, choking and gasping for air after dreaming that I was drowning in a vast sea of unopened yellow envelopes. Kevin the bank manager was throwing me a lifebelt from a cross-Channel ferry but try as I might, I couldn't hold on. When I tried to explain my dream to Matthew he refused to listen because I was speaking in the high-pitched whine I involuntarily adopt whenever the subject of money crops up.

Over the years, I have gone through several spells of refusing to open Barry's yellow envelopes. Once, when I went to see Barry in person, I took them all in a carrier bag, and as he sat there opening them Barry looked like a father greeting prodigal children on their return. The current bout of prolonged non-opening was triggered about two months ago by the contents of the last yellow envelope I did open. This informed me, or so I believed, that I owed the Inland Revenue a little over £111,000 in income taxes on money earned as a freelance writer in 1998, during what Matthew had described to me as a 'tax holiday'. On reading this letter I did what any modern career woman who grew to adulthood in the age of female empowerment would do in such circumstances. I collapsed on the nearest sofa, sobbed theatrically for half an hour and then rang my husband.

•

'I refuse to talk to you until you drop that high-pitched whine from your voice,' said Matthew. And then he said that I couldn't possibly owe £111,000 because I hadn't earned £111,000 and even under Harold Wilson no one paid more than they earned. 'Although,' he continued, 'I gather the rate of tax on unearned income in those days was nineteen shillings and sixpence in the pound.'

I said it didn't strike me as being the time for Matthew to show off his knowledge of tax rates down the ages, and I could only imagine he was driven by cruelty as he knows that phrases like 'nineteen shillings and sixpence in the pound' give me a headache.

Matthew apologized and asked me to read out loud the contents of Barry's letter, which I did.

'Look at the numbers carefully,' instructed Matthew, 'and tell me where the decimal point is.'

'The what?'

'The little dot. Somewhere in the number is a little

dot. How many ones are there to the left of that little dot?' This was downright cruelty (Matthew knows perfectly well that I go to pieces on my lefts and rights when under pressure).

'Two,' I squeaked. 'Two ones to the left of the little dot.' And so we established that I only owed £11,000 to the taxman. Not that this stopped the dreams.

•

In the first dream I was, according to my stationery, Rebecca de Winter III, which I took to mean Rebecca de Winter the one hundred and eleventh.

'How can I be your hundred and eleventh wife, Maxim?' I asked as we drove up the drive to Manderley.

'You silly adorable darling,' replied Laurence Olivier, patting me on the head. 'You dear priceless old ass, that's not one hundred and eleven – one hundred and eleven is the number of thousands of pounds you owe in tax.'

Last week, after the arrival of a letter from the bank telling me I am overdrawn (of course I'm overdrawn, I have just had to pay £1.11.11,000,000 in tax), I dreamt I was a guest on the Duchess of York's chat show. In my dream the caption on the screen read: *Rebecca is a numerical dyslexic and is unable to function in normal society*. Jan from Barry the accountant's office was with me, holding my hand, explaining to the studio audience that 'what people with this rare condition need is patience and understanding. Unfortunately, Rebecca does not receive the correct care in her home environment, and this has led to her developing an irritating high-pitched whine to her voice.'

In last night's dream, which was brought about by the arrival of two yellow envelopes, I was on *This Is Your Life*. Eamonn Andrews, not, interestingly enough, Michael Aspel, introduced Susan Hampshire, who embraced me warmly before telling a funny anecdote about how when we were in rep together in Weston-super-Mare she would sort out my bank statements and I would learn her lines for her.

Then she turned to the audience and said solemnly, 'But seriously, dyslexia of any kind represents a very real problem, and no one has done more to help the cause of numerical dyslexics than Rebecca. She has triumphed over tragedy and with no help, I might add, from her husband Matthew.' Eamonn then introduced the grand finale surprise, which in my case consisted of four men from the Inland Revenue with an arrest warrant and handcuffs. 'Rebecca Tyrrel,' said Eamonn, 'soon to be Prisoner 077668, this is your life.'

•

When I told Matthew about this dream (omitting Susan Hampshire's attack on him) he said I must open Barry's envelopes. 'Open them,' he said. 'It will be a catharsis. You will be cleansed. Until you open the yellow envelopes, you cannot be well again and the dreams will continue.'

Shortly after opening the first yellow envelope I started whimpering. Then I dialled a second-hand book-shop in Clerkenwell, but that was because I got the number wrong, and then finally I got through to Matthew.

'Barry's charged £4,500 for sorting out my tax affairs,' I squawked.

'Calm down,' said Matthew. 'Look for the decimal point. Where's the decimal point?'

'The what?'

'The little dot. Find the little dot . . .'

19 March 2000
Matthew Comes to Devon

For the first time in the week since Louis, Steptoe and I arrived in Devon, the sun has come out; the sky is proper sky blue and the clouds are Persil white. Normally, I am not much bothered by the weather when I am here because I love the place no matter what, and until now we have been splashing around quite happily in torrential rain; but today things are different. Something is about to happen, someone is about to arrive, and if I didn't know it for sure I would guess it from the air of expectancy and change about the place. The sun, like a recalcitrant adolescent who has finally agreed to tidy his bedroom, is obligingly drying out the sloppy sludge puddle just outside the front door. The birds, which have been silent all week, are now tweeting sweetly. Steptoe, after an early morning swim in the pond, is unusually clean and fragrant, and has yet to pay his daily visit to the decomposing badger carcass he has made his own since we arrived. Louis is quietly and thoughtfully dipping his pretend fishing-rod, a willow stick, in and out of the water. He has just caught a pretend fish – a sting-ray, he tells me. I suggest we have it for supper, a special occasion supper in honour of the new arrival who, traffic permitting, should be hoving into view any minute now.

•

Change of plan. We are having pheasant for supper tonight. It has been decreed by that new arrival and guest of honour, Matthew, who has never been here before because he says it is much too deep into the countryside for a Jewish man to be expected to go. We are greatly honoured therefore that this time he has agreed to pay us – his wife, child and dog – a visit, although when we spoke on the phone yesterday he said he was worried his inoculations were not all up to date.

He arrived saying he had almost run over a 'chicken' on the drive down to the cottage. Foolishly, I told him that it was probably a pheasant (he had never seen one with its feathers on before). So now, as if to get his own back on the bird, to punish it for humiliating him by not being a chicken, he is standing in the local butcher's ordering four of its close relatives – two brace of pheasant. I am mortified not just because he has affected a joke country squire accent which sounds like a cross between Michael Winner and Captain Mainwaring of *Dad's Army*, but because he keeps making cheap jokes about close-knit West Country communities. I am sure I am not the only one who just heard him mutter under his breath, 'And a packet of Knorr in-bred sauce while you are at it, my good man.' I am further mortified when, as we leave, the young man who served us, a young man with the teeth of Ken Dodd, the hair of Robin Cook and the body of Bernard Manning, wishes us a nice weekend and Matthew whispers to me, like a smirking schoolboy, 'Same to you and please send my regards to your wife and sister when you see her tonight.'

•

Matthew insists that Ken/Robin/Bernard could not possibly have heard the in-bred sauce joke. I am not so sure. Why, if he did not wish us ill, has he sold us pheasants that are unplucked and ungutted and which smell as if they were shot not less than a month ago? Unfazed, Matthew has set about the birds with gusto and the kitchen is now awash with feathers and entrails. Halfway through the process, leaving the giblets to congeal, Matthew decides it is time for a 'long, bracing walk' and he wants Louis and me to accompany him. Within a minute of leaving the cottage we come to a short hill which leads to a waterfall. 'A very nice incline for a Jewish gentleman,' he mutters several times as we climb. Then, moaning, he plonks himself down on a tree stump. He says his wellingtons, which are a great novelty to him because they are his first ever pair, are rubbing the skin off his heels – 'down to the bone.' He can go no further. We are 200 yards from the front door when we head for home. Matthew is leaning on me and limping like a soldier being helped away from the Somme.

•

The friends who have just arrived to stay for a few days, along with their three-month-old baby and attendant sterilizing equipment, are trying hard to ignore Matthew's forearms, which are decorated with a layer of feathers stuck to a layer of pheasant blood. They cannot, however, ignore Steptoe, who, having spent the afternoon in the company of his decomposing badger, determines to spend the evening in their baby's carry cot.

Matthew cheers them up by sampling his in-breeding jokes on them and is himself cheered when they laugh uproariously at them. He suffers a sudden mood change, however, when he discovers the plates in this self-catering cottage, which have always been big enough for Louis and me and countless other self-caterers, are not big enough for him. 'You have to have space to eat a pheasant,' he announces. The roasting dish is then deemed not big enough in which to cook a 'just-hatched sparrow', and he says he's going to have to boil half the sprouts in the kettle.

I remember thinking, not twenty-four hours ago, that this cottage – that Devon itself – would seem very small once Matthew had arrived. I was right. I can hear him now from the bench on which Louis and I are sitting on the other side of the pond. The kitchen window is open, and Matthew is grappling with four half-plucked pheasants and a Baby Belling. He is swearing loudly in his Captain Mainwaring/Michael Winner voice. Something to do with a pheasant plucker's mother.

26 March 2000
We Will Always Have Didcot

Never again will I mock the anorak. Never in my life have I been so in need of a quilted zip-up weatherproof jacket with a hood as I am now, standing on Didcot Parkway station with an ice-cold wind tearing at my bones and Louis, the youngest trainspotter in the world – the youngest anorak in the world – pulling at my arm. The man on the opposite platform actually has an anorak on. It's avocado green and he's just slipped his notebook and pencil into one of its Velcro-fastened pockets and taken a sandwich out of another. I am so hungry. It is, I decide, a corned beef with mustard sandwich. Never again will I mock corned beef with mustard – not, at least, when all Louis and I have between us is a packet of Hula Hoops and a banana. He (the anorak on the other platform, not the small insistent one on the end of my arm) has taken a flask out of another pocket now (I can hear the Velcro tearing from across the tracks), he's pouring himself a cup of tomato soup. He has his hands wrapped round the cup, all lovely and warm in his gloves with the cut-off fingers.

•

Never again, as I stand here with neuralgia creeping around my skull, hammering away at the inner ear, will I dismiss trainspotters . . . I will not be able to, knowing, as I now do, that I have produced one who is not quite three, and who has the rest of his life in which to fill infinite numbers of notebooks which he will no doubt keep under his bed, along with his newspaper clippings and cache of lethal weapons.

We have only been here half an hour so I can't possibly drag Louis away from his treat yet. This is his big day out. We are in Didcot to see Thomas the Tank Engine – but I got the wrong day. Thomas, who tours the country making public appearances, like Carol Vorderman, will not be here till tomorrow.

Things could not have worked out better for Louis, however. As a regular subscriber to *Modern Railways* magazine he had, quite frankly, far outgrown Thomas. Here at Didcot Parkway, they have the kind of state-of-the-art, cutting-edge rolling stock that he pores over at home. In the Thomas the Tank Engine books they have the Fat Controller, troublesome trucks and twee morality tales about being 'a really useful engine'. In *Modern Railways* magazine they have interviews with the Railtrack Regulator, a detailed rundown of passenger train orders for the year 2000, and a free Jubilee Line extension supplement given away with the March issue.

•

Matthew wants to know why Louis wants to know what the words 'haemorrhage' and 'staunch' mean. 'He wants to know,' I explain, 'because of the headline in *Modern Railways* magazine, "CHUNNEL HAEMORRHAGE

STAUNCHED". I read it out to him as we sat in a ten-mile tailback on the M4 on the way back from Didcot yesterday.'

Matthew is disappointed. He had thought for one happy moment that Louis was moving on from trains to hypochondria. Now, because he didn't see Louis all day yesterday, he has promised to spend the next half-hour reading out loud from *Trains*, an American magazine published in Wisconsin and Louis's favourite after *Modern Railways*. Matthew flags after fifteen minutes and then gives up, promising to complete at least an hour the next morning.

•

It is not quite 6 a.m. and I can hear Matthew and Louis in the next room.

Louis: 'What's that train called?'

Matthew: 'That's a . . . let me see . . . ah, yes, just as I thought, that is an SB Class 241 loco currently on trial in Amsterdam.'

Louis: 'That's a very handsome train.'

Matthew: 'Yes, it is. Louis, if you let me sleep for a few minutes. I'll buy you six new train magazines and as many sweets as you want. Will you let me sleep?'

Louis: 'Yes . . . Read that bit.'

Matthew: 'No, please let me sleep.'

Louis: 'Read it.'

Matthew: 'In 1994 the line in Okehampton and Meldon was sold by the British Railways Board to RCC Quarries, now a part of the Aggregate Industries . . .'

•

Dateline: Sunday evening. Matthew: '"On 30 October, NS empty hopper train 869, powered by ex-Conrail SD601 6727, was utilizing the reinstated connecting track at Diann, Michigan . . ." Louis, please let me stop, I can't take any more of this.'

Louis sighs and takes *Trains* magazine off to another chair where he leafs through it on his own, occasionally hurling a disconsolate look at Matthew, who appears to be resuscitating his numbed mind by reading the darts results on Teletext.

'Actually, you're right, this train thing isn't funny any more,' I say.

'Any more?' shrieks Matthew. 'Any more? And when, pray tell, was "Great Western 51XX 2–6-T No. 5167 is alongside a water tower at Buildwas Junction on a Wellington to Much Wenlock train" funny?' Matthew is showing off; he is reciting by heart a caption from *Steam World*.

'Oh, come on,' I say, 'there was a time when we thought it was very funny that Louis knew the difference between a City Line Tube train and a Docklands Light Railway carriage. But today we have a weirdo who knows that Uckfield will no longer be the end of the line under Connex's proposals for franchise extension.'

Now I'm showing off. Louis looks on proudly.

•

'Louis knows so much about trains!' says the day-nursery key-worker.

'I know,' I say, 'I'm a bit worried about it, actually. With your knowledge of pre-school children, do you think he's going to turn into a serial killer?'

The key-worker suggests we should try distracting Louis with other activities when he asks for his railway magazines. So this evening, instead of getting him (and me) off to sleep with an article about the increased number of diesel units in France, we stayed up for a bit and did some painting. Louis finished his – a horizontal streak of blue paint – quite quickly. When I asked him what it was he said, 'Eurostar.'

Mine was an anorak and a corned beef and mustard sandwich. Below it, in the corner, I had painted some brown stripes which I had thought of as decorative if meaningless abstracts, but which Matthew recognized at once as a cache of automatic firearms beneath some floorboards.

14 May 2000
My Father's Headstone

I cannot for the life of me remember now, five years after the event, why my family left to me the selection of a headstone for my father's grave. It was a solemn, but not unenjoyable task. Certainly I found the glossy 'Memorials' brochure quite entertaining as I contemplated lumbering my father for eternity with a twelve-foot-high black-and-white marble archway, with decorative doves meeting over a white marble tombstone engraved with his image. This model was called 'Aldershot'.

Among the other options offered was to have a personal memento of the deceased – his leather and horsehair fly swat, for example – dipped in liquid bronze and fixed permanently to his headstone. But in the end, despite my brother's belief that we should hold out for a Lottery grant to purchase 'Aldershot', I chose a simple upright pale grey flecked-granite headstone with no adornment other than name, dates and a biblical quotation.

That was five years ago and my stepmother, who passes the cemetery regularly, says it has started to blend in a bit now. There are more graves behind him and he is not quite so exposed. No one has erected an 'Aldershot' yet but there are a couple of recent memorials which are only a foot or two shorter than my father's. Even so, his is still the only one you can see from the other side of the cemetery wall as you drive out of Newmarket, but my stepmother says she quite likes this because she can wave at him from the car.

•

Time has done little to dull the shock of that first sighting. 'What have you done?' smirked my brother, as we walked through the cemetery gates five years ago today. And then he repeated himself. 'What have you done?'

I couldn't say anything. I was unable to reply. All I could do was survey acre upon acre of gravestones, and there was my father's, the one I had ordered, the one whose design and measurements I had been entrusted with, towering over all, soaring high above the rest.

'Did you actually specify a height when your ordered it?' asked my mother in a tone of polite enquiry.

'Well, I suppose he was large in life . . .' trailed off my stepmother breathlessly.

'Very tasteful,' said Matthew. 'I haven't seen anything so tasteful since Boot Hill Casino, Las Vegas.'

•

That same evening, when Matthew read through the 'Memorial Price List and Dimensions' document which I had used to order the headstone, he swiftly identified the cause of the confusion, or series of confusions: between width and depth and height, inches, feet and centimetres. He said, though, that he was surprised the company I'd ordered it from hadn't questioned it.

And then, flicking through the brochure, he saw the 'Aldershot', changed his mind and said he wasn't surprised at all. We could have had something done about it, had the top lopped off, but I had already committed my family to spending vast sums on an extraneous foot and a half of solid granite – my folly.

•

I haven't had the courage to return since and Matthew says that using my numerical dyslexia as an excuse for not visiting my father's grave is a bit rich. Not reading my bank statements, maybe, not opening letters from the accountant, fine, but this, he says, is different. I explain that I do not need to visit it – I have only to close my eyes to picture that granite stone dwarfing all the other poor souls whose misfortune it was to be buried nearby.

The fifth anniversary, though, must be observed, and it is apparently blending in a bit now.

•

'He must be happy here,' said my stepmother as we stood at the graveside, the wind blasting across Newmarket Heath.

'Hmmm. He loved windy days,' I said. 'On windy days you don't get flies and he hated flies. Remember the horsehair swat?'

'It was no age, though, was it?' she said thoughtfully.

'No,' I replied. 'Sixty-two is no age.'

'He wasn't sixty-two,' said my stepmother, swiftly morphing from ponderous to shocked, 'he was sixty.'

'No, he wasn't,' I said, 'look, it says it here – it's

carved in granite – "Born October 1st 193 . . ." Oh my God, what have I done?'

We are getting it changed. My brother has been put in charge.

21 May 2000
Putting Up a Parasol

It is a beautiful parasol. I don't deny it is a beautiful parasol. Even though it has yet to be unfurled I can see it is a queen among parasols. It is huge – ten feet high and probably reaching twenty feet or more in diameter when open, with acres of creamy white canvas waiting to burst forth. The bones of it, the spokes and spine, are solid, creaky golden-varnished mahogany. The fittings are made of old brass with pockets of verdigris where the rain has seeped in. A truly magnificent parasol.

Matthew and Michael, who is one half of the couple with whom we are staying in the country on Matthew's annual 'Bluebells! I must see the bluebells!' weekend, have been standing in front of this parasol for ten minutes now. I can hear their voices from my sun-lounger at least sixty feet away, a low muttering drifting across the swimming pool, alternating with profound troubled sighs. And I can see from the way they are staring at it, sometimes nodding sagely in apparent approval, sometimes stroking their chins in enrapt contemplation, that they are deeply intrigued by it. They look like two Manhattan art critics examining the latest hot thing in sculpture at a private view, one agreeing with the other, perhaps, that the *objet*, while tangentially representative of the artist's *œuvre*, is a shade regressive in terms of spatial awareness. A moment ago both Matthew and Michael put their heads in their hands at the same time, like members of the British synchronized head-holding team. Every so often they pace, Michael in one direction, Matthew in the other, like duellists. They are seeking new angles from which to examine the parasol and, who knows, perhaps unravel its mystical secret.

It's 11 a.m. They've got two hours to put it up if we are going to eat lunch under it.

•

'We're a pair of Jewish gentlemen of a certain age,' I hear Matthew saying from under the unfurled parasol. I have moved over, unnoticed, to within a few feet of them in order to eavesdrop. 'We're a pair of Jewish gentlemen of a certain age,' Matthew is repeating, 'and it isn't right that we should have to be doing this. It isn't natural.' Two heads then appear from within the canvas, notice me, nod pleasantly enough, and recommence the art-critic staring. To me, even from the outside, the solution seems simple enough, and I wish to help.

'Have you tried . . .' I begin, but two right hands go up, asking me to halt.

'Please,' says Michael, 'I know you want to be helpful, but please don't.' The staring begins again, and then, as though they are in the early, flirty stages of a tango, they very slowly begin to circle the parasol in opposite directions, eventually meeting on the other side for a conference.

'I imagine this pulley must be connected to something,' says Matthew.

'Hmm,' says Michael, 'well, obviously it's connected to something. The question is, what?'

'Yes. And what does that something do?'

'Mm. If anything at all.'

'Hmmph.'

'Hmmm.'

I leave them to it and spend the rest of the morning in a paddock with a man who has come to trim goats' hooves.

•

Lunch began a few minutes ago under a tree. When I go to inform Matthew and Michael I find them crouching on the ground, eyeballing the parasol like two grandmasters analysing a chessboard. They are deep in discussion about their failure and its connection to their cultural/religious heritage.

'Yes,' says Michael, 'but if it's genetic, why is it genetic? That's the question.'

'It might not be genetic,' offers Matthew. 'It might be that we are both conforming, subconsciously, to the stereotype that Jewish men can no more put up parasols than fix cars or read maps.'

For what seems like minutes, Michael considers this, pondering his next move. 'You don't think,' he says finally, 'that if we turned the thing upside-down, and jumped up and down on the struts for a while, it might do the trick?'

And then the goat man wandered across on his way to his car. He stopped, looked at the parasol for two seconds, popped his head under the canvas, withdrew his head and put his arm under the canvas in much the same way, I imagine, as he must, in his line of work, have put his arm up the occasional goat. The parasol shot up and the goat man continued on his way.

'Well, that seems all right,' says Matthew, wiping the sweat out of his eyes, and apparently accepting the result without embarrassment, rancour or even irritation.

'Yes, it looks absolutely fine,' says Michael neutrally, with perhaps the minutest hint of satisfaction that the natural order of things has been restored. 'I think I'm ready for lunch.'

Throughout lunch they discuss the possibility of a game of ping-pong that afternoon. Michael has a new tennis table.

•

The light is beginning to fade, and I have just loaded Louis and the luggage into the car. Only Matthew is missing. I can see him out there in a field, silhouetted against the setting sun. Michael is with him and even from this distance I can hear the long, lung-evacuating sighs and the deep grumble of the debate as they discuss the mechanics of assembling a self-assembly, flat-pack ping-pong table.

4 June 2000
The Garden Row

Tucked away in third place in the frequency tables of domestic disputes, quite a way behind the perennial leader, 'No, no, it was your tone of voice that started it,' and closing in on, 'You're a fine one to talk about wasting money,' is the row about the garden. Since this argument is confined to the summer months, I suppose it is doing pretty well to be up there ahead of, 'Tired? What have you got to be tired about? If anyone round here has a right to be tired . . .' But then at this time of year the garden row makes up for lost seasonal ground by being held every time Matthew and I are in the garden at the same time.

Reduced to an easy-to-follow seven-step plan, it runs as follows:

(1) Matthew walks out into the garden, looks around, and begins tutting gently and shaking his head. (2) I ask what is distressing him (or sometimes I ignore him but the result is always the same). (3) Matthew tells me that there is not enough colour in the garden, and that far from merely being drab, it is also unkempt. (4) I say it is not drab, it is subtle; that it is not unkempt, it is wild. (5) He does his sardonic humouring-the-madwoman nodding of head, and moves on to (6), which begins,

'And while we are on the subject, what's the point of having a south-facing garden if the sun never gets through that blessed tree?' (7) I say that it's a beautiful tree, I love the dappled light and to cut it down would be tantamount to murder.

It all takes about four or five minutes, it ends, and no more is heard of any part of it until, usually, the next day, though sometimes later that same day, Matthew goes out into the garden, starts tutting and off we go again.

We have held this ritualistic exchange of views two to three hundred times since we moved here a little over three years ago, and you would have thought I would be hardened and impervious to it. Indeed I thought I was, until this evening, when, for some reason, I snapped during section (3). I told him that if he really wants something that resembles the municipal gardens at Eastbourne I'll employ a gardener to plant three hundredweight of Busy Lizzies and geraniums, install a mini-golf course and a wrought-iron bench with a memorial plaque on it and replace the sycamore tree at the end of the garden with a topiary lighthouse.

•

Keeping firmly to the tradition which dictates that no self-respecting middle-class woman allows a cleaner into her home without cleaning up first, I have spent the day 'tidying' the garden – indiscriminately rending, ripping, hacking and generally getting rid of anything that looks as if it is (a) dead or (b) not a flower – before the gardener arrives. Matthew is reclining on a sun-lounger with a paperback book over his face.

He looks relaxed but beneath that book his mind will be whirring away. The sun has just gone behind a cloud and I know, I just know, that he is going to blame it on the tree . . . Yup, here we go . . .

'What is the point of having a south-facing garden . . .'

I don't hang around long enough to hear the end. Climbing down from the ladder, where I have been pruning something beginning with 'f', I retreat to the shed, sit symbolically on Matthew's log pile and, I am ashamed to say, contemplate adding to that same log pile by laying down the tree's life if only I never have to go through the garden row again.

•

The gardener has arrived, and Matthew is giving her his colour monologue, to which she replies, quite bravely and wittily I think, that gardening is not painting by numbers.

By lunchtime she has made a planting plan, asked who the vandal who hacked down the something beginning with 'f' was and agreed with Matthew that she will monitor the sun–tree situation throughout the afternoon.

By teatime she has planted several new tasteful but brightly flowered shrubs and pruned all the old ones, and by 6 p.m. we are all assembled on the lawn to discuss the future of the tree.

•

Fifteen minutes later it could still go either way. The gardener has agreed with Matthew that the tree does block out light. On the other hand, she agrees with me that it is a lovely tree and because of it the shade we are now standing in is rather prettily dappled. Matthew just manages to stop himself from telling her that we are not paying her to sit on the fence and talking of fences what are we going to do about the fact that the tree is now growing into the garden wall causing it to destabilize. Instead he saves that for later, after she has gone. Not that Matthew and I notice that she has gone because we are too busy arguing about the future of the tree.

9 July 2000
I'd Rather Be in Harvey Nichols with a Film Star

My friend Monica has just phoned to tell me that I must cancel whatever I am doing on Saturday afternoon. She is to accompany someone she describes as a 'major Hollywood actress' on a shopping trip around London because she, Monica, is by some extraordinary piece of blagging dressing the said actress (whose identity, Monica says, must remain secret) for her next film. 'I can take someone with me to help carry the bags,' she says. 'I'll pick you up at two thirty.'

When I explain in great earnest to Monica that I really can't cancel what I am doing on Saturday afternoon because I am helping another friend, Harriet, with a car-boot sale to raise money for a children's playground somewhere off the A3 in Hampshire, Monica says, 'Ha, ha, ha, very funny. See you Saturday.'

I have a sick feeling in the pit of my stomach. Monica just doesn't get it. Harriet is the friend who in 1981 persuaded me to cycle from London to Brighton in aid of distressed donkeys, in 1997 had me canvassing for the Liberal Democrats while heavily pregnant and as recently as 1999 had me manning the bowling for a pig stall at her mother's annual summer fete in the same field off the A3 in Hampshire that I will be standing in this Saturday afternoon. Or rather the same field that I will not be standing in when I have broken the habit of twenty years to do what I have always assumed would be beyond me without intensive psychotherapy. For once in my life I am going to say no to Harriet. I am feeling quite sick at the prospect.

•

'You need intensive psychotherapy,' says Monica when I ring her back to explain that I really, seriously am going to a car-boot sale off the A3 and that I have a debilitating sick feeling in my stomach which is preventing me from getting out of it. 'Give me Harriet's phone number and I will ring her for you,' says Monica.

This suggestion makes me feel faint as well as sick and by the time I put the phone down I have agreed to ring Harriet myself. Before doing so, clutching my stomach with one hand and my sweating brow with the other, I pay a visit to George Sanders, my imaginary psychotherapist who lives in the shed. Sitting cross-legged on Louis's inflatable bouncy castle, so that I now begin to feel seasick as well, I assert that if it comes to a choice between selling unwanted cruet sets out of the back of a Volvo or spending three blissful shopping hours in Harvey Nichols with a Hollywood actress then a line has to be drawn. Filing his nails with an ivory-handled, ebony-inlaid nail file, George Sanders tells me that he is pleased that I have decided to be true to myself but adds, 'Upon consideration, do you not think you are being a little shallow?'

I phone Monica and tell her firmly that the arrangement with Harriet has been a long-standing one that I really cannot cancel. I thank her for thinking of me and am about to hang up when she tells me that there are plans to return to the actress's hotel suite after the shopping trip is over to have tea with 'the major Hollywood director' who is directing 'the major Hollywood actress' in her major Hollywood film.

•

It has been two days now and I have yet to phone Harriet. I am pacing the floor and drinking whisky and Matthew is explaining to Tanja, the home help, that Harriet is the kind of woman who barracks Tony Blair at the Women's Institute. 'She is, in fact, a leader of the Continuity WI,' he says. The phone goes. It's Monica asking if I've phoned Harriet yet.

Two nights later, whisky at my side, I phone Harriet. 'Are you feeling all right?' she asks when she hears my voice.

'No, not really,' I say, suddenly sensing a way out, 'bit of a tummy bug.'

'Well, I hope you're better by Saturday,' she says, briskly, 'I've managed to bag you your own trestle table and I've bought you a supper ticket for the barn dance in the evening.' Apparently I am in charge of the raffle. Harriet then says goodbye after recommending I send Matthew out for 'a bottle of that lovely pink Pepto-Bismol'.

•

Back in the shed, I find George Sanders has had a change of heart. 'My dear, you cannot let this woman dominate your life. You are in your prime. Look inside yourself,' he says, buffing his nails on the collar of his smoking jacket, 'and you will find you are stronger than you think.'

So uplifted am I by this that I skip from shed to house. Freedom is a phone call away. I can taste it already.

•

The Hollywood actress is trying on an organza sun dress with ribbon trim. 'It looks amazing,' says Monica, and then she cracks up.

'I can't hear you,' I yell into my mobile. I am finding it difficult to give the woman who looks like Camilla Parker Bowles and wants to know the price of a toast rack my full attention and Harriet is giving me a disapproving look from behind her trestle table where she is presiding over a tray of chocolate crackle cakes. 'What colour is the sun dress?' I hiss down the phone at Monica and I can just make out her reply.

'Oh, it's a wonderful rich pink,' she says. 'Think Pepto-Bismol.'

16 July 2000
The Log Thief

On a navy-blue night, with a full moon high in the sky and a light breeze to part the leaves of the magnolia tree, the passer-by who glances at our house will be able to make out a silhouette through the blinds. Rocking very slowly to and fro, like Norman Bates's mother in *Psycho* – I can hear the gentle creaks floating up the staircase now – a watchful person is keeping vigil.

It is Matthew, rocking and taking occasional glimpses through the blinds to the front garden below. But, above all, he is listening for the sound of shoes on gravel. Listening, rocking and glimpsing and waiting. He is waiting, this creaking vigilante, for the Shepherd's Bush log thief to strike.

•

This is the second consecutive night Matthew has been down there, and when asked how long he is prepared to continue the stake-out he replies, grimly, 'As long as it takes.' His only other comment today about this latest episode in his life has been to repeat the phrase, 'This time it's personal,' over and over again, each refrain keeping rhythm with the creak, creak of the rocking-chair runners.

Initially, though, Matthew said quite a lot about his

missing logs. He said he was hurt that I hadn't told him that the log pile was diminishing. It is true that I had noticed a growing dent in the centre of the four-foot-high mound of what Matthew calls his 'small intermediate logs', as opposed to his 'large perpetual logs', or his 'starter logs'.

These 'small intermediate logs' were delivered after several heated phone calls to the log man, who also received a fax from Matthew. The fax contained a sketch to scale of a log next to a tracing of Matthew's hand with the words, 'This size, please. On no account must they be much bigger or any smaller and they must be two inches in diameter. Please deliver to garden shed. DO NOT LEAVE IN FRONT GARDEN.'

This was late January, the rainy season in Shepherd's Bush, and in an act that Matthew has, many times, since described as 'pointedly malicious', the log man, finding us out at the time of delivery, chose to deposit his cargo not within the dry sanctuary of the garden shed but right under the dripping magnolia tree.

For two months, long before the logs started to disappear, Matthew was unable to travel up our path without pausing to rail against the poor log man, bemoaning the fact that the logs were not uniform in size and wondering, indeed, if the log man ever got his fax. He would tut over the increasing soddenness of the logs and the limited chances of them burning without at least a week in the airing cupboard.

•

Why didn't I tell Matthew that his logs were being stolen and why did the very fact of their disappearance please me so? I certainly take no pleasure in Matthew's current misery. On reflection I can only think that it was the base simplicity of the theft which gladdened my heart, the purity and common sense of it. Every part of the country, I imagine, has its regional hobby or leisure interest. In Cornwall they cook pasties, in Lancashire they gurn, in Scotland they toss cabers and in Shepherd's Bush they steal.

If it's not tied down, it can and will be taken. It doesn't matter what it is; a cardboard box, a broken iron, a log in an area where the most unlikely thing you will be able to flog down the pub is a log, a log in midsummer when no one is going to be having a log fire for at least six months. Here in Shepherd's Bush an Everest mentality thrives; ask the thief why he took it and he will reply, 'Because it was there.'

•

Creak, creak, creak, creak. It is two fifteen on the third night of the vigil and I have just left Psycho to his rocking. He is more militant then ever – while he was dozing in the middle of last night more logs disappeared. Oddly, he is taking this much, much harder than any of our previous burglaries. The loss of his Psion Organiser containing 1,300 un-backed-up telephone numbers he merely shrugged off, and he scarcely batted an eye at any of the three car radios stolen in the last few months. The computer, the wallet, the mobile phone . . . All he said was that he hoped they brought their new owners pleasure. But with the stolen logs he's all for hanging and flogging. He has been talking about playing hardball. One plan involves electrifying the logs and blasting several thousand volts into the thief.

I will sleep uneasily tonight, if I sleep at all, accompanied only by menacing visions of Matthew behind bars.

•

I am woken by Matthew at 5 a.m. 'They've taken the lot,' he says, sitting on the edge of the bed but still rocking, as if his body has grown so used to the chair that it carries on without it. 'I must have fallen asleep,' he continues. 'It couldn't have been for more than ten minutes, twelve at the most. They must have been watching and now they've taken the lot.'

He doesn't seem angry, just quiet and reflective. In his hand is a piece of paper. I ease it from between his fingers as he drifts off to sleep, still rocking and muttering to himself. 'Next time. Next time I'll get you.'

I take the paper from his hand and read it. It is a fax to the log man: 'Please deliver half a hundredweight of logs. Same size as last time. Leave in front garden under the magnolia tree. DO NOT PUT IN SHED.'

23 July 2000
Cruising the Tube

The train magazine which Louis and I have been leafing through this long, sleepless night is the March/April issue of *Voies Ferrées*. 'SPECIAL MATERIEL MOTEUR SNCF 2000' boasts the cover and 'LE RETOUR DE LA 141 R207'. All gripping stuff, or so Louis thinks, but then he is only three and he isn't yet reading or speaking French. All he can do is look at the pictures of 'really fast trains' and demand that I tell him what the captions say. It is 3 a.m. and Louis can't sleep. He's not being naughty, he just can't sleep. It happens to us all but, while most of us opt for a milky drink and a book or a schlock horror film on cable TV, Louis reaches for his train magazine and the first available parent.

'*En poster*', begins the caption to the pull-out double-page picture of a really fast train on page 40, '*depuis le 28 novembre dernier, la mise en service des x73500 a totalement revolutionné . . .*' Louis nods knowingly as I read. I glance at the clock. It is 3.37 a.m.

'Louis,' I say, 'I really think we should try to get some sleep.'

'Why?' asks Louis.

'Because,' I say, 'if we go to sleep now I promise that tomorrow we'll go on a train from Hammersmith to Goldhawk Road.'

'Can we go on the Piccadilly Line,' asks Louis, 'and, Mum, can I choose where we go?'

'Yes and yes,' I reply. I was very tired and obviously not in my right mind.

'We'll go to Earl's Court,' says Louis, 'and then take the Piccadilly . . .' I tuck him up in bed, *Voies Ferrées* under his pillow, and he finally falls asleep muttering something about the Jubilee Line extension.

•

I am extremely grateful for the dedication of the French student sitting next to us on the Piccadilly Line train from Hammersmith. For fifteen minutes now she has been translating the captions in *Voies Ferrées*, and Louis has been throwing me 'See, this is how it should be done' looks.

'How far are you going?' asks the French student.

'Stratford,' says Louis, which is news to me. The French student says she is going to Paddington. 'That's where the Heathrow Express goes from,' says Louis, and the two people opposite us are visibly impressed, cocking their heads to one side and giving 'Aaah, bless him' smiles.

I continue to glow with pride as we sit in a tunnel just outside Earl's Court station, despite the fact that it is nearly twelve thirty and I promised Matthew we would be home by 1 p.m. Matthew is cooking an organic chicken purchased from the most expensive butcher in

England. He remortgaged the house to buy it and very soon it will be coming to a crisp finish.

•

We are now waiting at Green Park for the second time today. The first time was my fault, we got on the wrong train at Earl's Court, but this time it is due to a still unexplained decision of Louis's to switch lines and pay a fleeting visit to Victoria station. It is now 2 p.m. and when I last spoke to Matthew five minutes ago he said that he had been late putting the chicken on so we still had time.

'You promised I was in charge,' Louis is saying over and over and over again, and only for so long can I continue to stare straight ahead of me pretending I can't hear him. Louis is indefatigable. More importantly, he is right. I did promise.

We board a Jubilee Line train heading for Westminster. Louis doesn't know but I have a plan which involves travelling one stop on the Northern Line to Embankment, taking the District Line back to Hammersmith, one stop to Goldhawk Road and home in time for late lunch. Matthew said I needn't rush too much, it would give the juices time to settle.

•

I think the juices will be adequately settled now. It is just after 3 p.m. and we have just disembarked at Stratford, on the Central Line, and then immediately re-embarked because Louis left *Voies Ferrées* behind. The doors have closed and off we go, eastbound into Essex, further and further from home.

I call Matthew from Theydon Bois. Matthew says we might as well be in Leeds. He says he is feeding the chicken to the dog. Louis has fallen asleep on my bag so it is not possible for me to produce a ticket to show the inspector. 'Don't worry,' he says, 'I believe you, though thousands wouldn't.'

Thousands would be right not to believe me. My ticket is valid for just one zone. So far we have travelled through twenty-seven and clocked up three hours and fifteen minutes of Tube time. I consider waking Louis up as we board the Docklands Light Railway (my fault – a momentary lapse of concentration at Bank). He would be so excited. Then I consider propping him up under a station sign and taking his picture. In the end I decide it will be best if I never tell him he has been on the Docklands Light Railway at all.

Louis wakes just as I am remonstrating with the Goldhawk Road station inspector who is insisting I pay the full £10 penalty fare.

'Exactly how far have you been?' he asks.

'Earl's Court,' I lie.

'Stratford,' says Louis, 'I was in charge.'

The inspector looks for a long while at the time printed on the ticket. It says 11.53. It is now 17.05. I cough up the £10, which doesn't hurt too much given the cost of an equivalent day out at Euro Disney, and we arrive home just in time for an interview on the regional evening news with Rufus Barnes of the London Transport Users Committee.

Louis is so engrossed that Matthew has to wait until three the next morning to hear what a lovely day we had.

10 September 2000
Celebrity Invasion

It's nothing less than an invasion. An invasion of our privacy and indeed of our territory, and I don't know whose hackles are highest, Steptoe's or mine. Steptoe is making his feelings clear by barking relentlessly and pacing up and down between the front door of the cottage and the bridge over the stream, on the other side of which a tall, balding man is casually eating a sandwich out of the back of his car. I, on the other hand, am pacing up and down in the kitchen muttering: 'He's still there!' and, 'Who is he?' and, 'What does he think he's doing there eating his sandwich without so much as a by your leave?'

I'm going to confront him. I am going to point out to him that at the turn in the drive which leads down to this cottage, the cottage which we have rented until tomorrow lunchtime, there is a sign which states clearly in large red lettering NO UNAUTHORISED VEHICLES BEYOND THIS POINT.

•

'Lovely morning,' I say as I unnecessarily remove a pair of wellingtons from the back of my own car.

'Beautiful spot,' replies the man. 'You in the cottage?'

'Yes,' I say heading Steptoe away from his ankles and returning back up the path with the wellingtons under my arm.

'What did you say to him?' asks Giles, who is staying with us, eager for dispatches from the front line.

'I said it was a lovely morning,' I reply.

Giles says he is going to have a word with the man himself so I hand him my wellingtons, which he puts under his arm.

We've been to this cottage six times in the past three years and have spent a total of nine weeks here. I like to imagine that it is, in fact, ours, and that each time we leave it remains empty and just as we left it until the next time. Friends who stay here with us are told that if they must read the visitors' book they should do so in their own rooms at the dead of night. The visitors' book is the only thing which interferes with my fantasy that I own not only the cottage but the stretch of river that flows just 200 yards from its front door. I own the cattle grids, the trout ponds, the grassy paths that wind through the woods and the stony track. The stony track along which a Land-Rover conveyed Clarissa Dickson Wright, the one extant Fat Lady, just a week ago after a girl with a Madonna-style headset asked me if I would mind very much waiting under a tree while they finished filming.

'We want to make it look lonely and deserted,' she said.

'It was lonely and deserted until you got here,' I muttered as we took up a holding position on a fallen tree trunk.

•

It took Clarissa four takes before the film crew perched above my woods overlooking my river were satisfied. Clarissa waved cheerily each time she passed, giving a thumbs down as the Land-Rover set off for another take and we waved cheerily back as Steptoe growled and I muttered beneath a rictus grin, 'Who the hell do they think they are coming here on my land with their walkie-talkies and their clipboards and their celebrity chefs . . .'

Prince Charles visited the estate in which my cottage stands two years ago. I felt pretty proprietorial about it even then even though it was only my second time here. I hovered about in the lower field where his helicopter landed, pretending I was a country landowner and that it was my cattle that he and his entourage were unsettling.

•

'Actually there is an entry in the visitors' book complaining that this place isn't as quiet as it used to be,' says Giles's wife Kate.

'I know nothing of a visitors' book,' I say sharply, craning my neck through the kitchen window to see how Giles is getting on with the sandwich man. Silently Kate continues to spoon food into her baby's mouth. I can hear voices coming from the other side of the bridge

Giles is back and in a state of high excitement. 'You'll never guess who he is,' he says breathlessly.

'A trespasser,' I say, 'an intruder.'

'It's Sir John Nott,' says Giles. 'I'm not kidding, I'm sure it's Sir John Nott, the former Defence Secretary.'

'That's as may be,' I say, surprising myself with both the speed and vehemence of my response, 'in which case

I am General Galtieri and I am going to defend my sovereign territory. Who does he think he is, coming here with his sandwiches?'

•

The man Giles claims is Sir John Nott is now heading over the bridge, which quite plainly to anyone of a military bent acts as a natural exclusion zone. It is an act of war. He's finished his sandwich and is now brandishing a fishing rod. I sit down at the table outside the cottage and examine my wellingtons. Sir John Nott turns sharp left down the bank towards my pond. Giles joins me at the table with two beers.

My mobile rings. It is Matthew, who has gone on a shopping trip into Tavistock, wanting to know if we'd rather have sausages or lamb chops for supper. I am pleased when he takes the Sir John Nott problem seriously. 'Hold a watching brief for now,' he says, having weighed up the options, 'and keep Steptoe inside. You don't want . . .' The line cracks up, but I think he is saying something about not wanting Tam Dalyell driving us mad with questions for the next eighteen years.

•

Sir John is returning towards the exclusion zone. Now he is packing his fishing rod and driving away. Steptoe is hurling himself against the front door, an unlikely missile but ready to be launched at any moment.

'No, Steptoe,' I say regretfully. 'We cannot fire yet.' I sigh and then I brighten. Sir John has gone but there is someone who looks very like Anthea Turner heading towards the cattle grid.

17 September 2000
A Gravy Boat

Out of the smallest acorns the tallest oaks can grow. Who would have thought, for instance, that a passing mention of our gravy boat could lead to an introspective discussion about the emptiness of our lives? Matthew, who has known for a week that I have taken up smoking again, has just asked me why I am still going to the trouble of hiding my cigarettes in the gravy boat. 'Because no one these days uses gravy boats,' I say. 'It's a style thing. The gravy boat is to the new millennium what the Flokati rug was to the eighties. When was the last time we, or anyone we know – apart from my grandmother, who keeps her hairgrips in hers – used a gravy boat?'

Apparently I am missing the point. Matthew has repeated the question, saying it was not his intention to start a debate on what is or isn't de rigueur in tableware. An hour later, though, and I have only myself to blame for this, Matthew announces that he has been mulling over the dullness of our lives as encapsulated by the gravy boat. 'If what you are saying is true,' he says, with his head in his hands (obviously), 'the very existence of a gravy boat in this house singles us out as irretrievably suburban. It says everything about us.

When did we turn into the kind of people who own a gravy boat?'

•

Matthew has now had another twenty-four hours to dwell on our dullness and predictably this has led him to a staging of that ancient debate which he kicks off by proposing, 'We have no friends.'

'We do have friends,' I counter because this, traditionally, is the second line of the 'we have no friends' dialogue, and I cite an invitation this very evening to dinner with two of those friends, Charlotte and David.

What Matthew should then say if he is to stick rigidly to the script is, 'We don't have any friends because everybody hates us.' Instead he pauses and then says, 'You're right, we do have friends, but they are the wrong sort.' Matthew says that what we need are 'louche friends with loucher friends of their own. Bohemian friends with complicated lives and strange, slightly disgusting habits. Friends we can live through vicariously, to offset the suburban nature of our lives. To offset the gravy boat. A bit less Joanna Trollope seems to be the motto here, if I've got it right, a bit more Martin Amis.'

The last time we went to Charlotte and David's, three months ago, the main topic of conversation was not house prices or school league tables but the equally enthralling subject of exactly how much one can save on a family estate car by buying it abroad off the Internet. It was a pleasant enough evening, but I am dreading going again tonight because of Matthew's repeated threats to walk out at the first mention of (a) a nanny, (b) a mortgage, (c) a school league table or (d) a Volkswagen Passat purchased in Maastricht for £7,000 less than it would have cost at Dovercourt.

•

It is a big dinner party, nine people altogether. Matthew and I know only two of the other guests. I introduce myself to a man in an aquamarine shirt sitting on my left. His name is Craig and he is a novelist, although he has yet to find a publisher. 'Oh dear,' I say, sounding like the Queen and passing him the asparagus tongs, a kitchen accoutrement I note that I do not own. Matthew is sitting next to a young actress called Sky who has a tongue stud. Her boyfriend, George, who looks like Guy Ritchie, is sitting on my right. Craig's novel is about a gay serial-killer window-dresser who turns his male victims into mannequins for Bergdorf Goodman. When the main course appears I notice that Charlotte is using a gravy boat and ask Craig whether he thinks our hostess is being ironic. Matthew looks as if he is enjoying himself – he's telling Sky that if we didn't have a mortgage and school fees to think about he'd be more like someone out of a Martin Amis novel.

Sky and her boyfriend George then disappear upstairs for what seems to me a suspiciously long time. I imagine they are indulging in something louche and wonder whether to interrupt Matthew, who is now talking to David about how much he could save on an Audi A6.

I am toying with the idea of nipping into the garden for a cigarette when Craig leans very close to me and whispers in my ear, 'Don't tell Sky, but young George has been a very naughty boy.' I lean away, look shocked and then lean in again for more. 'Three nights ago,' hisses Craig, 'George and I became more than just friends.' I choke on a muscat grape, run to the kitchen for a glass of water and when I return find that Sky is sitting on David's lap and George is in my seat next to Craig, whose hand he is holding under the table. 'Matthew,' I say, now sounding like Lady Bracknell, 'it's time we went.' And then I go and fetch my handbag.

•

Matthew is furious with me for dragging him away. He had, he tells me, just broached the subject of negative equity and was about to ask Charlotte where she bought her Parmesan shaver. He refuses to believe that my wanting to leave had anything to do with not keeping the babysitter waiting, in fact he refuses to believe anything I tell him, saying that I must have imagined the whole thing because my life is so dull I am now resorting to fantasy. After checking the cricket results on Teletext, Matthew looks up and goes to bed. I wait until I think he is asleep then sneak out to the shed for a cigarette, which is just about as exciting and louche as it's going to get around here.

1 October 2000
We Will Always Have Crewe

Auntie Olive has gone missing and the worry of it is taking its toll on her relatives. Auntie Olive must be somewhere and she must be found quickly. But where to start looking? The crisis has reached the stage at which someone is going to crack and begin peering under a seat, or a table or even a newspaper. The air is thick with tension, as the relatives stand about shrugging their shoulders and giving long, lung-draining sighs. One of them – she's Auntie Olive's daughter but she calls her mother Auntie Olive – has slumped hopelessly into a seat. She is staring madly out of the window and repeating under her breath. 'Trust her. Honestly, trust *her* to go bloody missing.'

She glares, and then a new tension fills her voice. 'Where's Paul?' she says to a co-relative standing nearby.

'Paul,' says the relative, 'went to look for Auntie Olive.'

•

'So now Paul's gone missing,' says Matthew sighing with mock melodrama. He lifts Louis off his lap, stands up in the aisle and stares dramatically, hand shading his eyes like a sailor scouring the horizon, down the carriages of the Virgin train we are taking from Euston to Crewe.

I shall, I know, always be grateful to Auntie Olive, who is, or was until she went missing, part of a family outing to Blackpool. The state of emergency which has been declared across the aisle from us has diverted our attention from the sheer dreadfulness of the day ahead.

We are here because we have finally given in to Louis's nagging. Crewe is, he believes, the spiritual home of the railway. In his bedroom he has his train set arranged so that at one end is Euston, at the other Crewe. Crewe is the place to which, in his games, all trains and train drivers dream of travelling. It's where all trains go to be mended, and given a new shiny coat of paint because they have been good trains. Crewe, in Louis's head, is clean and brightly coloured with white picket fences and hanging baskets filled with geraniums. It is populated with happy-faced, large-stomached, rosy-cheeked railway workers who eat their packed lunches out of crisp white handkerchiefs, off lush green railway banks. They say things like 'Hello, little boy. Would you like a ride on a steam engine?' and they chuckle. Sometimes it rains in Crewe, but when it does there is always a rainbow. A trip to Crewe, according to Louis, is a rite of passage and to have embarked upon it and alighted there by the age of three and a half is something to brag about. Crewe will provide the ultimate experience, a taste of the very essence of life itself.

•

Both Matthew and I have accepted that this is Louis's day and whatever horrors lie ahead must be endured in good spirit. But it is not easy to reconcile the fact that we are about to spend six precious hours of our lives in Crewe. We will arrive at twelve thirty. The only second-class tickets available for the return journey to London are on a train which leaves at six twenty-seven. There will be no early escape. No time off for good behaviour. So the Auntie Olive situation is a godsend, such a godsend that Matthew is now actively participating in the search for her by ironically peering in Louis's rucksack and calling: 'Auntie Ohhliiiive.' Paul has returned to his seat, the train is leaving the station and her kith and kin can only hope that Auntie Olive is on board. For myself and Louis I pray that she stays missing well beyond Nantwich.

•

Auntie Olive was found at Milton Keynes. She miraculously appeared on the platform outside the window of our carriage and was hastily bundled into her seat. The ensuing debate among the relatives about what could possibly have happened kept us happy for the duration of the journey. It couldn't last, though. At Crewe station, we took a taxi to central Crewe.

'You've come at the wrong time!' said the taxi driver. 'You should have come when Adtranz had their open day.' Matthew makes sarcastic, mock-horror faces at having missed the biggest event in the railway enthusiasts' calendar and asks the driver to take us to Pizza Express.

After lunch we are going to the Railway Age museum, so Matthew wants to drag lunch out as long as possible. The taxi driver says he doesn't know about Pizza

Express, but there's a McDonald's and he deposits us outside it.

But Matthew is determined to find a Pizza Express and while he looks for it Louis and I station ourselves on a monument – a train axle elevated on a chipped and graffitied red-brick plinth. We are in the centre of the low-rise shopping mall which appears to represent Crewe in its entirety. Every few minutes Matthew passes us and calls out, 'Just hold on a bit longer.' His demented search for a Pizza Express has now reached the stage where soon he will start peering into Louis's rucksack again – only this time there will be no hint of irony.

•

It only cost £180 to travel back to Euston first-class on the four o'clock train. Louis would have been happy to spend the rest of his life at the Railway Age museum. In fact, Matthew quite enjoyed sitting in the driver's cockpit of an InterCity 125, operating the controls – on his own because Louis has an unexplained aversion to InterCity trains. After about an hour, though, the novelty wore off and Matthew and I realized we could be sitting on a real train with real, plush red seats; which was when Matthew announced he would remortgage the house if that is what it took to get out of Crewe.

He didn't have to because in the end I paid.

8 October 2000
To be Thin like Eliza

George Sanders, my imaginary psychotherapist who lives in the shed, has well and truly proved his worth this morning. I visited him because Matthew refuses to listen to any sentence which begins with the words 'Last night I dreamt . . .'

'I'd love to stay and hear about your riveting dream,' Matthew had said over breakfast, 'but I haven't finished reading the Yellow Pages, so if you will excuse me . . .' And then on his way upstairs he shouted down the suggestion that I ring the BBC news desk about my dream, 'just in case they've got a hole on the lunchtime bulletin to fill.' So I braved the torrential rain and the garden mud and settled myself down to tell George Sanders. In contrast to Matthew, he listens patiently, interrupting only to light my cigarettes with his silver Tiffany lighter and to swap places with me so that it is he who is positioned directly beneath the hole in the roof.

'Look upon my humble abode not just as a shed, dear lady,' said George, 'but as a watershed . . . a watershed in your life.' And then he used a navy blue silk handkerchief to wipe a large drop of rain from his monogrammed patent-leather slipper. 'We will interpret your dream, and from the turmoil of your mind new resolutions shall spring.' Then he shot his salmon-pink cuffs from under his shot-silk dressing gown, crossed his legs, leaned forward and with a look of intense but caring concentration urged me to start. 'Don't hold back,' he said. 'Tell me everything. I sit not in judgement. I am here to help. Is that egg yolk on your blouse?'

'Last night I dreamt . . .'

'Ah, yes,' said George, ' "Last night I dreamt I went to Manderley again . . ." Dear, dear Larry Olivier. Dear, dear Joan Fontaine.' George focused on the hole in the roof above his head, lost in reverie for a short while before instructing me to 'Pray continue.'

•

Last night I dreamt I was an attraction at a fete in the Dorset village where I grew up. People from the surrounding areas queued in their hundreds to guess my weight. My mother was there, seated behind a trestle table, taking the money, and my stepfather recorded the guessed weights in a ledger with a quill. The prize was an all-expenses-paid weekend at a health farm, with magnums of champagne for the two runners-up. The winner was my old school friend Eliza – skinny, beautiful, clever Eliza.

In real life Eliza would not have been at the fete because she now lives in America. I haven't seen her in three years, except in my dreams, but she writes to me often about her important job in publishing, and yesterday evening, the evening before my dream, Eliza phoned to say she was coming to England on a visit. And so it was that as I put the phone down, as I climbed the stairs to bed, I knew I had two weeks to put my life in order. Eliza is perfect. She is funny, kind and charismatic. She doesn't smoke, she doesn't overeat, she rarely drinks. She keeps fit, she reads, she is successful and she lives in an immaculate apartment in a converted meat-packing factory in New York.

Eliza is, as I explained to George Sanders, the antithesis of me. 'I think you are being a bit harsh on yourself, dear lady,' said George. 'But if you are to persist with this point of view then you must turn it to your advantage.' And so I left that shed, that watershed indeed, with a determination to become perfect too.

I began by joining Matthew on his annual tandoori chicken and pilau rice diet – a tradition with which, until now, I have had little truck. But I have learned from past experience with other, more finicky diets, that my life, unlike Eliza's, is not conducive to cooking up little dishes of steamed vegetables and fish. Matthew, who has been on the diet for a month, has noticeably lost weight.

•

The tandoori diet is not working. After one week of nothing but fruit and water during the day and takeaway chicken and rice at night I am not thinner. If anything I am fatter. There is a picture of Eliza on the fridge which this evening only served to depress me and provoke me into the violent ravaging of a Marks & Spencer bread and butter pudding. Matthew has just interrupted my nightly whinge by reminding me of an episode of *Absolutely Fabulous*. Edina (Jennifer Saunders) is expecting a visit from a thin and perfect friend. Like Eliza and me, they have not seen each other for years. The denouement, after a week of torturous dieting, is that the friend has gone blind.

I would not wish this on Eliza. I love Eliza. So much so that I am causing havoc in the lives of my nearest and dearest while I attempt to become saintly – saintly, and as thin as she is. Today I sorted out my sweater drawer, bought an embroidery kit. I have not given up smoking entirely. For the sake of domestic harmony I am allowing myself three cigarettes a day. Tomorrow I am going to buy one of those things you hang on the rim of the loo which turn the water blue. I will also launder the dog's blanket. I have arranged some cornflowers in a vase in Eliza's room and I have put Joanna Trollope's latest on her bedside table.

•

Eliza has arrived. She is inside with Matthew while I am in the shed with George Sanders. George is weeping with mirth, wiping away the tears with a lilac and ecru handkerchief. 'Stop, dear lady, stop! I can't take any more,' he shrieks.

'I promise you, George,' I continue, 'she is gargantuan. She makes Luciano Pavarotti look like Victoria Spice.' I am exaggerating, of course. Eliza has put on half a stone, but it is a very meaningful half a stone.

22 October 2000
A Trip to Peter Jones

It is a tribute to the staff at Peter Jones department store in Sloane Square that in the twenty minutes it has taken me to pay for two pairs of argyle socks I have never once lost the will to live. In fact, half an hour later, as I wait another twenty minutes to pay for a roll of cotton wool and a pair of scissors, I find myself adding 'sales assistant at Peter Jones' to the list of jobs I would like to have if I didn't do this.

Waiting for the lift (five minutes is traditional) up to boys' wear on the third floor, I decide that after 'agony aunt on *Dogs Today* magazine', and 'early retirement to a nursing home in Godalming', a job at Peter Jones really is what I would like best. Integral to this decision is the consideration that if I worked here, rather than just shopped here, I would be under no illusion that I would be home before nightfall. Indeed, as a customer of ten years' standing, I am no longer foolish enough to announce blithely to my loved ones: 'I'm off to Peter Jones, back before lunch.' Nor do I underestimate the time and energy required in preparing for such an expedition.

Tanja the home help, who this morning watched me pack my rucksack (sandwiches, a drink, a packet of Hula Hoops, a mobile phone, two sweaters of varying thickness and a novel), was prompted to enquire whether I had taken up fell-walking. But then Tanja is from South Africa; she is young and single and shares a furnished flat. Tanja has never needed to equip herself for the torpor, the hunger pangs or the erratic fluctuations in air-conditioning (hence the sweaters) that are part and parcel of a trip to the haberdashery department at Peter Jones.

•

If I'm lucky, I might just make it home before Louis has outgrown the pyjamas I am now trying to buy him. I decide to swap them for the next size up, go back three places to the back of the queue and then miss a go because a woman who has nipped in for vests says she has double-parked in Cadogan Gardens and would I mind 'orflay' if she pushed in before me. It is 12.55 p.m., I have been here one and a half hours, and I still have to buy wine racks, a toaster, a bathroom mirror, a hose attachment and curtain material. Peter Jones has all these things and more, which is why I love it. You won't get hose attachments in Harvey Nichols. A department store, like soup, is only as good as its stock.

Luck, it seems, is now on my side. I have thrown a six; the down escalator is working despite the major refurbishments currently taking place, and I expect to reach kitchenware via bed and bath linen sometime before 2 p.m. I am looking forward to my sandwiches, which I am saving for the long wait in furnishing fabrics, where the management has thoughtfully supplied chairs.

Seated there with my lunch and my novel, I will be comfortingly overwhelmed by feelings of resignation. I am here for the duration, there is nothing I or anyone can do about it. I will tell myself just to settle in and enjoy it. The outside world can go hang.

•

It was a wait in furnishing fabrics shortly after we were married that first caused Matthew to lose his patience with Peter Jones. For five years he avoided the place, and then I made the mistake of persuading him to come with me one day to the white goods department (we bought a blue fridge). It took two and a half hours to buy that fridge, during which time I wandered happily among washing machines, tumble-dryers and state-of-the-art cooking ranges. Matthew, meanwhile, stood in line, a thunderous expression on his face, muttering and comparing the sales assistants to the Autons in *Dr Who* – otherwise known, he says, as the Nestenes. Apparently they resemble waxy humans, and there is no way of knowing they are evil until their hands drop off to reveal deadly weapons. They are, according to Matthew, third in the scale of scariness after the Daleks and the Cybermen.

I am eavesdropping on a Nestene now as I queue (seven and a half minutes) to pay for a reel of navy blue cotton. The Nestene is telling his colleague about his week off and how he met up with a former Nestene, a Saturday girl he hadn't seen in two years. They met for a drink in a wine bar, ended up boogieing the night away (he is all of forty-five) and finally rolled home at four in the morning. That's what I would like about working here – the sense of camaraderie.

•

It is now four fifteen and I have just emerged from furnishing fabrics into glass and chinaware. A grey-haired woman in pearls and mohair is apologizing profusely on behalf of her pug, which has just cocked its leg against a ship's decanter. The sales assistant tells her not to worry – 'It happens to the best of us.' Then she bustles off, holding the decanter with outstretched arm. Perhaps she is going to make an entry in the ledger they are rumoured to keep for just this kind of dog incident.

The eggcup was purchased in a record fifteen minutes, but I have just discovered that owing to the major refurbishments I will have to take a courtesy bus to the annex where Peter Jones is temporarily housing, among other things, the mirror department. I have never been to the annex and am quite looking forward to the experience of the courtesy bus. On the other hand I could leave it till tomorrow, which is, after all, just another day.

3 December 2000
Bread Sauce

It is seven thirty in the evening. I am being blinded by the headlights of oncoming traffic, it is bucketing down with rain and I am surrounded on all sides by glowering juggernauts. But that is by no means the worst of it. The worst of it is that I have only two measly packets of the wrong brand of bread sauce on the seat beside me. Matthew, since his annual obsession with cooking game birds began in earnest two weeks ago, would refer to this as only one measly 'brace'. I've been to Tesco's in Shepherd's Bush, Sainsbury's in Ladbroke Grove, Safeway in Acton, Waitrose and Safeway in Ealing. Then the Hanger Lane Gyratory swallowed me up and spat me out on the North Circular and now I am headed for Golders Green. Matthew will be halfway through cooking the pheasant. There is, I determine, only one thing for it – come off at Golders Green and while in this neck of the woods head for Sainsbury's in the Finchley Road.

•

Finchley Road didn't have it. Neither did Camden. They didn't even have Coleman's, let alone Schwartz. Schwartz Luxury Bread Sauce is what we wanted but we made do with Knorr that night, reminiscing about the time when we'd have been happy with our lot, a time before my brother, a bread-sauce connoisseur who eats it on its own, happened to mention that Schwartz was, to his mind, much the best on the market.

So I went out and bought some. I remember the day distinctly. It was crisp and autumnal and Matthew was cooking grouse. I bought a 'brace' of Schwartz from Tesco's in Shepherd's Bush. If only I had known then what I know now, that just a few weeks later supplies in West London would have completely dried up. Matthew claims to have been to sixty-three convenience stores, or thirty-one and a half brace of store.

'Perhaps it is a knock-on effect of the petrol strike,' I suggest to Matthew.

'Yes, that will be it,' he said, 'people are siphoning bread sauce into their tanks.'

'Or the floods,' I continue, 'perhaps the Schwartz factory was flooded. That much river water combined with that much dried bread-sauce mix could have created a devastating poultice effect, swamping villages and hamlets for miles around.'

'Hmmm, interesting,' said Matthew in between mouthfuls of red cabbage (Marks & Spencer). 'It will be intriguing to see what the situation is in Devon.'

Louis and I are going to Devon for a week's break. Matthew is coming only for the weekend, returning to London on Monday morning.

•

We drive to Devon in convoy until Okehampton, where Matthew veers off towards Launceston so he can stop at Tesco's. Louis and I head for the Tavistock Safeway, where I fare well, scoring twelve packets of Schwartz. But Matthew is not impressed. 'I'm sorry,' he sighs, 'it's just not enough to keep us through the winter.' It turns out he failed miserably in Launceston. He has now gone to bed complaining of dizziness. He is worried he might have been poisoned by car exhaust fumes.

By lunchtime the following day the AA man has been and confirmed that the seal around the rear window of Matthew's car had rotted away and it is lucky he has not succumbed to carbon-monoxide poisoning. Matthew goes back to bed just in case. For want of anything better to do I examine the list of Safeway branches in Devon and Cornwall kindly drawn up for us by the AA man. I will start in Bodmin this afternoon.

•

It is seven thirty in the evening, I am being blinded by the headlights of oncoming traffic, it is bucketing down with rain and I am surrounded on all sides by glowering juggernauts. But that is by no means the worst of it. The worst of it is that I have only one more brace of Schwartz bread-sauce mix on the seat beside me. Matthew is leaving in the morning and says he will stop in Exeter, but as for my suggestion that he takes the scenic route via Budleigh Salterton, Dorchester and Wimborne . . .

It is, however, apparently perfectly feasible for me to spend the remainder of my time in the West Country driving between Totnes, Paignton, Bude, Torquay, Tiverton and Newquay.

•

It is Thursday and I now have a total of fifty-seven packets of bread sauce. I am overwhelmed by the sense of my own achievement. Plymouth is the one that stands out in my mind. When the checkout assistant asked me why I was buying fifteen packets I told her I was cooking a Thanksgiving meal for the Bovey Tracey Retired Ploughmen's Association.

•

It is seven thirty in the evening, I am being blinded by the headlights of oncoming traffic, it is bucketing down with rain and I am surrounded on all sides by glowering juggernauts. But that is by no means the worst of it. The worst of it is that we are more than three-quarters of our way back to London and I have suddenly remembered that there are fifty-seven packets of Schwartz Luxury Bread Sauce displayed on the sideboard in the kitchen of a self-catering cottage in Devon.

17 December 2000
The Log Cabin

I am overwhelmed by a cocktail of emotions from guilt to gratitude and from disbelief to childlike excitement. I have just heard Matthew on the phone booking a surprise holiday in a log cabin.

When he first mentioned to me a few days ago that perhaps we should get away for a break in the New Year I was petulant and ungracious in my response. I told him that it would be a guaranteed disaster, that his idea of a break which would inevitably incorporate at best a casino and at worst an amusement arcade in an out-of-season seaside resort was my idea of hell. I told him that I understood that, by the same token, my idea of a break – peace, quiet, mountains, elk, walks, etc. would, in turn, be his idea of worse than hell and that we would be better off staying put in Shepherd's Bush celebrating New Year in our own time-honoured way (bed at 10.30 p.m. with a *Silence of the Lambs* video and a half-bottle of champagne). I had thought that that was an end to it and I certainly did not expect and most definitely do not deserve a log cabin. And now I can't say anything, express my gratitude, ask for more details, plan my holiday wardrobe, because Matthew is obviously intending this to be a surprise. I can hardly believe it and have been trying to temper my excitement with some common-sense reasoning.

There have been moments in the past few hours when I have tried to come up with other meanings to the words 'log cabin'. But what else could he have meant but a cabin made of logs? And where else would you find a cabin made of logs but in the mountains of Vermont, Montana, perhaps on a lakeside – Africa or even Scotland would be heaven.

Whatever and wherever, it will be as far away as it is possible to be from either a casino or an out-of-season amusement arcade. There will be an open fire, rugs, mulled wine, elk. Louis may experience his first taste of just-fallen snow, a sleigh ride, roasted chestnuts. The selflessness of Matthew almost beggars belief. But believe it I must, for I most definitely overheard him saying, 'What we want is a log cabin. I'll leave the exact location to you.'

Dare I go and buy a Ralph Lauren snowflake-patterned hand-knit in Harvey Nichols? It would be perfect for Vermont.

•

I have been foolish. A log cabin in Matthew-speak, I now know, is a waterproof asphalt and chipboard construction in which to store logs in the front garden. The log man who has been coerced into building it is due to arrive this afternoon. He will advise on where it should go. Matthew, who is going out, wants to know if I will be in. I tell him I won't be because, more determined than ever to buy a Ralph Lauren snowflake-patterned hand-knit, I am going shopping. The log man's visit is therefore postponed until tomorrow morning and I have vowed to myself never, ever to overhear a telephone conversation again.

Matthew, meanwhile, who is finding my lack of interest in his 'log cabin' hard to fathom and is wondering why I have suddenly seen fit to splash out quite so lavishly on knitwear, is apparently experiencing a cocktail of emotions in anticipation of the log man's visit.

•

The annual obsession with logs started earlier than usual this year, after Matthew failed to catch the Shepherd's Bush log thief who, despite his almost constant vigilance, made off with an entire pile of logs. Night after night the log thief would strike, and morning after morning the pile would have diminished. This despite the night watches, booby traps and state-of-the-art trip switches.

The log cabin is a security measure, complete with an industrial-strength padlock – Matthew's last-ditch attempt at protecting the logs. It will also keep them dry. There is only one thing Matthew hates more than a stolen log and that is a damp log, and, while I am devastated that I will not be spending the New Year in the Little House on the Prairie, I am also relieved that there will no longer be logs in the airing cupboard.

•

The log man is here. He is young, good-looking, seems intelligent enough and yet he is apparently as obsessed with logs as Matthew. But then it is his job to be obsessed with logs. He is outside the kitchen window now and I can see from his face that after half an hour of intense interrogation by Matthew, even he is looking a bit glazed. Matthew is cross-questioning him about log types: size, shape, tree variety, age, etc. Finally, the log man leaves and I am invited out to view the log cabin. I decline on the grounds that I have to try on my new Donna Karan fake-fur-trimmed snow jacket. 'Of course, it will take a few days for the log cabin to take effect,' says Matthew, carrying a basket of logs up to the airing cupboard, 'but at least they will be safe and sound at night.' I tell him I am surprised he hasn't booked a fortnight in Vermont for them.

•

Two hours ago I overheard a telephone conversation and for two hours I have been trying to come up with alternative meanings to the words, 'I want you. I must have you ... I have to have you today ... All right then, tomorrow.' I can't think that Matthew is having an affair, unless it is with the log man. Perhaps my constant sneering at his log cabin has pushed him over the edge. I have become unbearable to live with after the Vermont disappointment and now he has found a kindred spirit, someone who cares about logs. When he returns from his trip to Grate Expectations, where he is buying new fire tongs and bellows, I will suggest we sit down and talk. I can hear someone coming up the path now.

It is the log man with a new consignment and he asks me to impress upon Matthew that, as requested, the logs are yew.

2001

4 February 2001
Matthew's Retreat

It is a freezing cold night with a large moon and a clear sky. If there were any cloud, it wouldn't be nearly so cold. The clouds would act like a duvet, insulating the heat of the city, bouncing it back down onto Shepherd's Bush. I open the back door to let the dog in. He is accompanied by a blast of icy, stinging air. I turn out the lights, lock up and head for bed.

The house feels very empty without Matthew, who has quite uncharacteristically taken himself off to the country for a few days on his own, which is a bit like saying Ann Widdecombe has taken up lap-dancing. It is not like him. Matthew fears even the most benign countryside. He is someone who begins to tremble on the approach roads to Hampstead Heath. However, after explaining melodramatically that the ordeal of getting through January had exhausted him, he said he needed to be somewhere quiet where he could recharge his batteries in readiness for the year ahead.

In much the same way that members of the Society for Pedants believe that 2001 marked the real dawn of the new millennium, Matthew believes that no new year, millennial or otherwise, begins until 1 February. This theory, along with his need for 'total silence and an open fire', was outlined over the phone to some poor soul who was just trying to do her job. Twenty minutes later they had narrowed it down to a tiny hexagonal Bath-stone property twenty minutes' drive from Stratford-on-Avon.

'The cottage has no television so I shall rest in total silence,' says Matthew. 'I must have silence. Silence is what I need. Complete and utter silence.' And then he heads upstairs to turn on Radio 5 Live at full volume and begin packing.

He left at eight this morning and so far I have heard nothing. I have tried unsuccessfully to call him. But I mustn't worry. He said he needed silence. He will have turned his mobile off. The phone rings at 11.30 p.m. 'I've been trying to get a mobile signal for five and a half hours,' says Matthew.

'Why didn't you go outside?' I ask him. 'It's much easier to get a signal outside, especially on a clear night like tonight.'

'I can't go out because there is a dangerous animal howling out there.'

'What kind of animal?'

'I don't know. One that howls.' Matthew's voice is very small and sad. I ask him to put the phone out of the window so I can hear the howling. It is very obviously an owl.

'It's hooting to its fellow owls,' I tell him.

'Are owls dangerous?' asks Matthew.

'No. Have you looked at the stars?'

'No, I haven't looked at the bloody stars. Why would I want to look at the bloody stars?' The line begins to break up. I can just about make him out. 'I can't stand the silence. I can't sleep because of the silence. I am going mad with the silence. This terrible, relentless silence . . .' Then there is silence.

•

The next call comes at nine the following morning. Matthew sounds tired but reasonably cheerful – like someone buoyed by the relief of having survived a mortifying ordeal. He is telling me how he nearly called 999 at 2 a.m. because when he tried to get to the car to fetch a bottle of whisky he got no further than the front step. 'It was totally pitch black. I was completely isolated. But I didn't panic.' I suggest that he buys a torch. Matthew tells me it is now snowing. 'It is quite beautiful,' he says, 'I just saw a deer. I think I might go for a walk after breakfast. Are deer dangerous?'

'No.'

'What about mantraps?'

I try to explain to Matthew that mantraps are illegal.

'So is crack cocaine,' says Matthew, 'but that doesn't stop people using it. The snow will be covering up the mantraps. I could easily stumble into one. It would be days before anyone found my frozen corpse. I think I will go to the shops instead for further provisions.' He is beginning to talk like Ranulph Fiennes.

•

At 11 a.m. Matthew calls from an electrical retailer in Banbury to tell me that he has bought a torch, a new PlayStation with integral DVD and a new television with integral video player. At eleven thirty he phones me to tell me he has bought some new videos and some DVDs and that he is now going to buy himself a chicken to cook for his supper tonight. He says he is sticking to 'plain, no-frills, manly food', which is not like him at all. At 5 p.m. Tanja took a call from the woods. Matthew had just seen a fox and wanted to know if they are dangerous. Tanja, quite understandably, asked Matthew if he was joking. 'I'm not joking,' he said, 'I am in a darkening forest with a fox, I can't get my new torch to work and I am most certainly not making jokes.' Then, Tanja tells me, the line broke up.

•

It is just after 10 p.m. and Matthew has called in a state of wild self-congratulation. He says he has managed to make his new torch work and he has been out in the dark. He says he was forced to go out in the dark because he needed to drive to the shops to get some sugar for his vinaigrette. He couldn't possibly have made vinaigrette without a pinch of Demerara sugar.

'What did the stars look like?' I ask.

'I didn't stop to look at the stars,' he says, 'because on my way back up the path I swear I was being chased by something, possibly a wolf.'

4 March 2001
The Jinx

One night last week Matthew and I returned home to find two brace of duck hanging from our front-door knocker. Neither of us knew how they came to be there or whether they were a thoughtful gift or a dire threat – like the dead crows you find hanging from barbed-wire fences around crop fields as a warning to other crows. In any other household this incident might have provoked discussion or debate. Here it simply fuelled our current theory that we, or rather our house, has been jinxed. 'I'll hang these ducks out the back,' I said casually. 'Hmmm, good idea,' said Matthew, running himself a bath and activating the faulty pump the plumber had installed earlier that day. Its reverberations were so violent the house shook like a giant tumble-dryer – not our tumble-dryer, though, because ours stopped working a week ago, half an hour after the man who came to fix it had gone. These things, we have decided, are part and parcel of the jinx and we have given up passing comment on them.

•

Next morning I can see very little through the window on to the back garden because, since the window cleaner left last week after telling me he had needed to use a 'heavy-duty cleaning agent' to cut through the accumulated dirt of four years, it has been frosted. The frosting was caused by a chemical reaction after it rained the next day. I phoned the window cleaner about it and he said only that it was a 'new one' on him. Matthew, though, has an uninterrupted view of the garden from the open sitting-room window and he informs me that there is a blood-and-feather trail leading to the back fence. It seems a fox has made off with three of the ducks. The fourth, or what remains of it, is lying in state on the garden bench.

'This duck business is the last straw,' I tell Matthew as I wipe entrail from my shoe. 'I believe it is an omen. We should sell up and move out before blood starts dripping through the ceilings.'

Matthew, who has, by now, managed to exorcize some of his own demons over the phone to the plumber, says we should get away for the weekend to put some distance between us and the house. He then books us into a hotel in Oxfordshire, arranges to meet our friend Jonathan for lunch on the way and suggests that in the interests of a relaxing and enjoyable weekend we make a solemn pact not to submit to the usual in-car bickering.

•

The usual bickering commences before I am even in the car and intensifies after I ask to stop and buy Nurofen. Matthew, who has to pick his suit up from the dry cleaners, says that he has not factored my headache into our journey time and asks why I couldn't have told him about it earlier. He then, in an exaggerated watch-to-face gesture, times how long it takes me to buy the Nurofen and informs me that 'We will now be three minutes and twenty-four seconds late for Jonathan because of you.' After timing how long it takes for him to then pick up his suit I tell him that 'We will be four minutes and thirty-five seconds late and it will not be because of me.'

Jonathan, it turns out, is five minutes and twenty seconds late and is understandably perplexed to find himself under such intense interrogation when he does arrive.

•

'Why are you driving away from the M4?' I ask in a thin and, I have to admit, extremely provocative voice as we head off in the wrong direction.

'Because we are going on the M40,' says Matthew.

Three further minutes of bickering ensue and finally we turn around and head for the M4. In order to have the last word Matthew accuses me of 'over-emphatic clinging to the door handle' whenever he turns a corner.

Once out of the car, though, we are fine and get along reasonably well apart from an incident over the soup I didn't finish at dinner that night because it was too peppery. Matthew, who swears he saw the sous-chef standing in the doorway to the kitchen sobbing, spends the rest of the evening speculating on a ruined culinary career which culminates in the sous-chef working in a Harvester, all because of my thoughtlessness. Otherwise we have a lovely jinx- and bicker-free weekend. In fact, by Sunday morning as we head for home we have decided that a reverberating pump, a broken tumble-dryer, chemically frosted windows and some mystery ducks hardly amount to a jinx at all.

On the journey back to London we ration ourselves to only two bouts of bickering. The first occurs when Matthew notices we are crossing the M4 on an elevated section of road and says he can't understand why we still have to drive a further three miles through 'pointless countryside' before doubling back on ourselves and finally reaching the very stretch of the motorway we have just driven over. He refuses to accept my logical explanation that if every small village had a motorway exit we would now be approaching junction 3,456. He then accuses me of 'Pavlovian pressing of an imaginary brake pedal every time we come within fifty yards of another vehicle'.

By the time we turn into our road, though, we have both agreed that a weekend away has done us the world of good and selling the house would be a bit of an overreaction to what are, after all, just a few minor domestic hiccups.

•

The Townsend's estate agent sign which has mysteriously attached itself to our gatepost and which reads SOLD SUBJECT TO CONTRACT is still there. We have no idea what it signifies but have decided that fate should simply be allowed to run its course.

25 March 2001
A Stolen Dog

Strangely enough Matthew and I had our 'Shall we get another dog?' conversation just this morning and I am now trying to remember quite what the outcome was – should we or shouldn't we get one, and if so when? The new dog, however, will be arriving within the hour, and I must prepare its basket. I could phone Matthew at the office and find out if, hypothetically, he would be up for the idea of coming home to a new dog in situ, but he would only start asking pernickety questions about breed, colour, age and sex – questions to which I myself do not yet know the answer. I didn't think to ask them when Camilla, the dog walker, rang to say that she had just rescued a stray from a busy road – did we want it? I thought, What a happy coincidence this is – we (hypothetically) want new dog, dog wants new home. End of touching and heart-warming story.

•

Camilla was for some reason wearing sunglasses and had a scarf wrapped around her face when she dropped off the dog (a bitch), saying cryptically that she couldn't stop but would phone later when she had spoken to her lawyers. I am puzzled not only by this but also by what breed this new dog is exactly. Enthused by the idea of a playmate for Louis (Steptoe, the Victor Meldrew of the dog world, has refused, literally, to play ball), I had imagined something like Timmy from the Famous Five – a shaggy, muddy-pawed mongrel with a stick in its mouth and a permanently wagging tail. Instead I am looking at an acrylic guinea pig which has been put through the spin cycle and dried off in the microwave. Louis is delighted with it and has named it Anne Robinson. Steptoe is upstairs and refusing to come down.

When I hear Matthew's key in the door Anne Robinson hears it too and seizes the opportunity to escape. She is through the now open door so fast and in such a blur of fuzzy, molten acrylic that Matthew does not wait for the answer to his question – 'What the hell was that?' – before chasing off after her.

This is the first time I have ever seen Matthew in anything resembling a heroic light. It is also the first time I have seen him run, and I shall treasure the memory. Ten minutes later he returns, with Anne Robinson tucked inside his jacket.

'I know my recall isn't what it was,' he wheezes, heading upstairs for either the whisky bottle or his stethoscope, possibly both, 'but I don't remember deciding to give a home to a pom-pom with teeth when I left this morning. What I do remember is that we agreed to wait until Louis is a bit older before getting a new dog and that we would probably go for a spaniel rather than an animated cot toy.'

Happily, the phone rings.

•

It was Camilla, sounding as if she was talking through a handkerchief. She confessed that Anne Robinson isn't exactly a stray, in that she has an owner, who is apparently a nice enough man but allows the dog to wander the streets unchaperoned, causing a danger to itself and car drivers. Camilla has, therefore, confiscated the animal.

I suggested to her that surely only the RSPCA is legally allowed to confiscate animals and that what she has done might well come under the heading of theft. Camilla confirmed that this is exactly what her lawyers have told her, and that a custodial sentence is indeed in the offing. But she also said that she refuses to return the dog to its owner, and would we please agree to provide a safe house for it until the matter is resolved. I said I would talk to Matthew and get back to her.

'So,' says Matthew who is now, inevitably, rocking back and forth with his head in his hands (the new dog is in his lap and seems to be enjoying the rocking sensation), 'let's just sum up the situation. We are in possession of a stolen dog. A stolen dog which many a dog expert would tell you was not, in fact, a dog at all but a mutant tea cosy. We are liable for prosecution for housing said tea cosy, and Steptoe has taken up residence in the airing cupboard and is refusing to budge. Is that it, or am I leaving anything out?'

'Louis likes it,' I say feebly. 'And we can't let Camilla down. And how do we know the dog won't be killed on the road if we return it to the owner?'

Matthew agrees to let the dog stay for one night. Or possibly a week.

•

Camilla has just been round to drop Steptoe and Anne Robinson off after their walk. Steptoe makes straight for the airing cupboard, Anne Robinson makes straight for Matthew, who is still rocking slowly back and forth with his head in his hands. Camilla has news. Anne's owner is threatening to call the police. 'We're fences. That's what we are,' says Matthew. 'We are receivers of stolen animals and we're going down.'

'It's a good cause,' I say, 'and one that is worth fighting for.'

Matthew starts comparing himself to Nelson Mandela. 'He did twenty-four years on Robben Island for fighting apartheid,' he says. 'I'm up for nine months in the Scrubs for handling stolen dogs.'

Camilla, worried about the police dragnet closing in on her (she has just received a call on her mobile from a friendly desk sergeant), phones her lawyer again. After a ten-minute discussion she removes the sunglasses and headscarf and says, 'We've been beaten this time. I'm taking her back to her owner but I'm not giving up the fight.'

Exeunt Camilla and Anne Robinson. Enter Steptoe, who is quite uncharacteristically wagging his tail.

3 June 2001
A School Reunion

I allowed myself two hours to get to my school reunion because reinforcing twenty-year-old prejudices is the last thing I wish to do. (See 1974 school report entry: 'Rebecca failed to attend the Summer Garden Fete and has yet to return her unsold raffle tickets.') This time, no one will be able to accuse me of not putting thought, time or effort into this event.

I have been on a diet in preparation for today, and although my original target weight was Geri Halliwell I am not displeased with the result (a comfortable Jennifer Saunders). I have shopped relentlessly and strategically for something to wear, not once, not twice, but on six occasions, covering the main shopping areas of central London, Oxford and Wimborne. One entire Friday evening was devoted to trying the outfits on at home and putting them into weather-dictated categories. Finally, after getting up at six this morning, I had, by eight, decided on the 'easterly breeze, possible light showers' option, in green linen. The skirt would have fitted better had I reached the Geri target, but I look fine as long as I keep my coat on. If asked, I will explain enigmatically that I feel the cold because I am so used to spending time in hot countries.

I have artfully applied, over a period of three days, layer after layer of fake tanning lotion, which represents a total of two and a half hours standing with my arms stuck out to avoid smudging. ('Rebecca demonstrates a lack of patience in seeing her projects through to the end', Autumn term '73). I now possess the sophisticated, cultivated air of someone who is anything but a stranger to the British Airways Executive Lounge.

•

And so here I am at last, parked in the road opposite my old school with half an hour to go. Beside me on the passenger seat is a collection of school-days memorabilia which I have painstakingly put together in case any show 'n' tell opportunities should arise. I have my end-of-term reports, my O-Level certificate and a photograph of me and two friends sitting on a wall eating Cadbury's Creme Eggs. Most noticeable, and most betraying of our interests at fourteen, are our hairstyles. It was crucial throughout the early '70s to keep your Charlie's Angel fringe flicks in place with several litres of hairspray. The resulting solidified hair wings crackled to the touch, and the memory of them reminds me now of the polystyrene-textured, low-calorie rice cakes I have been living on for the past two months. No, I think to myself, reaching for a school report, no one could accuse me today, as Mrs Pomfrey, English teacher, seems repeatedly to have done, of not making an effort.

•

The very fact that I am here outside the school, the first to arrive, a full half-hour early, also gives the lie to Mrs

Pomfrey's next accusation, concerning punctuality. I would, in fact, have been here a whole hour earlier if I hadn't driven ten nostalgic laps around Salisbury, past the Debenhams at which we bought the Elnett, past the newsagent where we bought the Creme Eggs, and past what was the Cadena Café but is now a Pizza Hut. It was here, amid the orange leatherette and brown melamine, between weak milky coffees and sliced white toast, that I attempted to tattoo 'Leo Sayer' onto my arm with a compass. And less than half a mile down the road is the infirmary where I went two days later for the tetanus injection.

'Rebecca lacks concentration and is absent-minded', reads another report. 'Twice this term she has left her violin on the bus.' What isn't mentioned, I notice, and what I am never given credit for, are the dozens of other occasions when I did concentrate and remembered not to leave my violin on the bus. No reference is made either to the fact that I still achieved 60 per cent in my Grade 4 Royal College of Music examination despite playing on a borrowed and unfamiliar instrument, my own being fifty miles away at the end of the line in Weymouth, in the Hants and Dorset Bus Company's lost property office.

And in response to Miss Drink the maths teacher's bald remark – 'Rebecca seems unable to grasp the principles of arithmetic at any level' – I would say this: 'You are absolutely right but perhaps things would have been different if you had shown even the smallest degree of patience or understanding.'

There are fifteen minutes to go and I continue reading. 'Rebecca has a brain but seems to have forgotten how to use it.' (Mrs Pomfrey.) 'She makes little attempt to join in with team activities.' (Pomfrey again.) 'Rebecca has been unusually helpful in the classroom this term.' (Undecipherable signature – entry possibly tampered with.) 'Unfortunately Rebecca proved that she was not up to the role of Form Captain and was demoted after three weeks.' (Pomfrey.) I put the reports down and inspect my ankles. They are skewbald: 'Rebecca has been slapdash in her attempts to self-tan.'

•

It is now exactly midday and I am back in the car. I have passed no one and seen no one. No other cars have parked beside me, no one has come and tapped on the car window as I was half-expecting them to do, recognizing me after all these years and noticing at the same time that my T-reg Audi A6 with air-con as standard (something I am very grateful for as I daren't risk removing my coat) has just been valeted.

A bleak, lonely half-hour later I telephone the organizer of this reunion – my fellow consumer of Creme Eggs and Elnett hairspray. 'You're a week late,' she says. 'It was last Saturday.'

'Oh,' I say. 'Was Mrs Pomfrey there?'

10 June 2001
Hilda

The Sainsbury's carrier bag containing a packet of fruited teacakes, a bottle of Fairy Liquid and a carton of macaroons is lying like a courtroom exhibit on the kitchen table.

'I don't like it,' I say, nudging it warily. 'I really think we should call the police.'

'Yes, you do that,' says Matthew, patting my shoulder. 'Tell them you've found some macaroons you believe are dangerous. The SWAT team will be round here in no time. They don't mess around with macaroons.'

The sarcasm is nothing new, but nor are the mysterious carrier bags. For three weeks now someone has been leaving deliveries of groceries outside our front door. The first contained teacakes, a mop-head and some flypaper. Then, two days later, there were teacakes, crumpets and Brillo pads, and later on the same day teacakes, stewing steak and firelighters. We've had sausagemeat, greetings cards, dog food, blancmange, potted shrimps and kitchen wipes. This morning we had teacakes, three economy-sized packets of digestive biscuits and a sliced white loaf. And now, less than five hours later, teacakes, Fairy Liquid and macaroons.

I have no idea who is leaving these things, or what their motive is. But I am beginning to believe that these deliveries, particularly the sausagemeat and the stewing steak, and possibly the firelighters and the potted shrimps, are meant to threaten. They represent something sinister. 'It's voodoo,' says Matthew. 'It's well known that in Haiti they use teacakes when they run out of dead rattlesnakes.'

•

'This is what the carrier bags are all about,' I say, leaping up from the sofa and then sitting down again. Matthew grunts and, although I am not entirely sure what he means by it, I think derision plays a part. We are watching *Seven*, a film in which Brad Pitt plays a young police detective investigating a series of horrific murders perpetrated by Kevin Spacey. Each murder depicts one of the seven deadly sins. The grossly obese man, for instance, is made to choke on his own vomit, for his gluttony. The sloth is tied to his bed and left to die in isolation and agony. And so on.

Matthew, in a display of gluttony and sloth combined, is lying on the sofa eating Maltesers. He takes a handful, waits for them to melt a little, then in one dramatic jerk flings his hand to his mouth and releases the Maltesers in a high-speed cascade. He finishes this off with a dainty sip of Scotch.

I ask him which deadly sin he thinks the macaroons are punishing us for. He says he doesn't know, but suspects our own Sainsbury's Slayer is employing the age-old method of murder by digestive biscuit.

•

The sausagemeat and stewing steak must, however, surely represent a pound of flesh. I am reminded of another film we watched recently, *Theatre of Blood*, in which Vincent Price plays a ham Shakespearean actor who punishes his critics by murdering them in the style dictated by the play they were criticizing. I make my way to bed nervously that night, stopping only to double lock the doors and collect a claw hammer from the toolbox. Tomorrow, I am expecting a delivery of jelly babies (*Titus Andronicus*, V, 3).

•

By 5 p.m. there had been no deliveries – and then I heard the crunch of gravel on the front path. By the time I reached the door only a carrier bag remained. It was laden with hidden meaning but it also contained tea-cakes, twelve custard tarts and a pair of ankle socks (orange). The perpetrator had fled but, taking the carrier bag with me, I set off after a small figure walking in the direction of the Uxbridge Road. As I closed upon what turned out to be an elderly woman wearing a pink coat and diamanté brooch I called out. She turned around and, spotting the carrier bag, grabbed it from me quite violently: 'That's not for you,' she said, hugging the bag to her, 'it's for Tony,' and as she marched defiantly back in the direction of our house I attempted to explain that I don't know anybody called Tony. 'He's an officer,' she said. 'But don't you go saying there is anything between us!' Then she gave me a look which suggested that I am not someone either she or an officer would want to know, quickened her pace and hung the carrier bag back on the door knocker.

•

Matthew and I are intrigued by our old lady, who I have discovered, by opening a birthday card from her to Tony, is called Hilda, and have come up with a romantic *Upstairs, Downstairs* style scenario; the officer, Tony, was the handsome, heart-throb son of a well-to-do Shepherd's Bush family, and Hilda was in love with him. They had an illicit affair, conducted mostly in our broom cupboard, and then he was killed in action. Fifty years on, fuddled with age, Hilda wishes to spend her last days taking care of her lost love.

It is a touching story, and a part of me thinks we should just leave things be, because where's the harm? But I am worried about the amount of money Hilda is spending on imaginary Tony. So when she calls again the following morning (teacakes, mackerel and suet) I am ready and waiting.

'These are for Tony,' she insists, handing me the carrier bag. 'They are not for you.'

'But Tony doesn't live here,' I plead.

'You're lying,' she says. 'You're a bossy cow whore and you're making me unhappy.'

•

Since then we have had no deliveries, which is just as well, because this morning I caught Matthew taping a shopping list to the front door. On it he had written: 'teacakes (fruited), custard powder (Bird's), six apples (Granny Smith's), Maltesers (large box), white loaf (sliced), tuna (tinned)' and finally, 'whisky (Scotch)'. It was signed, 'The Officer'.

24 June 2001
Hilda and the Pianola Man

The hall is not the best place for the pianola. In the hall it gets swamped with junk mail, unopened letters from the accountant and, for some reason which I have yet to fathom, Matthew's socks. I would like it moved to a more convenient place and I would also like to find a buyer for the 582 music rolls which came with it – all a gift from my parents-in-law. The rolls are stacked up in the spare room and, though I don't wish to seem ungrateful, they are getting in the way of my new carpet plans.

The reason we need new carpets is that the existing carpet is infested with moth (the possibility that the moth came as part of the pianola package cannot be ruled out), and the resulting devastation is particularly evident in the spare room, under the 582 music rolls. Worse is that in recent months, the moth, and their relatives, have been going on regular family outings to my sweaters and are currently enjoying the stair carpets and the landing curtains. Soon they will reach the hall and with a whoop and a flutter pay a visit to their alma mater, the pianola, only stopping for a quick snack on Matthew's socks.

•

I have tried looking in the Yellow Pages for a possible buyer for the music rolls before but without success. Today, though, I have found a new entry, which is odd given that this is not a new Yellow Pages. It says, 'Pianola restoration and repair'. I am reminded by this sudden discovery of a story I once read, about a small boy who came across a toyshop that had never been there before. It was an old shop run by an old man and a few days later the shop and the old man vanished as quickly as they had so magically appeared.

It soon became apparent that the pianola-restoration shop was also an old shop run by an old man, and, as things turned out, it would not have surprised me if the next time I opened the Yellow Pages I found the entry was gone.

I rang the number while it was still there and spoke to someone with a gentle, quavery voice who asked me to 'Hold on a minute while I get a pen.' And then Cyril, as he has since asked me to call him, disappeared for a very, very long time. I could hear him shuffling about and riffling through papers, a cup and saucer clattered, and a dog barked. Simultaneously I heard the crunch of gravel outside my own front door, followed by two violent knocks. I knew who it was. It was Hilda delivering her daily bag of groceries to her imaginary sweetheart, Tony the Officer. Today she has bought teacakes, a bottle of Sancerre and a packet of latex surgical gloves. (The gloves have since been appropriated for hypochondriacal purposes.)

As Matthew opens the door to Hilda, the noise of her shuffling on the gravel amplifies and coincides with Cyril's very slow, shuffling return to the phone. I wonder if for a moment I am going mad. 'No,' says Matthew, 'not mad. But we have both been drugged and kidnapped and are being held in a parallel universe. We are like Patrick McGoohan in *The Prisoner*. We are numbers, not free men.'

•

'Sorry to keep you waiting,' said Cyril, finally picking up the receiver. 'I made myself a cup of tea, put my lunch on, watered my geraniums and let the dog out while I was at it.'

He said he would come and take a look at the music rolls at seven on Sunday morning, and I decided it was not for me to question his working hours. He also gave me the number of someone to move the pianola and I remember thinking at the time that Rita was a strange name for a removal man.

So I was barely surprised at all when I rang the number Cyril had given me and found that Rita is, in fact, a retired Spanish teacher. 'I do know Cyril,' she said. 'But at seventy-six, I don't know how useful I'd be moving your pianola.' We had a long conversation which was finally interrupted by Hilda paying her second visit of the day (teacakes, ant-killer and corn plasters).

•

It is six thirty on Sunday morning, as Matthew has mentioned several times from under the duvet, and the doorbell has just run for the second time. Cyril reminds me of Norman Wisdom without the slapstick and with added Brylcreem. After accepting a cup of tea and a biscuit and apologizing for being a little early – 'The traffic was better than I expected for the time of day' – he makes a very reasonable offer for the music rolls and I ask how quickly he will sell them. 'Oh, they'll go like teacakes,' he says, spookily confusing his metaphors and raising the spectre of Hilda. 'I'll sell them at my roll parties. You'd be amazed how many people come. You should come and see my shop one day.'

'I'd love to,' I said, showing him to the door.

'I've kept all the old gas lamps. You could meet my Doberman, he thinks he's a lapdog—'

Cyril is interrupted by the phone ringing. It is his friend Rita, the Spanish teacher, confirming the time of my first lesson and making no apology for the fact that it is still only seven thirty on a Sunday morning. When I return to Cyril he is holding a carrier bag. (Teacakes, soup and a pair of nail scissors.)

'A lady just dropped this off,' he said. 'She said it was for Tony.'

I took the bag and thanked him. 'That was your friend Rita on the phone,' I said.

'Oh,' said Cyril. 'Is she going to shift your pianola for you?'

Matthew is now standing behind him mouthing the words: 'We are not free men. We are just numbers.'

1 July 2001

Gillian and Julian's

I really had not envisaged needing the services of George Sanders, my imaginary psychotherapist, this weekend. Louis and I are staying with friends – Gillian and Julian and their children at their house in Somerset – and we have been looking forward to it for weeks. It would have been nice if Matthew, who is working, could have been here, although he most certainly would have balked at the four-mile hike to the pub (it would have come under the heading of 'activities not suited to a Jewish gentleman of a certain age', i.e. thirty-seven). He would also have spent his entire time worrying about foot and mouth: checking between his toes for blisters and inspecting his tongue in the enormous gilt rococo mirror hanging in the flagstoned hallway of Gillian and Julian's Jacobean home. But even without the presence of the world's greatest hypochondriac I am finding the mirror disturbing, especially when tallied up with all the other nice things that Gillian and Julian have which I don't. It is impossible for me to turn around in this house without spotting something to covet, and there is a very real danger that before the weekend is out I could start turning nasty. Already I can detect a certain tone in my voice.

'Is this from Cath Kidston?' I asked, fingering the floral print dressing gown hanging behind the bedroom door.

'No,' said Gillian, 'actually, it's made from an original antique textile.'

And when I replied: 'Oh, really, isn't it lovely,' my tone implied that what I really meant was: 'Ooh, hark at you, with your perfect life and your Jacobean firedogs.' I can only hope that Gillian hasn't discerned the tone, because I am very fond of her and Julian. I am not quite sure what has come over me.

As well as the hall mirror, there's the navy blue Aga in the kitchen, the Roger Oates border-striped carpets, the toile de Jouy curtains in the vast, echoing bathroom, the sweet-scented Diptych soaps arranged in a carved bowl which Gillian found in a French flea market and the thick white towels from Frette.

Overcome with bitter envy I take refuge in the television room, which is strewn with things more familiar to me: colouring books, Thunderbirds, a Sony PlayStation and a copy of the *Racing Post*. I pick absent-mindedly at a bowl of cherries until I have revealed enough of the fruit bowl to see that it was not only designed by John Pawson but signed by him too. Moving on to the kitchen I find Gillian making sorrel pesto for the children's supper. She is chopping the home-grown sorrel and basil with her Japanese porcelain-bladed chopping knife on her five-inch-thick round maple chopping board (just like Jamie Oliver's, £92 from Divertimenti). Julian is buffing the walnut humidor he bought at a car-boot sale in the grounds of a local stately. He puts down his duster and offers me a drink. I tell him I'd rather wait until supper and head off to check on the children, who are playing in the knot garden just beyond the orchard.

•

I am furious about the orchard. If I had a flame-thrower, I'd torch the orchard. All my adult life I have wanted an orchard, and a knot garden. And a dovecote. George Sanders sits on a deckchair beneath the dovecote in a sea of wild grasses and lupins (much like the sea of wild grasses and lupins at Highgrove). He wears a bee-keeper's hat with the veil down to protect his face from the early evening midges.

'Dear lady,' he exclaims in greeting, 'aren't we having the most perfect time? Just smell these roses!' He minces towards a trellis, picking his way through some artfully arranged, picturesquely chipped terracotta pots. I swipe at a midge.

'Yes,' I say in a weary, thin-lipped voice, 'it really is very, very lovely.'

'Do I detect a tone?' says George. 'Was there not a smidgen of envy in your words? Do you begrudge your friends this wonderful house in this idyllic setting? Do you covet their Gaze Burvill garden benches, their Le Prince Jardinière watering can?'

From past experience I know there is no point in lying to George, so I tell him about my only just controlled urge to slash Gillian and Julian's Timney Fowler shower curtain, and after much pacing beneath the vine-clad pergola, George speaks.

'Dear lady, what you need is a psychological device to get you through what remains of the weekend. I suggest that if the total perfection of this paradise is what distresses you, make it imperfect. Sully it. Do something that will be imperceptible to your friends, that only you will know about, and I guarantee you will be able to enjoy the rest of the weekend. Now, if you don't mind, I am meeting Dame May Whitty for a swim. Have you seen the pool? It really is quite something.'

I return to the house and sit on the edge of my bed wondering how rude it would be if I simply went to sleep here and now under Gillian and Julian's Chelsea Textile eiderdown. George Sanders has obviously gone mad, and has been no help at all.

•

Louis and I are saying our goodbyes the following evening and Gillian is politely placing the orange lava lamp I have just given her as a thank-you present in pride of place on the kitchen table. 'I just loved its kitschness,' I said as she unwrapped it. 'I found it in that bric-a-brac shop in the village.'

'Oh, yes. It is certainly kitsch,' said Gillian. And then before we left I asked the children to pose in front of the lava lamp for a photograph, so that I will have a lasting memento of the weekend.

22 July 2001
A New Puppy

The good thing about getting Louis a five-month-old puppy, rather than a three-month-old one, as we had originally intended, is that a five-month-old is already house-trained and civilized. This is my line of defence as I explain to Matthew, over the phone from Devon, why I have suddenly acquired a black Labrador bitch today instead of waiting as previously agreed for a liver-and-white spaniel in September. 'She desperately needs a home,' I tell Matthew. 'At five months they've pretty much grown out of the chewing thing and she knows not to climb on the furniture.'

'And how's Steptoe?' asks Matthew. This is an important question because one of the conditions of getting a new puppy, as stipulated in the endless debates over the past year, was that Steptoe must be considered. His needs, as senior dog, are paramount.

'And although Labradors are renowned for their greed,' I continue, studiously ignoring the Steptoe question, 'this one seems almost discerning about what she eats!'

'How's Steptoe?' repeats Matthew and then, before I can answer, the line goes dead, which could either be because of the bad signal, or the fact that I just turned the phone off.

•

Steptoe is, in fact, not handling the situation well. He is furious, which is why Izzy the puppy has sought refuge on the sofa. She is chewing on the sponge I am about to use to clear up the mess she has just made in the kitchen – the direct and deeply unpleasant consequence of the punnet of strawberries she stole off the table. They went straight down (reminding me of Matthew with a bag of Maltesers) and straight through her, barely touching the sides. At least she is safe on the sofa. On ground level her life is in grave peril because Steptoe is patrolling up and down in front of her like a German guard in a prisoner-of-war camp, hackles raised like bayonets.

I admit that I have been putting an optimistic interpretation on the Izzy situation, but, like any good spin doctor, I have not told Matthew any actual lies. I have retained 'plausible deniability', although when I phoned him this morning to say we were leaving for London, I did not tell him that I was having to call from a phone box because Izzy has chewed my mobile phone.

We stopped eight times on the way home. Three times because Izzy was carsick, once because Louis was carsick and five times because of canine violence erupting on the back seat. Matthew, who had been a bit worried, was extremely relieved to see us and seems delighted with Izzy.

•

On the green sofa: me, Izzy and Louis. On the blue sofa: Matthew and Steptoe. We are a house divided. Matthew's head is in his hands. Steptoe's is between his front paws. They are both sighing heavily, and in sync. Steptoe has been on the blue sofa for two days now. For two days he has sat in judgement on the new puppy, watching as she shredded newspapers, chewed CDs, graunched on shoes, rended cushions, and (rather lethally) tossed Matthew's darts about like hot potatoes in her jaws. He watched as Izzy chewed her way through an electric cable, bravely masking his disappointment when it turned out not to be plugged in, and he watched as I silently set to with bucket and sponge and reprimanded Izzy in high-pitched whispers that I hoped Matthew couldn't hear.

Matthew joined Steptoe on the blue sofa – the seat of the righteous – when he found his copy of today's *Racing Post* shredded and scattered to the four corners of the kitchen. At first I tried to convince him that it was me who had shredded it. 'Why?' he asked. 'Why would you do that?'

'Because I was fed up with it,' I said.

Matthew looked at me as if I were mad and was asking me precisely how I had shredded it ('With your teeth, perhaps? Or was it a frenzied knife attack?') when Izzy walked in, at one end wagging merrily and at the other holding between her teeth several pages of the *Daily Telegraph*, including the back page with Matthew's half-completed crossword.

•

Any moment now Matthew's head will emerge from his hands, and the examination of the facts will begin.

Finally he looks up. Then Steptoe looks up. They both stare at me accusingly. 'I don't blame the dog,' says Matthew. 'I blame you. You have pulled a fast one. She is not, as you insisted, house-trained, she is not over the chewing thing and Steptoe is miserable.'

I search my mind for a straw at which to clutch, but without much luck. 'I will go out now and buy you a new *Racing Post*,' I say. 'And she is house-trained but has yet to grasp fully the difference between inside and outside.'

Matthew stands up and walks slowly up the stairs. Steptoe is following him.

I await the ultimatum.

•

I was very worried but I am not any more. I had thought that I would have to fight to keep Izzy. But now I know things will be all right because Matthew has just found her chewing the controls of his Sony PlayStation and I am eavesdropping on his conversation with her.

'Oh, Izzy Wizzy,' he says. 'What have you done-ums? You naughty doglet.'

I peer round the door. Izzy has rolled over with her paws in the air and Matthew is reaching down to scratch her tummy, cooing gently. With one foot he is surreptitiously pushing the damaged electricals out of sight, under the sofa.

26 August 2001
Leave Her Be

I know why Matthew is unravelling the hose, marching it through the house and aiming its nozzle through the front-door letterbox. I also know that he is a kind man who is not generally given to violence, and that he has no intention of actually firing his DIY water cannon at the seventy-something-year-old lady standing on our path.

It is six months since Hilda announced herself by leaving a Tesco's bag containing groceries on our doorstep. Since then she has been visiting at least once and sometimes as many as three or four times a day. The things she leaves are for 'Tony', also known as 'my officer'. Tony is a figment of Hilda's imagination, or perhaps someone from her past, who, she believes, lives in our house. Sometimes she leaves food for him: teacakes, sardines, suet. Sometimes it's bric-a-brac: an egg timer mounted on a piece of wood painted with a seagull from Budleigh Salterton, for example. Yesterday she left a shopping bag on wheels; a while back you could get them in fluorescent neoprene as a kitsch postmodern joke, but the one Hilda left was in Black Watch tartan. It comes in very handy because once a month I take Hilda's leavings – although obviously not the perishables and certainly not the egg timer from Budleigh Salterton – to the charity shop.

The problem was, Hilda saw me setting off down the street with the Black Watch tartan shopping bag on wheels, full to the brim with all non-existent Tony's other unreceived gifts, and she turned quite nasty.

'That's not for you, it's for Tony,' she shouted. 'It's for my officer. You bring that back here, you slut.'

•

There has been a lot of this kind of language (and worse) lately. Hilda, it has to be said, is becoming a menace, and this new aggression presents a dilemma. Matthew and I like to think of ourselves as easy-going liberal folk, and whenever I have suggested following Hilda home to see if there is a carer or a relative I could have a word with, Matthew has always advised that I 'leave her be'.

This is an odd phrase for Matthew to use, but he does tend to come over rather quaint when referring to Hilda. He imagines the officer to be a romantic Edwardian figure like Captain Bellamy in *Upstairs, Downstairs*, so whenever he talks to Hilda he says things like, 'Run along now, my good woman.'

Yesterday, however, when I gently tried to persuade her to go home because she was being spectacularly rude to passers-by, and she said, 'I shall shoot you dead with a Kalashnikov,' Matthew was forced to agree that this was a most un-Edwardian threat and that a Kalashnikov, come to that, was not an especially *Upstairs, Downstairs* sort of weapon. I wouldn't have minded so much – it is unlikely a septuagenarian in a hairnet would ever actually get hold of a Russian military rifle – except that Louis was standing beside me at the time, and such language is not easy to explain to a four-year-old.

So when Hilda did finally meander off down the street, I announced to Matthew that I'd had enough and was going to follow her.

•

Far from discouraging me, Matthew patted me supportively on the back and wished me well. Louis said, 'Be careful, Mum,' and offered to lend me his water pistol.

I have never followed someone before, and it was only after crouching behind first a bollard, then a dustbin and then a Mini Metro (Hilda, who is clearly experienced at being trailed, turned round every few paces) that I realized how hard it is and how easy they make it look in films. Two hundred yards up the road she took a sharp left and then left again and then she rang the bell on a black front door which was opened by another seventy-something-year-old woman in curlers.

'All right, Hilda,' said the woman, 'I'll watch you go in.' Hilda came back down the steps, walked across the road and in through the gate behind which I was hiding. She saw me, lunged at me with her shooting stick (the one she uses to sit on when she puts our house under surveillance), missed me, and I made a run for it.

A few minutes later, when the coast was clear, I returned and rang on the doorbell of the woman with curlers. 'Hilda?' she said. 'Oh, she's harmless. Best thing is to leave her be.'

•

Hilda, though, has no intention of leaving us be. She is here now, on her shooting stick, teacakes in her lap, staring at the front door. Matthew is staring back at her through the letterbox, and this Mexican stand-off has been in progress for ten minutes. Every so often Hilda will wave her fist and shout, 'I know he's in there, you let me see him,' to which Matthew responds by waggling the hose. Louis did turn it on for a moment but, fortunately, the resultant dribble of water would not have troubled an anarchist sparrow.

Finally Matthew opens the door. 'Now come along, my good woman,' he says. 'This is all very silly and it's time to stop.' His tone is kind and paternalistic, like Lord Bellamy talking to Ruby.

'Don't you "come along" me, you filthy toff,' says Hilda, and Matthew now metamorphoses into Hudson the butler (I am sure I can detect a faint Edinburgh twang to his voice).

'It's getting late and we've had quite enough of this horseplay,' he says, to which Hilda replies: 'I am the Queen and I can have you executed. I'll have you beheaded.'

And then all of a sudden the fight goes out of Matthew. He visibly deflates, bows before Hilda and says, 'You are very kind, ma'am, very kind,' and then he comes back inside and says that, in his opinion, we should, after all, just leave her be.

2 September 2001
Losing Sydney

'There is,' says Matthew, pacing the room, sighing and gesticulating, 'a clear and present danger that something monstrous is about to happen. If we are not extremely vigilant we will before long become one of those couples who call each other Mam and Dad. I mean to say. I'm a fan of Alan Bennett, but . . .'

'If ever there is so much as the merest hint of that happening,' I continue, 'we must book ourselves immediately on to some kind of twelve-step self-help programme.'

Matthew and I are waiting for an express delivery which we hope will bring a happy ending to a terrible week. It all began when Louis left Sydney, an orange-and-blue duck-billed platypus, behind on a train after a trip to Brighton with his grandparents. Sydney (actually the official 2000 Olympic mascot) has been Louis's constant companion since Matthew returned with him off a Qantas flight last October. To Louis, Sydney was not just a stuffed toy. He was a stuffed toy with a voice, opinions and a surprising capacity for Castlemaine XXXX. At the end of each day Matthew, Louis and the platypus would settle down and chat. (Matthew gave Sydney a strident Dame Edna voice, and the manners of Les Patterson. He would call Louis his 'little mate'.)

Louis, not surprisingly, was racked with grief at the loss of Sydney – and so, rather shockingly, were Matthew and I. Battling the lump in my throat, I immediately phoned National Railway Enquiries and reported our loss.

'It's a platypus,' I said in a quavering voice, 'an orange platypus with a blue beak, about one foot in height.' The man on the end of the phone assured me that a report would be put through to the lost property office in Purley.

'If your platypus is found, madam,' he said, 'you will be contacted immediately.'

•

Louis is sitting in my lap eating a large slab of chocolate fudge cake. The cake is all mixed up with his tears and occasionally he gives out a gaspy sob. Suddenly Matthew leaps to his feet.

'You forgot to say he was duck-billed,' he cries. 'Don't you think you should ring them back and make it clear that he is duck-billed?' From his tone I believe for a moment that he is serious, and I wonder if it is only the look of absolute horror on my face which brings him to his senses.

'What is happening to us?' asks Matthew, pouring himself a large whisky.

I take Louis upstairs – he has now stopped crying and within half an hour is happily rediscovering his Action Man. So much so that when the phone rings, and it is Matthew pretending to be Sydney, Louis asks him to call back later. I, meanwhile, dig out an old photograph of Sydney and for a few seconds allow myself to give in to the lump in my throat. I quietly sob for a boy and his lost toy. I wallow in the misery of it, imagining Sydney, frightened and alone in the lavatory cubicle of the 3.56 Connex South Central service from Brighton.

•

Once Louis is tucked up in bed, with Action Man nestling uncomfortably in the crook of his arm, I return downstairs and find Matthew on the phone to our friend Mike in Australia. It is only six in the morning in New South Wales and while Mike understands the urgency and is keen to help locate a replacement Sydney, he wonders if we would mind if he waited until the shops open. But by three in the morning British time Mike is back on the phone with the news that all Olympic mascots were removed from the shops last December. He has found a Sydney, though, on eBay, the Internet auction site, and has put in a bid of US$30. 'It's a special limited-edition platypus wearing a pilot's uniform,' explains Mike, and then, after suggesting that Matthew and I log on and take a look for ourselves, he says goodbye and promises to ring again if there is any more news.

•

Matthew and I stare at my computer screen long into the night, monitoring Mike's US$30 bid, and, in a moment of mild hysteria, actually bidding against him, raising the eventual price to US$90.

'That'll do it,' says Matthew.

'Please God,' I say, 'I don't know how much more of this I can take. It's the waiting which gets me. The terrible waiting and not knowing.'

By the following evening Louis and Action Man have bonded to the extent that when Sydney/Matthew phones again, Louis asks me to tell him he's not in and won't be back for a week. Mike, on the other hand, has had time to become as obsessed with Sydney as Matthew and I are, and has tracked down an American website which specializes in Olympic memorabilia – pins, banners and soft toys (or plush mascots, as Sydney must henceforth be known). At three forty-five on the third morning of the crisis, Matthew shakes me awake with the news that we have received a charming email from a Larry Elmer of www.pin-marketplace.com informing us that a thirteen-inch plush mascot is on its way via Federal Express. Our successful bid for the pilot Sydney is also confirmed, and that too is winging its way to us.

•

'Hello, little mate!' says Matthew/Sydney round Louis's bedroom door, and it's not that Louis isn't pleased to see him. It's just that this reunion scene between a four-year-old boy and his beloved toy is not nearly as tearful and emotional as the one which just happened downstairs when Matthew and I unwrapped a Federal Express parcel containing a fourteen-inch duck-billed platypus dressed as an airline pilot.

'Oh, Mam,' said Matthew. 'Sydney is home.'

'He certainly is, Dad,' I said. 'And doesn't he look smart in his uniform?'

7 October 2001
Going to the Ritz

We thought about Morocco for our tenth-wedding-anniversary treat. We considered Paris, Rome and Venice. We came horribly close to Warwickshire before they cancelled the Ryder Cup, but in the end, this time, after three days and nights of intense deliberation, we have decided to go to the Ritz. This way we still have a treat, there is very little travelling involved, and Matthew is adamant that our total expenditure will be considerably less than four nights in Taroudant, or even two nights at Le Bristol in Paris.

He has booked a large room, a table for dinner and a cab, which will be picking us up any minute now. How sophisticated is that? I think to myself, as I teeter out on to the pavement in my special-occasion heels, clutching my special-occasion clutch bag.

After an uneventful cab ride (Matthew did question the route seven times, but for once only under his breath), we have arrived at the Ritz, where he is now tipping lavishly after noticing that a plate of eggs Benedict costs £23.50. This time around, instead of repeating over and over again that 'We are damn well going to get our money's worth', he has, in fact, gone more than slightly mad and has been handing out fivers to anyone who comes within arm's reach – disconcerting, to say the least, for the Spanish tourist who just happened to know the way to the lift. He insisted she keep the money and say no more about it.

By the time we are ensconced on our emperor-sized bed in our fantastically gilded and swagged room, drinks in our hands, watching *The Weakest Link* on television and congratulating ourselves on our decision to stay in London because this way we can still verbally abuse Anne Robinson, Matthew has spent the equivalent of a week's shopping in Tesco's on tips. Judging from his cheery demeanour he believes that this is a fitting way to celebrate ten years of, as he puts it, 'being shackled together by the bonds of holy matrimony'.

•

It's lucky we didn't decide on a sightseeing break in a foreign city because I doubt we would ever have summoned the energy to see any sights beyond the airport and the interior of the hotel. It is 8 p.m. and we have spent the last fifteen minutes attempting to justify not going downstairs to the restaurant because we feel too tired and *EastEnders* is on the telly.

'We must go,' I say, praying Matthew will overrule me. 'You've booked a table in the most spectacular dining room in England. We can't not go. Don't you agree?'

'Yes,' says Matthew. 'You are right. We do have to go, it would be sacrilege not to go. Or, on the other hand, we could stay here and order room service.' Half an hour later we shuffle reluctantly down to the restaurant like a pair of institutionalized inmates on their way to the macramé class.

Towards the end of dinner, during a review of our ten years shackled together by the bonds etc., we get to the bit in 1997 where I am pregnant, it is a fortnight before Louis is born and Matthew is suffering from really bad acid indigestion. 'I wonder what Louis is doing now,' I say, by way of distracting Matthew from reliving the indigestion publicly. He has done this before and I am worried it might not be seemly in the Ritz.

'Well,' says Matthew, sensing an opportunity for some biting sarcasm and therefore happily forgoing the indigestion, 'it's a quarter past eleven, so I imagine Louis will just be coming home from the pub, probably stopping for a takeaway in the Uxbridge Road.'

I say nothing – ten years of being shackled etc. has taught me to say nothing at times like this. 'It is 11.15 p.m. and Louis is four years old,' continues Matthew. 'What do you think he is doing? He'll be tucked up in bed fast asleep.'

Neither of us speaks for a few minutes and then, both at once, we look up from our Turkish delight petits fours. 'We could just go home and check up on him,' I say.

'Now you are being ridiculous,' says Matthew. 'If we were in Marrakech we couldn't go home and check up on him. If we were staying at the Danielli in Venice we couldn't go home and check up on him.'

•

It takes us all of three minutes to get out of the restaurant and into a taxi headed for Shepherd's Bush. We arrive home just before midnight and Louis is, of course, fast asleep.

Matthew and I must go to sleep now, too, because we need to be up bright and early if we are to catch breakfast at the Ritz.

•

It is 7.15 a.m. and a complimentary newspaper is hanging in a bag on our bedroom door. Three chambermaids are hovering like midges around the DO NOT DISTURB sign and Matthew is nudging me hard in the ribs. 'They suspect something,' he hisses loudly so that they hear him and immediately suspect something. We smile breezily, hoping to give the impression that we have been out for an early-morning walk in Green Park. Matthew hands one of the chambermaids a five-pound note as we pass, so now they really suspect something.

•

After our breakfast (eggs Benedict £23.50, kedgeree £4,569,874,000.50), we set about distressing our room so it looks a bit more lived in. Matthew takes a long time arranging the towels all over the floor, gently tweaking their corners and rippling them with outstretched fingers, like an abstract painter working on a canvas. 'They must look as if we have just dropped them carelessly,' he says, and I try to point out to him that the best way of achieving this effect would be simply to drop them carelessly. But he isn't listening because he is too busy jumping up and down on a fluffy bathrobe. And this is the sight that greets the chambermaid as she opens the door.

21 October 2001
Radio 2

Radio 2 has changed my life. Whenever I listen to Johnnie Walker, for instance, I experience a comforting sensation – a feeling that I have come home, a sense of familiarity and belonging. I mention this to Matthew, and he says he came home to Johnny Walker twenty years ago. But once he understands that I mean the disc jockey rather than the Scotch whisky, he looks at me incredulously for a very long time.

'It's true,' I say. 'I have become addicted to Radio 2. I love Ken Bruce and Terry Wogan and Steve Wright in the afternoon and I really, really love Ed 'Stewpot' Stewart.'

Matthew pours himself a glass of Johnny Walker and says that what I am experiencing is a second childhood. 'Most people have the sense to wait until after middle age before regressing,' he says. Then he suggests that we rush forward our plan to retire to an old people's home in Godalming, and I envisage being wheeled around a closely cropped lawn listening to *The Tracks Of My Tears* (David Cassidy picks the records that mean the most to him).

•

While I was making my pre-bed milky drink at 9 p.m. this evening, gyrating in front of the microwave to Billy Ocean's 'Love Really Hurts Without You', Matthew said he thought I had gone mad and asked me first my name, which I gave him correctly, and then who the Prime Minister was. 'Ted Heath,' I replied, and for a moment his alarm seemed genuine.

It all began when the car went in for its 40,000-mile service, and the mechanic retuned the Kenwood detachable radio from Radio 4 (93.5 FM) to Radio 2 (89.2). Until now my only experience of Radio 2 has been while visiting Mr Ede the dentist, who never listens to anything else. I had always assumed he was using it as a back-up anaesthetic, in case the injection didn't work.

Then the car came back from its service, and, instead of hearing *Woman's Hour*, I found myself listening to Terry Wogan joshing smoothily with Ken Bruce during the 10 a.m. handover. At first I panicked. I pressed every button. I pressed every combination of buttons in search of *Woman's Hour* but I kept coming back to Terry and Ken. Then Ken played Diana Ross's 'Chain Reaction' and quite involuntarily I started bouncing rhythmically in my seat.

I'll be taking a notebook with me when I go out at lunchtime so I can take down Jimmy Young's daily recipe. Matthew is quite right to look incredulous once more when I tell him about this, for it is unlikely I would ever actually make the recipe. But it is nice to feel as if I am part of the whole JY Prog family, whereas I never felt I really belonged on Radio 4.

I listened to John Humphrys and James Naughtie, to

Melvyn Bragg and Jeremy Paxman, but I never felt at home with them in the same way that I do when I listen to *Seminal Soul* on Wednesday nights – in bed with my milky drink.

When I was younger I certainly felt I belonged with Radio 1 – and that, of course, is where I first encountered Ed 'Stewpot' Stewart. Perhaps Matthew's second childhood theory isn't quite so unlikely after all.

•

On my way back from taking Louis to school this morning I became stuck in a traffic snarl-up at Shepherd's Bush Green. A truly dedicated listener would have phoned Radio 2's Sally Boazman so she could have announced it on the travel news. Unfortunately I was unable to think of a pseudonym for myself before Ken Bruce had segued softly into the Chi-Lites. Radio 2 callers always give themselves pseudonyms when they phone in with the traffic news.

'A consignment of chip fat has overturned on Dollis Hill,' Sally will say, 'so thanks to Cheeky Bunny for that, and Big Saddo has just phoned, informing us of a twelve-mile tailback on the A74 past Anorak Corner.'

That evening I composed a request to the Ed 'Stewpot' Stewart show. 'Please can you play "Puff The Magic Dragon" for Louis who will be five next April and send all our love from Mum, Dad, Grandma, Grandpa, Granny, Uncle Noel, Auntie Penny, Ian and Ginny. Please don't forget to mention Steptoe and Izzy the dogs and Nana Dorothy.'

'Nana Dorothy?' said Matthew, when I showed it to him. 'Nana Dorothy?' And then he went downstairs to listen to the emergency twenty-four-hour football news on Radio 5 Live – a station I really can't abide.

•

I have just collected the car from the garage. It needed a new headlight after I ran into the back of a caravan while trying to take down a JY recipe – meringues – and to my distress I find that the radio has been tuned back to Radio 4. I panic and press every button. I press every combination of buttons in search of Alex Lester who is standing in for Johnnie Walker who is standing in for Terry Wogan. By the time I drive back to the garage, it is shut.

The dentist is my only hope. I will make an emergency appointment with Mr Ede for 10.30 a.m., just in time for tomorrow's round of the Pop Master Quiz with Ken Bruce. There was a time when I had to undergo hypnotherapy before going to the dentist but not any more. Radio 2 has changed my life.

4 November 2001
Goodbye, George Sanders

The incident that provoked the crisis that propelled me to a consultation with George Sanders, my imaginary psychotherapist, was relatively trivial. Just before lunch Louis asked me to pass him his Pocket Pop, a lollipop which, after licking, can be folded away into its integral plastic case until the next time it is required. The Pocket Pop is kept with various other delights on top of the fridge. 'No, Louis,' I said in the pursed and prim tone used by parents, teachers and dog trainers. 'We are about to have lunch and I don't want you ruining your appetite.' Louis stuck his bottom lip out at me defiantly for a few seconds, buried his head in his hands and muttered something about how one small lick wouldn't ruin a whole appetite. He then wandered off, tutting, to draw a seasonal picture of me in a witch's hat, riding a broom.

Two minutes later he watched as I passed by the fridge and absent-mindedly broke off two squares of the Cadbury's Fruit & Nut kept there. The first square had been consumed and the second was on its way when I noticed he was staring at me. He didn't say a word, just put his hands on his hips and pursed his lips primly. I stared back, chewing and swallowing quickly, and said: 'Do as I say, Louis, not as I do.' Then I gasped, appalled at myself, and marched swiftly towards the garden shed where George Sanders resides.

'So what you are saying, dear lady,' said George, shaking Trumper's Essence of Limes cologne into his palms, 'is that your own gluttony and lack of self-discipline, willpower, et cetera, et cetera, et cetera – all these things are beginning to affect your parenting skills.' I nodded, speechless to hear the word 'parenting' coming from George's lips.

'First, let us deal with the gluttony, self-discipline, et cetera, et cetera, et cetera,' said George, making me wonder why he felt it necessary to use so many et ceteras. He was lowering his knees in order to check his hair in the mirror hanging next to the hoe. Finding a troublesome strand, he repeatedly pecked at it with his fingers.

'When my second wife, Zsa Zsa Gabor, came to me feeling depressed,' he continued, 'I would recommend to her the purchase of a new negligee.'

George turned away from the mirror for a moment to look at me, then turned back and said: 'But no. Not in your case. You look shocked at the very thought.'

I was shocked, but not about the negligee. I had forgotten that George was married to Zsa Zsa.

'It lasted less than a decade,' said George, as if reading my thoughts, 'and in 1970 I married her sister, Magda.' And then, just as I was wondering why I had chosen for an imaginary psychotherapist someone whose idea of rational behaviour was to marry not just one Hungarian sister who can't act but two, George ushered me to the shed door. 'Let us continue our conversation later,' he said. 'You are right. "Do as I say and not as I do" is hardly a suitable maxim for young Louis. But we will talk about this another time. I must leave you because I have an appointment with Joan Greenwood. We are lunching at the new Gordon Ramsay at Claridge's.'

•

'Oh, yes,' said my friend Gerri, who is a bit of a film buff, 'George Sanders had four wives in all. He not only married Zsa Zsa and Magda, he was also married to Susan Larson and Ronald Colman's wife Benita Hume. Of course, he was a terrible depressive,' she continues.

'Really?' I say.

'Oh, don't you believe it!' says Gerri, who is American. 'At one point he was seeing seven psychiatrists, not that they did him any good. He took seven tubes of Nembutal in Barcelona and ended his life. His suicide note read: "Dear World, I am leaving you because I am bored. I feel I have lived long enough. I am leaving you with your worries in this sweet cesspool." '

George was not in when I visited the shed this evening. He had left a note written in turquoise ink, Blu-Tacked to one of Matthew's logs. It read: 'Dear Lady, I am leaving this shed because I am bored and it is too close to your neighbour's cesspool. You will find me on the steps of the Albert Memorial.'

•

I was taking the dogs for a walk anyway when I came across George in the dusk. He seemed dwarfed and small as he sat there on those expansive steps, his huge, enveloping coat wrapped around him. 'Ah, dear lady,' he said as I sat down next to him. 'Please try to keep those dogs of yours away. I have an allergy to Labradors, and West Highland terriers wear away at my nerves.' George sounded sad, despondent, out of sorts. Plucking a stray leaf from his turn-ups, he said: 'Dear Joanie always tires me out and I should never drink port at luncheon. But now we must talk about your problem. I have been thinking about it a great deal and I repeat my earlier advice. "Do as I say and not as I do" is not a suitable maxim for a child. It is not at all suitable, madam. Not suitable at all.'

Moments later, he got to his feet, stumbling slightly on the steps, and wandered slowly off towards the Serpentine. When I started to follow him he said: 'Leave me now, dear lady. I must urge you to look for a new imaginary psychotherapist. You see, I am not suitable, madam. Not suitable at all.' Then he turned and walked off into the mist. But before disappearing from view, he called to me over his shoulder: 'Errol Flynn was a marvellous man,' he said. 'Why don't you try him?'

2 December 2001
Arrival of a Treadmill

Despite the fact that neither Matthew nor I have said very much about the scheduled arrival on Friday of a Horizon Quantum Treadmill exercise machine, there is a tangible air of resolution and change permeating the house. Once the treadmill is safely installed it is surely only a matter of a few weeks before we metamorphose into Anthea Turner and Grant Bovey. As it is, we have just two days left before those first endorphins start making themselves felt – in fact I wouldn't be at all surprised if the simple excitement and adrenaline rush of having such a machine on the premises burn up a few calories.

In preparation for the new regime I have already begun quickening my walking pace for short intervals when taking the dogs out to the park, and Matthew's preparation is even more intriguing. It seems to involve an increase in the amount of Terry's Chocolate Orange segments consumed per evening – a last, decadent fling, perhaps, before Boveydom.

•

We weren't in when the treadmill arrived. (I was out buying some sweatbands, a leotard and a new book on food-combining which promises to help me lose weight, feel great, beat stress and look amazing. Matthew was out buying six three-packs of coffee-flavoured Walnut Whips.) But Tanja the home help was here to welcome the treadmill and learn how to get it from the stow-away position into the working position.

When I return from the shops it is in the stow-away position. Matthew is standing, transfixed, in front of it. Tanja has gone home without, apparently, telling him how to put it into the working position. Matthew is gazing at it in disbelief as though its presence here in our house makes no sense whatever: as though its very existence has turned his entire view of the world on its head. 'What have we done?' he rasps. 'My God, what have we done?' He sounds like Charlton Heston finding the Statue of Liberty, crumbling in the sands, in the final scene of *Planet of the Apes*. 'Look at it,' he says, 'just look at it. How in the name of sanity are we supposed to get on it?'

That Matthew's concern about the treadmill is merely technical, rather than philosophical as at first seemed the case, comes as a relief. Telling him not to be so defeatist, I pick up the manual, turn to the relevant page and start reading it out loud. But Matthew isn't listening, he is tapping a Terry's Chocolate Orange on the coffee table. Its segments fall away from each other like unfurling petals. He pours himself a glass of Jim Beam bourbon and settles down to the old regime. It is almost as if the treadmill didn't exist.

•

It is Sunday morning and, after spending the whole of yesterday in denial about the treadmill, Matthew has now decided to go to work on it. He has just appeared, dressed as I have never seen him before, in black shorts, a white T-shirt, black trainers and Nike sweatband. 'Right,' he says, 'I'm ready.'

Louis turns off the television, the two dogs sit upright in their baskets and I put down my food-combining book. We all turn to watch Matthew as he slowly circles the treadmill, slyly glancing at it from the corner of one eye as if he hopes to catch it off-guard. He stops, studies the instruction manual with intense concentration, circles the treadmill once more, nods to himself in apparent satisfaction and then makes a mad lunge, pressing down on the lever at the bottom with his right foot and grabbing the central bar with both hands. For a few seconds, the treadmill and Matthew are locked in combat. Then, with Matthew standing bolt upright and the treadmill leaning on him, they begin to waltz around the room with the treadmill taking the lead. When finally they come to a standstill Matthew gives the treadmill a despairing kick, wipes his brow with his Nike sweatband and heads upstairs for a shower.

•

By Monday morning Matthew is dressed in a pair of startling red shorts and some rather modern zip-up trainers. He is also wearing a fuchsia-pink headband. Tanja has just arrived, and in one deft movement she has manoeuvred the treadmill into the working position. It is now operational and Matthew is standing on it. I leave to take Louis to school. Half an hour later I return and Matthew and the treadmill are fairly flying along. Matthew, red in the face with the sweat pouring from him, gasps: 'Bloody marvellous . . . really good workout . . . endorphins . . . two stone by Christmas.'

Another half an hour later I hear him running in a sprightly, tippy-toe fashion up to the bathroom for his shower. 'Excellent investment, that machine,' he says, putting his head round my office door. 'You should have a go. Nothing to be frightened of.'

•

I have just returned from picking Louis up from school and I notice the treadmill is back in the upright position. Matthew, however, is not. It is six hours since this morning's workout, just enough time for his muscles to have stiffened up. He is lolloping around the kitchen and as I look at him, bent double with his arms hanging limply at his sides, I wonder who he reminds me of. And then I know: it is Roddy McDowall in *Planet of the Apes*.

9 December 2001
A Basil Street Suit

As part of what Matthew calls 'the drive towards early retirement', he has selected the Basil Street Hotel, in Knightsbridge, for his thirty-eighth-birthday lunch. He could have chosen any number of 'destination' restaurants throughout the Greater London area, but no, he has gone for the creaky, elegant, doughty old Basil Street, the sort of place you'd take your great-aunt to if she came up to town for the day from Hampshire. The real treat, Matthew says, will come after lunch when we will retire to the lounge and he will drop off while reading the Sunday papers. He has given me permission to nudge him, or even, if necessary, douse him with iced water when he snores.

Unusually, I am completely with Matthew on this one (with him on the Basil Street, if not necessarily the snoring). But then we have always agreed upon the necessity of an early and genteel retirement. In fact, the only source of worry about Matthew's birthday is what to buy him for a present. The backlog of Matthew's birthday presents, along with all his other presents (Christmas, Valentine's Day, wedding anniversaries), has become something of an issue lately. I owe him more than one: in fact, I owe him about four. Every so often, at random moments, he will say, apropos of nothing at all: 'Shall we just review the backlog?' The sequence of the recital that follows is identical each time.

He begins with the dartboard, which I did manage to buy him but then took a year to have attached to the wall.

Next up is the antique office chair he requested which I have yet to purchase. Then there is his tenth-wedding-anniversary present, now three months overdue. This one is a secret. Matthew has no idea what it is going to be. And, to be perfectly honest, neither have I.

Finally comes the soda siphon, another item I did actually buy but which has never worked. Three years have passed and I still haven't quite got around to taking it to the shop, with the result that Matthew pressurizes anyone who comes to the house into having a whisky and soda, so that he can go over to the siphon, pick it up and then exclaim in mock regret that he has 'quite forgotten' that it does not technically dispense any soda water. 'But it's early days,' he will conclude apologetically, offering wine to whoever never wanted whisky and soda in the first place, 'very early days.'

The issue of this year's birthday present, though, will be resolved tomorrow. I have set the whole day aside to buy him a corduroy suit. If there's time, I might get myself a cashmere twin-set, which will look just right in the Basil Street, but the suit is the priority. If I fail in this and add to the 'backlog', there is every chance that Matthew will start greeting visitors to the house wearing pants and T-shirt, with the words: 'I'm so sorry. I thought I was wearing my new corduroy suit, but I've just remembered Rebecca hasn't bought it yet. Now, let me fix you a whisky and soda.'

I have come to Regent Street, where there are a number of shops selling corduroy suits – Hackett, Austin Reed, Aquascutum and Liberty. I decide to start at Liberty, which is more familiar to me than the rest because of its extensive women's wear department, and find that there are major renovations going on in the store at the moment. This means that instead of being able to enter straight from Regent Street into the men's wear department I have to go via the jewellery department and the cosmetics department before realizing that I have completely missed the lift up to women's wear. There is also a French Connection in Regent Street, and, of course, Bond Street is but a stone's throw away. But by the time I emerge from Liberty the carrier bags are weighing me down, so I take them to the car, via Gap Kids (gloves and hat for Louis), before proceeding to Armani on the corner of Brook Street.

It is now four o'clock and I have yet to find a cashmere twin-set so it's back to the car with the Armani bags and a quick march up to the Burlington Arcade, which should leave me a good half an hour to concentrate on Matthew's suit.

It took me much longer in the cashmere shop than anticipated – so many colours to choose from – and by the time I made it to a men's wear shop time was running out; the car was on a meter with just ten minutes to go. I did actually buy him a suit, but unfortunately the trousers are several sizes too big, which didn't seem to be such a problem because I could always change them next week.

The important thing was to have a present for Matthew to open on his birthday morning and I think I made the right decision. Matthew was very pleased with the suit, although, of course, he couldn't wear it out to lunch today because of the oversized trousers.

I am, therefore, puzzled this evening to hear him telling his cousin Nick, very loudly, so I can't fail to hear, how he had to walk from the restaurant to the lounge wearing ties knotted together over each shoulder and then secured through his belt loops as a pair of makeshift braces. 'How else do you keep a pair of forty-six-inch-waist trousers up?' he is saying. 'The belt to do the job hasn't been made.

'Now then,' he says, turning to me, 'have you seen the siphon? I've managed to persuade Nick to join me in a whisky and soda.'

16 December 2001
Scratching the Car

A territorial war has broken out in the kitchen over Louis's blackboard. Louis himself is very keen to use it because he wants to draw a picture of Peter Davison, his favourite Dr Who, and since it is his blackboard, and also since he is only four, you might have thought this would have given him the edge. However, Matthew has bought Louis off with a packet of fizzy cola lances and now appears to be drawing the outline of a car on the blackboard. Imagine a crime scene at which a car is the corpse and someone has drawn around it and you will get the picture. Matthew has written *Rebecca's car* at the top and now he is highlighting the areas of the vehicle that have been damaged in the last year, in various traffic or parking incidents. I have seen this done before on insurance claims forms.

'Why have you drawn three wing-mirrors on the left side?' I ask.

'Because as an artist I find myself ever more influenced by Salvador Dali,' he replies. 'Or could it be,' he continues drolly, 'because three is the number of new wing-mirrors that the left-hand side of your car has required since you took possession of it a little over one year ago?'

And now I understand what Matthew is doing. He is making an issue of the fact that this morning I reversed into a wall and smashed the car number plate. In a minute he will deliver a sarcastic lecture on the subject of safe motoring.

•

It is true, I suppose, that in the fourteen months since I have had this car there may have been a marginally higher than average number of incidents. Driving back up our road this afternoon, I run over the catalogue in my head and wonder whether Matthew is right to blame it on me letting my mind wander at the wheel. It is just as I am wondering this, in fact, that I hear the sound of scraping; the sound of metal scrunching against metal, the sound of a couple of hundred pounds' worth of damage being done to an innocent victim's wheel arch. Either the Japanese sports car that was parked (very badly, I think) at the side of the road has gone into me, or I have gone into it.

I consider driving off, more because I can't face another sarcastic road-safety lecture from Matthew than because I don't want to own up to the owner of the Japanese car. But then I imagine burning in hell-fire for eternity, and knock on the nearest door. 'It belongs to the lady in number 283,' says a man with a baby. There is no answer at 283 so I drive home, where Matthew and Louis – who must have been practising – ask me in perfectly synchronized unison if I managed to get here without any road-traffic incidents. I tell them that I did and thank them for asking. I go to bed early that night and lie awake, the flames of hell-fire lapping around the room. At midnight I dress, write a note, drive to the Japanese car and place the note under its windscreen wiper – which I may have bent back a little too far in the process.

The rest of that night I am kept awake, not by the flames of hell-fire, but by the threat of Matthew answering the phone when the woman in number 283 rings and the inevitability of the ensuing sarcastic lectures about road safety and owning up to things. So, when I drive past the Japanese car the following morning, I stop and remove the note.

•

Two days later I have barely slept and when I do sleep I have terrifying hell-fire dreams. Six days later, however, I am sleeping dreamlessly because I have satisfactorily convinced myself that the owner of the Japanese car must be pretty well off and that she can easily afford to get it fixed. She will also, of course, be getting sympathy from her family for her bad luck whereas if I own up I will get no sympathy at all, just sarcastic lectures.

By day seven I have persuaded myself that I have behaved not only justly but even honourably. My biggest worry at the moment is what to tell Matthew when he notices the new scratch down the left side of my car. By Sunday evening, a week almost to the minute since the incident, Matthew has noticed the scratch down the side of my car. 'Hello, hello, hello,' he says, irritatingly. 'What is this scratch doing here?'

I tell him I have no idea. At first he doesn't believe me but I do a very convincing impersonation of an indignant injured party. 'Someone has run into my car and damaged it quite badly,' I whine, 'and instead of showing me any sympathy at all you are accusing me not just of a hit and run, but of lying to you.'

Matthew finally apologizes and makes me a cup of tea which I didn't ask for. Then he gets angry. 'I can't believe someone would do that,' he says. 'Why would someone do that? Why wouldn't someone leave a note? It makes me so angry.' And then his anger turns to fury. 'Just for once I wish someone would get caught doing it,' he thunders. 'It's a serious offence, not leaving details after an accident. You can be sent to prison for that.'

•

That night I lie awake with a mental image of the man with the baby in the witness box and at midnight I write a note, drive up the road and put it under the windscreen wiper of the Japanese car which is, I can now confirm, slightly bent.

2002

20 January 2002
Izzy's Bitch-pants

The scene greeting a visitor to our kitchen would have been reminiscent of a 1950s American TV commercial. The two dogs were charging around the room together, with Louis excitably joining in. Resplendent in freshly laundered gingham apron (a Christmas present), I was standing at the stove reheating a takeaway for supper, and Matthew . . . Well, Matthew was letting the side down a little. He was sitting on the sofa, his arms crossed at the chest, hands tucked under his elbows, staring straight ahead while rocking to and fro and humming quietly. When he continued to do this even as the two dogs landed on him at high speed, I asked him who he thought he was today.

'Today, dear bride,' he said in a strange, spooky voice, 'I am Randle McMurphy, the Jack Nicholson character in *One Flew Over the Cuckoo's Nest*.'

'Why?' I asked.

'Because,' he said, 'like McMurphy, I am a sane person in a madhouse and the only way for me to survive is to pretend to be mad myself.'

I then asked him what was so very crazy about a small boy frolicking with the family dogs while his mother prepares a meal.

'On the surface,' he said, 'nothing at all. Except that then I look at that clock and see that it is five forty-five in the morning.'

•

The reason for this prompt start to the day was that Izzy went into season at 4.45 a.m. At least, that was the time when Steptoe began howling like a very small wolf before revealing himself as a frothy-mouthed sex beast. What woke Louis was not the howling, or the scurrying that ensued, but Matthew's wailing: 'It's a madhouse. It's a madhouse. How could you let this happen?'

When I phone Nancy at the vet's later that morning she says dogs need at least twenty minutes for a successful coupling, so every ten minutes or so I separate them by putting Izzy behind a baby-gate which we never got round to dismantling; it is now, in fact, operating as an anti-baby gate, or more accurately, an anti-puppy gate.

By 1.30 p.m. a terrible gloom has set in. We are sitting in the kitchen with Izzy but Steptoe is not here. The howling and the frothing (Matthew's, not Steptoe's) have become too much, and I have sent him (Steptoe, not Matthew) away to Camilla the dog-walker, who said she could have him for eleven days but then she was going to Northamptonshire. 'This is unforgivable,' says Matthew accusingly. 'That you could let this happen. That Steptoe should be ejected from his own home like this. And him senior dog as well.'

•

Three days later Camilla phones to say that the top of Steptoe's head is going bald. 'I think it might be stress,' she says, 'separation anxiety.' She says she will take him to the vet and keep me informed.

Matthew, who is now examining the top of his own head in the bathroom mirror, says he is keen to know what treatment the vet suggests and that he too would like to be kept informed. He also mentions, in passing, that he cannot begin to fathom how I have allowed this to happen. Two hours later Matthew says he can't wait to hear from Camilla and that I must phone the vet myself.

'Ah, yes,' says Nancy. 'Steptoe has just been in. It was a food allergy. Nothing to worry about, Camilla is going to give him fresh chicken and rice for the next few days and it should clear up on its own.' Matthew seems rather disappointed by this diagnosis and suggested treatment, and stops examining his scalp in the mirror.

•

Eleven days later Steptoe is home because Camilla has gone to Northamptonshire. However, according to the Labrador book which it has only just occurred to me to read, Izzy is apparently going through her most 'receptive', 'fertile' period. Her season, according to the book, and Nancy confirms this, is set to last a total of twenty-one days. 'Marvellous,' says Matthew.

So that afternoon I drive seventy miles to Northamptonshire and deposit Steptoe with the very kind and accommodating Camilla. I arrange to collect him a week later, when Izzy's season should have well and truly finished. Just to be on the safe side, though, I invest in a pair of 'bitch-pants' made of black elastic with shiny metal stud-fasteners and a hole for Izzy's tail.

Having taken the bitch-pants out of their package I decide to store them in the cupboard with the broken door in the downstairs loo until Steptoe's return. Here, they are clearly on display and visible to the friends who come to dinner that evening. No one says anything at the time but the following morning, when I realize what has happened, I ring to explain. They admit they were curious.

•

Steptoe is now home once more, but, despite the fact that we are now well into Day 22, he is still frothing and occasionally groaning. Izzy is wearing the bitch-pants. Matthew, who says helpfully that he is finding it harder and harder as each day passes to keep a grip on reality, heads upstairs to watch television. Tiring of the constant sound of our pets' heavy petting, I go with him.

Twenty-two minutes later both dogs appear at the door. Steptoe looks very pleased with himself and Izzy is no longer wearing her pants. Nancy at the vet's says there is a 'morning after' injection available if I'm at all worried.

27 January 2002
Louis's Hypochondria

Louis has just remarked that he can 'hear Dad shuffling about'. It is true. I can hear Matthew myself. He is one floor above us and, since it is January, the month which, tradition dictates, is set aside for depression and non-specific ailments, he has given up lifting his feet when he walks. Louis and I temporarily cease making biscuits in the shape of Dr Who's Tardis in order to listen to the rhythmical shuffle on the floorboards above – shuffle, shuffle, stop; shuffle, shuffle, stop – and I can picture Matthew as we listen. He will be stopping every third step to put a hand to the small of his back and grimace. I often wish, at this time of year, that we had had the house carpeted throughout so the shuffling wouldn't be so audible.

The noise gets closer and closer, and louder and louder, until, as Matthew reaches the top of the stairs, it turns into a series of slow, evenly paced downward stomps. He arrives in the kitchen with his left hand clutching his chest, his right hand holding the back of a chair for support. 'I don't know,' he says, 'I just can't shake this thing off.'

Out of the corner of my eye I catch Louis mouthing the words as Matthew says them, 'I just can't shake this thing off,' he echoes silently. What exactly the 'thing' Matthews refers to is I don't know. I have asked him repeatedly but I never get an answer. Perhaps there is no answer. Or perhaps it is just 'January'.

'How old is Dad?' Louis asks after Matthew has returned, shuffling, from whence he came. I tell him that he is thirty-eight. 'Will he be in a nursing home soon,' asks Louis, 'like Great-Granny?'

'No,' I explain, as I attempt to mould a piece of leftover dough into the shape of Jon Pertwee, 'Great-Granny is ninety-three, and Dad has a long way to go before he reaches a nursing home.'

'Will he shuffle all the way there?'

'Probably,' I say, swiftly reworking Jon Pertwee into Tom Baker and slipping him into the oven on gas mark 4.

Louis gets down from the chair he has been standing on and shuffles over to the other side of the room. When he stops he bends down, dramatically clutches his right shin bone and, contorting his face into a terrible grimace, says: 'I just can't shake this thing off.'

'What thing?' I ask.

'This broken leg,' says Louis. 'It's a spinal fracture of the lung bone.'

•

Living with a hypochondriac of Matthew's calibre is bound to have had an effect on Louis. The 'lung bone' reference is to do with Matthew's chest X-rays (an injury eleven years ago) – an apparently permanent exhibition of these X-rays, about which Matthew always insists he doesn't like to talk, is arranged on the sitting-room table. And by 'spinal fracture' what Louis means is spiral fracture, something he suffered when he fell off a playground slide one and a half years ago.

'I just can't seem to shake it off,' repeats Louis, who obviously believes that a bit of timely bother from an old wound will get him off school tomorrow.

'But, Louis,' I say, 'you are clutching the wrong leg.'

Louis, it turns out, has an answer for this because be has been talking to Matthew. 'It's cycle-automatic,' he tells me, 'and cycle-automatic is just as bad as real. It means I am making it up but it still hurts.'

I ask Louis if Matthew has told him about his own psychosomatic illnesses, about the time perhaps when he thought he needed a new heart and woke up with a swelling ('oedema' in Matthew's vernacular) on his ankle – a classic symptom, so Matthew claims, of cardiac failure. 'But when he went to the doctor and he said there was nothing wrong with him, the ankle swelling disappeared as if by magic.'

'Yes, he has told me that,' said Louis.

•

It is 5 a.m. and the entire household including both dogs is gathered at Louis's bedside. We were woken three hours ago by his screams of agony, and even now he is still clutching his left leg and insisting that a warm flannel be placed over the lower part of it. Matthew and I are doing that thing that worried parents do, sitting on the edge of Louis's bed, whispering the same questions to each other over and over again.

As well as being genuinely worried that something is seriously wrong, I am also racked with guilt about dismissing Louis's complaints as an attempt to get off school.

'What do you think?' asks Matthew.

'I don't know,' I say, 'what do you think?'

'It isn't cycle-automatic,' interrupts Louis.

•

'We always take a limp very seriously,' says the casualty doctor, 'and this one is certainly very pronounced.' She then asks Louis to hop onto the couch, a request he takes quite literally and with surprising dexterity for someone with such a seriously injured leg.

'Mmmm,' says the doctor suspiciously, beginning a series of experiments. She taps Louis's left knee. She asks him to lie down and lift one leg. Then the other leg. She picks up one leg and draws a circle in the air with it. And then the other leg.

'Mmmm,' she says again. 'What do you think is wrong with your leg, Louis?'

'I don't know,' he replies, 'it could be cycle-automatic because my lung bone hurts as well but I just can't shake it off.'

In a tone which unmistakably implies that we have wasted enough NHS time, the doctor suggests Louis and I go home.

3 February 2002
New Copper Saucepans

Fanny Craddock, who (on a trial basis only) has replaced George Sanders as my imaginary psychotherapist in the shed, does not seem at all impressed with the new copper pans. 'All very well, darling girl,' she says, balancing precariously on a bag of logs, 'but what on earth are you going to cook in them?' She stares at me intently, terrifying in her mink coat and sheer stockings, like an angry, puffed-up hen. 'From what I can gather,' she continues, now dabbing nail varnish ferociously onto her hosiery, which she has snagged quite badly on a scythe, 'you are hardly Nigel Lawson in the kitchen.'

'Nigella,' I say, 'I think you mean Nigella Lawson.'

'It doesn't matter,' barks Mrs Craddock, who will not, especially during the trial period, allow me to call her Fanny, 'what matters is that these pans are far too good for you. You are not worthy of them. These pans were destined for great feats of culinary genius, and from what I can gather your repertoire in the kitchen extends no further than a burnt fishfinger and a reheated take-away. Am I wrong, sweetie, or am I right?'

Mrs Craddock is absolutely right. Although I am quite good with eggs. I've always had a way with an egg.

Even Matthew will admit that I am quite good with eggs.

•

It was Matthew who gave me the copper pans. They were my Christmas surprise. I had been asking for them for some time but held out little hope of getting them. 'Why, in the name of all that is gastronomically unviable, would you want a set of copper pans?' he had said. 'Although you are quite good with eggs. You have always been quite good with eggs.'

And so it was with tremendous surprise that on Christmas morning I unwrapped a set of fantastically beautiful and immensely heavy copper pans which, for over a month now, have been arrayed picturesquely on the kitchen table. Recently, however, the pressure has been mounting for me actually to cook something in them. Tanja the home help has twice asked me if I want her to dust them, and Mathew keeps offering to take them out for a walk, 'just to give them a sense of purpose'. Finally, after much deliberation, I have decided upon Delia Smith's ragù as my maiden dish and with this recipe I will prove to Mrs Craddock and Matthew that I am worthy of these pans. 'Delia who?' sniffs Mrs Craddock.

•

Matthew, who has just consumed a large bowl of Delia's ragù with spaghetti and Parmesan, is saying the nicest things. In fact, he is slightly overdoing it, making 'mwah, mwah' noises while kissing his encircled fingers. 'A triumph!' he says. 'Tell me, was there not a hint of nutmeg in there somewhere, the perfect foil for the basil and tomato?'

Modestly I thank him and admit, 'It wasn't bad for a first attempt.'

Except that he then goes on to list seventeen 'very minor' points ranging from the spaghetti being too al dente by thirty seconds of boiling time to whether it should have been green or purple basil. 'A good cook,' he says, 'has to fine-tune, to hone, until it is just right. A good cook experiments, becomes one with his or her utensils.'

It was at this point that I put down the heaviest of all the copper pans, which I was carrying to the sink, for fear I might cause Matthew's head to become one with it.

•

Something else that Matthew said was how he had always dreamt of coming home after a morning walk with the dogs, followed perhaps by a trip to the pub, to a roaring fire and the smell of Sunday lunch cooking. And today, for the first time in ten years of marriage, if you don't count the times when he has been greeted by the smell of polystyrene burger carton warming in the microwave, his dream shall be fulfilled. I began preparing the lunch at eight o'clock this morning. Matthew, who said he wasn't going to interfere – in fact, he said, he wasn't even going to ask what I would be cooking because he wanted it to be a surprise – set off with the dogs at eleven.

At eleven thirty he phoned me from his mobile to say that he was working up quite an appetite, and at eleven thirty-five he phoned again to say that he was heading for the pub. At twelve thirty he phoned to say he had bumped into a friend, and at one o'clock he phoned to say that he was running a little late. I was wearing my gingham frilled apron at the time and I quite enjoyed the experience of tutting and rolling my eyes to the ceiling as if to say, in Oxo Katie-fashion, 'Boys will be boys.'

•

'I am not questioning the quality of your cooking,' said Matthew later that afternoon, 'and I commend you, as I have on many recent occasions, for your new-found talents in the kitchen.' Then he fell silent, stood up and walked over to the fireplace. 'It's just that, to be honest, I had not envisaged a bowl of spaghetti Bolognese for Sunday lunch. A roast would have perhaps been more like it, or even a hearty stew.'

'It wasn't spag bol,' I whined defensively. 'It was Delia Smith's ragù, as you well know.'

'Yes, indeed, it was,' sighed Matthew, 'and a very fine ragù it was too. Every bit as fine as the one you served last Wednesday and the Monday before last.'

'You're bored with the ragù,' I said. 'Admit it. You think it is time I tried something new.'

Matthew said nothing and we sat in silence for a few minutes until he looked up and said, 'Why not have a go at something with eggs. You have always been very good with eggs.'

10 February 2002
We Are Most Definitely Moving to the Country

'If you go down to the woods today,' sang Louis as we made our way across the field adjacent to our Devon holiday cottage, 'you're in for a big surprise.' And how right he turned out to be, for as we opened the wicket gate leading into the copse, and headed down the path towards the river, there, just a few yards in front of us, ambling – and not just ambling but whistling in a hail-fellow-well-met-kind of way – was Matthew.

I'm not convinced that black leather shoes were an inspired choice of footwear during the rainiest, muddiest period in post-war West Country history, but who cares? Those shoes were moving squelchily along, one after the other, and even to my well-trained eye their wearer seemed to be enjoying himself.

•

Matthew's behaviour still gives cause for concern. This morning, he embarked on a quaint speech about listening to the rain on the cottage roof. 'If you go up to Louis's room,' he said, 'and curl up with a book, *The Cat in the Hat*, perhaps, or, depending on your reading age, something a little more ambitious such as Daphne du Maurier or a Brontë sister – and read to the soothing background music of rain falling on the skylight . . . well, there is no cosier feeling in the world. And even the knowledge that you will eventually have to unfurl yourself and take the dogs out for a walk, or fetch in some logs, doesn't detract from it, because outside, wrapped up against the weather, it is even better.'

I swear that is what Matthew said. The same Matthew who has always insisted he could never spend more than two consecutive days in the country, the same Matthew whose objections to moving to this part of the world are as follows: (1) while he likes and admires people with such a strong sense of family that they insist on breeding within it, he doesn't want to live among them; (2) it's a twenty-minute drive to the nearest betting shop; (3) it would be quicker to go to Milan, buy a wood-fired oven, transport it to Devon, install it and then make a pizza on it than actually to have a pizza delivered; and (4) 'I'm a Jewish gentleman of a certain age, and it's just not natural.'

If his current behaviour continues, I might even find the courage to broach the subject of moving out of London, something I haven't dared to do since a holiday in Cornwall in the summer of 1992. I have to get the timing right, though. The timing is vital.

•

Today we went shopping. On our way into town we were held up behind a tractor and not once did Matthew shout or shake his fist. We went to no fewer than six shops and not once did he offer a shop assistant his traditional country farewell, the one about giving 'your mother and sister my best when you see her this evening'. When we bought bread sauce he even forwent his usual line about 'in-bred sauce'. And then he volunteered, actually volunteered, to buy himself a new pair of wellingtons.

We drove back at 23 m.p.h. behind a man at the wheel of a Morris Traveller, who was wearing a flat cap and smoking a pipe, and Matthew made not a single reference to the appeal of owning a hand-held missile launcher. This evening we went to the pub and Matthew got into a game of darts with a fellow human being. At home in London he plays alone in the kitchen, and several times a week I am dragged over to the dartboard to 'verify' a score of 180, or something called a bull finish. Here, in the pub, he kept shouting, 'Oh, good darts,' or, 'Arrghh, darts!' and his opponent would reply, 'Good darts,' or 'Arrghh, darts!' or sometimes just, 'Darts!'

'If we lived here all the time, you could join the team,' I said as we walked home. But Matthew didn't hear me, he was too busy staring wide-eyed at the moon which, appropriately, was full.

•

We have just returned to Shepherd's Bush, after a five-hour journey, to find our road closed, or, more precisely, closed twice – once for resurfacing and a second time because of a shooting. The entire area is crawling with police and Matthew's bucolic glow is fading fast. He is white-faced and dejected and just as I am about to suggest that perhaps we could consider moving out of London one day, not now, of course, but perhaps in a few years, he turns to me and says, 'I think you should get on to the estate agents in the morning.'

I would quite like to shout, or jump, or dance on the table even, but I don't. I wait and later that evening, while Matthew plays darts on his own, I creep upstairs and unearth my collection of estate agents' house brochures from the summer of 1992.

10 March 2002
Using the Treadmill

The problem with the exercise treadmill which Matthew and I bought five months ago and which conveniently folds upright for easy storage so that it resembles Robbie Coltrane's ironing board at rest, is that it is extremely cumbersome to manoeuvre into the ready-for-action position. That is why I have only used it twice.

I don't know what excuse Matthew, who has used it once, wishes to offer. The last time he attempted to explain his estrangement from the treadmill he babbled incomprehensibly, reminding me of that scene in *Kind Hearts and Coronets* where Louis D'Ascoyne tries to pass himself off as a Swahili-speaking bishop. Subsequently we both fell into a heavy and meaningful silence on the subject from which we show no signs of ever emerging.

That unspoken pact of silence is maintained each time Matthew stubs his toe on the treadmill's iron extremities. He hops about silently, his features seared with agony until the pain subsides and we carry on as before. We also maintain the silence each time I bang my hipbone on the jutting handle of the treadmill. In fact, we never actually use the treadmill word at all. Even when the dog chewed through its electric flex (and I have suspicions that she was encouraged in this; that someone in this house arranged the contents of an entire bag of doggy snacks around and beneath the flex in such a way that she had no choice), we just said, 'Izzy has chewed through an electric flex,' without identifying the flex's host appliance.

Meanwhile it looms enormous over our collective conscience like The Thing from a 1950s sci-fi film. Its presence is permanently felt. So much so that I have been thinking of auditioning it for the role of my imaginary psychotherapist, in succession to George Sanders and Fanny Craddock. At least then I could move it out of the kitchen and into the shed.

•

This morning, I referred, unwittingly, to the treadmill. Matthew shouted down to me from two floors up, 'Have you seen my blue sweater?' and I replied, 'It's hanging on the treadmill.' A sticky, atmosphere-laden minute followed before Matthew arrived downstairs wearing his green sweater and we said no more about it.

Then, this afternoon, Tanja also said the 'T' word. She had no idea why I abruptly left the room when, in answer to the question 'Have you seen the dogs' leads?' she replied, 'Yes, they're hanging on the treadmill.' And then Louis came home from school and spent fifteen minutes attempting to throw his cap onto the treadmill. 'I did it!' he cried when he finally succeeded. 'Can I phone Dad and tell him?' he asked.

'No,' I said, 'your father is far too busy.'

•

On those rare occasions when I actually sit down to have a phone conversation instead of talking on the hoof with phone wedged between shoulder and chin (according to my osteopath, this is why my neck is out of alignment. An effective cure would, she says, be some kind of regular exercise regime), I have taken to putting my feet up on the jutting arm of the treadmill.

It was while in this position this evening, during a long chat with my former personal trainer, now just a good friend, that I rediscovered my lost grey cashmere scarf hanging just above my head, its fringe caught in the treadmill's hinges. Still talking, but with the phone now wedged, I idly pulled the scarf to one side and found that underneath it was the paisley stole left here by Louis's best friend's mum last bonfire night. It was like one of those conjuring tricks in which the magician keeps unravelling knotted chiffon from up his sleeve. Underneath the stole was my lime-green macramé handbag containing some Nike sweatbands, still in their cellophane wrapping, and beneath that were Louis's swimming goggles. Then came the lucky tie Matthew always wears when he goes to the casino.

The treadmill, presumably through some sense of injustice at its lack of proper use, has been consuming accessories like a famished, furious beast.

•

'Has anyone seen my black moleskin jacket?' asked Matthew.

'Is it really made of moles?' asked Louis, buying me time to sneak across the kitchen to fetch the jacket, which had been kidnapped by the treadmill.

Several minutes later a button on Louis's school coat got jammed between the upturned base of the treadmill and the control panel. 'Hurry up!' called Matthew, who was waiting to leave the house. 'What's keeping you?' I didn't answer, I just continued wrestling with the treadmill – then Matthew appeared in the doorway, saw what I was doing and backed off like a startled rabbit.

'Go upstairs, please,' he told Louis, as he pulled me by the arm to safety, 'and fetch your school blazer. You can wear that instead.'

•

I have just put the phone down, after speaking to my ex-personal trainer.

'Do you or Matthew ever use that exercise machine you bought last year?' she asked. 'One of my clients is looking for one, and I thought you might like to sell him yours.'

'Sorry,' I said, 'but yes, we do use it. We use it a lot actually. A great deal. Every day, in fact.'

'Oh,' she said. 'Well, I just thought I'd ask.'

I am looking at the treadmill now. It is draped, furnished, upholstered, hung about with coats, bags, hats, scarves, dog leads, two dressing gowns, Louis's feather headdress, an apron and a copper saucepan. I wasn't lying.

We do use our treadmill, all the time.

17 March 2002
A Family Outing

As parents, both Matthew and I understand the significance of family outings and the quality time they allow. We have therefore avoided them like the plague, realizing that it only takes one parent to escort a child around an attraction, thereby allowing the other parent to enjoy proper quality time at home, having a lie-in or watching the telly.

Under this arrangement outings involving anything cultural or educational traditionally fall to me, while Matthew's responsibilities lie in swimming on a Sunday morning and taking Louis, who wants to be a train driver as well as an actor in *Dr Who*, to Liverpool Street station to spend a few carefree hours watching the Stansted Express arrive and depart. We have gone on full, tripartite family outings before but thankfully Louis was too young to remember them.

And then this morning, quite shockingly, Matthew suggested he join Louis and me on our trip to the Science Museum. 'I loved the Science Museum when I was a child,' he said. 'I loved pressing all the buttons.' I pointed out to him that he is currently suffering from a 'non-specific' virus he simply cannot shake off, and ought to rest. But he was insistent. 'Don't worry, I'll manage,' he said.

If he's still in the museum after twenty minutes, it will be a medical miracle.

•

Ten minutes in the Science Museum and all the signs of fidgety boredom to be expected from someone of almost five are already evident. Needless to say, they are coming from Matthew, who is nearly thirty-nine. We are in the aeronautical section, and while Louis is thoroughly absorbed, Matthew is only interested in pushing the buttons, something which in each case loses its allure after anything between two and seven seconds. After twelve minutes he is looking very, very bored indeed and I suggest that, since he has a virus he cannot shake off, he might prefer to go home and catch whatever football is on telly. 'No,' he says, 'I'm going to enjoy this if it kills me – although I have to say I remember the buttons being far superior in my day.'

•

By the time we reach the 'flight lab' on the third floor Matthew has undergone some kind of metamorphosis (perhaps it was one of the buttons he pressed), and has turned into the Competitive Dad from *The Fast Show*. He has just broken into a trot to beat Louis to the Bernoulli blower machine, which allows you to direct an air flow in different directions to make a beach ball dance around. Five minutes later he is persuaded to let Louis, who is much better at it than him, have a go and wanders off to crash a helicopter on another machine.

I sense that he is on the verge of calling it a day when there is a tannoy announcement. In ten minutes there will be a demonstration of water rockets involving volunteer children. Matthew grabs Louis's hand and marches him across the room only to find that another father and son have got there first.

Pretending that he doesn't realize it is a queue, Matthew insinuates himself between the other father and the water-rocket launcher. The other father retaliates by pushing in front of Matthew and since there is now no more room for anybody to push in anywhere, Matthew instructs Louis to take up his position on the raised platform. The other father prods his son in the back and he, too, takes up his position on the platform.

Nine painfully silent minutes later an 'explainer' from the museum staff arrives with a box full of water rockets.

'Hello, everybody!' she says.

'Hello,' we mumble.

'Ooh, that wasn't very good, was it?' she says. 'Shall we try again? Hello, everybody!'

'*Guten Tag!*' exclaims the rival father.

I knew full well what was coming next. Matthew looked at me and mouthed the word 'German'. I looked away, pretending not to have noticed. He nudged me hard in the ribs. I looked back at him. 'German,' he mouthed again.

'Stop it. Please stop it,' I begged in a stage whisper. But it was a futile plea because Matthew was already whispering loudly back to me: 'I'm surprised they didn't bring their beach towels.'

•

The jet-propulsion rerun of the 1966 World Cup Final is over and Matthew has announced his intention to leave when he spots a sign directing us towards 'History of Medicine'.

'Oh, my word,' he exclaims. 'Louis, look at this. Isn't it stupendous? That's the first kidney-dialysis machine ever used in Britain. Look at the size of it. And look at that walnut finish. It's exquisite.' Then he spies an early MRI scanner and says simply, 'Wow.' Looking around to check there are no staff watching, he steps delicately over the cordon and starts pressing buttons. 'Louis, come here,' he whispers. 'This is what we call a magnetic resonance imaging machine. And – oh, that's just unbelievable, it's a prototype radiotherapy machine. Louis, look at this. Louis? Louis?'

I find Louis by the lift, asking to go home. We leave the museum together, without Matthew, who has said we are not to worry about him. He will be home in time for supper.

24 March 2002
Interviewing Katarina

I often wonder as I drive back from Devon along the M4 into London what first impression people coming from Heathrow airport must get of this country. I imagine seeing it all for the first time through their eyes: the grey, the dullness, the small sky, that stupid, prissy little bus lane of John Prescott's.

I am applying the same technique now as I embark on a tour around our house – a critical eye on the sitting room, surveying the kitchen, inspecting the bathroom. What will Katarina, the girl who is coming to be interviewed tomorrow evening, the girl who will in all likelihood sit on the sofa cushion that I am now so uncharacteristically plumping, make of us? What will her first impressions be? Will she want to be our new home help when that fly-by-night Tanja, who has only been with us for three and a half years and who has only given us a year's notice, makes the reverse journey to Heathrow for the last time and so selfishly buzzes off back to Cape Town?

•

To analyse our lives objectively it seems to me that the first thing to be considered must be Matthew. He is bearded at the moment, having announced his intention not to shave until he has reduced his weight by a stone. He has also decreed, knowing how much I hate beards and how keen I am to lose weight, that I have to lose nine pounds before he goes anywhere near his razor. There's a fair chance he will be ready to join ZZ Top before it's over. He has already moved past the Jesus look into the dangerous madman stage, and the scales are refusing to budge for either of us.

Watching him now at his dartboard, I attempt to see him through Katarina's eyes.

'Laydeesungentlemen,' he proclaims, 'the very best of order. Third leg. Matthew to throw first. Game on!' For the next few minutes, the only sound to be heard is a lacklustre 'twenty-six' here, a delighted 'one hundred and forteeeee!' there. Then in a far shriller tone he announces: 'Matthew, you require forty.' His dart flies into the red section at the top of the board. 'Yeeeeessssss! Game, shot and the leg, Maaaathewww!'

The next person to be considered through the eyes of Katarina is Louis. He is in the laundry basket – or 'Tardis', as it has become known. He is humming the *Dr Who* theme tune. Every so often he will pop his head out and announce the discovery of a new tear in the fabric of the space-time vortex. Hopefully Katarina won't find the incessant humming too wearing. And what of the dogs? At the moment they are relatively clean and placid. In fact, if Matthew stays away from the dartboard, and we cite 'medical problems' as a reason for the beard, we might be all right. Katarina might even like us. She might even think we are vaguely normal. Just to be on the safe side, I plump some more cushions.

•

Louis has in fact decided to wear his Sulley the Monster outfit from *Monsters, Inc.* for Katarina's interview, and has only lapsed into four or five unintentional outbreaks of the *Dr Who* theme tune, duh duh duh duh, duh duh duh duh duuuurrrgh, since she arrived. I am beginning to think that we might just get away with this when things take a worrying turn. Steptoe has just mounted Izzy with intent.

Unfortunately, this has happened while Katarina is stroking Izzy. Steptoe is behaving like this because Izzy is having a phantom pregnancy. Her hormones are up the spout and Steptoe, never one to miss the opportunity of becoming a frothy-mouthed sex beast, has chosen this precise moment to demonstrate just how virile yet sensual he can be.

Then there is a knock on the door. Matthew answers.

'Where's Tony?' squeaks Hilda the confused neighbour, who thinks we are housing a Second World War army officer called Tony.

'Come on, Hilda, run along now,' Matthew tells her.

'Don't you speak to me like that, you greasy wop,' she hisses scarily. 'You've done away with my officer. I shall take my Kalashnikov to you and your cow-whore woman.'

•

'More tea, Katarina?' I ask.

'Lovely,' she says.

The tour of the house has finished, and when we come back down to the kitchen Matthew is at his dartboard. 'Matthew, you require one hundred and twenty-seven . . . triple nineteen? Yessss! Triple eighteen? Yesssssss! Double eight? Yeeessssssss! Game, shot and the leg . . .' He does a little lap of honour around the kitchen.

Then there is a knock on the door. Matthew answers.

'All right, Matthew?' says Chris, our friendly local junkie, who collects and then consumes the bags full of groceries which Hilda leaves for the non-existent officer.

'You've got pineapple chunks and teacakes today,' says Matthew, handing over a bag.

'Ta very much,' says Chris, nodding politely at Katarina but ignoring the entangled mass of shagging dog by her feet.

•

'Well, that went well,' I say to Matthew when Katarina has gone.

Matthew is sanguine. 'It was absolutely fine,' he says. 'Just so long as the only other job offer she gets comes from the Addams family, I can't see any problem at all.'

The agency has just rung. Katarina, they say, is very keen indeed to work for us. Apparently she thinks we are very nice.

'That is very worrying,' says Matthew, 'the girl is obviously mad.'

'Worth giving her a try, though,' I say. 'Although she's going to need watching like a hawk.'

31 March 2002
Yummy Mummies

I am just popping out to the shops and, because it is still quite wintry, I am wearing my lovely black velvet embroidered coat by Ghost. Actually, 'popping' is hardly the word because although the entire shopping list amounts to barely enough for a meal for two, what I am about to embark on is an odyssey around four of the world's most upmarket food retailers, each one of which would regard being 'popped' into as far beneath their dignity. My shopping destination is Holland Park Avenue (because Louis's school is conveniently situated on it), where my fellow shoppers will include a phalanx of pencil-slim, youthful, fashionably dressed American women buying mache (a trendy green salad leaf) from Michanicou the trendy greengrocer. There will also be a handful of fellow mothers who have children at the same school as Louis, many of whom, depending on which side of the Shepherd's Bush roundabout they live, can accurately be described as 'yummy mummies'.

'Yummy mummy' was not a tag I was familiar with until recently, these being two words Louis has rarely had the opportunity to speak consecutively. He says things like: 'The food Alex's mum cooks is really yummy, Mummy, much yummier than yours and not burnt.' But he has never said: 'This apparently char-grilled fishfinger is really yummy, Mummy.' However, I gather the phrase refers to mummies who look yummy, who have retained their aching fashionability despite having given birth. Holland Park is swarming with them. Hence the necessity of the black velvet embroidered coat by Ghost. Come to think of it, 'swarm' is the wrong word for the yummy mummies of Holland Park. They don't swarm, they parade like Jane Austen characters. Holland Park in the twenty-first century is the equivalent of eighteenth-century Bath: somewhere to be seen and admired. They don their Prada and their Gucci and their Ferretti and they glide through the four key Holland Park shops in a sequence so rigidly observed that I sometimes think there must be some kind of local by-law which they dare not disobey.

•

They glide into the interminable queue at Lidgate's the butcher, stopping to say a 'Hello, we must have Ferdy over for a play date' here, or a 'Where did you get that adorable black velvet coat?' there. Then they glide off round the corner to the queue outside Michanicou, pausing only to admire Francesca Annis as she picks out the plumpest artichoke. Then they glide back in the direction of the patisserie, Maison Blanc, next to the butcher, to swap weekend-cottage-in-the-Cotswolds anecdotes while surveying the *tartes aux poires*. Finally they glide on to the Italian delicatessen, Speck, where they will spend the national average weekly wage on a small tub of mozzarella with cherry tomatoes.

What wouldn't I do to be a yummy mummy? I think

as I join the Lidgate's queue. A real yummy mummy I mean, someone who would feel happy taking their black velvet etc. coat off in an environment such as this. The tiniest hint of sun is giving me tremendous cause for concern. I pray for cloud cover and pull the collar of my black velvet coat protectively around my ears. But by the time I get to Michanicou I am forced to pay attention, for the first time this year, to how taut and trim are the exposed upper arms of my fellow shoppers. The sun is now well and truly out, the chill wind of earlier this morning has dropped and much of the population of Holland Park has shed its outer layers. In fact, only me and the tramp who is sitting outside the flower shop are still wearing coats.

•

It is particularly hot in Maison Blanc today. Norman Lamont is looking quite red in the face, and he's usually so pasty. In Speck I catch sight of myself in the mirror and see that I am just as red as Norman, if not more so. I am as red as one of those aforementioned cherry tomatoes nestling in the tub of mozzarella. Beads of sweat are beginning to form on my forehead. An American woman in a thin-as-a-wisp chiffon blouse is stroking my arm.

'I lurve your coat,' she says. 'Where did you get it?'

'Thank you,' I pant. 'It's by Ghost.'

'But you must be so hot,' says the American woman's American friend, who is wearing a sleeveless poloneck.

I tell her that I am coming down with a cold and feeling quite feverish, leave my cooked and marinated baby chicken with sultanas and my pannacotta pudding on the counter, and head for the vet's in Addison Avenue, where I have to pick up some dog shampoo.

Anna Chancellor is buying some puppy food. She is wearing a light hand-knit and jeans. She is not wearing a coat. It is hot in the vet's, the sun is streaming in. By the time I get to the car I feel quite faint. A mother with a child at Louis's school stops to say hello. 'Are you feeling all right?' she asks, rolling up the sleeves of her cool crisp cotton Boden shirt. 'You look very flushed.'

I tell her I am coming down with something, mutter feebly that I must rush home to some paracetamol and get in the car. I turn the air-conditioning up high and head for the wrong side of the Shepherd's Bush roundabout. Safely home I remove my coat and settle down to dwell on my shopping trip with a slice of *tarte au chocolat* and it is not long before I reach the satisfying conclusion that my fellow shoppers are not Jane Austen characters after all, they are Stepford Wives.

•

'And where does that leave me?' I ask Matthew, who has just come home and asked where the marinated baby chicken with sultanas he specifically asked for is.

'You?' he says. 'You are from Shepherd's Bush – you are a Step*toe* Wife.'

He's right, of course, and therefore from now until next winter when my lovely black velvet embroidered coat from Ghost can come out with me again I shall be doing my shopping in the Uxbridge Road.

5 May 2002
A Dalek to Tea

I have just finished apologizing to our new next-door neighbour for our behaviour yesterday evening. The unacceptably loud shouting at the television, which must have penetrated his walls despite his polite insistence that he had not heard a thing, did not, I explained, have anything to do with football or boxing. 'Although you will certainly have plenty to complain about in that department in a few weeks' time,' I added, 'what with Lennox Lewis fighting Tyson and the World Cup coming up. I'm afraid my husband will become extremely over-excited, almost animal-like.' I then went on to explain that last night's shouting was, in fact, directed at an episode of *Room 101*. 'Michael Grade was on,' I said, as our neighbour barely stifled a yawn, 'and you won't believe it, but he only nominated *Dr Who*! *Dr Who*!' At this point the poor man was saved by Hilda, carrying her usual bag full of teacakes for her imaginary war-time lover. She insinuated herself between us and told him he should have nothing to do with me because I am a filthy slut.

•

I may or may not be a filthy slut but I am loyal to my son, and our new neighbour's indifference to the axeing of *Dr Who* – something Mr Grade actually did do when Controller of BBC1 – has infuriated me.

'Do you know,' I told Matthew this evening, 'he seemed completely unconcerned. Blithe, even. It's amazing.'

'Quite extraordinary,' said Matthew, 'that this man, who arrived in England a month ago from Tangiers, where he's lived all his life, that this man, this callous monster, showed no interest in a long-defunct British children's science-fiction series . . . I think I'll take a drop of brandy for the shock.'

Perhaps he had a point. It is true that I, and Matthew, too, for all his sarcasm, have adopted Louis's latest obsession wholesale. Not that we have much choice. When you live with a person approaching his fifth birthday who spends six hours a day humming the *Dr Who* theme tune, can discuss the command structure of the Daleks for several hours without a break and much of the time refuses to answer unless addressed as 'Doctor', there is no alternative. If we didn't join in the obsession there would be no common ground between us all. Our relationship with Louis would break down at once. Louis has just appeared in his uniform. Not his school uniform. The Peter Davison as Dr Who uniform, a birthday present we had had made for him. I think it is fair to say that he cuts an eccentric figure for a still-four-year-old. He is wearing a long Regency frock coat over a cricket jumper, white Edwardian trousers and white plimsolls. Only the hat has yet to arrive.

'Mum,' he says.

'Yes, Louis?'

'Mum.'

'Louis, what is it?'

'Muuummmm!'

The penny drops. 'Yes, Doctor?'

'Have you ordered the Dalek cake for my birthday party yet?'

'No, Doctor. Due to a problem with the fabric of the space-time continuum' – Louis nods sagely – 'it's not possible today. But I'm going to call Jane Asher Party Cakes in the morning to order it.' I am considering asking if it would also be possible to have five wax effigies of Michael Grade made for birthday candles. How dare Grade axe *Dr Who*? How dare he?

•

Jane Asher's representative was extremely obliging about the cake, although when I asked her if she thought a Battle Dalek, a Command Dalek or a Supreme Dalek would be best she said that the decision was entirely mine. She said this very politely but there was a faintly discernible tone to her voice which suggested that Jane Asher doesn't pay her to know about the intricate hierarchy by which Daleks operate. I decided against mentioning the Michael Grade effigies because Louis was listening, and is unaware of the *Room 101* situation, and I don't know how he'd take it if he found out.

'Why were you phoning Jane Asher?' asked Matthew. 'Tell me it's because you wanted to congratulate her on never marrying Paul McCartney. Tell me it wasn't to order a cake.' When I failed to answer, Matthew's head clunked into his hands. 'Well, if you'll excuse me for a moment,' he said, 'I'll just go and ring the Bristol & West about a second mortgage.'

Funnily enough, the thing I failed to discuss with Ms Asher's helpful employee was cost. It hadn't occurred to me that it might be slightly higher than the £7.99 Tesco's charges for a *Thunderbirds* or *Monsters, Inc.* cake. Unfortunately, when Jane Asher's people called my people to confirm the order and ask for credit card payment over the phone, my person turned out to be Matthew because he happened to be passing the telephone at the time. However, when the Dalek cake arrived, it was so spectacular even he admitted it was worth relinquishing any plans we might once have had to retire one day in order to pay for it.

•

The party is going very well indeed. Mr Loonney the entertainer has also dressed as Peter Davison and is really getting into character. Even some of the children seem to be enjoying themselves.

'What was your favourite bit?' I asked one boy who came up to thank me for a lovely party.

'The *Monsters, Inc.* Monster Juice,' he said.

'And how much did that cost?' asked Matthew that evening as we sat nibbling the left-over Dalek cake.

'Ninety-nine pence from Tesco's.'

'Fortnum and Mason don't stock it, then,' said Matthew. He was being sarcastic, but actually he was right. They don't. I checked when I was in the area, buying a Peter Davison-style panama hat from Lock's of St James's.

12 May 2002
Desiree's Cottage

Loyd Grossman was wearing a moleskin waistcoat, riding boots and breeches in last night's black-and-white dream. 'Who would live in house like this?' he said, flicking a speck of dust from a portrait of Catherine Earnshaw (me) with his riding crop. 'Here at Wathering Hoights, this bleak, secluded outpost, this godforsaken—'

Loyd was interrupted by the front door banging open on its hinges. Leaves swirled in on the howling wind and a deranged madman (Matthew) strode across the flagstoned hall wearing a black cape. 'If I have to sit behind another Vauxhall Cavalier driver wearing a hat and going at thirty-five miles an hour . . .' he said, pouring himself a whisky. And then the picture faded into colour.

'Let this be a warning to you,' said Loyd. 'Moving to the country is seldom a good idea.'

'This is a public information film,' said Tess of the D'Urbervilles (Carol Smillie). And then I woke up.

•

It is not the first time since Matthew and I decided to move to Devon that I have had this dream. Sometimes Loyd appears as an itinerant parson, and often the Carol is Vorderman not Smillie. Otherwise it is always the same. I was thinking about mentioning it to Matthew this morning, when the phone rang. 'Sorry to ring at this bleak and godforsaken hour,' said Lydia, the professional property-seeker who is helping us to find our dream home, 'and you'll think I've gone mad because I know you are looking for a full-sized house, not a weekend cottage, but . . .'

Lydia went on to tell me that a three-bedroom property on the very country estate where we currently rent a cottage, the very country estate which inspired our move to Devon, has come on the market. I told her I would ring her back.

Matthew and I digested Lydia's news, our complexions flushed with excited anticipation, or at least mine was. I have been sensing a certain reluctance from Matthew over the Devon issue ever since Good Friday when an accident on the M5 forced him to turn back to London after eight hours of 'utter, suicidal, bloody, pointless, murderous misery', as he put it, 'which raised the gravest doubts about the very purpose of human existence'.

•

Lydia arranged for us to view the cottage and we drove down in just under five hours (Matthew said if it hadn't been for that piece of plankton in a Nissan Cherry we'd have done it in four). We have put in an offer for just under the asking price, and nothing can go wrong because the cottage is not officially on the market yet – this is the purpose of clever Lydia, to find properties before anyone else does so there is no competition, no danger of being gazumped. We expect to be moving in within the next five or six weeks or so – certainly before the summer holidays start.

'What were we thinking of?' says Matthew as we drive back to London (just over six hours because of an 'overturned half-wit' on the A30). 'Of course a weekend cottage is the answer. You know, I never could quite picture myself actually living in the country. I am a Jewish gentleman of a certain age and I know my limits.' Matthew's limits, these days, are approximately a hundred yards before he develops an old wound in his leg, which he says he doesn't like to talk about, and turns back.

That night Loyd appears in my dreams as an estate agent showing a coachload of prospective buyers over our cottage. 'Be warned,' he says to the camera, 'nothing is ever as easy as you think it is going to be.'

'Gazumping is a very real danger,' says Carol (Vorderman), 'and it could happen to you.'

I tried to tell her that the property wasn't even on the market yet but she started doing a sum on a blackboard and explaining the intricacies of stamp duty so I woke up.

•

We haven't been gazumped. It's much, much worse than that. Lydia phoned this afternoon. The vendor's girlfriend has instructed the estate agent to increase the price by £55,000. 'The vendor's girlfriend,' I tell Matthew, 'fancies herself as a bit of a property expert. She's called Desiree and wears an ankle chain and tights under stonewashed denim with a diamanté appliqué . . .'

'How do you know all this?' asked Matthew. 'Did Lydia tell you?'

'Yes. Well, no. Lydia told me that she was probably called Desiree. She was just guessing but it did seem fitting that she should be named after a potato, and we worked out the ankle chain and the appliqué from there,' I said.

'I see,' said Matthew. 'How very rational, grown-up and egalitarian of you.' He then sat down with a large whisky in one hand and his head in the other, and after a short but frenzied bout of madman rocking, looked up and said, 'Desiree has a hairy upper lip. And six fingers on both hands. She must be destroyed.'

•

Matthew and I have slept on it and decided not to raise our bid. We have also decided on a slightly less emotional response to Desiree. 'The first thing to do now,' says Matthew, 'is make an appointment to view the cottage under an assumed name, and then, while the estate agent is showing you the immersion heater, I'll put the prawns inside the curtain poles.'

'Then we find out where Desiree lives and bombard her with hate mail,' I say. 'And then we put acid in her moustache bleach and daub her red BMW convertible with graffiti.'

'No, no, no,' chides Matthew. 'Now you are being childish. If we're going to do this, we have to be serious. You phone the estate agent and I'll go and buy the prawns.'

19 May 2002
End of a Dream

Matthew and I have agreed not to put prawns in Desiree's curtain poles, not to daub her red BMW with graffiti, not to sneak up on her in the night and connect her ankle-chain to the national grid. If Desiree thinks that she can sell her boyfriend's cottage in Devon for half a million quid to someone a lot richer and more stupid than us then that is her business and we can only commend her for her ambition, although some might call it avarice. In fact, Matthew and I have decided not to move house at all. We will not be buying a weekend cottage, least of all Desiree's boyfriend's cottage. Desiree, if she only but knew it, has saved us from the most terrible mistake. But for that woman's ambition (some might call it extortionate greed), we would now be exchanging contracts and preparing to spend the rest of our lives on the M5 or adjoining B-roads.

•

'I think that we've made the right decision,' reaffirmed Matthew, turning down the radio. He had been listening to the traffic news on Radio 2: a ten-mile tailback on the A30; sheer weight of traffic causing delays on the A303 near Stonehenge; two lanes blocked in both directions on the M4. Then he went out into the garden and, lowering himself into a deckchair, sighed, 'This is the life. You wouldn't really know you were in Shepherd's Bush on an afternoon like this.' Then the sound of the local drug-dealer's in-car stereo started up, realigning the foundations of our house.

'I've often wondered,' I mused, 'if the drug-dealer works on the same principle as an ice-cream van's jingle – local residents hearing the sound of Eminem at 129 decibels say, "Ooh, there goes the drug Saab. I think I'll nip out for a crack-cocaine ice lolly. Anyone else want anything? A heroin 99 perhaps, with a flake?" '

Matthew is right, though: much as I might hate Shepherd's Bush, our marriage would never have survived those traffic jams. But still I grieve for the future I will now never know – the village life I was set to hurl myself so wholeheartedly into, the Victoria sponges I will never be baking, the church flowers I will never arrange, the cheery greetings I will not be imparting to my fellow Women's Institute members, the thought-provoking articles on the evils of second-home buyers from London I could have penned for the parish magazine.

•

But Shepherd's Bush is not without a community spirit, it's hardly as if we don't know our neighbours. Here's one now, knocking on our door. It's Hilda, the confused seventy-something who leaves groceries for the long-lost wartime lover who she believes we are holding captive. Hilda does not knock, she bashes. For a woman of her age she puts an awful lot of weight behind a door knocker. Matthew opens the door to her, bows ironically from his waist, takes the carrier bag (Spam and a light bulb), nods affectionately at the stream of abuse ('You filthy wop, what have you done with my officer? I'll report you to the police, you and your filthy slut wife'), and says, 'Lovely to see you, Hilda,' as always. 'Until tomorrow, then.'

'You see,' he says, shutting the door, 'this is just like village life and that was our idiot.'

'I'm popping out to the dry-cleaners,' I say.

'Send him my regards,' says Matthew.

Now that might seem odd, that a resident of an inner-city area like ours should send the dry-cleaner his best. I think about this as I drive off, and marvel at the realization that we have now known Ray, the proprietor of New Look dry-cleaners, for eleven years.

'Good afternoon,' shouts the man at the tyre shop.

'Good afternoon,' I shout back. I don't know the name of the old-age pensioner who lives off the Shepherd's Bush Road and dresses like a cowboy but today, not for the first time, he informs me that with 'a little bit of surgery' I'd be a dead ringer for Tammy Wynette. I tell him I'd be flattered if only Tammy hadn't been dead for years, and he slaps his thighs and roars with laughter as if this was the first time he'd heard it. Then, as village folk do, we exchange local gossip.

'Did you hear about that raid a couple of streets down towards the Askew?' says the cowboy. 'They found an arms cache.'

'Don't tell me,' I say as though hearing of an outbreak of TB among David Archer's herd over a pint of Shires at the Bull.

•

Ray the dry-cleaner has been almost as worried as we have about Louis's Peter Davison *Dr Who* outfit and has worked wonders. The braiding around the frock coat hasn't run at all and the Ribena stains are mere shadows of their former selves. I thank him profusely for the trouble he has taken, and as I drive home past a church I make a mental note of the vicar's name in case he needs any Victoria sponges.

Pulling up outside our front door, I see Chris the junkie and an integral part of the local food chain (he collects Hilda's carrier bag each evening). He is standing on the corner apparently pleading with a man in a brand-new Saab convertible who eventually gives a hopeless shrug, then reaches into his pocket and hands over a small package. It's a moving sight, someone doing some-one else a little kindness. This is English village life at its most precious, right here in Shepherd's Bush. Who needs Devon? Devon, as I have said before, can wait.

26 May 2002
The Garden Furniture Row

It's been two months since I last ventured into the shed because Fanny Craddock, who replaced George Sanders as my imaginary psychotherapist, is in there and she finds me irritating. She can't be doing with me, so I've been steering clear of her. Sometimes she wanders about the garden wearing a headscarf and sunglasses and waspishly snapping at the dead heads, casting withering glances at the forget-me-nots as if they were Johnny and she would like to forget them. Today, though, I am forced to make an excursion into her lair because it is the time of year when Matthew reminds me about the garden furniture.

•

The annual garden-furniture row should be given a name in the way that hurricanes are. Matthew and I can perfectly happily – contentedly, even – bumble along with our married life, no arguments, no tension, harmony prevailing. But then one day in spring we will erupt at the merest mention of garden furniture. Sometimes I can predict it, see the storm clouds gathering, feel the chill wind that suddenly whips through the house. Then I can clear the decks in preparation, and the neighbours can be warned to put tape on their windows and keep their children indoors.

The row harks back to a phone call I took all of five years ago. We were in the process of buying our house, and Matthew, because he understands concepts such as mortgages and interest rates, was dealing with it all. Except that one day the vendor rang and spoke to me.

'As you know,' she said (I didn't), 'we have been quibbling over the final sale price of the house and I have a suggestion.'

'Oh, good.' I said.

'How about we throw in our dining-table and chairs and call it a deal,' she said.

'Oh, right,' I said.

'Good,' said the vendor, 'that's sorted, then.'

'Yes,' I said. 'Goodbye.' Well, then I phoned Matthew to tell him I had made this deal and that I thought I had been rather smart because I remember from viewing the house that the dining-table and chairs were really pretty chic.

'Chic!' shrieked Matthew. 'Chic! For £3,000 they've got to be more than chic!' He went on the explain, extremely aggressively, that he had been on the verge of negotiating a £3,000 reduction for the price after seeing the survey and that I, with my 'moronic interference', had just blown it. 'You are totally bloody stupid!' he said.

I thought that this was quite extraordinarily rude but was aware that Matthew was under a lot of pressure and that buying a house has often been cited as the third most stressful thing after a divorce and watching Esther Rantzen on *Celebrity Stars in their Eyes*. On the other hand I was eight months pregnant and the vendor had put me on the spot, and I was not in the mood to be told that I was totally bloody stupid. So I slammed down the phone. What's more, I took it off the hook so Matthew couldn't get hold of me and would spend the afternoon worrying in case I had gone into labour.

We didn't speak that night and then it got worse. The chic dining furniture that I remembered so clearly turned out to be chic garden furniture made of stainless steel – the kind you find on pavements outside Parisian cafes, or Café Rouge in the Shepherd's Bush Road. But because the vendors of our house were very trendy they were using it indoors.

Matthew does not and will not do trendy, and I have to admit that in this instance I could see his point. The tables were too low, for a start, and the chairs were a nightmare in the small of the back. But it was far too late to admit a mistake so, when he said he wouldn't have them in the house, I told him he had no sophistication, and that if he had his way we would have antimacassars and a sideboard – a look which a couple of years later actually became a rather fashionable option. The trendy vendors, ahead of their time as they undoubtedly were, were probably going for the antimacassar look themselves in their new house, while we stood and yelled at each other over their reject stainless steel, which I insisted we keep – as garden furniture.

•

This year, like every year, the beginning of the garden-furniture row was heralded by Matthew saying in a weird Dracula voice: 'I think you will find it is time to get the garden furniture out of the shed.'

'I think I've been punished enough,' I retaliated. 'I think I should now be allowed to buy some new garden furniture, and you should stop being so bloody childish.'

'Oh, no,' says Matthew, 'not until we have got £3,000 worth of use out of those lovely chic ones that you liked so much. They are exceedingly chic, are they not? Abundantly chic. Indeed, almost supernaturally chic, wouldn't you say?'

Then I threw a pineapple at him which ever so slightly grazed his neck.

•

Matthew's neck bandage is still on, and because we are not speaking he has written me a note. 'Admit you were wrong and the tables and chairs will be gone by sundown,' it reads. I decide to agree to his demands but only on the condition that he apologizes for being so horrible to me when I was eight months pregnant and promises never to mention £3,000 again. Ever. 'You mean as in the £3,000 you swapped for these astonishingly chic tables,' he says.

And that does it. I storm out – I'd rather be with Fanny in the shed. It will be another year at least until we get new garden furniture.

9 June 2002
Lying for Izzy

Animals are supposed to have a calming, positive effect on humans. Medical research has shown that the company of dogs lowers the blood pressure, and pets are even taken into prisons so they can bring out the gentle side in violent offenders. Izzy, on the other hand, is having the opposite effect on me. She is turning me into a pathological liar, and despite the several megatons of disbelief in Matthew's voice every time he is asked to swallow another of my lies, I still tell them.

The reason is that I am not prepared to admit I was wrong about Izzy. To all doubters and detractors who insisted that Labradors were thieves and chewers and wreckers of furniture I argued that she was going to be trained within an inch of her life, that she would be a model Labrador. 'A trained dog is a happy dog,' I said as I set off to training class, an experience which proved to be possibly the most humiliating of my life. I was so bad at dog-handling that the trainer made me sit at the back of the class while she took Izzy, and I gave up after two sessions. Meanwhile Izzy thieved and chewed and wrecked furniture and I told lies in her defence. I said, for instance, that it was I who had eaten the entire box of Bendicks Bitter Mints last October.

'Indeed,' said Matthew, employing his best Sherlock Holmes voice. 'But you hate bitter mints and why did you suck the silver foil wrappers and leave them in a heap in the dog basket?' I told him that actually I used to hate goat's cheese but now I like it, that palates change and that I hadn't sucked the wrappers, I had washed them and put them in a handy spot so I would remember to give them to Louis to take into school for art.

I became an expert in the art of lying, and although they were seldom good or credible lies, they were always imaginative lies and I was quietly proud of them.

•

'Why wasn't your uncle Arthur at your grandmother's funeral last week?' asked Matthew this morning. And so began the unravelling of one of my more absurd lies – one which, unfortunately, I had for the moment forgotten.

'Uncle who?' I said.

'Come now, come now,' said Matthew, so Holmesian that he was on the verge of sucking on an imaginary Meerschaum. 'You told me after the cod-liver-oil incident of last Thursday that you had an uncle Arthur who suffered from arthritis. In fact, you said that his name was Arthur Itis and that he was a distant cousin of your grandmother from Cheshire.'

I don't think I did say he was called Arthur Itis. I think that is Matthew's childish invention. But I do remember saying that the reason I was drinking cod-liver oil was that I had an arthritic uncle and that I could easily have inherited the weakness.

'But why consume the whole bottle at once?' asked Matthew. 'Did you perhaps look at the label and where it said "One teaspoon per day" misread this as "One bottle per day"?'

'I didn't drink all of it,' I explained. 'I spilled most of it over the sofa. It was an accident.'

The truth is that I have been putting the cod-liver oil in Izzy's food because Labradors are prone to arthritis. Then last Thursday she found the bottle, chewed the top off it and drank half the contents, spilling the other half over the sofa. The smell was awful and it clung. It still clings, in fact. Matthew's hideous green towelling dressing gown somehow got into the same wash with the sofa covers and it clung to that so badly that it had, tragically, to be thrown away.

The sickly, sour fishy smell still hangs over Izzy, over all the other furniture she has been on or near and through the entire house. The upside is that Izzy has a very shiny coat, the downside that Matthew keeps sniffing melodramatically and saying how nice it is to get the flavour of Grimsby without having to go to the trouble of visiting Lincolnshire. And now he has remembered Uncle Arthur.

•

'Of course he wasn't at the funeral,' I said. 'He died in arthritic agony ten years ago. If only he had drunk more cod-liver oil, like me. Poor Uncle Arthur.'

And then Matthew went to Tesco's and came back with six bottles of cod-liver oil. 'Go on then, drain a bottle,' he said. 'We don't want to end up like poor Uncle Arthur, do we? Knock it back in one or admit that it was Izzy. Admit you haven't trained her properly and then I propose we have an amnesty. You can confess to all the other lies you have told over the past year and I will agree never to say "I told you so" the next time you find your hairdryer in her basket.'

I refused. And for the past week, as well as giving Izzy her teaspoon a day, I have been pouring some cod-liver oil down the plughole, because Matthew is checking the levels every mealtime.

'I've never seen you actually drink it,' he says, holding it up to the light. 'I sincerely hope you are not just pouring it down the plughole. Now just remind me, were you very close to your uncle Arthur?'

'Yes,' I said. 'He used to dandle me on his knee when I was a child.'

'His arthritic knee?'

'No, his other one. Mostly it affected his elbows.' Behind Matthew's back Izzy is heading for the garden with a cold chicken in her mouth. Luckily Steptoe, our other dog, is following her so I will make sure that he gets the blame. I shall say he has been thieving a lot lately, it's an old-age thing and he is nearly eight. I might even get Izzy off yesterday's kipper-nicking charge.

16 June 2002
Chilling Out in Deauville

There's a strange hush in the house tonight. It's quiet, too quiet – as the nervous colonel always says from behind the walls of the desert fortress. It's because Matthew has gone away. He left this evening, heading for the sibling towns of Deauville and Trouville in Normandy – the only holiday destination he will tolerate, for its unholy trinity of casinos, restaurants and a racecourse. He loves it, too, for its total absence of anything that might be called culture; he has made a point of never going to Deauville during the film festival, while always being there for the racing in August. He has gone now because he says he is 'fatigued' and he insists that a 'few days of sheer, untrammelled mindlessness' is what he needs. 'I'm sure you'll have a lovely peaceful time without me,' he said, and then he promised not to plague me with phone calls because he just needed a few days on his own and I wasn't to worry if I didn't hear from him for a while.

•

He has just called for the first time from the Channel Tunnel terminal. 'Listen, I don't want to alarm you,' he said, 'but I think I've found a lump.' Matthew may not want to alarm me but he has: this is *most* alarming. Normally, when he goes to France the first medical emergency doesn't arise until midway through the second day. For it to come when he's still on British soil is unusual, if not unique – and very alarming. I am not going to have a peaceful time at all. I am going to be plagued with calls.

I asked him where the lump was. 'At the bottom of my tongue,' he replied, 'and it's very sore.'

'I'm sure it's nothing,' I replied. 'But have a look in the rear-view mirror, with the light on. What does it look like?'

'Ayr alt, hiboo, alt aoht,' said Matthew.

'Put your tongue back in and then repeat what you just said,' I said.

'There's a little white spot,' he said.

'It's an ulcer,' I told him. 'You're run-down. That's why you have gone away.'

Matthew was unusually easily reassured by this. He said his train was being called and repeated his earlier words that I wasn't to worry if I didn't hear from him for a while.

•

'But, Matthew, it's one o'clock in the morning,' was my initial response to his second call.

'I don't know what you're moaning about,' he replied, 'it's worse here. It's two fifteen here. Listen, I've found another lump, a pea-like lump, under the left ear.'

'It's probably a lymph node,' I said. 'It's fighting the infection in your ulcer.'

'I don't think so,' said Matthew. 'I've got a feeling

it's something much more serious.' And then he added tetchily, 'Look, I've had a long day. I'm worried sick, and I need some sleep.'

I apologized sincerely for keeping him up all night chatting and we said goodnight.

By late morning on the first full day of his holiday Matthew had called in for the seventh time. Calls three and four concerned whether he should summon a doctor, five was to report that the doctor had been summoned, number six was to say that the doctor had been cancelled and number seven was to inform me that the doctor was on his way.

'Will you have to pay?' I asked.

'Oh, no,' he hissed sarcastically, 'French doctors always give freebies to English visitors. They like to thank us for liberating them. Of course I'll have to pay. It'll cost a fortune, but I'm on holiday so I think I can afford to treat myself.' He then said that if it was bad news on the medical front he would be leaving for home at once. 'Otherwise, I won't be calling again for some time.'

•

Matthew has just called, sounding ecstatic. 'It was a lymph node, and it only cost thirty euros.' He said he had asked the concierge to block-book the doctor for the rest of the week. At that price, he said, he could afford a potentially fatal illness three or four times a day; he was sure he'd be coming up with another one very soon and he'd let me know what it was.

In fact the ninth call in less than twenty-four hours did not come for another 190 minutes. It was to report that the sun had come out.

'It's wonderful here. I've had a sauna, and now I'm lying by the pool, reading a book and listening to the Mamas and the Papas on my portable CD. I feel so good, I've had to cancel the doctor.'

The tenth call came shortly before midnight and it was in its way the most disturbing yet. 'I'm calling about Mama Cass,' he said. 'She was the obese one in the Mamas and the Papas and she died in 1974. She choked to death in London. I've never got over it. My mother was heartbroken too; so, I remember, was my mother's friend David Wolf. I thought I'd got over it. But you know, today, lying on that sun-lounger, listening to the CD, it brought it all back. I don't know how I'm going to begin to get to sleep. It was such a tragedy, she was only thirty-three. I may not call you again for a while. I just need some time on my own.'

23 June 2002
Louis's Mummy

When Louis asked just now for a mummy, I could have played for time. I could have stalled and said, 'But, sweetheart, you already have a mummy. I'm your mummy.' Louis, though, knows perfectly that I know what he meant. He meant 'mummy' as in his current obsession with death. He meant he would like to mummify something, and he went on to ask if I could think of anything dead that would fit the bill. As he spoke he was looking with intensity over my shoulder in the direction of Anthea Turner's cage, and I wondered where I was going to get bandages small enough to mummify a hamster.

Louis's obsession with death started a few weeks ago when his great-grandmother died, and now seems to have merged in his mind with his other obsession, *Dr Who*. We have already covered his theory that coffins are like the Tardis: infinitely large on the inside, so that all of heaven is contained within them. We have moved on from thoughts of regeneration (the process by which one Doctor changes into the next), bringing Great-Granny back to us in the guise of Tom Baker, and are now deeply involved with a video called *The Pyramids of Mars*.

The villains in *The Pyramids of Mars* are mummies in the service of the ancient Egyptian god Sutekh the

Destroyer, who has been imprisoned inside a pyramid on Mars by all his fellow Osiran gods, but is now planning to escape and lay waste the entire cosmos. In the story, these mummies, far from being dead, stalk around the English countryside. And now, in the same way that he wants me to find a spare cardboard box large enough to make a Tardis out of, Louis also wants me to help him make a mummy.

And so, after dropping him at school this morning with the promise that before the week was out I would procure the necessary materials for both Tardis and mummy, I began by ringing Peter Jones.

•

In much the same way that it is necessary to pack a rucksack and get your affairs in order before setting off on an actual visit to Peter Jones, I have this morning discovered that it is also worth informing your next of kin before phoning to ask if the shop has a spare cardboard box the size of a Tardis.

Perhaps the most interesting stop-off point on my complex telephonic journey was the Peter Jones Warehouse, which is just off the A40 in somewhere called Park Royal. Once through to Warehouse I was, puzzlingly, transferred to Garments, where the very young-sounding man was so helpful that I began to wonder if he wasn't about to tell me that Peter Jones actually stocks cardboard Tardises for people to wear. But then it all went horribly wrong. 'I am sure I will be able to help you, madam,' he said, 'but before I go and look in dispatch, can you tell me this: will the box actually have "Tardis" written upon it?'

Mentally, I backtracked through our conversation: the bit where I explained I was looking for a box large enough to turn into a Tardis; the bit where I patronizingly asked if he was old enough to remember *Dr Who*. But it was beyond me to imagine where and how the conversation could have gone quite so badly askew. So I said, 'Not to worry,' and hung up.

•

Having informed my next of kin that I was 'back', I set off, in person, for Hamleys toy shop in Regent Street. Here at Hamleys the plan is to find some kind of inflatable doll which Louis and I can wrap in papier mâché before getting on with the serious business of mummification. I have no idea which of Hamleys' five floors will sell the inflatable, so I make my way methodically through the entire store, only stopping when I spot a pair of toy handcuffs, something which Louis has (already) put on his Christmas list. Finally I give up my search and approach a salesperson.

I put the handcuffs down on the counter and say, 'I'll have these handcuffs, please. And perhaps you could tell me where I can find an inflatable doll?'

The salesperson looks very worried indeed, as if she is trying to reach for the panic button without alerting me. When she finally speaks, she says firmly, 'I think you would be better off in Soho, madam.'

•

This was an extremely helpful suggestion and I have ordered something from the back of a magazine which will be arriving in a plain brown-paper wrapping within the next few days. In the meantime I have only to buy the bandages and find a cardboard box large enough to make a Tardis. The man in the chemist at the end of our road who is always very understanding towards Matthew and his hypochondria (he has been known to feel for lumps in places I myself would never dare venture) does have bandages but not nearly enough for Louis's purposes. He does, though, have a large cardboard box because he has just had a new fridge delivered. I can't believe my luck, thank him profusely, buy the bandages he does have and ask him where he thinks I can get some more. 'Why don't you try looking in your bathroom cupboard?' he says. 'I feel sure your husband won't mind parting with some of his for such an important cause.' So it has all turned out very well, and – Daddy willing – Louis should have his mummy by the weekend.

30 June 2002
World Cup II

I do not have an imaginary psychotherapist at the moment. George Sanders resigned months back, having entered his very own black pit of despair. Meanwhile his successor, Fanny Craddock, has moved out of the shed and into the next-door neighbour's kitchen, where she stands about all day flicking fag ash over their free-standing butcher's block and bitching about me. Far from being distraught, though, far from plunging head-first, like a skydiver without a parachute, into an abyss of self-doubt, I find myself soaring dove-like towards a state of unalloyed happiness. This is because I have joined a club and in doing so I have made my life complete.

It was the World Cup that made me do it. It was vital I had somewhere to escape to, somewhere removed from this house, which is full of people. They come and go, these people, visiting Matthew, who sits, like Marlon Brando in *Apocalypse Now*, in his lair. They shout, suck their teeth and punch the air and occasionally one of them will suddenly charge down the stairs and out into the back garden to perform some victory laps. There are days when these people exit with their heads down in morose silence, leaving behind them a thick, bad atmosphere. At other times they drive away parping out a moronic but jubilant tattoo on their car horns.

So two weeks in, the day before England played Denmark, I joined a club – not just for me but also for Louis, who, to his father's utter disbelief, has absolutely no time whatsoever for football.

•

The Park Club in East Acton puts me in mind of the 1960 film of *The Time Machine*, in which Rod Taylor finds the population of the earth's distant future sitting about on pastel-coloured fibreglass pouffes in a drugged state, wearing shortie togas and plucking wantonly from an array of mouth-watering fruits. Families frolic in the water gaily throwing a ball to and fro, and young couples wander dreamily under exotic flora. There aren't in fact, any pastel-coloured fibreglass benches at the Park Club, more blonde wood with chrome, but you can eat a honeydew melon with a cocktail umbrella stuck in it. Couples don't wander dreamily here either, instead they work out aggressively in the gym. But families do frolic in the pool and this is where Louis and I can be found. We spent an hour in the water on our first day, followed by another hour in the changing rooms, where the children run around naked and mothers cluck and fuss and pretend not to be checking out each other's cellulite. In here we are insulated from the shouting and the teeth-sucking and the chanting and charging and parping by an abundance of soft, thick, white towelling and sweet-smelling body lotions.

•

When I told Matthew that Louis and I had joined a club he looked up from the highlights for long enough to say, 'Oh, marvellous,' and proceeded to calculate out loud that if past experience was anything to go by the novelty would wear off within a week and therefore the estimated cost of our one-hour swim would be £230. But he is already wrong because we spent two more hours in the pool the following day. Then we had lunch in the restaurant, and while Louis played in the children's play area with its cushioned flooring, I read magazines in a suedette chair in the club's lounge area. And although the England–Denmark match was on and the television screen is several feet square – it is made up of many screens – somehow the shouting and teeth-sucking and air-punching didn't bother me so much. In fact, when England scored their second goal I did a spot of air-punching myself – before looking around to make sure no one had been watching me. By the end of the match, however, I was on my feet and shouting and I didn't care who saw. Louis was horrified.

The next day we spent an hour and a half in the pool, five minutes in the changing rooms and two hours in the children's play area (Louis) with cushioned flooring, or in the lounge (me) watching Ireland versus Spain on the multi-screen television. Louis came to find me just as Ireland scored the first penalty in the shoot-out. He wanted to go home. 'Not now,' I said, nudging him gently out of my line of vision, 'I'm not leaving without seeing the end of this match.'

•

I rang Matthew when Ireland lost. I was so upset I couldn't keep it to myself. I could no longer keep my football habit a secret, so I phoned him and confessed.

'You are not my wife,' he said. Since then he has refused to talk about it. I tried a couple of times to draw him into a discussion. When South Korea beat Italy I rang him from the club but he just said, 'This isn't funny any more. Please could you leave the line clear for those who genuinely wish to discuss the result of the match with me.'

And so, as the day of the final dawns, Marlon Brando will be in his lair, the usual troupe of people will be filing their way up the stairs at about eleven thirty and Louis and I will be going to the club where I can watch today's match with people who understand how very much it means to me.

4 August 2002
In Search of Inner Peace

The latest manifestation of Matthew's midlife crisis, the one that began on his nineteenth birthday and is soon to celebrate its twentieth anniversary, is perhaps the unlikeliest yet. He has enrolled at a school to learn the ancient art of meditation. A letter (which I read because it was left open on his desk) arrived this morning. It confirms the date for his first lesson as 6.30 p.m. next Thursday evening at a house in Victoria, and asks that he take along various 'presents': four pieces of fruit, six long-stemmed flowers, a piece of white linen or cotton (new) and a donation to the school charity (one week's wages after tax and National Insurance; or, for those on benefits, a minimum of £100).

There is, of course, no way he will turn up; absolutely no way will Matthew travel through the rush-hour traffic on a Thursday afternoon, laden with flora and napkins, to meet a guru. It is simply asking too much.

I have suggested several times that he has the courtesy to ring now and cancel, but each time he closes his eyes, adopts an idiot savant grin and starts chanting the syllable 'ommmm', which I think he picked up not from any of his eleven unread books on the subject of meditation but from a *Dr Who* video of Louis's in which malign meditators chant in order to unleash the power of giant spiders on the blue-crystal planet Metabilis 3. 'You're not going to stop me,' he said this evening when I had another go at bringing him to his senses. 'I will find my inner peace.'

•

The day of Matthew's lesson has dawned, and, amazingly, over breakfast, he has started preparing for the journey (physical and metaphysical) to Victoria. He has located a relatively clean linen napkin, and the four pieces of fruit – an apple, a mango, a lime and a lemon – are lined up on the kitchen table. He has also been to the cashpoint for the money, and seems determined to attend his lesson.

As I leave the house in the late afternoon for a long round trip that will culminate with an appointment at the vet's just off Holland Park Avenue, Matthew is sitting in his big chair smiling foolishly and muttering about how calm he feels. 'It's already working,' he says. 'Even before my lesson, I can sense my inner peace. Ommmmmmm. Ommmmm.'

•

Matthew has just called me on my mobile to say that he was about to leave for Victoria when he realized he had forgotten the six long-stemmed flowers. Please could I buy him six long-stemmed flowers. From the sound of him I'd say he is suffering a temporary loss of inner peace but I am rather relieved that he has called since I have forgotten something too, namely the dog. I am within a hundred yards of the vet's and I do not have the dog. Matthew and I arrange to meet in twenty minutes when we will exchange fauna for flora.

•

The last remnants of Matthew's inner peace evaporate in the waiting-room at the vet's. He arrived saying he would rather boil his head in acid than endure the traffic in Holland Park Avenue again as long as he lived, and he would be going on to Victoria on the Tube. He said he would be late and would be 'in trouble' with his headmaster. Miraculously, though, he found time to practise his apology for the benefit of the vet's receptionist: 'I've let you down, I've let the school down, I've let the entire world of meditation down but, most of all, sir, I've let myself down.'

When I handed him the peonies I had bought he said, 'Why such long stems? I have never seen such ridiculously long stems. I can't go on the Tube with stems that long.' Then he jumped up and down on the spot for a while, calmed down sufficiently to ask the receptionist politely for some scissors and began hacking manically at the peony stems, leaving them where they fell, before sprinting out of the vet's in the direction of the Tube station.

•

It is eight thirty and Matthew has just called from a phone box. He didn't get into trouble for being late but he refuses to discuss his lesson or to reveal his mantra, because these things 'are very secret'.

'But what about the flowers?'

'The flowers were fine.'

'What about the linen?'

'Fine. They've given me back the napkin.'

'And the fruit?'

'Don't talk about the fruit, I don't want to talk about the fruit.'

'Why? What on earth happened with the fruit?'

'OK. I'll tell you, if you really want to know. They gave me back three of the four fruits, keeping one for themselves. Guess which one they kept? Go on, guess.'

'The lime?'

'No, not the lime. Why would they keep the lime? Of course they didn't keep the lime. They kept the mango.' Then he stopped talking and let out a long, vibrating 'ommmm'. It didn't work. Inner peace was eluding him. 'They could have kept the apple or the lemon,' he continued, 'but no, they had to keep the mango. The prince of all fruits. Ommmmm. They're not so spiritual and unworldly that they didn't know to keep the mango. Oh no. They kept the mango. Ommmmm.'

•

It is a week now since Matthew returned from his lesson and this morning he opened a letter from the School of Meditation. 'Dear Matthew, we are sorry not to have seen you for any follow-up appointments.'

The quest for inner peace apparently put on hold, he scrunched up the letter and rammed it into the waste-paper basket. The mango is apparently still nagging away at the forefront of his mind and no amount of ommmms are going to shift it.

11 August 2002

The Decorators Are In

We have the decorators in. Or rather, to be precise, they are scheduled to be in at nine o'clock tomorrow morning – which could mean, going on past form, that they will arrive at noon tomorrow, at 5.30 a.m. on Wednesday, at some apparently random time of their own choosing in November or never. The last time we had the decorators in I fell out with the decorator-in-chief so badly that if ever I see his van parked in our neighbourhood I will be compelled to drive to Beachy Head, leave my clothes in a pile and start a new life as a reflexologist in Vancouver. This time, though, it will be different. This time it will be worse, because Matthew will be here. Last time he was in Australia at the Olympic Games. Now he is in the sitting room watching the Commonwealth Games, and if there is one thing Matthew won't brook – actually, there are so many things he won't brook that I've often thought it would be quicker to make a list of the things that he will brook – it's abandoned trestle tables and buckets of wallpaper paste on the landing while he is trying to watch athletics.

But Matthew's presence is not the only factor dictating that this time it will be different: this time I, too, will be different. I am going to make those men wish they had never set foot in this house. My name will go down in history in decorator circles and will forever be spoken in an awed, respectful whisper. Also, I am going to ration their tea.

'Oh. They'll be terrified of you,' said Matthew, going straight to auto-sarcasm. 'Decorators are the samurai warriors of British workmen, the elite SAS of bone-idle wastrels. Oh, yes, they'll be very frightened of you.'

•

The doorbell has just rung. It is 8.55 a.m. The decorators are here, and it seems their game plan is to bamboozle me with punctuality. There are two of them. Ali I know already, because he is also an electrician and computer technician. He assembled and installed the computer and the chandelier in my office, and stayed on at no extra charge to show me how to work it (the computer, that is; even I knew how to work the chandelier). But charming and helpful though he was in the past, today he is the enemy. Today, and for the next fortnight, or however long it takes, he is a decorator and must be handled as such. He smiles at me from the doorstep but I do not smile back and when he introduces his accomplice, I nod silently with lips pursed.

'Hi, Ali,' calls Matthew on his way down the stairs. 'Cup of tea?' He is doing this on purpose to undermine me. He knows my policy is to offer no kind of refreshment until mid-morning, depending on their progress.

'No, thanks,' says Ali. 'We'd rather get on.'

Matthew and I look at each other in naked alarm. 'Well,' I say stumblingly as they make their way upstairs, 'are you sure you won't have a cup of tea? And a piece of toast? Or maybe an egg?'

•

It is 6.45 p.m. and the decorators are still at it. They haven't stopped all day. I have tried eleven times to persuade them to come down to the kitchen, but they've bought their own sandwiches and Thermos flasks. Matthew is wandering around in shock, unable even to watch the Commonwealth Games.

'Don't worry,' I tell him, 'they start all keen and whistly like the Seven Dwarfs heigh-ho-ing away. But just wait till tomorrow.'

'Yes, of course you're right,' he says. 'Tomorrow they won't even bother to turn up.'

They arrived at 8.40 a.m. 'Have a cup of tea before you start,' I begged. But they just pointed at their Thermos flasks and bounded up the stairs like gazelles. We can't even hear them while they are working. They don't even have the obligatory paint-spattered transistor radio turned up to three times its normal volume.

Matthew has gone into a decline. He is sitting in his chair gazing vacantly into space, and he has been like this ever since they declined his offer of a cold beer.

•

'We haven't seen their work yet,' I tell him, in the hope that this might cheer him up. 'It might be quite shoddy.'

The minute they leave (10.45 a.m.) we bound upstairs like more gazelles to find the top landing is all but finished. Matthew stealthily approaches a wall and taps it with his index finger, obviously anticipating some kind of avalanche. Nothing happens. He shakes his head. Then he cranes forward and begins sniffing the wall-paper. Then he backs away and in a whisper says, 'It's perfect. Absolutely perfect.' We trudge disconsolately downstairs.

•

In ten days they have not asked for or accepted a single cup of our tea, and when Matthew just happened to leave his own radio turned up to three times the normal volume on the stairs, they turned it down. But then, three days before they are due to complete the job, Ali appears in the kitchen saying that while they thought they would be finishing off today, ahead of schedule, they have just run out of paint. This is my fault because the paint I have chosen comes from a specialist supplier in Arbroath and, not being good with measurements, I have ordered too few litres. Even if they Red Star it, there is no way the decorators are going to finish on time.

'Ah, well, no surprise there,' sighs Matthew happily.

8 September 2002
Name that Mantra

Matthew is meditating and I am hovering outside the sitting room pretending to sift through the post. My real aim, though, is not to open any of the accumulated yellow envelopes from Barry the accountant but to overhear Matthew's deadly secret mantra. The deadly secrecy surrounding it has created in me a pathological need to discover exactly what the mantra is. Plus, lovely though it may be to have serene Matthew, calm, open-minded, easy-going Matthew, in fact almost lobotomized Matthew, there is something fantastically annoying about the aura of self-satisfaction which surrounds him each time he emerges from a meditation session. It sets my teeth on edge and makes me want to inflict grievous bodily harm.

And call me childish, but I am ever so slightly jealous of Matthew and his new-found ability to meditate. Not that I am in need of meditation myself. Of course I lose my temper from time to time, who doesn't? But it takes a lot to push me over the edge. I continue to sift post, straining my ears until I think I catch the sound of something recognizable. It sounds like 'yup'. Matthew is repeating the word 'yup' over and over again. Odd for a mantra. I had expected something softer, something less terse and more honeyed than 'yup'. Irritatingly, I have been concentrating so hard on overhearing that I have inadvertently opened a letter from Barry the accountant. It is bad news. The kind of bad news that can only be responded to by a wholly irresponsible shopping spree.

•

I am in a department store in West London. Matthew, who came to the gate to wave me off (a new and intensely annoying habit of his), was, it turned out, not meditating at all. He was confirming his order with the local tandoori. 'Yup' is not his deadly secret mantra after all, which means I have to spend more of my valuable time standing about outside the sitting room as if I haven't got better things to do.

The girl at the till is being remarkably slow with my Calvin Klein pyjamas. I tut at her and then I scowl. She scowls back. The word 'yup' is repeating itself over and over in my head causing it to ache.

Finally I march towards the exit with my purchases and 'Wheeeeeeeeeee,' goes the anti-shoplifting alarm.

'I'm sorry, madam,' says the guard, taking possession of my pyjamas. 'This is obviously our mistake. If you could just show me the receipt for your goods, I will have the security tag removed immediately.'

I scowl at him and then search through my wallet for the receipt. It is not there. 'It's in the carrier bag,' I snap. 'Yup, yup, yup,' goes the mantra in my head.

'I'm sorry, madam, but the receipt is not in here. Please follow me while I make further enquiries.'

I follow him, obedient but scowling, until, halfway through the perfumery, I stop dead in my tracks and screech, 'I am not moving another inch! How dare you frogmarch me across a public place like this, as if I were some petty criminal?' They let me go. 'Yup, yup, yup.'

•

Matthew is meditating again. This time I have my ear pressed against a glass tumbler and I can hear much more clearly. 'Mmmm,' says Matthew, then, 'mmmm,' again. He says it a few more times but then he starts talking. He says, 'Oh, dear. No, she hasn't told me a thing about it. How embarrassing.'

He wasn't meditating at all. He was on the phone to the friend who happened to be passing through the perfumery during the climax of my tantrum.

'I don't wish to sound smug,' said Matthew later, 'but you seem to have rather a short fuse lately. Perhaps you should learn how to meditate too, it really does help.' He stops on receipt of my scowl. 'Aaah, well, perhaps not,' he says, smiling the smile of Grasshopper in *Kung Fu*. 'Perhaps this weekend in the country with your mother will do you some good.'

•

The thing that really annoys me about the new meditating Matthew is the air of piousness; it's as if he has never flown off the handle or screamed abuse at the pizza deliveryman. If, for instance, he were here with Louis and me now, in a five-mile tailback on the M4 caused entirely by John Prescott's stupid prissy little bus lane, he would be demented with rage and questioning the very purpose of human existence. And he wouldn't even be able to meditate in case we overheard his deadly secret bloody mantra.

'The car in front has moved on, Mum,' says Louis and I lift my head from my hands and see that he is right. But it's only twenty yards: twenty yards in as many minutes. I phone Matthew. 'Oh, you poor thing,' he says, and it is his tone which gets me. 'Just sit tight. Not long now and you'll be home.' What is he talking about? Not long now and we'll be home! Is he mad? I sit behind the steering wheel, my head in my hands once more, and reflect upon the old days, the happy old days when Matthew was a pioneer of the social substratum recently identified as 'the Meldrews'. Before he morphed into a grinning hippy.

•

Matthew, it turned out, was quite right. It wasn't long before we were home because after another five minutes of banging my head against the steering wheel and questioning the purpose of living I finally decided to pull out into the stupid prissy little bus lane, which I proceeded to drive up with my horn blaring. Perhaps the most gratifying thing was the subsequent outbreak of anarchy among my fellow motorists, the stampeding herd of other drivers who followed my lead. Those that didn't, I concluded, probably practised meditation and therefore deserved to spend the rest of the weekend in a five-mile tailback on the M4.

22 September 2002
She's Back

The Kentucky Fried Chicken carton containing a coiled sock has survived another night in Shepherd's Bush. I am beginning to wonder if someone hasn't nailed it to the pavement. Perhaps I am the intended victim of some Jeremy Beadle prank; footage of me grappling it into the bin will be shown on television. Why hasn't it been blown about? The rest of the rubbish in this road has managed to make its way into our front garden, yet the Kentucky Fried Chicken carton with the coiled sock stays put, slap-bang outside our gate.

Further along the road a maroon-and-beige-fleck velour sofa is being unloaded from a lorry, while opposite, outside the bail hostel, a man and a woman are eating Kentucky Fried Chicken and smoking. At the end of the road two men are busy replacing the window in the launderette, which has been decorated with bullet holes since the last drug-related shooting three months ago. Maybe now is the time to put our house on the market – 'spacious four-bedroom family house in an area which boasts a new launderette window and no drug-related shootings for three months'.

•

It is also three months since we discovered that Hilda, the confused old lady who believed that Matthew and I were harbouring Tony, her wartime 'officer', disappeared. Given her tendency to threaten me – 'I'll shoot you with my Kalashnikov' – we wondered if perhaps she'd been involved in the launderette shooting but, in fact, we learnt, she was sectioned. So it is three long months since we last returned home to find, propped against the front door, one of Hilda's carrier bags containing groceries for Tony. Sometimes it would be Spam, suet or a meat pie, but more often than not there would be teacakes. She once brought blankets and towels for 'Officer Tony' and bizarrely, four cropped T-shirts and some ankle socks. When I tried to give these things back to her she spat at me and called me a 'cow whore'.

That was another thing that Hilda did – she called me names. Her voice was high-pitched and it seared itself resolutely into my brain. When she knocked on the door she put all her strength behind the knocker: it was so loud that the neighbours would come to their doors as well. So, though I am sorry she was sectioned and I hope they are treating her well, I quite enjoy being able to get from the car to the front door without being accused of harbouring Second World War army officers in the spare room.

But Chris the junkie, who, by collecting Hilda's carrier bags, completed a neat little local food chain (he is very fond of Spam and teacakes), is missing her dreadfully. So is Matthew, who was always very courteous to her. When she referred to him as an 'oily wop', he would bow and say, 'Thank you, Hilda, you are very kind.' 'Sod off,' Hilda would reply. And from this brief but meaningful exchange Matthew would derive much pleasure.

•

The maroon-and-beige-fleck velour sofa was, it turns out, not being unloaded so much as dumped. It is now outside our house, and, intriguingly, the Kentucky Fried Chicken carton has made its way on to it. There is no sign of the coiled sock. The couple are outside the bail hostel again, this time eating Magnums (white chocolate), whose wrappers are making their way slowly across the road on the prevailing wind. Also making his way across the road is Chris. He is calling out to me but a council 'street-cleansing vehicle' comes between us. Thankfully it doesn't stop to do any actual cleansing and it is only a moment before Chris is by my side asking me if I would like him to 'buff up' the scratches down the left-hand side of my car. I thank him but decline. 'Why don't you ask that couple over there if they'd like this lovely sofa to sit on while they eat?' I say. 'Save their bottoms on those cold steps.'

'Good idea,' says Chris, and I hand him a fiver in advance for getting the sofa moved to the other side of the road.

•

What happened next, as I entered the house, is something I have often seen in British situation comedies – where Person One walks past Person Two and says, 'Good morning,' and then performs an exaggerated double-take because they suddenly remember that Person Two is supposed to be dead.

'Good morning, Hilda,' I said, and, though it may only have been half a second before I remembered that Hilda was supposed to be in a care home for people who deposit groceries for imaginary army officers on other people's doorsteps, there was a definite comedic delay. There she was sitting on our sofa (the one indoors as opposed to our new one in the street) in her coat and scarf, her Black Watch tartan shopping trolley parked up beside her.

'The lady knocked on the door asking for Tony,' explained Suzanna, our new home help. 'So I said she could come in and wait for a while.'

Hilda didn't stay long. She finished the tea Suzanna had made her, said she wanted to see Tony, called me a cow whore and went on her way. Her voice seems lower than it used to be, not so searing, and when she passed Matthew as she left and told him to 'sod off', she seemed rather half-hearted about it. He was thrilled, though, bowing lower than ever before and booming, 'Hilda, a delight. Welcome home.'

•

'Hilda's back,' said Chris.

'Hilda's back,' said the couple from the bail hostel.

'I know,' I said, and I was all the way to our front door before performing another exaggerated situation-comedy double-take because they were all sitting outside our gate, on the sofa eating her teacakes.

29 September 2002
Dancing at the Wedding

I have been trying to explain to Louis why he has not been invited to the wedding we are going to next week-end. I have told him that if all the guests turned up with their children the place would be over-run and there might be a coup. I have also said that some anarchist babies screech during the service. Eventually, in desperation because Louis is clearly not prepared to let it lie, I sit him up on the kitchen table so that his eyes are level with mine and say, 'OK, you want the truth, you want the real reason why children aren't invited?'

'Yes,' says Louis defiantly.

'Then I'll tell you,' I say. 'Are you sure you are ready for it?'

'Yes,' says Louis resolutely.

'Well, then,' I say, lowering my voice for dramatic effect, 'at weddings something happens that is so frightening it gives children nightmares for the rest of their lives. Some are struck dumb if they see it and never speak again; others grow a tail.'

'What is it?' asks Louis worriedly.

'Are you absolutely sure you want to know?'

'Yes.'

'Ready?'

'Yes.'

'OK, then, here goes. Grown-ups do disco-dancing.'

•

When I said grown-ups I was not necessarily referring to Matthew and me. Not once in eleven years of marriage have we danced together. We didn't dance together at our own wedding, let alone at anyone else's. We have sat in many marquees surrounded by empty chairs, which were vacated at the opening bars of 'Hi-Ho Silver Lining', without once giving in to the urge to get up and dance. It's not an issue and it is not something we have ever discussed. It's just not something we do.

Or at least it wasn't, and with hindsight I can see that I should have left things as they were. But the more I thought about it, the more convinced I became that there must be something wrong with us. When we die our joint headstone will have carved upon it 'In memory of Rebecca and Matthew, a devoted couple even though they never danced together'. Why don't we dance? When other people hear the first strains of 'I Will Survive' by Gloria Gaynor they say to each other, 'Oooooh, I love this one,' and off they go, handbags down, glasses swiftly drained, to flail about on ten feet by eight feet of specially sprung flooring under a glitter ball. Matthew and I just sit there and smile wanly at each other. And so I resolved that next weekend, as soon as the bride and groom have done their traditional opening turn around the dance floor, I will take Matthew's hand and say quite blithely, as if it is something I have said a thousand times before, 'Shall we dance?' No doubt Matthew will remove his hand and ask if I'm running a high fever. But I have to try. If nothing else, I owe it to Louis.

•

It is hard to describe what happened on that dance floor in that marquee on that lawn in front of that house just outside Sidmouth, and I have not yet learnt how to cope with the repercussions. I will tell it slowly. The music started, the bride and groom danced, the parents of the bride and groom danced, gradually old university friends and some aunts and cousins got up to dance. But Matthew and I remained seated. 'Hi-Ho Silver Lining' came and went, as did 'Lost in France' by Bonnie Tyler, but when Gloria Gaynor started up I seized the moment, took Matthew by the hand and said, 'Shall we dance?' I wasn't expecting him to leap to his feet; I wasn't expecting him to hurl himself on the dance floor with abandon; but neither was I expecting him to say, 'I'd rather wait and see if they play "It's Raining Men".'

It was the way he said it, as if it were something we had discussed a thousand times, as if we had long ago decided that 'I Will Survive' is OK as dance records go, but given the choice we'd rather wait for 'It's Raining Men'.

'Oh,' I said, 'and which version would you prefer, Geri Halliwell or the Weather Girls?'

Matthew said he wasn't particularly bothered, so I lodged a request with the DJ and five minutes later we were both heading for the dance floor where I proceeded to dance like someone's mother at a wedding disco, gyrating stiffly and self-consciously with absolutely no abandon whatsoever. I just about survived 'Tragedy' and

'Night Fever' and then, even more self-consciously, made my way back to our table. Matthew, on the other hand, remained. He danced to 'Celebration' by Kool and the Gang, he rather eccentrically pogoed to 'We Are Family' by Sister Sledge and he contrived to moonwalk to Michael Jackson's 'Billie Jean'. Finally, after thrashing about enthusiastically to 'Come on, Eileen' by Dexy's Midnight Runners and 'Who Let the Dogs Out?' by the Baha Men, he returned, only to head straight back the moment he sat down, unable to resist Blondie's 'Atomic'.

•

It wasn't an issue. Matthew's dancing was not something we discussed as we made our way back to the hotel. I simply didn't mention it and neither did he, except indirectly when he said he couldn't remember when he had enjoyed himself so much. 'I might almost start preferring weddings to funerals,' he said as we drew up outside our hotel. 'Fancy a drink in the bar?'

'Good idea,' I said, at that stage unaware that Saturday night was dance night in the Belmont Hotel, Sidmouth.

The band was playing 'Dance in the Old-Fashioned Way', and Matthew said he didn't mind if he did. We were the only people there under sixty. We were the only people who had no idea how to foxtrot, waltz or two-step. We were the only people who had never danced to the theme music from *Last of the Summer Wine* before. And we were the only people left when the band packed up to go home.